Hot Picks

COLLECTION

Hot Picks:
His Bride of
Consequence

ABBY GREEN

MILLS & BOON

First Published in Great Britain 2020
By Mills & Boon, an imprint of HarperCollins*Publishers*
1 London Bridge Street, London, SE1 9GF

HOT PICKS: HIS BRIDE OF CONSEQUENCE © 2020
Harlequin Books S.A.

The Kouros Marriage Revenge © 2007 Abby Green
Chosen as the Frenchman's Bride © 2006 Abby Green
The Spaniard's Marriage Bargain © 2008 Abby Green

ISBN: 978-0-263-28143-9

MIX
Paper from
responsible sources
FSC™ C007454

This book is produced from independently certified FSC™ paper to ensure responsible forest management.

For more information visit: www.harpercollins.co.uk/green

Printed and bound in Spain
by CPI, Barcelona

THE KOUROS
MARRIAGE REVENGE

PROLOGUE

'KALLIE, you have to tell him you love him tonight. If you don't, he'll never know. You're going home in two days, next year you'll be at college or working…this is it, your last chance to tell Alexandros how you feel.'

Kallie's arms were gripped by her older cousin Eleni, her dark face close to Kallie's, her eyes fervent. In some dim part of herself she did wonder at that moment why Eleni cared so much about this. And stifled the thought, feeling mean. Hadn't Eleni been her confidante, having had to listen to her wax lyrical about Alexandros for years on every summer holiday? She was only helping her.

Nerves made her voice shaky. 'But, Eleni, I haven't seen him in ages, he's always in Athens now…' She shivered. *And a little remote.* Which he'd never been before…

Eleni shook her head emphatically. 'Doesn't matter. He's always had a soft spot for you. He's exactly the same, the only difference now is that he's loaded.'

Kallie gulped. *And way more grown up…he's going to laugh at me.*

'Kallie, come on. Don't chicken out now.'

She looked at her cousin. She had that impatient look that always scared Kallie a little.

Kallie nodded jerkily, her heart thumping like crazy. Over

Eleni's head she could see the object of her affections. Alexandros Kouros. Twenty-five years old and so handsome it hurt. Midnight-black hair that shone almost blue-black in the light, curling softly on his collar, a touch too long. His skin a deep olive. His face had a harsh masculinity that made Kallie's insides feel weak. An arresting, utterly captivating quality that drew the eye and kept it there with little effort.

He stood at least six feet four, broad across the shoulders and chest. His body was finely muscled, potently masculine. Sometimes it frightened Kallie, the response she felt around him. Like it was something she couldn't control, didn't fully understand…

They were in his palatial family villa, which was right beside her grandmother's in the hills above Athens, where she always spent her summer holidays. Every year, the end-of-summer party in the Kouros villa was the highlight of the social scene. Kouros Shipping was one of the biggest companies in the world. And since his father's untimely death two years before, Alexandros had taken full control without even breaking sweat.

'Kallie, he's never going to see you as anything but a friend unless you go and take things further.'

'I know.' Kallie was anguished, her attention brought back into the room, to the events that her cousin seemed to be determined to set in motion. She'd never done anything so bold in all her life, usually preferring to hide behind a book or in the hammock at the end of her grandmother's garden, dreaming. She didn't even know if she really wanted to do it. Suddenly she saw Alexandros across the room take a bottle of something off a table and disappear. Eleni had followed her gaze. She turned Kallie to face her.

'This is it, Kall—now or never. You'll regret it for ever if you don't. By the time you see him again he'll be married with three kids…'

The thought made Kallie feel physically ill…or maybe

that was the wine Eleni had been plying her with to get her courage up. Eleni held up the glass again. Kallie shook her head, as it was it was already swimming slightly. The sight of it made her feel nauseous. It was the first time she'd drunk anything alcoholic and she really wasn't sure she liked it.

'Go, Kallie. *Now.*'

Fuelled by something bigger than her—the wine, the sense of finality about everything—Kallie moved forward as if in a dream, through the crowd in the room, out the door that Alexandros had disappeared through and onto the patio. The warm air washed over her, bringing her to her senses somewhat. She almost turned around and went back inside, but saw Eleni at the door. No going back.

She didn't see Alexandros at first—he was hidden by an overhanging tree that trailed its leaves along the stones of the grand patio. Then she saw him, his tall lean body, jacket off, leaning against the wall, and it made something inside her flutter to life. She moved forward. Thoughts swirled around her head, like a drumbeat…a mantra…as she approached him.

It's now or never. If I don't do it then I'll never know, he'll never know how I feel…

She held her breath and stepped into the space where the tree formed a kind of hidden clearing. The faint sounds of the party drifted out on the breeze but Kallie was oblivious to that. Her heart nearly jumped out of her chest it was beating so hard. Alexandros had his back to her but she could see that he had a bottle in his hand and was lifting it up, drinking from it. She must have made a noise because he whirled around, the bottle clenched in one hand.

'Who's that?' He peered into the gloom and Kallie stepped forward slightly. 'Kallie? Is that you?'

She stepped forward. 'It's me.'

He turned away. 'You should go back inside to the others.'

She was stung at his obvious desire to be alone. His dismissal. She realised a little belatedly that he'd been in a strange mood all evening, dark, brooding, as if a black cloud clung to him. And it seemed even more apparent now.

Having come this far, she ignored him and kept walking till she was almost beside him, the twinkling vista of Athens laid out below them at the end of the garden. Her heart was beating so rapidly she felt light-headed.

'I'd like to stay, if that's all right.'

He shrugged and took another swig from the bottle. Kallie grabbed it from him, taking him off guard, and took a drink herself before he could stop her. She coughed and spluttered as the liquid burnt her throat. He stood up straight and clapped her back, sitting her back on the low wall beside him. A wry grin on his face.

'What were you expecting? Wine?'

Tears streamed down Kallie's face, shocking her out of her nerves for a moment. 'What *was* that?'

'Ouzo.'

She shivered suddenly when she realised that they were close together, his muscular thigh burningly close to hers.

He reached for his coat and draped it over her shoulders. She had to fight not to give in to the sensation, not to close her eyes and breathe his scent deeply. They sat in silence for long minutes, neither one moving. That brooding energy emanated from Alexandros. The air seemed to grow thick around them, tension mounting, and Kallie wondered feverishly what to say, how to break it. But Alexandros turned to her suddenly.

'Kallie…why did you come out here? You should go back, it's getting dark.'

She looked at him, hurt in her eyes. 'I just…I don't mind just sitting here with you…'

He groaned softly and ran hands through his hair. 'Sorry. I'm just…not the best company tonight.'

She laid a hand on his arm, and looked at him. 'Do you want to talk about it?'

He looked at her for a long time with an intensity that made something coil deep in Kallie's abdomen, something alien and tight...*hot*. He seemed to be fighting some inner battle, struggling with something. Then it passed. She held her breath as he reached out a hand and caught a lock of her hair, letting it slide through his fingers.

'Your colouring is amazing, do you know that?'

Kallie grimaced, felt like squirming under his gaze. 'It's horrible. I burn too easily. I blush too easily.'

And I'm too fat...

Every insecurity rose up all too easily.

He shook his head. 'No, you've got your mother's colouring. A typical English rose...'

'That's why my father says he fell in love with her.'

Something dark crossed his face and he let her hair go. The moment was gone. And in that same moment she knew she didn't have the guts to do this. She should leave Alexandros alone. To fight whatever demons were chasing him.

'I'll go...'

She got up to leave and promptly stumbled when the ground swayed as she stood up. Alexandros's arms came out automatically, swinging her into his chest to regain balance. Her wish to leave dissolved in a flash of heat. His chest was against her hands, strong and broad and warm, his heart beating steadily. His scent surrounded her. She looked up into those dark, fathomless depths and was lost, no more capable of moving than hiding the blatant desire in her expressive eyes. She was in a bubble of sensation so acute that she'd lost all sense of reality, space and time.

She lifted a tentative hand and with one trembling finger traced the outline of Alexandros's mouth, the hard sensual contours. She could feel his breath against her palm.

'Kallie…what are you doing?'

Her eyes jumped up to his and for the first time in her life she felt bold, filled with some unknown, unexplored feminine power. Not knowing how she had the nerve, she just said simply, 'This…'

And she reached up, closed her eyes and pressed soft, warm lips against his.

For a long moment he didn't do anything. Kallie felt something move through her, an aching *wanting*. It stunned her with its intensity. And then hope sprang in her breast. He wasn't pushing her away. Would he kiss her back? She wanted him to, so much. Her lips moved tentatively against his…and then abruptly her world erupted and tilted. Alexandros stood and pushed her away from him with two harsh hands so quickly that Kallie was dizzy and would have staggered back except for his unwitting support. His jacket fell to the ground behind her.

'What the hell do you think you're doing?'

He let go and somehow Kallie managed to keep standing. She could feel a tide of red heat climb her chest, her body throbbing painfully with all the newly discovered sensations clamouring for release.

The way Alexandros was looking at her, with such disdain, disbelief and *horror*, made her turn to jelly.

Her voice was hesitant. 'I…I was kissing you.'

He was scathing. 'I know that, Kallie, I'm not stupid.'

Mortification twisted her insides. 'I'm sorry… I don't know what…' She shook her head and stumbled away a little.

He caught her back with his hands on her shoulders. 'No, Kallie, what the hell was that? Why would you try and kiss me?'

'Because…' She looked at him, backlit by the falling dusk. So handsome. And it made something burn in her belly, dissolving her embarrassment. She had to tell him.

Now. 'I did it because…' she swallowed painfully '…I love you, Alexandros.'

He straightened, his whole body taut, bristling. 'You *what?*'

'I…love you.'

Nothing moved. Kallie saw Alexandros looking at her and the blatant shock on his face changed to confusion and then something else…disgust.

He took his hands off her shoulders suddenly as though he'd been burnt.

'Look, I don't know what you're up to, Kallie, but I don't appreciate it. I'm announcing my engagement tonight and if someone had seen… *Hell.* Just go, Kallie.'

His words dropped into her brain but didn't register. Engagement? Married? To whom?

Kallie felt a mad desire to burst into hysterical laughter and then just as suddenly felt very silly. And very small and very young. Like a child caught playing dress-up, her face smeared with make-up. Acutely conscious all of a sudden of her not exactly svelte figure and her dress, which she'd borrowed from Eleni, hoping to be more grown up, and which was a little too tight.

Her lips felt stiff and numb. Her body cold.

'I'm sorry, Alexandros, just forget this…all of it. Forget it happened, forget *me.*' She whirled away and ran, down the steps, into the garden, away from the patio, away from everything. She heard him call after her once but she didn't stop, and he didn't follow.

The tears came as she ran and when she finally stopped she hunched down and cried and cried until she could hardly see. She cried for being so naïve, so silly and for listening to Eleni. She must have been emboldened by some lunar magic or madness, the wine… As if someone like Alexandros Kouros would *ever* notice someone like her, would ever even want to kiss someone like her. She cringed when she thought of how she'd thrown herself at him. He'd as good as had to pry her hands off him. She wiped her cheeks. One thing was for sure, she was *never* going to touch alcohol again if it had led her to do something so stupid and ill-judged.

Miserable, Kallie went back up towards the house, unable to avoid going around it to return home. And as she passed the open patio doors, she couldn't help but look inside. The room was hushed, the designer-clad, jewel-bedecked crowd with glasses high in the air as they toasted the newly announced union of Alexandros and the stunning woman at his side. His fiancée. Pia Kyriapolous, the famous model. They looked so beautiful together Kallie's eyes watered again.

She felt a tap on her shoulder and whirled around, very aware of her tearstained cheeks. Eleni. Looking at her with sympathy written all over her face.

'Oh, Kallie, I'm so sorry…'

Something in the way she said it made Kallie very still. Her stomach churned as she suddenly remembered her cousin's words. *By the time you see him again he'll be married with three kids.* 'Please, tell me you didn't know about this, Eleni.'

Eleni looked defiant. 'I did you a favour, Kallie. If you'd known, would you have gone near him?'

Of course not!

She lashed herself again at her phenomenal naïvety and knew it was in that moment that something in her died, or grew up.

She pulled away, physically and mentally, curled up somewhere inside herself. Something in Eleni's face made her want to protect herself. It was something she'd never seen before. *Or noticed.* She contrived to toss her head, exactly how she'd seen her cousin do it a thousand times, usually when Alexandros was around, and shrugged. 'It's no big deal, Eleni. I can hardly compete with Pia, now, can I?' She even managed a small laugh from somewhere. 'But, like you said, at least I tried…*ne?*'

And for the first time in her young life, she summoned all the adult poise she could, and swept away, leaving the party, her cousin and Alexandros behind.

When Kallie woke up the next morning, the tight ache in her chest didn't seem to have dissipated one bit and she had the horrible sensation of thinking it could have all been a bad dream, but of course it hadn't. Her only consolation was that she knew Alexandros would probably be in Athens, and that she was due to go back to England the next day. She prayed Alexandros would stay in Athens till she was gone. And that no one would ever know what had happened. Except them. And Eleni. Who at least, Kallie thought with a shudder of relief, hadn't witnessed her humiliating efforts.

However, she came downstairs to noise and confusion and commotion, Her parents and Alexandros in the middle of it all. Her father was shouting at him, thrusting a newspaper in his face.

'How could you? We trusted you. She's seventeen, for God's sake. Little more than a child. Isn't it enough that you're getting married to one of the most beautiful women in Athens? You had to mess around with Kallie.'

They didn't see her come down the stairs behind Alexandros. His voice came low and blistering. 'Pia's family have surprisingly little regard for their daughter marrying someone splashed across the middle pages of the biggest tabloid in the country. They also have surprisingly little regard for her marrying someone who, and I quote, "never wanted to follow his father into business." Thanks to your daughter, my engagement is off as of today.'

Her mother, who hadn't seen her either, stepped forward at that moment and slapped Alexandros across the face. Kallie saw his head jerk back. In the shock of silence afterwards, her mother's voice was shaking with emotion as she said, 'Surely you *know* she's always had a crush on you? You were like a son to us.'

Kallie's legs stopped. They wouldn't work and she felt herself going icy cold and clammy, an awful sick feeling in her stomach. She must have made some kind of noise because they all turned and saw her.

She couldn't believe what she'd just witnessed, *the violence,* and how her mother had just laid out her innermost feelings for all to see. Alexandros grabbed the paper out of her father's hands. The anger and disgust on his face made her want to turn around and run away. She saw the livid red hand imprint on his cheek.

'*You—*'

Her father cut him off. 'Kouros, get out of this house. You are not welcome here, now or ever again.'

Alexandros turned away from Kallie and back to her father. 'Believe me, I don't want to see any of you again. Especially *her.*' He flicked her a look that was so contemptuous that Kallie took a step back. And then he was leaving, walking away, out the door.

Acting on pure impulse, Kallie ran after him, ignoring her parents' calls to come back. Alexandros's long legs nearly had him at the gate that separated their neighbouring properties.

'Wait, Alexandros…wait!'

He stopped so suddenly that she almost ran into his back. He turned and gripped her arms with hard hands, his face close to hers. And suddenly he didn't even look angry any more, he looked sad. And that was even more confusing. Her head swam as she tried to understand what could have happened.

'I thought we were friends, Kallie. Why did you do it? You've ruined everything…and all because I didn't want you?' He shook his head. 'You were the one person who didn't seem to expect anything from me. I trusted you and you set me up, blabbed everything.'

What was he talking about?

'I don't know what—'

He shook his head, cutting her off with a fierce look in his eyes, his lip curling in distaste. An image came back into his head of her reaching up to kiss him with a bold look in her eyes. One thing he knew now, without a shadow of a doubt, was that he'd never really known Kallie Demarchis. Just like he'd never really known any of them. Kallie's family had been like a second family to him and yet they could throw him out of their lives, their house. He'd been a fool to trust them. *To think he'd thought her innocent, untainted... sweet!*

'These last two years you've really grown up, Kallie, haven't you? Become just like the others. You heard about the engagement and thought you could have a go, too? Try to get in there?'

His face was so harsh that Kallie didn't know how she still stood in front of him. And he wasn't finished. 'Seventeen is just a little too young for my tastes, though, and you don't have what I need.'

He shoved the newspaper at her. 'Oh, and next time you want to do a kiss and tell? If you're trying to keep your identity a secret, it's a good idea not to submit the copy from your own e-mail address. You're nothing but a spoilt little bitch, Kallie, and not even a particularly bright one.'

She watched as he disappeared from view, her mouth open...words stuck in her throat. *Her e-mail? Kiss and tell?* As if in an awful sick nightmare, she looked at the paper which had fallen at her feet. It lay open on a very bad-quality, grainy black-and-white photo. As if taken with a camera phone. But one person was unmistakable. Alexandros. The golden boy of the shipping world. And the woman with her arms wrapped around his neck, straining against him, was most certainly *not* Pia Kyriapolous. The girl in the picture would be unidentifiable to any but those who knew her well, and was far too chubby to be the well-known model. A screaming headline. THE GROOM! THE NIGHT HIS ENGAGEMENT IS ANNOUNCED...!

CHAPTER ONE

Seven years later, The Ritz Hotel, Paris

ALEXANDROS KOUROS was bored. It was like a heavy mantle around his shoulders. A black cloud that spread outwards from his very depths, pervading everything. He was oblivious to the fact that he was surrounded by opulence. The opulence that came with being one of the wealthiest men in the world, in one of the world's most exclusive hotels. Hushed whispers encircled him. He tuned them out, the superlatives bouncing off him. They'd surrounded him for years, but he'd never courted them, never needed any assurance.

So handsome…so young! The most successful shipping magnate since Onassis… Even more money… Most eligible bachelor…

Now the constant murmurs that followed him wherever he went only added to the ennui he felt. He'd achieved a pinnacle of success attained by just a very few, and only imagined by most. And it had been hard won, which should make it all the more sweet. But was this it? How could he be feeling like this when everything he'd ever worked for lay at his fingertips, when he could snap those fingers and influence the world's economy with just a word, a command… And if this wasn't what he wanted, then what the hell was? A distant memory, an old faded dream, reared its head. *That* had long turned to dust.

A touch on his arm, not gentle. It was predatory, possessive and brought his attention back to the room. To the woman at his side. She was considered one of the most beautiful, desirable women in the world…and she was the latest in a long line of similar women who had graced his arm, his bed.

'Darling…'

He felt irritation prickle across his skin. Unfortunately, for the sake of politeness, he couldn't remain oblivious to her. He turned to face her and smiled tightly, taking in the platinum blonde of her hair that suddenly looked too garish, too bright. Took in the heavily made-up face, the hard, avaricious glitter in her eyes. The diamonds flashing around her neck. Diamonds that he had bought with scant regard to their worth. He made a split-second decision, suddenly aware that he didn't find her at all attractive any more. Had he ever?

Isabelle Zolanz didn't know it yet, but she was on her way out. He felt relieved for the first time in weeks. The thrill of knowing he'd be free again already helped to diminish the crushing boredom. He didn't want to spend another minute with her. In fact, he decided there and then that they would leave, he'd take her home, break it off now. His suit felt constrictive and he had to school his features into some semblance of neutrality.

Just as he was about to open his mouth and speak, to say some platitude, something flashed in the corner of his eye and he turned on a reflex to look. The room was packed, and in the doorway on the other side of the room stood a woman. She'd obviously just arrived, craning her neck looking for someone, standing on tiptoe. For a split second the noise in the room faded. He couldn't take his eyes off her. Goosebumps broke out on his skin. The hubbub rushed back.

She was utterly captivating. But in a way that he couldn't

define, in a way that confounded him. Not model gorgeous. Not preened or buffed. But something about her caught his attention. She was only of average height but was perfectly proportioned, his expert eye assessing in seconds the way her curves dipped in and out in all the right places. A little more voluptuous than he'd normally go for but calling to him on some deep, primitive level. The simple black V-neck dress drew the eye to her waist and the slopes of her breasts. A pendant hung around her neck, the gem resting in her cleavage. It sparkled as the light hit it and he dimly recognised where the flash had come from.

Just as he also recognised with shock that he felt a compelling desire to walk over, take her hand and lead her back outside to see for himself if her skin was as soft and silky as it looked. The urge was so strong that he actually felt his feet shift, his whole body turn, as if to move in her direction. He wanted to touch the place where her gem rested. And he had to admit with sudden chagrin, as possessiveness was an alien emotion to him, that he wanted to lead her away from the other men who he could see already taking note of her arrival, too. She was like a breath of fresh air in a musty room.

She was pale. Her face had clear, clean lines, cheekbones clearly delineated, eyes wide apart and almond-shaped, making him want to see them up close, see their colour. Honey-streaked hair hung in loose waves over her shoulders and a heavy fringe, swept to one side, hid and alternately revealed tantalising glimpses of her eyes.

His hooded eyes followed her as she walked with effortless feminine grace, her hips swaying, the inward curving line of the small of her back and the jut of her rounded bottom making Alexandros feel a twinge of reaction in his trousers. More than a twinge, in fact.

He felt a tug on his arm and almost shook off the hand that rested there, still completely engrossed in watching this woman. And only remembered then where he was, who he was with. He felt shocked. For a moment he had become entranced. Forgotten nearly everything. He shook his head mentally. Definitely a sign that he needed to move on, if he was lusting after a complete stranger across a crowded room.

But there was *something* about her. Something he couldn't put his finger on, some kind of familiarity, as if he knew her or had seen her somewhere before…

He tore his gaze away with more of an effort than he liked to admit and looked down at Isabelle again. A smooth smile was in place as he remembered wanting to leave, her harsh beauty even more jarring now after *that*.

He murmured, 'Forgive me…I have an important early meeting tomorrow. Would you mind if we left?'

'Not at all, darling. I'll get my coat from the cloakroom.'

She squeezed his arm and smiled, clearly anticipating, somewhat misguidedly, that he wanted them to be alone, and walked away.

As he watched her walk away, Alexandros felt no compunction, no guilt at what he was about to do. A woman like Isabelle Zolanz was well versed in the way he worked, and men like him. He had no doubt she'd be put out, but as no emotions were invested, he knew it'd be for the loss of his money, his largesse and the social standing that came with being seen on his arm. It was a state of affairs he was used to. He enjoyed the thrill of the chase. But lately, if he was honest, every conquest had become stale…flat. And there was invariably very little chasing involved.

Even so, he conversely felt the relief flood him again and unconsciously sought out the other woman. But she had disappeared. He grimaced slightly. It was probably for the best. He knew all too well that seeing something like that, building up an image, no matter how beautiful the woman—*and she wasn't even that beautiful!*—always led to disappointment.

They were all the same. All the ones that hovered around him like bees around a honey pot. In the rarefied circles he moved in, he didn't encounter another type. Sex and money. They were the two currencies that he understood and knew all too well. He played the game like a virtuoso. In bed and out of it.

A cloud crossed his mind. Was he ready to be free again? There was a certain amount of protection to be had in keeping a mistress. A respite from the tiresome attempts of other women to get his attention. And then he was forced to remember something. He scowled. He actually did need a woman right now. He needed a lot more than that and it irked him beyond belief. But even as he saw Isabelle in the distance, collecting her coat, his stomach felt acidic. He certainly wouldn't be asking her.

Kallie pushed her way through the crowd. She craned her neck looking for her uncle and finally spotted him in a far corner. When she reached him she kissed him on the cheek. 'Sorry, Alexei, I got held up at work.'

'No matter, my dear. Let me get you a drink.'

He spoke quickly and seemed a little jumpy to Kallie. Which was reinforced when he grabbed a glass of water from a passing tray and practically shoved it at her. He avoided her gaze, looking distractedly over her head as he did so, and Kallie felt an uneasy sense of foreboding. Her uncle looked almost…nervous.

'Alexei…'

He suddenly jostled her behind a plant and screened her from the room with his body.

'Alexei…?' Kallie's voice was indignant. She knew her uncle was given to dramatics but this was ridiculous. He was acting as if they were in a bad spy movie. 'What on earth is wrong with you?' She smiled widely and then whispered *sotto voce* in his ear, 'Are we hiding from your mistress?'

He turned back to face her, affronted, 'Kallie Demarchis, you know I would never look at another woman.'

She put her hand on his arm, soothing him. 'I'm teasing…but you're acting so strangely. Do you think I can come out from behind this plant?'

He paled for a second as he took in something across the room. Kallie frowned and couldn't hide a spike of fear. 'What is it? You're scaring me now.'

He looked back at her and loosened his collar. 'Kallie… it's someone…someone is here, someone you haven't seen in a long time…someone…'

'Who?' she asked, beginning to feel a little exasperated.

Her uncle avoided the question. 'I tried to call you on your mobile just now but they wouldn't let me use it…then I got waylaid by someone else and couldn't stop you coming in…before…'

She tried to be reasonable, patient. 'Before what? Alexei, why wouldn't you want me to come in?'

She could see her uncle gulp visibly. 'Because…well, because…Alexandros Kouros is here…'

Alexandros Kouros…

The noise in the room became a buzzing sound in Kallie's ears. She was vaguely aware of her uncle practically wringing his hands and very dimly, in a far-away place, his words slowly sank in with the same devastation as the *Titanic* hitting the iceberg. She felt an icy numbness take over her limbs and would have dropped her glass except that her uncle caught it in time. The water slopped onto her dress. At least it's only water, she thought with banal shock, it won't stain.

Alexandros Kouros…

It was just a name, she rationalised somewhere within her still buzzing head. Just a name, attached to someone very famous. Well known. Very wealthy. Very handsome. Influential. Someone who didn't even enter her sphere or orbit. But yet…it was the name of someone infinitely memorable. Intimately tied into her past, who had once been in her orbit—*had been her orbit*—as big a part of her past as if he'd been one of her own family.

Someone she'd never dreamed of having to face again. And now he was here, *somewhere,* possibly even just mere feet away. Panic gripped her, making her skin clammy.

Her uncle had grasped her hands and was looking at her. She forced stricken eyes to his, her face leached of all colour.

'Kallie, darling…I'm so sorry. The thing is, you can't be here… If he sees you…'

She nodded slowly, not even really sure why she was nodding, only seizing on the words "if he sees you". She didn't even want to imagine for one second what that reaction might be like…or what *he* might be like now, in the flesh.

She was more than dismayed that she couldn't be feeling just a mild curiosity, to be able to shrug it off, declare the fact that he was in the same room as a funny coincidence, uncaring whether or not they bumped into each other. She was stunned by the strength of her own reaction after all this time, the well of emotion that was still so close to the surface. It shook her to the core and scared the life out of her. She'd never guessed it was still there.

It had only been a kiss, for God's sake, little more than a kiss. Yet it had led to so much more. She chided herself that he must have moved on from what had happened…but then she had to remember with a sudden upsurge of nausea that *she* and her stupid actions had been instrumental in the calling off of his engagement…the ruination of the so-called marriage of the decade. To the woman he loved… How would he have possibly forgotten that?

Her uncle was getting more agitated, looking slightly shifty. 'The thing is, Kallie…I didn't tell you before now as I knew it might upset you, but I've started doing business with him again. Since your parents died, that is. Obviously your father wouldn't have approved but, you see, I *had* to, Kallie. I had no one else to turn to and when he gave me an appointment…' He laughed a sudden brief laugh, sounding like a little boy. '*Me!* An appointment. It would appear he's willing to let bygones be bygones, with me at least. Now, if it had been your father, that would have been a different story—' He seemed to catch himself, realising he was starting to babble, and gripped Kallie's hands tighter. 'But if he sees *you*…'

The familiar clench of grief at the mention of her parents went unnoticed for once. Her uncle was referring, of course, to the scandal that had gripped Greece for weeks. The press had devoured the story of how Alexandros Kouros had taken advantage of his family friend's young daughter. Just when he was about to become engaged to Pia Kyriapolous. And even though Kallie had cried tears of frustration, trying to defend him, no one had listened, too intent to paint him the villain and her the poor innocent victim.

It had been even more futile trying to assert her own innocence with regard to the photo and story, and only recently had she confirmed for herself who the real culprit was. The story had since faded, of course, and since her grandmother's death the summer after that, Kallie had only been back to Greece a couple of times. She'd never seen him again.

Her uncle looked so comically terrified that it brought her back to reality. Kallie's heart went out to him. No doubt he was watching his entire business float down the river if Alexandros Kouros took one look at her and decided to wreak belated revenge.

'Alexei, I don't care if you're doing business with him…really. Look, I'll go. Believe me, I have as little desire to see him as he must have to see me.' *Liar. You'd love to see how he's turned out…*

Her heart beat a staccato just at the thought. A whole

Pandora's chest was being opened and Kallie was helpless to stop it. This was too close a call and she had to get out, get away. She kissed her uncle on the cheek and squeezed his hand. 'I'll call you tomorrow, we can talk more then.'

He nodded with obvious relief and Kallie walked away quickly, head down, not looking left or right, just focusing on getting through the crowd in front of her. She comforted herself with the thought that even if he did see her, she'd changed a lot in seven years, and she would come so far below the radar of his usual women that he'd be unlikely to recognise her straight off, thus giving her time to escape.

Almost at the door, she had to duck out of the way of a waitress carrying a loaded tray and she careened into someone's back. They twisted to look around and Kallie was horribly, familiarly aware of someone very tall, very broad, with black hair curling on his collar. The back of her neck prickled and afterwards she wondered at how she hadn't had a stronger sensation, a stronger warning of imminent danger. Quite the opposite, it seemed, some evil force had directed her straight into the lion's jaws. She couldn't move. She was rooted to the spot. Unable to flee the danger.

CHAPTER TWO

SHE looked up…and up again. And her eyes met all too familiar dark, fathomless depths. In a heart-stoppingly handsome face. A face she knew well, because it had stayed vivid in her consciousness. Her mouth, which had opened automatically to apologise, stayed open.

'Alexandros Kouros…' She wasn't even aware of saying his name out loud. It was as if she had to say it to make it real or to pray that he was a figment of her imagination. But he was no figment of anyone's imagination. He was too vital… too dark…too big and too…gorgeous. *Why* did she have to bump into him? It was too cruel.

'Do we know each—?' He stopped and turned fully. Black brows pulled together, frowning.

It was her! The woman… But he knew her…

His eyes raked her up and down. They both knew that the way she had said his name had been more than just the banal recognition of someone famous.

Kallie, while praying he *wouldn't* recognise her, was conversely stung somewhere very vulnerable when he clearly had no idea who she was. She forced her stricken limbs to move, to try and get away. She couldn't believe her awful luck. Why hadn't she just stayed where she was? Why hadn't she taken more notice of where she was going? Why was he looking at her like that? She had to get away.

'Sorry…'

She turned and just when she thought she could let her breath out, when she'd taken a couple of steps, her arm was taken in a punishing grip. His deep voice rang with stunned incredulity.

'Kallie Demarchis?'

She closed her eyes. The worst thing had just happened. Her breath came back but it was painful. She longed to be able to keep going, to walk away. The burning humiliation was still so vivid that she had to open her eyes again to halt the images rushing through her mind. His grip was painful on her arm and yet it lit tiny fires that raced up and down over her skin. She finally turned, with little choice to do anything else.

She turned, hitched her chin and looked up. 'Yes.'

His face was unreadable, but she saw something flare in the depths of his dark eyes. Anger. Shock and anger. He moved his intense gaze from hers and looked her up and down, slowly and thoroughly.

'Well, well, well. Little Kallie Demarchis. All grown up.'

He spoke almost musingly, as if to himself. 'Your eyes give you away. They're such a distinctive colour. Blue and green. Only for that, I don't think I would have recognised you. You must have had work done. If I remember, you always were insecure…but it's definitely been worth it.'

It was only when his eyes insolently dropped to her breasts that Kallie gasped with outrage, welcoming it because it crashed through the numbing shock. She finally managed to tear her arm out from his grip. 'How dare you? I've done no such thing. I'm sorry I bumped into you, believe me, but I'm sure you'll be only too happy to excuse me.'

'Don't you mean you're sorry for wrecking my engagement all those years ago…or sorry for dragging my name through the tabloids…or sorry for publicly humiliating me, for getting me thrown out of your house like a common thief?'

So much for hoping, or even praying that he might have forgotten…

Two spots of colour burned in her cheeks and her eyes flashed. Alexandros had to suck in a breath against his will.

She was magnificent…and how had she transported him back to a time he had believed he'd forgotten for good, so easily and so quickly?

He reeled. Reeled with the shock of coming face to face with the very woman who'd captivated him across the room. Reeled with the force of her beauty up close. And now reeled with the knowledge that it was *Kallie Demarchis*. The girl who had taken petty spite and used it to almost ruin him. He looked down at her. Except now she wasn't a girl. She was a woman. A very sexy woman. A woman who was making the blood hum in his veins and an arrow of desire shoot straight to his groin. An instant chemical reaction.

Kallie had opened her mouth again to speak, but before she could do, a blonde vision appeared beside Alexandros, a scarlet-tipped hand on his arm. A blatant indication of ownership. And who could blame her? Kallie thought fuzzily, closing her mouth, words dying unsaid. Even without studying him—*she didn't have to*—he was the most handsome man in the room, head and shoulders above all other men. A perfect, potent specimen of manhood, sexual energy radiating off him in waves that she fancied were almost visible to the eye.

He'd been a gorgeous young man but now…he was quite simply devastating. The years had filled out his frame, had added maturity to his face, the lines starker, harder but no less beautiful. He now had an edge of sexual charisma that came only with age, confidence and experience. His hair still had the curls of his youth though, and that made something poignant erupt in Kallie's chest. The other woman's slightly, delightfully accented tones broke through Kallie's reverie.

'Darling…aren't you going to introduce me?'

Alexandros couldn't stop staring at Kallie. Again. He'd been mesmerised *again*. To the exclusion of everything else. He could see Kallie flounder, too. As if they'd both forgotten they were in a public place, surrounded by people. But Isabelle had to be attended to. Kallie cut in, though, before he could speak. She looked apologetically at Isabelle, cutting out Alexandros.

'Please, excuse me. I have to catch someone before they leave. It was…nice to see you again, Alexandros.'

And she was gone, had melted into the crowd. All he could see was her shining head every now and then as it bobbed and weaved away from him. The urge to snatch her back was strong. Very strong. And the gnawing, clawing feeling of boredom that Alexandros had felt earlier was gone. As though he'd just been injected with vital energy. And desire. The kind of desire he hadn't felt in a long, long time. The fierce elemental kind that made his insides burn for completion, for fulfilment.

Reluctantly responding to Isabelle's urging to go, he was already making plans in his head. Plans that didn't involve her, but that did involve Kallie. He couldn't believe how she'd strayed into his path, like a plump, succulent piece of fruit.

He hadn't thought about her in years—*hadn't had the time*—and only fleetingly had she crossed his mind when her uncle had approached him recently. Agreeing to meet with her uncle, he'd congratulated himself that he'd left all that behind…*until now*.

Kallie Demarchis.

He couldn't stop repeating her name in his head.

He'd seen her uncle earlier, and had acknowledged him briefly across the room, but who would have known that she'd have come there, too? Who would have known that she'd be the very woman who was stoking the dying embers of his desire? And who would have known that he'd ever get the chance to do something about her petty, spiteful act all those years ago? An act with ripple effects that had vastly eclipsed the actual incident involved. She'd never been made accountable for those actions. The feelings of betrayal and anger from those days surprised him now with their resurgence, with their freshness. He didn't like being reduced to such primitive emotions.

The initial anger that had gripped him fed his energy. Seeing Kallie again tonight, the timing was so perfect that he almost laughed out loud. The linkages that existed in place for him to take advantage of this opportunity were mind-blowing with their simplicity. If there was such a thing as karma, this was it. And he was going to enjoy every minute of it. And enjoy every piece of her.

Two days later, Kallie stared at the blinking light on the intercom of her phone. Her PA's disembodied yet unmistakably awe-struck voice floated through again. 'Kallie…did you hear me? Alexandros Kouros is on line one for you.'

Just like that. Alexandros Kouros is on line one…

Her heart, which had stopped, started to beat again, slowly. She'd somehow, in the past forty-eight hours, tried to convince herself that she hadn't actually seen him. That it had been some sort of bad dream. She tried to speak but nothing came out and with a huge effort she shook herself out of the inertia that seemed to have taken control of her every limb. 'Thank you, Cécile. I'll take it now.'

She picked up the phone, pressed the button under the blinking light and took a deep breath.

'Hello?'

'Kallie.' The deep authoritative voice sounded close in her ear and made her sit up straight.

'Alexandros.' She marvelled that she could sound so cool when her head and insides seemed to be self-combusting. The treacherous unfurling of desire that had started the minute she'd seen him again was still there. And that knowledge scared her. What did he want? Kallie swivelled around in her chair and didn't take in the view of Paris outside her third-floor window, the Eiffel Tower going unnoticed in the distance. Her voice was clipped, tense.

'What can I do for you, Alexandros? I'm sure this isn't a social call.'

Even if they didn't share history, the most successful Greek shipping magnate in the world wouldn't be ringing up her small Anglo-French PR firm.

His slightly accented tones came like silk down the phone into her ear again. 'It was certainly a shock to see you the other night. It's been, what, six years?'

'Seven.' She had answered far too quickly and easily. Her hand tightened around the phone, hoping that he hadn't noticed. He didn't seem to as he spoke again. And took the wind out of her sails.

'I was sorry to hear about your parents...'

Kallie was feeling more and more bemused. This man had been thrown out of their house by her father. Slapped by her mother. He had told her he never wanted to see her again. He must have picked up something in the silence because he said, 'Despite the past, Kallie, I *was* sorry to hear of their deaths.'

The shock at hearing his voice was beginning to wear off. 'Well...thank you.'

She repeated her question again. 'What...what can I do for you, Alexandros?'

He didn't speak for a long moment, and she was almost about to repeat her question when he said with devastating banality, 'I want you to have dinner with me tonight.'

Kallie took the phone away from her ear for a second and

looked at it. Alexandros was up to something. That was one thing she was sure of. She existed on his list of people to call for dinner somewhere alongside Attila the Hun. He whizzed around the world on his private jet, doing billion-dollar deals, meeting heads of state and dating what seemed to be an endless stream of models and actresses, like Isabelle Zolanz. It was only afterwards, when she'd got away from him, that she'd realised who the other woman had been: a famous French actress. He certainly didn't ring people he despised to ask them out for dinner. People who had ruined his chance for marital happiness. And even by some accounts a huge merger with his fiancée's family shipping company, but she wasn't sure about that. She'd avoided listening to anyone talk about it at the time and in England, at least, it hadn't hit the news with the same force.

'Somehow I don't think you do, Alexandros.'

'But I do, Kallie. I'd like us to catch up,' he returned easily. Far too easily. As if he'd anticipated exactly how she'd respond.

Kallie's hand tightened even more on the phone and she felt dizzy. This had to be some kind of bad dream, a sick joke. He was playing with her.

'Alexandros, I don't want to go out for dinner. You said you never wanted to see me again.'

'Well, I've changed my mind.'

'Why?' she almost pleaded.

'Let's just say you owe me at least this, don't you think?'

Kallie closed her eyes weakly. What could she say? She searched frantically for an excuse but, as if reading her mind, his voice trickled down the line like dark honey, weaving around her senses.

'I had a nice chat with your assistant. She was most helpful in informing me how clear your diary is this evening.'

Kallie cursed Cécile mentally. And yet she couldn't stop the entirely uncontrollable part of her that was intrigued…that wanted to be able to say yes. She had no excuse not to, and to fight was to invite him further into a dialogue that might take them down a path she didn't want to go.

Her voice was stiff with obvious reluctance. 'It would seem that I have no choice. I'm finished work around six this evening…when would suit you?'

'I have a table booked for dinner at the Hotel de Crillon at the Place de la Concorde. Eight o'clock. I can pick you up…or send my driver?'

Kallie thought of her tiny flat in the Marais district and spoke quickly. 'No. There's no need. I can meet you there.'

She could almost feel him shrug on the other end of the phone. 'As you wish. Eight, then. I'll wait for you in the bar.'

CHAPTER THREE

ALEXANDROS put down the phone and stood up from the leather chair. In custom-made Italian trousers and shirt, he walked over to the window of his office and stuck his hands deep in his pockets. The action drew the fabric taut over his buttocks, the shirt stretched over broad shoulders. He cut an impressive, very masculine figure silhouetted against the window. He thought back to the other night. The remnants of the shock of seeing Kallie again still lingered. Along with the shock of how much she'd changed, and the desire that had pounded through his entire body. That still pounded through it just from hearing her voice.

It had been harder to extricate himself from Isabelle than he had thought. It had taken two nights. More jewellery. And dinner in the newest, most expensive restaurant. She'd been more tenacious than he'd realised and he was relieved the episode was over. She'd begun to fancy herself as perhaps being in line for marriage and had not been pleased to discover that, instead, he'd wanted to end things.

He looked out at the horizon, his gaze skipping absently over the Eiffel tower in the distance. His thoughts centred on Kallie. Her blue-green eyes flashed again in his mind's eye. Seven years might as well have been seven seconds. He'd been transported back in time that quickly. Felt all the old emotions surge up. Emotions he'd long thought he had under control. Apparently not.

He'd been such a fool all those years ago. How had he missed seeing her true colours? How had he ever thought for a second of her family being closer to him than even his own? His hand clenched into a fist as he remembered how vindictive she'd been. And how he hadn't seen it coming at all.

He'd been fooled into somehow believing that she of all people wouldn't have changed. He could still remember seeing her across the room that night, smiling sweetly at him. It had been like balm to his ravaged spirit. A cool reminder of happier times, more carefree concerns. And *then* to have her morph into some kind of temptress, right in front of his eyes. He could still feel the astonishment that had slammed into him. So immobilising that he hadn't even pulled away from her kiss immediately.

Everyone along the way had shown their true colours in the end. Not least his own family. But for Kallie to join those ranks…and to behave in a way that he would never have even imagined. She'd had him thrown out of her house, his fiancée's life, and his name had been dragged through the mud.

By using her own e-mail to send the photo and story, it had been so obvious she'd meant it like a taunt! And she'd had the nerve to reveal deeply personal details to the newspaper that only she could have known…because she had been the only person he'd ever told them to. Details like wishes and dreams…aspirations that had had nothing to do with what had been expected of him.

His mouth slashed into a grim line. The vultures who had already smelt a possible weakness on his father's death had circled for a long time. He repressed a shudder. And they'd nearly got him.

He had to acknowledge that when he'd told her those things he'd been two years younger, before his father had died, and she'd been fifteen. He hadn't yet been flung at top speed into a reality that had torn any rose-tinted dreams away. A reality that had mocked him for having been so open. The fact that she would have stored those conversations up to use in such a way made his stomach turn.

That period had been the turning point for so much. A turning point that meant he'd never, ever let anyone get that close again. He operated on his own now. He didn't need anyone.

He slammed a fist against the wall beside him. *How* could she have changed so much in those two years? He closed his eyes. He'd asked himself the questions over and over. The fact was, he'd been betrayed. All he'd ever represented to anyone around him had been a means to make money. To generate wealth. When he'd turned his back on her that day, he'd turned his back on a lot of things.

Enough. Kallie Demarchis was about to learn what it meant to cross Alexandros Kouros. It was time for her to taste a little of the reality he'd had to taste.

His mind went to the plans he'd set in motion since seeing her again. It was true that he'd never been one with a lust for revenge, seeing it only as a device that could betray a weakness to the opposition. That could betray emotion. When all around him had descended to that visceral level in business, he never had. And it was part of the secret of his success. Part of what had helped him claw back control, get to the top. Go further than even his father had done.

He thought of how, when Alexei Demarchis had come to him for help, he'd debated for a long time whether or not to entertain the man. He smiled grimly. He'd made the right decision. Fate had just told him so.

Now he was willing to rethink his views on revenge… especially when it was laid out for him so enticingly, so temptingly, when his loins ached with a hunger that was all too rare. It was time for him to lay the ghost to rest and indulge a little.

* * *

Kallie took in the passing streets of Paris. She'd never normally take a taxi, the métro being more than efficient for her needs, but a last-minute crisis at work and a derailed train had meant she was under pressure to make the Hotel de Crillon for eight. She felt nervous and jittery. Her hands felt clammy, so she smoothed them distractedly on her dress. What would it be like, seeing Alexandros again? He was even more handsome than she could have imagined. The stark, masculine lines of his face were indelibly imprinted onto her retina. He'd seemed even bigger to her. Six feet four of nothing but lean, hard muscle. Her belly clenched in a pure spasm of sheer, unadulterated lust and she tried to take her mind off his physical attractions.

He hadn't ever married, there had been no talk of it since the debacle with Pia Kyriapolous. He obviously hadn't managed to mend bridges there. From what Kallie could remember, Pia had quite quickly married someone else. No doubt further rubbing salt into Alexandros's wound. Pia had been one of the most successful models in Greece, the daughter of another very wealthy shipping magnate. The day after the engagement had been announced, Kallie had had to endure everyone saying that it was a match made in heaven.

Kallie knew now with maturity and hindsight that her developing sexuality had been hopelessly snared by Alexandros. But, of course, he hadn't noticed that. Hadn't noticed *her* like that. So that's why, with the very vocal, almost bullying encouragement of Eleni, she'd gone out to find him that night. She closed her eyes and gulped. She did *not* need to go there now, not when she was going to be seeing him in mere minutes. She was a grown woman, in control of herself and her emotions.

She smiled grimly to herself, opening her eyes. She'd confused immature, infatuated lust with love. And as for Eleni… Kallie sighed deeply. There was no point thinking about that now, there was nothing she could do anyway. It was all water under the bridge.

She saw that the taxi was pulling into the area outside the main door of the hotel. She went hot and then cold in the space of seconds. They came to a halt. The porter stepped forward to help her out. She looked up at the distinctive name on the awning over the door and, with her legs feeling decidedly wobbly in her high heels, stepped into the distinctively honey-coloured marble foyer.

At the door to the small bar she saw him immediately. And felt the urge to turn around and step back outside. Go home, pack up and move back to London. She straightened her spine and walked forward. He was sitting on a high stool, a glass with dark liquid swirling around the bottom in his hands. He didn't see her approach and there was something so intense about the way he was studying the liquid…almost as though he was looking for some kind of answer. Kallie dismissed her fanciful notions and came to a halt near him, doing her best not to be bowled over by his physicality.

She cursed her voice, which sounded unbearably husky. 'Alexandros…'

He looked up and those dark, deep depths caught her and sucked her in. She was in trouble. He stood with lithe grace, no hint of expression on his face. He reached to take her coat. Reluctantly she let him help her out of it, studiously avoiding touching him anywhere.

'Sorry I'm a bit late. I got held up at work.'

He smiled. It didn't reach his eyes. 'No problem. We'll have a drink here and then go through.'

He was charm and urbanity incarnate. And he didn't fool her for a second. Kallie followed him on legs which had become like cotton wool. He led her over to a table and gestured for her to sit down. She was glad of her simple silk shirt and plain back skirt. Glad she hadn't made an effort. The waiter arrived and Kallie ordered water.

Alexandros lifted a brow and ordered a whiskey for himself. 'No alcohol tonight, Kallie?'

An immediate blush stained her cheeks as the meaning of his loaded question cut through her. He was referring to *that* night, the way she'd grabbed the bottle from his hand. Again she was aghast at his memory. Had he forgotten nothing? She shook her head tightly.

She wasn't going to tell him that ever since that night she'd never touched a drop of alcohol. She'd had plenty of opportunity but somehow, when it came to it, she just couldn't. Something would flash back into her head, and she'd find that even the smell turned her stomach. She had the very uncomfortable suspicion that her bizarre reaction was somehow tied in to the fear that something out of her control would happen. Like it had that night.

'Look, I'm sure you're busy. We really don't have to do this whole dinner thing. Do you want to just tell me—?'

'All in good time, Kallie.' He bent forward and Kallie fought against arching back into the chair. She felt very keenly as though she were involved in something huge, but something she had no clue about. Like a fly caught in a web. And she didn't like it. Not when Alexandros smiled at her like the hungry spider.

'Tell me,' he asked equably when her water arrived, 'how have you ended up here in Paris? Didn't you go to college in the UK?'

She nodded slowly, determined not to show her fear, her sense of being intimidated. But despite her wariness, she found it surprisingly easy to talk.

'After my mother and father died, I wanted to get away from London. I've always loved Paris. I had spent a year here during my business degree, taking French…' She shrugged, awkward under his intense gaze. 'It seemed like an obvious choice. I had money from my inheritance and set up our small firm. We got busy quickly as we seemed to corner the niche in doing PR for English companies setting up here and vice versa for French ones in London…'

Alexandros thought of the rapid research he'd done on Kallie that day. The countless pictures he'd unearthed of her at various parties, looking like the life and soul of each one. Although her appearance opposite him begged to differ, as she sat there in her plain skirt and blouse, which did little to disguise the curves he'd seen on display the other night.

And despite her abstinence from alcohol so far, he didn't doubt that she used *it* and maybe more to enhance her partying. He felt inarticulate rage start to rise, some indefinable sense of disappointment, and forced himself to be civil. For now.

'You've done more than corner the niche. I read about your company in the financial press—you were awarded best new small business last year. That's some achievement.'

Kallie was too surprised at his praise and it was given in far too much of a backhand manner for her to feel a glow of pride. She shrugged again modestly. 'Like I said, we just got in at a good time. Britain has never been so close to France with the tunnel, and plenty of people are capitalising on it. I'm one of many.'

'Yes, but not everyone makes a success of it. You obviously have the Demarchis genes.'

'Which are nothing compared to the Kouros genes,' she pointed out with a wry smile, feeling herself start to relax slightly. The smile surprised her and she pursed her lips immediately. She knew that to feel relaxed was entering very dangerous territory.

'Maybe so.' Alexandros's eyes dropped to her mouth and rested on her full bottom lip. Her sudden smile had caught him off guard. His head felt uncharacteristically hazy as all he could imagine was how it might feel to take that bottom lip between his, explore its lush cushiony softness, parting them softly with his tongue…

With relief, he saw the head waiter from the restaurant approach the table. 'Mr Kouros, I'm sorry to bother you. Will you be having another drink here or taking your table now?'

He stood with the grace of a huge jungle cat, making Kallie shiver. 'Now, Pierre. Thank you for waiting.'

He waited for Kallie to stand and precede him from the bar, curling his hands into fists when an urge struck him to reach out and place a hand on the curve of her hip, feel it sway against his hand, explore how the silky fabric of her shirt played across her skin. He took in the sheen of glossy hair, longer at the back than he'd thought, the soft waves tamed from the unruly curls of her youth.

The crippling ennui was definitely fading, and he had to admit that he was looking forward to the future for the first time in a very long time.

'Good?' Alexandros's soft question came across the table. Kallie looked at him warily. He lounged back in his own chair. At obvious ease in the sumptuous, gilded surroundings, the famous restaurant, Les Ambassadeurs. She'd heard that this was the hotel that hosted every year an exclusive ball for debutantes, where twenty-four privileged young women from all over the world, aged from fifteen to nineteen, would have their introduction into society. Kallie's insides clenched when she thought of herself at seventeen.

She dragged her attention back, nodded and set her knife and fork on her cleared plate. A slight flush of colour entered her cheeks. Why couldn't she have just ignored the plate of food? He must be disgusted by the way she'd tucked in. Stress for her meant eating more, not less, and she hated to be reminded of the fact. It wasn't so long ago that she'd still carried around her puppy fat.

'Amazing,' she said tightly with a bright smile. 'My appetite has never been a problem, as I'm sure you remember.'

His eyes ran down her body, what he could see of it. To where her waist curved in before swelling out again to her hips in a way that was fast becoming a provocative invitation to him.

Kallie felt her insides heat up under his look. Why had she drawn attention to herself? She remembered his nasty jibe that she must have had work done. His eyes thankfully rose to meet hers again.

'You seem to still be self-conscious. You were a little chubby maybe, but what teenager doesn't go through that?'

Chubby...!

Humiliation flooded Kallie when she thought of how impassioned she'd been that night on the patio. How her body had burned for him, how for once she'd been unaware of anything other than the sensations that had overwhelmed her, her untutored, gauche advances. And how she'd ever imagined for a second that he might be turned on by her. But, of course, he hadn't been. It hadn't taken long for him to come to his senses. She wanted to close her eyes, block out the potent sight of him.

'Alexandros, surely it's time to tell me—'

He ignored her plea, butting in. 'No. It's not.'

She flinched back slightly at his harsh tone and he seemed to notice. She could see a pulse flicker at his jaw, as if he was controlling something.

'Tell me, Kallie. Why did you feel it necessary to tell that rag about our conversations? Wasn't it enough to just publish the photo?'

She flushed a dull red. It had killed her when she'd found out just how her own trust had been abused so abominably. But by then it had been too late. And would he understand what it was like to be a teenage girl in the throes of young passion? How she'd merely confided in someone she'd thought she could trust? Of course he wouldn't. The Alexandros she'd known a long time ago might have…but this man wouldn't.

She gave thanks for having held her tongue about Eleni…for not having blurted out the truth. Eleni's situation meant that Kallie couldn't use her as an easy excuse for vindication. She had to find out just what he wanted. Because *that* was as clear as the nose on her face. He wanted something.

Kallie hardened her heart. She had to. Those conversations he mentioned had belonged to another time, a more innocent time when she'd believed he'd had different sensibilities, like her own. But, she had to remind herself, once his father had died and he'd taken over running Kouros Shipping, he'd changed. Under his hands it had gone from million-dollar profits to generating billions. That wasn't the same person she'd known who had confided a wish to go to art college. He'd obviously smelt the chance to make money, lots of it, and he'd changed.

But, pathetically, she couldn't stand the thought that he would tar her with the same brush, despite the evidence she knew was stacked against her. 'I didn't… It wasn't how you think…' she said ineffectually, miserably.

He leant forward, his face hard. 'Oh, and just how was it, Kallie?'

Now they were getting to it. Kallie felt something like relief flood through her. This she could handle. Alexandros being angry, hating her.

She looked at him slightly defiantly. She could, at least for the moment, be honest about this. 'I never intended to hurt you, Alexandros. Believe what you want—you made up your mind that day.'

He was derisive. 'Oh, you didn't hurt me, Kallie. But you did wreak a trail of destruction with your careless, cruel actions.'

She swallowed painfully. She hadn't been intentionally cruel. But he was right—she'd been careless, and foolish. She couldn't argue with him about that.

'Your uncle Alexei…'

He didn't finish the sentence. His rapid changes of subject caught her off guard. He was like an opponent conducting some form of mental martial art. Immediately she was wary. She clenched her hands into fists under the table.

'What about him?'

Alexandros shrugged negligently. 'I hear he's having some difficulties…'

Guilt flooded Kallie. She suddenly remembered her uncle's words from the other night, how he'd mentioned he'd *had* to get in touch with Alexandros. It hadn't occurred to her to question him, she'd been so distracted.

'What kind of difficulties?' she bit out. Hating Alexandros with passion at that moment. He was milking every single moment of this dinner. Her nerves were on a knife edge of sensation so acute that she thought she might break in two.

'The kind that would be solved with a cash injection of a few million euros.'

Kallie tried not to let shock show on her face. She had a sudden very acute fear that they could be vulnerable to Alexandros, who was clearly out for some kind of revenge now.

'You don't even have your shares, do you?'

How did he know that?

She shook her head warily.

'Apparently you couldn't even wait until your parents were cold in the grave before you cashed them in…'

She gasped at the cruelty of his words. It had been nothing like that. She'd handed them over to Alexei and *he'd* cashed them in, giving her the small amount she'd needed to set up her business. She hadn't wanted anything else to do with them and her uncle had needed them.

She leant forward, unaware of how it gave Alexandros a tantalising view of her cleavage beneath her shirt. She quivered with rage and injustice.

'What I did or didn't do with my shares is none of your business, Alexandros.'

He shrugged like he didn't much care and Kallie felt impotent, wanted to walk around and slap the look of smug superiority off his face. It held all the arrogance of his forebears.

'The fact of the matter is that your uncle has come to me for help...for a loan, if you will.'

Kallie sagged back against her chair. *Oh, Alexei, what have you done?* Her uncle had never been the brains behind Demarchis Shipping. That had been her father, until... Her mind slammed down on painful memories.

'Look, Alexandros, what do you want? Surely...surely this can't be because of what happened all those years ago?'

'Why not, Kallie? Do you think that what you did wasn't so bad after all? That time might have diminished it? You tried to seduce me and when it didn't go your way, in a fit of spoilt pique you lashed out. You singlehandedly stopped a marriage from taking place—'

'But, Alexandros.' Panic was making her insides liquefy. 'Surely Pia would have given you the benefit of the doubt, let you explain? I'm sure you could have convinced her that it meant nothing, was nothing...' she had to stop for a second when her heart clenched in remembered pain '...if she loved you...'

Her remark caught him on the raw, caught him in a place he'd shut off long ago.

'You're priceless. *Love?* It was never about love, Kallie, it was a business arrangement. A merger between two families. Needless to say the merger never happened as soon as they lost faith in my ability to do the job. Thanks to your revealing titbits...' The rage rose up again. '*Theos,* Kallie...'

She was speechless. She'd always assumed that he had loved Pia. And even though she hadn't leaked the kiss-and-tell story to the paper, and had had nothing to do with the damning photo, she'd always felt guilty for trying to seduce Alexandros when he'd only wanted to be friends.

Her vulnerability and pathetic weakness for this man *still* made her blood boil. She opened her mouth, about to proclaim her innocence, and stopped. Eleni. And it wasn't just Eleni. Even *if* he knew, Kallie was still in her own way responsible, too. She couldn't say a thing…angrily impotent at the way she was trapped, she put down her napkin and went to stand but he reached across the table and caught her hand.

The feel of her smooth warm skin, the frantic pulse beating like a trapped bird, called to Alexandros, scrambled his brain for a second. He had to fight for control and remember what he was there to do.

'I'm not finished with you, Kallie. In fact, we haven't even started.'

She pulled her hand away, uncaring if people were looking. 'There's nothing starting here, Alexandros. I'm leaving.'

His voice was low and lethal. 'No. You're not. If you stand up, so help me, I will pick you up and carry you out of here over my shoulder. Don't think that I won't. So we can do this here and now, or we can cause a furore of interest, give the paparazzi outside something to photograph and do it back in my apartment.'

She had been in the act of standing and sat down again slowly. She knew without a doubt that she didn't want to be alone with him and that he wouldn't hesitate to do exactly what he'd said.

When she had sat back down he continued agreeably, as though discussing the weather. 'As I was saying, your uncle is in need of a substantial loan. A loan to keep Demarchis Shipping afloat…literally. This puts me in an interesting position, wouldn't you say?' He didn't wait for her answer. 'I was quite prepared to do business with Alexei, as it suits my needs, too, but *now* things are intriguingly different. Needless to say, it won't make the slightest bit of difference to me should I choose not to help him. But it would make all the difference in the world to him…and your family.'

The lines in his face were unbearably harsh and Kallie quailed at how time and circumstances had turned this man into such a lethal combination of sheer ruthlessness and icy cool. And at the part she had unwittingly played.

He continued unflinchingly, 'He's a tough old dog, but he's exhausted every other avenue and, as he told me himself, I'm his last hope…'

Kallie was stung with guilt that she hadn't known, that her uncle hadn't confided in her. That she could somehow be instrumental in potentially doing damage to her family hurt her unbearably. Yet still, even through this, she was so aware of Alexandros across the table that she felt dizzy with his presence.

'How have they not told me—I mean, how is this possible?'

She suddenly looked very young and lost and alone to Alexandros. Her eyes were huge, shimmering, blue and green. And he felt something twist in his chest before he ruthlessly quashed it back down.

'Who knows? By selling your shares so promptly, by coming here to Paris, moving away from the UK—your mother's own home, and your father's adopted home— perhaps Alexei and your family thought you were taking a stand away from them, weren't interested in their problems.'

It killed her that he could deduce this, but she hadn't. And the familiar wave of grief washed through her. She lifted pain-filled eyes to his, speaking without thinking. 'It wasn't like that. It just became too much. After the funeral, the business was all they could talk about. All they ever talked about. My father had as good as taken his own life, and my mother's with him and no one wanted to talk about that. It was Demarchis Shipping this, Demarchis Shipping that…' She broke off when her voice caught and she desperately blinked back the sting of tears, hating that he might see any hint of vulnerability.

She strenuously fought to hide the brightness from his narrowed gaze and only looked back when she felt more under control. He had an intense look on his face. And then it was gone. Replaced with that implacability again. She hardened her own jaw.

The emotion that had softened her features could have been a figment of Alexandros's imagination and he felt himself flounder slightly. This wasn't going exactly how he'd imagined it. He wanted to reach over and run the pad of his thumb across her cheeks, down to her lips…cup her delicate jaw. He was fast losing the thread of why they were there. All he wanted was to stop talking and take her to bed. Spread her underneath him. The speed with which this woman had taken over his senses shocked him.

Kallie felt anger boil up at the unfairness of it all. All she had done had been to bare her heart and soul to this man. And he had crushed that into the dust. *Before* the story had even erupted. She jabbed a finger towards him. 'Look, Alexandros, I can't undo the past any more than you can, with all your money. And I wasn't alone out there that night. I may have… initiated things. I tried to tell my parents, to explain…but they wouldn't listen.'

He held up a hand, derision on his face. 'Please. It's a bit late to try and tell me that you defended my honour when you cold-bloodedly arranged for the photo and the breathless story in the papers—that shows a level of premeditation on a par with the most corrupt politician. But…' he silenced her protest with a look '…there is one way that Alexei need never know about this, one way that I will give him his loan, help him out of this situation he's become embroiled in.'

She flushed at yet another indication of how much he knew

and focused on how she could avert a disaster within her family. 'How's that?'

'You, Kallie.'

And then before his words could sink into her head, which felt like it might explode, he asked her abruptly, 'Do you remember my uncle Dimitri?'

She nodded, her brain still scrambled, trying to make sense of everything.

'He died a month ago.'

'I didn't hear that he was unwell. I'm sorry,' she said stiffly, wondering where this was going.

He shrugged, his face closed, belying the fact that he had loved Dimitri like a father. Something he would have credited Kallie with knowing…once.

'It was sudden.' His black gaze fixed on Kallie. 'It's part of the reason I've asked you here.'

Along with the burning desire that holds you in a grip so tight you have to shift in your seat every two seconds.

A pulse beat at his temple.

Kallie's face felt rigid. She couldn't help the sarcastic response. 'Well, I was wondering… You were hardly calling to reminisce about old times.'

Shut up, Kallie!

He didn't seem to notice her self-flagellating turmoil. The waiter appeared, removing their plates. Kallie refused dessert, ordering a coffee, Alexandros asked for a liqueur. He waited until his drink arrived before fixing her with that intense gaze again. He wasn't going to make this easy. Kallie's full armour was erected against him.

'I have to admit that bumping into you was a shock…but also perfect timing, a certain kind of serendipity, if you will.'

She looked at him warily. 'Timing, for what exactly?'

He looked at her across the table. He clenched his jaw and refused to let his gaze drop to that shadowy line of her cleavage, the gem on the end of that same pendant swaying back and forth, kissing her skin. Skin that looked soft and… He clenched his jaw even harder and focused with effort.

Think of what you need. Focus on business. This is business. And revenge… Nothing else.

Alexandros valiantly concentrated on that and not on Kallie's all too grown-up charms. There'd be time for that later, he vowed.

'I need a convenient wife, and *you,* Kallie, I've decided, are going to oblige me.'

Kallie looked at him dumbly, shock washing through her body.

CHAPTER FOUR

'I'M SORRY?'

'You should be, Kallie. It's time to start atoning for what you did seven years ago. I bet you never thought it would catch up with you. I have to admit, I hadn't planned on doing anything, I was quite happy to settle for never crossing your path again, but bumping into you the other night, together with a slightly…' His mouth twisted as he looked for words. 'Unfortunate set of circumstances that I'm in, has all been very fortuitous.'

A nightmare. She had to be stuck in some kind of nightmare. This couldn't be real. Kallie's mind disengaged from everything. She looked around dumbly and could see couples dining. Lovers holding hands. Men having business dinners. They looked real. And then everything seemed to rush back into focus. Someone was calling her name.

'Here, drink this.'

Alexandros was reaching across the table with dark amber liquid in a glass. His after-dinner drink. She shook her head violently and pushed his hand back, snatching hers away abruptly when she felt the strong bones of his wrist.

He looked at her, his voice unbearably harsh. 'What's wrong with you?'

She shook her head, ignoring his question. 'Why on earth do you want to marry me, Alexandros?' She waved a jerky hand that still tingled from the contact with his. 'Why would you want to do that?'

He put down his glass, smiled grimly. 'Don't worry, Kallie, I don't *want* to marry you. When my uncle Dimitri died, he left me his share of Kouros Shipping. It's the last piece not in my control.'

She looked at him blankly. Still in shock.

'It was expected. He'd always made it clear where his inheritance would go.'

She nodded vaguely, incapable of speech.

'But there was a surprise in his will. Dimitri had a sense of humour. He knew how I felt about marriage.'

He answered the look that Kallie hadn't even been aware of giving. His face was carved from stone as he said the words, 'I'll never willingly marry. The woman doesn't exist who I would marry.'

A knife seemed to enter Kallie's heart, stunning her with pain and surprise. She felt herself pulling inwards as if to avoid a blow. Alexandros was oblivious to the havoc he was wreaking within her. The havoc she couldn't even begin to understand. *She* had done this to him?

He cut through her thoughts. 'He made it a condition of his will that I marry within six months of him dying or I won't receive his share of Kouros Shipping.' His mouth twisted. 'It's as if he knew it was the only way I might ever give in to his foolish romantic notions for me.'

Kallie dumbly seized on words to try and avoid feeling the emotions swirling in her head and body.

'But how could you lose everything? Surely his share isn't that big?'

'It's not, but he controlled a key part. As you know, on my father's death, I took full control of the business.'

She felt an unbidden surge of sympathy, remembering the chaos of that time. But Alexandros wouldn't appreciate her concern or interest, certainly not her sympathy. And *how* could she even be feeling sympathetic?

'Dimitri's will states that if I don't marry within the time frame, his share will go to Stakis Shipping.'

Kallie gasped audibly. Stakis Shipping was the mortal enemy. Even she knew that. Underhand deals, rumours of links to drug rings, sex trafficking. They were the black sheep of the shipping world and the only conglomerate powerful enough to possibly take over Kouros Shipping. If what Alexandros said was true, and if he didn't marry, they would be handed an invitation on a silver platter to take a sizeable potshot at his company.

Alexandros couldn't stop the unbidden dart of pleasure seeing the expressions cross her face, at her immediate understanding of the world he came from. He quickly schooled his features again, slightly shocked at how easily the accord had crept in.

'My uncle, in an effort to see me happily wed, has set me up for professional suicide if I don't.'

'I know this is bad but can it really be *that* bad?'

He nodded. 'The share he controlled has strategic importance in the stock markets. It's the link that holds everything else together. *That* gets weakened and it could all crumble. And he knew how abhorrent I find the practices of Constantine Stakis. He's been waiting for an opportunity like this for years. A marriage seems like a small price to pay to keep my family's legacy intact and Stakis out of harm's way.'

That word again. *Marriage*. It crashed into her brain. Kallie shook her head. 'Impossible. I couldn't. I can't.'

Alexandros felt a surge of irritation and anger. Why was he even telling her all this? He slashed a hand through the air.

'This is all beside the point. You don't even deserve an explanation. All you need to know is that I hold the fate of your family in my hands. And the only way you can influence that for the better is by marrying me. If you don't, your family can kiss their fortune goodbye.'

'But that's…ridiculous…archaic. You don't want to tie yourself to me—you hate me.'

He leant forward again. 'Hate is the other side of love, Kallie. I certainly don't hate you.' He swept a look up and down that was so hot she felt it on her skin, 'But I do desire you.'

Little fires of shock raced all over Kallie's body. His eyes had darkened, eyelids lowered slightly so that they looked slumberous.

He desired her?

Why did that make a treacherous curl of excitement lick through her body…and not pain, or disgust?

Her back was so stiff it hurt. Her voice sounded stilted, desperate and glaringly insincere to her ears. 'Well, I certainly don't desire you, Alexandros, so it would be a little one-sided.'

Before she could move out of danger, he had reached across and taken her hand again. Engulfing it with his own. She felt a traitorous pulse start up between her legs and clamped them together. His eyes made a thorough study all the way from her face, the rapid pulse at her neck, down to her chest, where shallow breaths did little to hide her agitation. She could feel her breasts tingle, her nipples hardening, and prayed that he wouldn't see the reaction.

His eyes came back to hers, smug. 'You did once, Kallie, and you still do. If I were to stand up, walk around this table and kiss you right now, you'd be begging for it within seconds.'

The very thought of him doing that made her mouth go dry.

'You flatter yourself…' she said faintly, knowing her words would have no effect. He was coming at her like a two-tonne lorry and there was nothing she could do to stop it. She seized on something, her hand still trapped by his. 'Isabelle Zolanz! You're hardly going to marry me if you're seeing her. Why don't you just marry her? You two are lovers after all…'

Something twisted in her gut when she said that and she had to hide her reaction.

He let her hand go and flicked his dismissively in a very Greek gesture. 'Isabelle is no longer a part of my life.'

Kallie had to suck in a shocked breath at the coldness of his tone. 'It didn't look to me the other night as though she was aware of that.'

'She is now.' His tone brooked no further comment on the subject. Kallie felt a twinge for the other woman and could only imagine how brutal he'd been.

She had to face it. If she hadn't already. The young man she had known, the young man who had once been her friend, her confidant, was gone. In his place was a ruthless man of the world. A truly alpha male. And she had played her part in creating him. She should never have gone to him that night. Regret and recrimination burnt its way through her. But it was too late for all that. Far too late.

She tried to reason with him. 'I won't do it, Alexandros. It's crazy. I'm sorry for what happened. Truly I am. I never meant for anything to happen.'

Liar… You went in search of him that night…

She swallowed and cut off her painful thoughts. 'You can't punish me for something that happened when I was seventeen.'

'Seventeen?' He laughed harshly. 'You were no ingénue, Kallie. I remember the way you were with Giorgio…you had the poor guy panting after you like a dog. You were almost eighteen, about to go to college, on the brink of adulthood—you knew exactly what you were doing.' He waved an impatient hand. 'This isn't about the past any more. In fact, that whole episode just bores me. It's about the present. All the past is doing now is serving to give me a little leverage where you're concerned. A little retribution, sweetened by very strong desire.'

Sadness filled her. He had it all so wrong. Giorgio. She

hadn't thought about him in years. Another friend of her cousins, she'd taken advantage of his dogged pursuit of her to try and make Alexandros jealous. To little effect and much to her shame. But it had been done with the innocence and disregard of a typical teenager. She didn't doubt that Giorgio had been robust enough to accept her rejection and knew he hadn't been too wounded as he had quickly sought the affections of another cousin. Was she to be punished for every little thing?

She shook her head desperately. 'I won't do it. You can't make me.' *Please,* she added silently. He had no idea how much of a punishment this would be.

'Too late. I've made up my mind. If you don't marry me, who would suffer most? I think possibly your uncle Alexei, as he has the most invested. Doesn't he have three grown-up children at college in the States?'

'Stop it…' Fear and panic laced her voice. 'You're a bastard.'

He inclined his head. 'No, Kallie, I'm not.' He lifted a hand and ticked off long fingers. 'I need to get married more or less immediately, you've fallen into my path like a ripe plum, you are available…and you've grown up into a very attractive young woman.'

'So that's it? You only want me now because I come up to your standards of physical perfection?'

He smiled and it didn't reach his eyes. 'You're no image of physical perfection, Kallie, don't flatter yourself, but for some reason I find myself wanting you more than I've wanted any other woman in a long time…so I don't anticipate that there's going to be any hardship on our wedding night when you come to me…'

His insulting choice of words barely impinged her consciousness, she reacted purely to his assertion that she would ever choose willingly to sleep with him. 'I'll never—'

'Yes. You will,' he cut in ruthlessly. 'And I am going to enjoy every moment of this sweet revenge, every step of the way, every piece of flesh that's going to be uncovered as you give yourself to me, as you offer yourself up as you did seven years ago. In the place of the marriage that *you* made sure didn't happen, don't you think when I need a wife now that it's only fair that you step into that role?'

She couldn't control the shiver that shook her frame at his words. And she knew it wasn't a shiver of fear. She *hated* this man. He had her backed into a corner with no way out.

'How can I be sure you'll still deliver on the loan?'

He shrugged. 'I *could* watch your family flounder. Heaven knows, I have the right. But contrary to what you think, Kallie, I'm not that cruel. On our wedding day when I get my convenient wife, you can consider the loan approved.'

She had an overwhelming urge to jump up and run as fast as she could, as far away as she could. But he would find her if she did. She knew that without a doubt. She sank back against the chair, unable to sit up straight in the face of his condemnation.

She looked miserable. 'I don't want them to suffer, despite what you might think.'

And suddenly Kallie had to do something, had to try and make him listen. There had to be a human being in there somewhere. The old Alexandros. She appealed to him now, sitting up straight again.

'Alexandros—'

He started to cut her off and she put up a hand. 'Please. Just let me say something.' Her eyes were an intense green on his. 'I never went to the paper with that story. I would never have done something like that. You *knew* me…' *Better than nearly anyone.*

He said nothing and Kallie searched her brain frantically. 'Why would I have done it, Alexandros? *Why?*'

There was unmistakable tension in his huge frame, just inches away from her. He shrugged dismissively. 'Because you were just one more in a long line of people who thought they could cash in on the Kouros money.' *Except that was a myth by then!*

'Did your father put you up to it, Kallie? See his ticket out of debt? Or did you just do it for the hell of it, to see if you could turn my head yourself? I told you that day I didn't go in for seventeen-year-olds.' His mouth twisted mockingly. 'But if you'd come to me as you are now…'

He flicked an openly appraising look up and down her body. It should have disgusted her. It should have made her angry. But it didn't. It made her feel hot and bothered and confused and out of her depth.

But he wasn't finished. 'To tell the truth, seven years on I'm not much interested in why…' He shook his head. 'You changed, Kallie. The girl I knew would never have tried to seduce me and get someone to photograph the evidence.'

Her insides stung with acute hurt and the humiliation rose up again so sharply she felt sick. To think that he would have believed that of her.

Kallie bit her lip hard and could feel blood. As if his rejection hadn't hurt enough that night, he had to reiterate just how unwelcome her advances had been and how futile it was to try and get him to listen to anything, any explanation.

'I'm sorry. I can't tell you how sorry I am.'

'It's a bit late now.'

His words flayed her like a whip, cutting so deeply that she winced inwardly. 'But really it wasn't like that. I didn't—'

'Give me a break.' Derision and disbelief stamped his features, his mouth a bitter slash. 'There were three people there that night, you, me and whoever your loyal photographer was. Pity they were so amateur…but they got enough.'

She slumped back again, defeated and diminished by his derision and cruelty. And now that she knew what he wanted, all avenues of escape were closed off. She couldn't assert her innocence any further, and she couldn't explain what had happened as that would involve someone who wouldn't be able to handle this much more dangerous Alexandros. Eleni had come up to Kallie at her parents' funeral, nearly hysterical with remorse and guilt. She'd told her everything—how she'd followed Kallie out to the patio, taken the picture, hacked into her e-mail and sent in the story.

For one blissful moment, unaware of *him* across the table, Kallie's mind was fixed on that awful day of such tragedy. The added pain when Eleni had revealed the truth. Kallie had always had her suspicions but, still, to hear it explained… She'd been shocked and angry. Dismayed, hurt. About to lash back, already filled with grief and now anger. But Eleni's husband had stepped in. He'd explained everything, exactly why Eleni had been acting so on the edge. Which was the reason why Kallie couldn't defend herself now.

She'd discovered that her cousin had had a nervous breakdown, and had been undergoing intense therapy after suffering numerous miscarriages. Kallie had seen the pain on Eleni's husband's face. Her fight had left her. It had only been after that incident and with the benefit of maturity and hindsight that Kallie could see just how Eleni had also been captivated by him. And how highly strung and manipulative her cousin had always been. Especially with regard to Alexandros.

The man who sat opposite her now, looking so calm and so devastatingly at ease as he toyed with her life. He had been on a mission ever since he'd seen her again. It was as if she'd awakened the sleeping dragon. And she had to take it, had no choice.

She didn't need to remind herself that, despite Eleni's involvement, if *she* hadn't pursued Alexandros that night, there wouldn't have been an excuse for a story in the first place. She had no one to blame for this except herself. No matter what the consequences had been, or how unwittingly she'd played a part. And now he held the future of Demarchis Shipping in his hands.

She lifted dull eyes that were mute with an appeal she was unaware of. Weary beyond belief.

'I have no choice, do I?'

He answered slowly, 'Of course you do, Kallie, we always have a choice. Yours is very simple. If you walk away now, your uncle will not receive one euro from me, and as he's been turned down by every bank, and no other shipping company will touch him, he and, consequently, the family, will be ruined. If you agree to marry me, he'll be fine.'

Some choice…

She asked the fateful question. 'How long would we…?'

He shrugged one broad shoulder. 'For as long as I want, Kallie. The day you start to bore me, the day I lose interest, is the day we'll divorce and you can consider this marriage over.'

CHAPTER FIVE

AND just like that, from the moment she'd fatefully bumped into Alexandros Kouros again, he'd come back into her life with the force of an atom bomb and turned everything upside down and inside out. And all because he needed a convenient wife. Someone who wouldn't expect a happy ever after when he discarded them by the wayside of his fast-paced life that had no room for a real marriage.

Kallie moved through the next three weeks as though in some kind of a fog. Where once Alexandros had been blissfully absent, now he was everywhere she turned. In her office, at the door of her flat, on the phone, barking terse instructions. The paparazzi had snapped them coming out of the Hotel de Crillon that night after dinner. Kallie had been so shell-shocked coming out that she'd barely noticed the flashing, popping bulbs. And only the next day when she'd opened the papers had she seen the pictures. Headlines screamed of a possible romance...which was promptly confirmed by Alexandros's PR people. Before she even had time to draw breath, the net was being drawn tighter and tighter around her. And no doubt, she thought bitterly, he saw the justice in dragging her name through the papers now, too.

She drew the line, however, when he sent over a credit card one day close to the wedding with an order to kit herself out, and called him angrily on the phone.

'I will *not* be paraded like some gilded lily. And I will *not* go and buy clothes with your money, to your specifications. You may be as good as blackmailing me to buy yourself a convenient wife but I will not be your chattel, Alexandros. I've been dressing myself successfully with no complaints for some time now and I intend to keep doing so.'

'Well, believe me, you're going to need a little gilding to be my wife. Your look is far too casually natural—'

Kallie gasped in consternation, seething. 'Weren't you the one who implied that I might have had work done? Make up your mind!'

He was quite unconcerned, drawling, 'That was before I saw you again properly. I'm quite sure now that you've had no…surgical enhancements and, believe me, I'm looking forward to finding out for sure.'

That was when Kallie slammed the phone down. She cut up the credit card and sent it back to Alexandros with a courier. Which he received with a wry smile. The first woman, *ever,* to refuse his money. He wondered what game Kallie might be playing but couldn't deny that he was growing more and more intrigued by the day. Having to take a convenient wife was turning out to be far more entertaining than he'd first anticipated.

The day before the civil marriage was to take place at the office of the *mairie* on the Place Du Panthéon, Kallie was meeting her uncle for lunch near his office on the Champs Elysées. The Arc de Triomphe was a mere shape in the distance as she steeled herself and went into the restaurant.

He stood as she approached and they kissed on both cheeks in a warm greeting. She hadn't seen him since that night at the Ritz. They'd spoken on the phone when she'd delivered her news of the wedding and now she couldn't put off the inevitable any more. Finally, after she'd prevaricated for as long as possible, he got to the point. Taking her hand across the table, he said gently, 'Kallie, darling, you know how important to me you are, you're like another daughter.'

'I know…' She tried to keep the emotion out of her voice, aching to be able to confide in someone, anyone.

'Are you telling me the truth about Alexandros?' He shook his head. 'I just find it a little hard to believe that you bumped into him that night and have had this whirlwind romance. I know him, Kallie. He's not given to random romantic whims…and *this*, well, it's completely out of character. Especially with the history between you. I remember how angry he was. That story in the paper—'

Kallie cut him off before he could delve too deeply into the past—the present was hard enough to deal with. 'Alexei. Please. believe me when I say you don't have to worry about anything.' She crossed her fingers under the table on a superstitious reflex. 'It is true. We met that night and… I don't know.' She shrugged and pasted a bland smile on her face. 'He's changed. Seven years is a long time. He doesn't harbour any grudges.' Her fingers were clenched so tightly that Kallie could feel the blood flow stopping. 'Trust me, Alexei, I don't want you to think about it, really. I *want* to marry Alexandros.'

She prayed that her hopelessly romantic uncle wouldn't push her to say anything about love. He looked unconvinced for a long moment but then something seemed to pass over his face and he smiled. 'I do trust you, Kallie.' He squeezed her hand. 'I know it can happen like that. After all, didn't I fall in love with your Aunt Petra in just a week?'

Kallie smiled weakly.

A rogue part of her needed to check something. 'Alexei, that night at the Ritz, you mentioned that you'd had to go to Alexandros. Is there anything you want to tell me?'

He paled and Kallie's heart fell. Confirmation…as if she needed it at this stage. Even so, a tiny part of her had clung to some mad, irrational hope. He blustered slightly, clearly embarrassed, his macho Greek pride painfully evident and obviously the reason why he hadn't said anything about the loan. 'My dear, don't be ridiculous, we're just doing business, that's all.'

She read far more into his reactions than he suspected. She'd checked up on what Alexandros had said and every word he'd uttered had been true. Things were even worse than she'd anticipated. She didn't know how Alexei had been managing for so long without a loan. His efforts to secure loans elsewhere were dismayingly documented in financial papers. Guilt made her feel cold inside again. If she'd been the slightest bit interested, she would have noticed. Her shares had long been sucked into the haemorrhaging business.

She had to comfort herself that at least this way she was keeping Alexandros's lust for revenge to herself. No one else would ever know and the Demarchis shipping fleet would be safe. It was cold comfort, however, as she said goodbye to her still uncomfortable-looking uncle. She'd never felt so alone and vulnerable in her life. As she walked back down one of the most famous boulevards in the world, she felt as if everything was closing in on her and her last chance of possibly avoiding her fate had just disappeared. Snuffed out like the light of a candle. She shivered in the warm spring air.

When she got back to her office Alexandros was waiting for her. Her whole body stiffened in blatant rejection of what was to come the next day. He noted it with narrowed eyes as he watched her walk in from behind her desk. As at home as if he sat there every day. He made a thorough study of her, up and down, taking in the black pencil skirt, the cream high-necked shirt, which she was supremely grateful for now.

'Can I help you with something?'

He uncurled his tall length from the chair and came around the desk. Devastatingly compelling in a dark suit and dark shirt. Kallie took a step back. The room seemed to have become as hot as hell in seconds. Alexandros flicked his head to indicate the window and looked out. Kallie walked over very warily, keeping a good distance, but even that couldn't stop the frisson of awareness running through her.

Outside, swarming on the pavement, were what seemed to be hundreds of photographers. The circus that surrounded Alexandros Kouros. She hadn't seen them before as she'd come in through another entrance. He came and stood beside her. Her skin prickled uncomfortably. So far he hadn't said a word. The moment seemed to stretch for ever. And finally with silky deadliness he said softly, 'You see that? They're all going to be waiting outside the office of the *mairie* tomorrow. Waiting to see you arrive, go in and then come out on my arm. And they're going to get the pictures they want. If you're planning any little surprises, like not turning up, then I will find you, Kallie, and I will take you as far away from here as I can, and we will be married where you will have no escape.'

She turned to face him, dread in her body at his cold tone. This stranger before her. Bitterness laced her voice. 'I've already told you I'd marry you. I'd do anything to save my family from ruin. Even if it means marrying you and subjecting myself to a period of purgatory.'

He turned to face her, his face stamped with arrogance and a sensuality that even now called to her on some base, carnal level. She hated him. She knew she kept telling herself that…and knew it felt as though she was trying to convince herself.

He reached out a finger and trailed it along her jaw. She clenched it and he tapped where it bulged out against her smooth skin.

'Such dramatic language, Kallie. When you set me up all those years ago, when *I* was considered as close as family, it made me very wary. I'm just warning you what will happen if you decide to leave your family to their fate. That's all.'

He was so far off base from how Kallie felt that her head

swam. She would never, *ever* do something to hurt her family. It seemed as if everything, every conversation that had ever passed between them, had turned to poisoned ashes. And amounted to nothing. He'd decided to judge her solely based on what he'd perceived her to have done seven years ago.

She straightened her shoulders and stuck her chin out.

'I will be there tomorrow, Alexandros, and, believe me, you're going to be sorry you ever married me.'

'Somehow I don't think so. But I admire your attempt at bravado. One other thing. I've asked members of our families, just as a little added…insurance.'

Kallie felt her throat clog and wanted nothing more than to hit him right in the solar plexus, wipe that smug smirk from his face. But then he snaked a hand around the back of her head through her hair and pulled her softly to him. Panic coursed through her. Her hands came up in an instinctive and classic defense pose between them.

'What do you think you're doing?' She tingled with anticipation.

'Just the one other thing I need to confirm for myself before I make you my wife…check the levels of compatibility…'

'Levels of—'

And before she could speak another word, his head had dipped, daylight disappeared and his mouth was on hers. Warm and intoxicating and hot and…words disappeared. Kallie found her hands resting against his broad chest, his heat coursing over her skin, making *her* heat up all over. She felt herself wanting to melt into him, against his hard length. His lips moved against hers, hard and insistent. A completely instinctive unbidden response made her open her mouth and at the first touch of his tongue to hers, an explosive heat erupted deep in her belly.

She felt him pulling her in tighter, lifting her up against him. She wanted nothing more than to give in…lean against him, savour the support. Her eyes flew open. His were shut. Hidden.

What was wrong with her? What was she thinking?

She welcomed reality, letting it flow through her like ice, dousing the flame of desire that wanted to burst into flame like a flash fire. His mouth was still moving over hers, and a weak part of her was an insistent voice saying, *Give in, give in.*

She clenched her hands into fists with a huge effort and pushed against his chest. It was like a steel wall, immovable. She twisted her mouth away from his and was shocked at how ragged her breathing was. Pushing her chest against his, making her very aware of how her breasts had begun to ache, her nipples so hard they chafed against her bra. He tried to twist her head back and Kallie struggled in earnest now, beating against his chest, her breath coming more and more ragged and jerky. She still couldn't speak.

He finally loosened his hold and Kallie used it to push herself out of his arms, staggering back against the desk behind her. If it hadn't been there, she would have fallen to the floor, she knew that for sure. Her hands clung to the ridges behind her, her entire body pulsed, heat melted the ice and she had the strongest urge to throw herself back into his arms and beg him to kiss her again. She tried to bring her breathing under control and marvelled that kissing him so chastely at seventeen certainly hadn't prepared her for *this*...

She was undone. In the space of seconds. Had given in spectacularly before she'd stopped, letting him know of her weak acquiescence. She couldn't look up and saw his feet come into her line of vision on the floor in front of her. A hand came under her chin, tipping it up to face him, and she shut her eyes.

'Kallie, closing your eyes isn't going to make the truth go away.'

Against her better judgment she opened them and tensed herself for his look of triumph. But it wasn't there. Instead was a look she couldn't read and his eyes were dark, darker than she'd ever seen them. With deep glowing embers in their depths. Embers that *she* had lit? The thought made something rip through her. She trembled.

She had to try and claw back some modicum of dignity and found a voice from somewhere.

'Truth…' She didn't even have the energy to voice it as a question.

'That there's enough electricity between us to power the national grid.' His eyes fell to her mouth and Kallie felt it quiver in response as if it were begging for his own lips again. 'And that tomorrow we get married and…*this* we'll come back to. We'll have plenty of time on our honeymoon.'

Kallie opened her mouth and couldn't speak for a few seconds. *Honeymoon!* 'That's ridiculous. There's no way this is going to happen.' Panic was making her sound breathless. 'I am not going anywhere with you for any honeymoon. I have to work, I can't just leave—'

He put a finger to her mouth. 'Oh, yes, you are. It's part of the deal. Make sure you're packed…'

Alexandros strode through the mass of photographers outside Kallie's office. Unlike with other celebrities, who they would crush around, intimidate into submission, a space was left around Alexandros. That held a certain kind of respect. As if they knew that with one swipe of his hand, one word, he could do some serious damage. He ignored the barrage of questions and got into the back of his car. The blacked-out windows concealed him from view immediately.

He tersely instructed his driver to take the long way back to his office. He needed to think, to collect himself. And this was as alien a concept to him as the thought of taking public transport. But the fact of the matter was that his body still throbbed with a level of arousal he'd never experienced before.

What the hell had just happened back there?

He ran a hand through his hair and stared unseeingly out

of the window. He hadn't planned on kissing Kallie. But when she'd walked in, so prim and proper in her buttoned-up shirt and tight skirt that drew the eye to the toned length of thigh, he hadn't been able to resist.

All he did know was the moment he'd taken Kallie into his arms he hadn't felt like he'd thought he would. Oh, he'd felt the desire. That had been like a neon sign that lit up whenever he was near her…it hadn't been that. It had been something else, something he'd never felt before. He'd expected to feel detached…but he hadn't. He'd felt anticipation that had gone beyond the mere physical. As if he'd finally had something within his grasp that he'd been searching for. A sigh had gone through him when his mouth had touched hers. *A sigh of relief…*

His whole body tensed in the back of the car in absolute rejection of his thoughts. And for the first time since seeing Kallie again, he questioned whether or not he was doing the right thing. His mouth pulled into a thin line. The fact of the matter was, though, that he'd left it too late now. He would need to find a wife to marry within twenty-four hours if he was to make the deadline of Dimitri's will. And he certainly couldn't afford to let this slip through his hands merely because he was having these…doubts.

For Alexandros, who never ever doubted a decision he'd made, this was also a new concept. Not a welcome one. His mind even seized on Isabelle for a moment. He grimaced. There were plenty of women who would be only too happy to comply with his need for an immediate wife. But he had Kallie so well trussed now, not to mention the arousal that hummed in his every vein, why shouldn't he use her? Have her. Sate himself with her.

After all, wasn't this just meant to be just a diversion for him? An amusement? A timely revenge and a way to get his needs met, both in and out of bed?

It was only then that the belated thought struck him—he'd called at her office to see if she'd received the pre-nuptial agreement. He'd never before had a lapse like that in his concentration. He found himself ignoring the need to dwell on why he'd been acting so out of character and quickly instructed his bodyguard to go back and pick it up.

It was a couple of minutes after Alexandros had left that Kallie fully realised that he'd gone. She still hadn't moved. She felt as though she'd been flung into another dimension. He'd just kissed her, she told herself rationally. *And told you that he expects you to go on a honeymoon...*

She felt dizzy, disjointed...her head was fuzzy. She went on shaky legs and sat down behind her desk. Her glazed eyes took in a note on the top of her pad. The big brusque handwriting that could only belong to one person. *Him.*

'Please sign the pre-nuptial agreement and send it back.'

Kallie read it and reread it, finally, slowly coming back to her senses. She heard the bells of a church ring ominously in the distance. Like a nail going into a coffin, her fate was sealed, this was it. He hadn't even had the decency to tell her this much. He'd gone from issuing terse instructions to leaving curt notes. He'd waltzed into her office, tested her out like some Arabian prince buying a new girl for his harem. To see if she met with his approval. Her mouth twisted, she couldn't help the shudder of reaction that went through her. Well, apparently she did. Lucky her.

Her assistant popped her head around the door at that moment, diverting her thoughts, and when Kallie nodded she came in. Holding out a manila envelope, she said, 'Sorry, this came earlier, but I got distracted when Alexandros...' She blushed prettily and Kallie scowled. 'Sorry. When Mr Kouros arrived.'

She beat a hasty retreat and Kallie scowled even harder. Another female ready to drop at his feet. Was no one immune to the man's charm? She ripped the envelope open and a sheaf of papers fell out. The agreement. Kallie skimmed it feeling numb. It outlined the terms of the marriage—basically she was entitled to nothing in the event of the divorce. That didn't surprise her. It also specified the terms of the loan to her uncle, the generosity of which surprised her. He genuinely was reserving all punishment just for her. It suited her fine. She didn't want to touch a penny of his money.

She signed quickly, without thinking, and shoved the papers back into the envelope. About to call Cécile back in, she looked up when a shape appeared at the doorway. She almost thought it was him until she saw his bodyguard come in. She pulled herself together and held out the envelope.

'Mr Kouros sent you for this?'

He took it and left.

The reality was stark. From now on, as long as he desired, for as long as they would have the reaction they'd both just had to a simple kiss, she was Alexandros Kouros's property. For better or worse.

CHAPTER SIX

'FOR better or worse…'

The words swam over Kallie's head. She stood in the *mairie*'s office with Alexandros by her side. Everything seemed to be swimming, ever since she'd come in the door with Alexei and seen Alexandros standing there. In a steel-grey suit, looking so tall and dark and vibrantly handsome that she'd stumbled on her walk towards him.

Members of both their families were seated behind them. The speed with which the last few weeks had flown, the reaction of her body just standing beside this man…was overwhelming. She struggled to fix her gaze on a point in the distance and only belatedly realised that Alexandros was turning her towards him, having been told he could kiss his wife.

His wife…

Kallie looked up into his face, helpless now. Bound to him in front of everyone, in front of society. Wordlessly she tried to communicate with him. Willing the harsh, stark lines of his face to relax…just for a moment so that she could reach something of the person she'd once known. But they didn't. That person was gone. As his head bent towards hers for the second time in two days, she felt every treacherous cell in her body leaping in response, hungering for his touch, his mouth on hers. She fought it, though…tensed her entire body and willed herself with every fibre of her being not to have the same reaction as yesterday.

He took her face in his hands, tilting it up to his. Why did he have to do that? Why couldn't he just plant a dry kiss on her lips, quick and efficient? With his big hands cupping her jaw, face close to hers, his thumbs feathering across her cheeks, she felt her body temperature soar and imagined he must be able to feel her heart about to explode from her chest.

Slowly, and surrounded by a hushed quiet in the room, his head came closer and closer. Kallie's eyes were trapped by his. When the drowning sensation became too much she closed them, the lids feeling heavy. And then…his mouth angled over hers and fitted so perfectly that her every nerve ending seemed to meet and connect with every one of his. The reaction in her blood to just the touch of his lips to hers made her knees weak and she had to put out her hands and cling to his waist in an effort to stay upright. The scent of him intoxicated her, his body heat enveloped her in a haze of sensual warmth. Just like yesterday—and she was being played like a violin, *again*.

He had intended for it to be a quick kiss. As much as he wanted Kallie with a desire that was fast running out of control, Alexandros had no intention of being surrounded by people when he plumbed the depths of that lush mouth again. So this was just going to be chaste, dry—certainly not *this*. This *fire* that had taken over his blood as soon as he'd touched her skin, as soon as their lips had made contact. Light exploded behind his eyes. And when he felt her eyelashes flutter against his cheeks, it tugged at a thread of a memory from long ago…

When he felt the tremor run through her, felt her hands reach out to steady herself, it was too much. He was only human. He pulled her in close and dropped a hand to her back to anchor her against his body. The crowd, witnesses forgotten. The world was reduced to this moment, this woman, these lips under his which were opening to him so enticingly, with such potent sweetness. And he was lost in a maelstrom of passion that made him shake with the effort not to stroke and explore and plunder the moist, hot interior.

A child's cry pierced Alexandros's consciousness and went through him like shock of cold water. Feeling every impulse in his body wanting to stay, he somehow managed to pull back. When he opened his eyes they felt dazed, hazy, and Kallie's were still shut, her lips pink and plump, lashes curled against her cheeks. He could feel the uneven raggedness of her breath.

Kallie knew he had stopped kissing her. She knew it like a bizarre intellectual fact but could not seem to open her eyes or move. When she felt him tap a finger against her cheek it unlocked the stasis she'd been stuck in. Her eyes flew open to meet his. They were full of heat and darkness. A sound made her look and when she turned her head she saw their relations staring, open-mouthed. She felt her insides go cold, even as she felt hectic colour flood her cheeks.

Kallie couldn't look at him. Instead, she smiled brightly, breaking the spell that seemed to encompass the room. The crowd started clapping and Alexandros took her hand and led the way back outside. Only when Kallie was sure she had regained some semblance of control did she turn to him. Before they were sucked into a round of congratulatory hugs, she said coolly, 'Don't think that just because I can put on a performance for the family, it'll be the same in private.'

His face visibly darkened and Kallie rejoiced in needling him, even a little, even as she had to realise that this was not a man to trifle with. He would exact revenge for every petty point she scored. She was saved from a caustic response as they were surrounded in seconds and before she knew it they were getting out of a car and stepping into an exclusive discreet hotel for the lunch reception.

A few hours later, the only thing keeping Kallie back from the brink of sheer white-knuckled panic was the sight laid out in front of her in the glittering ballroom. Members of her family that she hadn't seen in years and some of Alexandros's family were seated at little round tables dotted around the room. Petra caught her eye beside her beloved husband Alexei, and waved at Kallie, who waved weakly back.

When they'd come out of the office earlier, into the Place Du Panthéon with its massive monument to the glory of secularism dominating the magnificent square, her uncle's wife had rushed up to Kallie with tears in her eyes and, taking advantage of Alexandros talking to someone else, had whispered in her ear, 'Kallie, darling, I'm so happy for you. When Alexei told me about how you two got together, I have to say I was a little worried, but after seeing you now…' She'd raised her hands high. 'It's obvious you're in love.'

Kallie couldn't believe that people patently saw what they wanted to see. Not what was right under their noses. She was doing this against her will and no one could see it.

The lunch was finally over and Kallie could absent herself from Alexandros's disturbing presence beside her. Thankfully he'd agreed that they wouldn't make speeches—that would have been pushing things too far, even for Kallie. She excused herself to go to the bathroom and once inside splashed water on her wrists and on her neck to cool her pulse which had been racing since that kiss.

She sent up silent thanks that he obviously hadn't thought to invite Eleni and her husband, and then chastised herself for her churlish thought. Perhaps Eleni was back in hospital again? She looked at her pained face in the mirror. Why couldn't she be more like him? Emotionally cut off from the neck down?

Wearily she straightened her hair, fixed her make-up and made her way back into the huge room, firmly diverting any line of thinking that involved the future or even later that evening. She hadn't yet figured out how to handle Alexandros because there was one thing she was certain of—she was not going to be sleeping with him.

Alexandros couldn't focus on the conversation around him. Kallie's shining head stood out like a glowing beacon from all the darker ones. He watched her progress as she walked back into the room, the only member of the family who wasn't entirely Greek on both sides. She'd tied her hair back in a loose, tumbled knot. With an orchid caught in the glossy strands and minimal make-up, Alexandros thought he'd never seen anyone lovelier.

Her outfit was simple, highlighting her natural elegance, and he had to admit that he hadn't been entirely fair when he'd criticised the way she dressed. A knee-length cream silk dress with a gossamer-light golden-coloured shawl, high strappy golden sandals that drew the eye to slim ankles and shapely calves. And when she moved, like now, to greet one of her family, the silk of the dress moved with her and tightened across her hips… again, he was blown away by the beauty that had been lying in wait through her younger years. Yet hadn't she always possessed it? Her eyes had always been that distinctive blue-green colour, her lips always as soft… Desire surged through him fast and urgent as he thought of the kiss in the registry office.

Acting on blind impulse, he strode through the crowd. It was time to get out of there and take her with him.

Kallie was still talking to one of her aunts when she felt a presence behind her like an electric frisson, and her skin tingled in reaction. She closed her eyes briefly in despair and when she opened them again a strong arm had come around her waist. She didn't look up at Alexandros but smiled brightly at the older woman and chattered on nonsensically. She could feel the tension in the man beside her as his arm tightened on her waist, causing a whirlpool of sensations in her belly.

'Are you ready to go?'

As if she had a choice, Kallie thought slightly hysterically. She just nodded, realising that she actually did want to get away from the attention, the looks, the questions. They said their goodbyes.

In the lobby, with her hand in the firm grip of his, Kallie stumbled, trying to keep up with his long-legged stride. And in that moment, the enormity of what had just happened hit her. They were about to walk outside, away from any last piece of protection. She would be alone with Alexandros and he would expect—

She stopped dead in her tracks, forcing him to come to a halt, too. He looked back, a dark look on his face. 'What is it?'

'What is it? *What is it?*' Kallie's voice was rising as her fear rose, too, like an unstoppable volcano that had just blown its top. She yanked her hand out of Alexandros's with an effort and stood there shaking.

'What is wrong with you? This isn't real…this is a farce. And everyone in there thinks that we're in love, that this is a proper marriage.' She started to back away, back towards the room, babbling, 'I can't do it. I can't do this. I'm going to tell them. I'll work for Alexei, I'll do anything to help him get another loan… But don't make me… I just can't do this, I can't—'

With lightning speed Alexandros reached her as she turned and hauled her into his arms, his mouth crashing down on hers, silencing her words. She struggled and fought but he kept kissing her, and kissing her. Finally he felt her body grow pliant, and her mouth had softened. He'd forgotten the reason he'd started to kiss her in the first place.

Kallie forgot, too, in a shamingly short amount of time. The anger drained away under the intense building of desire that started low down and rose throughout her entire body. Her hands were trapped against Alexandros's chest and she revelled in the close contact with the hard muscle under his shirt. When she felt the strength of his arousal through the flimsy silk of her dress she couldn't pull away. Her hips rocked, aching to be closer, and he pulled her up and into the cradle of his lap.

When he lifted his head after long minutes. Kallie's mouth clung…until the cool air swept over her skin as someone came out of the door behind them. She tensed immediately and her eyes flew open, clashing with dark brown ones. This time there was a look of triumph on his face.

She was still too stunned by the strength of her reaction to do anything, feel anything other than the blood that coursed through her with the force of a crashing wave.

He smiled down at her, and trailed a finger along her jaw. He, unlike her, seemed to be capable of speaking, of being rational.

'It's too late, Kallie. We're married. As you seem to have conveniently forgotten, you've already signed the agreement that seals my promise of the loan, and this…' He moved his hips slightly, his erection sliding tantalisingly against the silk-covered apex of her thighs. The burning desire still held her in its grip. '*This* is very much the next part of the plan.'

She was held and mesmerised by his eyes. She had to wonder for the first moment since seeing him again what he would do when he discovered she was woefully inexperienced. That suddenly made her brain freeze. He wouldn't want to sleep with a novice. She wasn't a virgin but may as well be compared to him! She should tell him now before they went any further. This was the thing that would make him dump her faster than a hot piece of coal. She opened her mouth to speak but nothing came out. Two sides of her went to war, the side that wanted very badly to get away right now, forget she'd ever seen Alexandros again, and the other side that wanted nothing more than for him to lay her down, right where they were, and take her to paradise and back.

They were still locked together, as close as they could be. She had to say something, she couldn't be this weak. A flashing pop made Kallie flinch in his arms as suddenly, within what seemed like seconds, they were surrounded by paparazzi. The hotel doormen, along with bodyguards that had materialised out of thin air, were trying to beat them back, and in the mayhem that followed Kallie was bundled out and into a car with Alexandros so fast that they were speeding away before she could even get her breath, never mind launch into a declaration of her sexual inexperience.

CHAPTER SEVEN

WHEN she was finally able to articulate a word she bit out, 'Are you going to tell me where we're going?'

The thought of a honeymoon, just her and Alexandros together, was causing waves of panic through Kallie's tense body.

Alexandros looked at her. Her arms were folded across her chest. Everything about her screamed, *Get out!* And made him more determined than ever to slake his lust, experience the passion that ignited with just a touch of their mouths.

He forced himself to relax, to try and dampen the spark that was ready to be fanned into a burning flame at the slightest provocation…or encouragement, which he figured was unlikely in the near future.

'Our bags are following so we're going straight to the airport.'

Was he being deliberately obtuse? Kallie emitted a frustrated sigh.

'And is this a magic mystery tour or are you going to tell me where we're going?'

She was all too aware of the strained edge in her voice. Alexandros regarded her coolly from his seat. Looking casual and relaxed and at ease, when she felt as tightly wound as a spring.

'We're going to my villa just outside Athens.'

Kallie frowned and automatically slipped into the familiar Greek name for her grandmother. 'The villa beside *ya ya*'s?'

He nodded. 'My mother has moved into town. It's easier for her, and closer to the doctors if she needs them. I've had it completely refurbished in the interim.'

She'd bet he had. And she could only imagine the opulence. It had always been very grand, effortlessly overshadowing her grandparents' more humble villa, with its deceptively simple design.

She saw that they were driving into a small airfield, approaching a private jet. She tried to quell her panic and looked at Alexandros as if to block out the evidence that very shortly they would be on a plane, flying to Athens, to be alone. She knew she was talking quickly, inanely.

'I haven't been back there since *ya ya* died. Her house is sitting empty now. Some of the family go there sometimes, I think, but…'

A sudden upsurge of sadness gripped Kallie, taking her by surprise. That house held such special memories for her and the thought of seeing it again without her beloved grandmother hit home.

She didn't see how Alexandros's gaze narrowed on her face. 'Is this your first visit back to Athens since then?'

And was that moisture in her eyes?

She swallowed the lump in her throat and looked at him, shaking her head, desperately willing the emotion down. 'Not to Athens, just to her house…'

She'd had no idea the thought of going back there would affect her so strongly.

The car came to a smooth halt and thankfully she clambered out into the cool air. Anything to avoid that intense, laser-like gaze. Within minutes they were ensconced in plush cream leather seats in the plane, sitting opposite one another. Kallie felt a little more under control again. She couldn't be her normal self around Alexandros. But it was so hard, watching everything she said, having to control every impulse. She was used to living honestly, openly. But, of course, they were the last things he believed her to be. Open and honest. As they took off and she avoided meeting the dark gaze she could feel resting on her, Kallie had to admit to herself that being open and honest hadn't exactly worked for her in the past. She'd found out that people didn't appreciate it. Would step all over it…

A host of conflicting uncomfortable emotions were ripping through Alexandros. He took in Kallie's averted profile, the way she swallowed convulsively. He'd seen the sheen of tears in her eyes in the car and it had thrown him completely. He'd even found himself about to ask if she'd prefer to stay at his apartment in Athens, rather than go to the villa. His jaw clenched. Thank goodness he'd come to his senses. Kallie Demarchis at the age of seventeen had shown a mercenary streak that had stunned him. Seven years on, it would only have been honed and developed.

The only reason she'd be letting tears fall would be to manipulate a situation for her own ends. And he had to concede that she must be seething…perhaps even plotting something. How could she not? He'd made sure that she would get nothing from the marriage and he'd checked up on her financial status. The money she would have got from her shares, which would have gone into six figures, was long gone. The girl had expensive tastes. Goodness only knew what she had spent the money on.

He looked away moodily and stared out the window at the ground dropping away beneath them. Bed her and get her out of his system. That's all he wanted to do. He didn't have to think about anything else. He sent up a fervent prayer that by the end of the two weeks he'd be thoroughly sated and he could file for divorce. He'd even told his solicitor to have the divorce papers drawn up and ready, not intending this to be a long marriage *at all*.

Kallie sent a quick curious look to Alexandros and was shocked to see his face in such stern lines. She'd felt his withdrawal, as if he was pulling in, pulling away from her. And as if to confirm her suspicions, he looked at her then, but it was so cold, so black that she had to repress a shiver.

'Are you hungry?' he surprised her by asking brusquely.

Kallie shook her head and felt a wave of tiredness wash over her, which she succumbed to with relief and not a little cowardice. She was confused by her own turbulent desires. She welcomed some respite, however flimsy. Allowing her eyes to close, shutting out the evocative and disturbing image of Alexandros, her body sank into the reclining seat.

Kallie woke to a gentle touch and found the stewardess standing over her. Someone had put a blanket over her, too.

'Mrs Kouros, we're landing in a few minutes.'

For a second she was about to assert that she wasn't Mrs Kouros until she remembered that she was. She scrambled up inelegantly, relieved to see that Alexandros was missing from his seat. She pushed her hands through her tumbled hair and secured it back again. The orchid came out in her hand and she looked at it. What had possessed her to put it in her hair earlier? She threw it down on the table beside her, disgusted with herself that she might have somehow unconsciously done it for *him*. She wanted to get out of the dress, which clung far too much, and get into jeans…or overalls, or something. Anything else.

And who had put the blanket over her? The thought that it might have been him made her insides liquefy. Silly, she chided herself. It was far more likely to have been the stewardess. She looked up and saw Alexandros emerge from a cabin at the back. He looked pristine. Her cheeks felt hot and her eyes sticky from sleep as he came towards her.

'Good, you're awake. We're landing now.'

She just nodded, didn't trust herself to speak, and diverted her attention to the view outside. The vista of Athens in the distance got closer and closer until they finally landed. A warm feeling spread through her as she saw the familiar skyline. Coming back to Athens had always felt like coming home, and she'd missed it.

Once they had landed everything happened so quickly it was a blur. They were out of the plane and ensconced in a luxury four-wheel-drive with tinted windows within minutes. One bodyguard in the front with the driver, the other following in another vehicle with the luggage. She was caught out by feeling suddenly happy at the thought of being back here. She needed to feel close to the Greek earth again.

The warm air caressed Kallie's skin like silk as she stepped from the vehicle outside the Kouros villa. Dusk was claiming the sky, lines of pink strewn across it like ribbons as the sun fell. Her own family villa was hidden in the trees just a couple of hundred yards away. She sucked in the warm spring air and drank in the sight of Alexandros's home. It had always had a slightly crumbling grandeur that Kallie had been in awe of, but the refurbishment was total and stunning. It was painted a warm off-white that reflected the glow of the setting sun. Its low front and flat roof made it look almost unassuming, but the wide veranda leading up to the huge front door hinted at the luxury that lay inside.

What kept the villa from looking almost too linear, flat, were the trees that lined the entire front façade. Tall and willowy, the typical pine trees of the region were spaced in such a way as to enhance the view of the villa, not detract from it. Kallie knew the first modest impression was deceptive.

The villa was built into the hillside, almost wrapped around it, in fact, giving it two stunning views over Athens—one from the garden, the other from the pool that was at the bottom of several levels cut into the earth, among trees and olive groves.

Just then the front door opened and a familiar full-bodied figure rushed out and down the steps, a round brown face wreathed in smiles. Kallie tried to keep track of the rapid Greek as Alexandros's long-time housekeeper greeted him with a big hug. But when it came to Kallie Thea merely skated a glance over her and barely acknowledged her. Kallie's stomach dropped. So Thea hadn't forgiven her either. There had been a time when she had been the housekeeper's favourite, when she used to sneak over and spend happy hours in the kitchen learning how to make traditional Greek recipes. But Thea had never forgiven Kallie for the way Alexandros had been treated. Kallie had tried to explain, feeling that out of everyone Thea might listen to her, but to no avail. And with seven years gone by, Kallie knew she'd be even less likely to listen now.

In the entrance hall Thea called a young maid and asked her to show Kallie up to her room, as coolly as if she'd never even known her. Kallie was determined not to reveal how hurt she was and followed the young girl upstairs. She was relieved to see that it wasn't the master bedroom, although her relief fled when Alexandros appeared at the door, leaning against it nonchalantly.

He took her in, standing like a startled fawn caught in the headlights. The raw, visceral way he felt, the almost overwhelming urge he had to go over and tip her onto the bed, made him very, very wary. The maid had mistakenly brought her to a guest room. He'd intended her to be in *his* room with *him*…but now he wasn't so sure that was the best idea, despite the clamour of his pulse. He was a civilised man of the world. Not someone ruled by his primitive desires, like some kind of caveman. He made a decision to play around with the truth slightly.

'I've given you your own room, Kallie,' he said as he came

in. She backed away against the far wall, watching with huge eyes as he walked to another door and opened it. *That* led into the master bedroom. He left it open.

'There's no lock in this door… Like I said in Paris, you'll come to me. And I'll be ready when you do.'

He walked over and stood very close. He reached out a hand and trailed fingers over her collar-bone, which was bared in the dress. Her breath hitched. The energy crackled between them, like a live wire as his hand went down, lower and lower until his fingers grazed the slopes of her breast. Watching her intently, Alexandros let his hand cup one breast. Her nipple sprang to immediate hardness against the silk of her dress and pushed insistently against his palm. He struggled not to haul her close and take her mouth with his, ravaging her breast with his hand.

Kallie's breath had long stopped and she'd given up trying to figure out how she still stood. She could feel a bead of sweat break out on her brow. Her lips quivered under his look and she could feel her body wanting to push…push against his hand, have him caress her breast, have his fingers close over her nipple, which throbbed. Then abruptly, cruelly, his hand was gone, his warmth was gone, his scent was gone as he stepped back. Not a shred of evidence that he was as in the same turmoil as she was.

'So don't take too long, Kallie. There won't be a divorce until this marriage is consummated so you see…it's in your hands. You have the power to make this go as quickly or as slowly as you want. In the meantime, I'll enjoy the anticipation.'

Kallie wanted nothing more at that moment than to have the nerve to reach up, pull him back to her and give in. Once they'd slept together she was sure she wouldn't satisfy him…a man with his reputation, used to women like Isabelle Zolanz! One night with Kallie would cure him of whatever madness she was sure was just tied up with his lust for revenge.

He turned and stalked to the door, turning back just as he reached it. 'Dinner will be served at eight.'

She stood for a long time, waiting for her body to cool down. A curt knock came on the door and Kallie steeled herself, expecting to see Alexandros again. But it opened to reveal Thea, who put her bags inside the door. She was almost gone when Kallie called to her. 'Thea…' She walked over when the woman stopped, her heart aching that Thea could be so cold.

'Thea…it's good to see you again.'

The older woman just looked at Kallie, grunted something unintelligible and left.

Kallie went and sat down on the bed. Her head reeled. Little had she known that when Alexandros had stormed out of her life seven years ago she'd be back to face her demons. And how…

CHAPTER EIGHT

'YOU look tired.'

'Thanks,' Kallie replied dryly, noting that *he* looked vibrant, vital and more alive than anyone she'd ever known. They were sitting at a wrought-iron table, covered with a white linen tablecloth, on the back terrace. The French doors to the salon inside had been thrown open. Thea had insisted on serving dinner out here, more, Kallie was sure, for Alexandros's pleasure than hers. But Kallie had to admit that it was magical. Chinese lanterns threw shapes on the ground at their feet, she could just make out the glimmer of water from the pool on the next level down and the glinting, twinkling lights of Athens and the Acropolis in the distance were mesmerising.

'I'd forgotten how breathtaking this view is.'

'Yes. It is.'

The tension was giving Kallie a headache. Their conversation over dinner had been stilted and forced. And Kallie dreaded to think what Alexandros might expect that night. She stood up, her chair sounding harsh on the stone.

'I'm going to turn in. It's been a long day.' Her voice sounded too forced. He looked up at her and Kallie knew that if he was to stand up and take her in his arms, she'd be lost. He just nodded and she felt an irrational surge of disappointment. She went to walk past him and just when she was nearly clear, he grabbed her wrist in a loose yet firm grip. Her heart skidded to a halt. She looked at him warily, eyes glinting green and blue in the light.

His voice was silky. 'Kallie, that door will be open. Don't forget.'

Kallie jerked her hand out of his grip and fled. As much as she perversely wanted him to make a move, she knew she couldn't. Not yet.

Alexandros swallowed the last of his wine with almost a savage movement. This evening had been purgatory, sitting opposite Kallie with the lanterns and moonlight bathing her skin in a warm milky glow. It had looked so smooth, so silky that it had taken all the strength he'd possessed not to reach out and touch her. But she'd caught him off guard again. Every time he'd moved, she'd flinched slightly and looked at him with those huge wary eyes. Even though he'd seen the blatant desire in their depths.

She'd come down to dinner dressed in loose trousers and a long flowing cardigan, its low neckline hinting at the naked body beneath. Her hair had been soft and loose over her shoulders. Why did he have to desire her so much? It was quite possible that he could have met her with her uncle, not found her attractive and let it go at that. He knew that the lust for revenge had been born out of that fierce desire he'd felt on first sight, before he'd recognised who she was…

The view became a blur. She certainly wasn't like any other woman he knew or had been with. With them things were easy, it was like a dance he knew well. With Kallie… He shook his head abruptly. Enough! It was their common links, shared history, that was all. Being back here in Athens. He hadn't been here for a long time and now to be back here with Kallie, it was only natural his thoughts would turn inward. Making him think about the past and things he hadn't thought of for a long time.

He stood with a brusque movement and finally went inside, doing his best to shut down the wayward thoughts that made him nervous. He wondered if he was a complete fool to let her dictate when she'd be in his bed. He comforted himself with the thought that it wouldn't be long. She had as little desire for this marriage as he did. And apart from that, *their* desire, unchecked, would soon burst into flames.

The following morning when she woke up, Kallie had a quick shower and dressed. Choosing a plain skirt and vest top and sticking her feet into flip-flops, she headed downstairs and found herself in the kitchen. It brought back so many good memories that she was lost in a dream and jumped when Thea surprised her. A terse greeting. Kallie sighed and went into the dining room, as it was obvious she wasn't welcome in the kitchen. When Thea came to clear the plates after breakfast, Kallie asked casually about Alexandros, who she still hadn't seen that morning. Thea told her he'd gone to Athens to his office for the day.

Kallie's insides plummeted. A whole day alone in the villa, being frozen out by Thea. She felt something rise up and told herself fiercely that she wouldn't miss Alexandros's company.

Oh, be honest with yourself. When he's near you your whole body comes to life, your brain clicks into high gear and you've never felt so aware...or stimulated...

With the mocking voice in her head, Kallie explored the Kouros villa from top to bottom again. Although she studiously avoided going anywhere near the patio, as her heart started to thump erratically when she passed near it. She couldn't bear the thought of seeing it again, the place of her original humiliation.

And though she knew she could get a key from Thea and

go next door to see her grandmother's house, she knew it wasn't time. She was feeling far too vulnerable. Afraid of what it might spark off within her, what feelings she might be forced to face.

That evening when Alexandros returned he felt hot and sticky and cross with himself for having gone into Athens. A visit to his mother hadn't helped his mood. She was as cold and wrapped up in herself as ever. He didn't need to remind himself that she hadn't even been bothered coming to the wedding. His own family had been in woefully short supply. After making sure she had everything she needed, he'd left. Which she'd barely noticed.

When he'd been born, as an unplanned late arrival, ten years after the youngest daughter, his parents had only been happy for the fact that they'd finally had a boy, and a proper heir. Their own interests always had been in themselves, not their children, and Alexandros's sisters had all been married by the time he'd been in his early teens. He'd long ago shut himself off from the pain of his family's indifference.

Climbing up the hill to the villa in his four-wheel-drive he found his thoughts straying in an annoyingly familiar direction. Kallie. Wondering what she would have done that day. He'd needed space, had gone into Athens primarily for that…and yet bizarrely he felt slightly guilty. He frowned at his capricious emotions.

It was quiet when he entered, the coolness inside bathing and soothing him. Soothing his frayed edges. He walked from room to room. There was no sign of Thea or Kallie, and he finally descended down the levels until he came out by the pool. At first the setting sun dazzled him and he had to put on his sunglasses, then he saw her. His body tightened and his breathing quickened in an entirely involuntary response. She was dressed in tracksuit bottoms and a tight vest top and was doing a series of movements facing the sun. He knew what she was doing, yet even though he knew it was yoga, it seemed like something more mysterious, reverential.

Without the cover of layers, he could see her body in all its supple glory. It wasn't stick thin and muscly, which he usually associated with the yoga physique, she had curves and a soft belly and full breasts. Her movements were controlled and so graceful that it almost hurt to watch. Holding his breath without even realising, he stared transfixed as she came to a standing halt and pressed her hands together at the centre of her chest and bowed her head in the universal symbol of prayer and thanks. She looked so serene and peaceful that Alexandros felt a twinge of jealousy. And then she turned and saw him.

'Oh…'

He could see her chest rise and fall after the exertion and was glad of the dark glasses that shaded his eyes. That hid what he knew would be an almost feral gleam, as she brought that instinct out in him. A need to possess…to devour.

She picked up the towel that she'd been using as a mat and drew it across her chest as if to try and hide behind it.

'Alexandros.' Her voice came out cool and yet slightly breathy, making fine hairs stand up all over his body in reaction.

He strolled towards her, hands in pockets, devastating eyes hidden. How much had he seen? She hated the thought that he had been witness to what was a very private thing for her. He was enjoying her discomfort.

His hands, deep in the pockets, stretched the fabric across his pelvis. Kallie's eyes dropped in a reflex and hurriedly she lifted them again, her cheeks scorching with mortification when she registered the bulge.

'Yoga?' He lifted a mocking brow. 'Not something I would have associated with you—the ultimate party girl.'

'Why?' asked Kallie sweetly, burning up under his shaded look. 'Doesn't it fit with your view of me as a heartless seductress?'

His big body went very still and Kallie almost took a step back. She should have known by now not to provoke him. He stepped very close, but she stood her ground.

An X-rated image raced into his head at that moment and had him clench his jaw in reaction to what it might be like to see Kallie, her strong supple body naked, under his, legs wrapped around his back as he sank in…deeper and deeper…

'Not at all. Quite the contrary, in fact. It's certainly going to make our time in the bedroom more…enjoyable.' His gaze dropped down her body and she knew her nipples had peaked and were pushing against the thin fabric of her top. She clutched the towel even tighter to her body and felt a drop of sweat roll down between her breasts and wondered perversely if he'd seen it.

After long moments Alexandros stepped back and indicated for Kallie to precede him back into the house. Her spine straight, back stiff, she walked in. She fought the urge to run and just then remembered his other comment. She whirled around.

'And what's that supposed to mean—party girl?'

He stopped short, surprised by her question. 'Just that. I looked you up, Kallie. Never out of the society pages. In fact, I'm surprised we haven't bumped into one another long before now as you seem to hit every night spot with alarming regularity.'

Kallie simmered when she thought of the long hours, the back-breaking work she had put in to get her business off the ground. Invariably on those nights that he had talked about, she'd been up the next morning to go back to work at six a.m., and certainly not sleeping off the rigours of a mad night out. Especially when she didn't even drink!

'I'm surprised, Alexandros. For someone with a seemingly insatiable desire to take over the world, that you don't recognise another workaholic when you see one.' She shrugged. 'Think what you will, though, I really couldn't care less.'

Liar…

Her words caught at him, tugged him into a memory from long ago, and he felt an immediate need to justify…something. And how could she claim to be a workaholic? If that work included being out among the B-list and C-list celebrities till dawn every morning? He'd always had a scathing disregard for her profession and only used his own PR in a very calculating way. Unfortunately, the way the media worked today, as he knew all too well, his need for such a company was imperative. He strode on ahead of her, taciturn and dark.

'We're eating out tonight.'

Kallie's rage dissipated like lightning. Her mouth dried up. *And then…?*

'OK,' she blurted out. Anything to avoid being alone with him in the villa, being wound up, suited her just fine. In fact, it'd be easier if she didn't have to look at him at all. She hurried after him. 'You know we don't have to eat out together. If you want, you could go out. I don't mind staying in.'

He ignored her, not even looking back. 'We'll go out in a couple of hours.'

She stuck out her tongue in a ridiculously childish gesture at his back and curiously it actually did make her feel a little better. She followed her autocratic husband into the villa.

Alexandros sat sprawled in a chair in the hall waiting for Kallie to come downstairs that evening. His body had a satisfyingly tired ache. After their little exchange, he'd gone back to the pool and swum lengths to try and forget the fact that he wanted Kallie more than he'd ever wanted another woman. And that he was very much afraid that he'd be the one to go through the door first. The fact that she could arouse him to the point that he couldn't even control his impulses made him seethe.

She appeared at the top of the stairs at that moment and the mere sight of her made a complete waste of his punishing physical exertion in the pool. As if he'd just received an injection of pure adrenalin, Alexandros shot to his feet. What killed him about watching her come down the stairs was that she wasn't even dressed to impress. She was wearing jeans and a white shirt. Hair loosely tumbled over her shoulders. With barely any make-up and a fresh, light scent pervading the air around her lightly, she came to a halt in front of him. She smiled tightly but even that rocked his foundations.

'Good. I'm glad we're not dressing up.'

He was transfixed by her eyes, her mouth. 'What?'

She indicated his clothes. He was dressed casually like her, in jeans and a shirt. He thought to himself that if he could hardly handle her dressed like this, how would he even begin to control himself around her if she *was* dressed to impress, to seduce? Before she could read anything on his face, he ushered her out and into his vehicle. The ever-present bodyguards followed in another one and Kallie shivered at the knowledge of how important Alexandros was. Somehow, in the intensity of the ongoing battle between them, she'd forgotten that.

She couldn't help the fizz of excitement at the thought of going into the city, she'd always loved the hustle and bustle of Athens. At least, that's what she told herself was causing the fizz of excitement, not the man beside her.

'Where are we going? It's been so long since I've been here I'm sure things have changed quite a bit.'

When Alexandros shot her a quick glance, she saw that he was avoiding her eye. 'There's a new place just opened in Kolonaki I'd like to try out.'

As if he'd even care for her opinion on the matter…

'Is that still *the* exclusive area?' she asked idly, determined not to be bothered by him.

'Yes, but it's fast being taken over by areas like Gazi which are becoming the in place to be.'

Kallie shook her head. 'That place was just full of derelict buildings…don't tell me, some bright spark converted an old industrial works building into some kind of an art space and now it's become a home to all sorts of bohemians and trendy restaurants.'

She saw his mouth quirk, and was transfixed by the sudden lightness that seemed to surround them.

Alexandros was amused at the way she'd assessed the situation in one.

'Yes, those damned bright-spark shipping magnates have a habit of regenerating dead areas.'

Kallie gasped and looked at him. 'You?'

He nodded and shrugged. 'With a few others. Well, it was better than letting it crumble. Now there's galleries, restaurants, clubs…' His mouth tightened for an instant. 'Constantine Stakis had taken control of the area and it took years to clean it up. It was becoming a haven for the black market, cheap, dangerous housing, prostitutes…you name it, he had it there and made a killing from it.'

She turned to face Alexandros fully, unaware of the natural glow on her face that was lit up with sudden enthusiasm. 'Could we go there instead? Please? I'd love to see what you've done to the area. I always thought it had great potential.'

Alexandros felt an uncustomary punch to his gut, a burst of pride. He just answered with a shrug and turned the vehicle in the other direction. It had been so long, if ever, since he'd felt shared pleasure in the accomplishment of something that it kept him silent for the rest of the journey.

CHAPTER NINE

KALLIE loved it. The area he'd invested in had become her dream of what was possible. She turned to look at him outside one tiny gallery that had prints in the window, smiling. Alexandros had the irrational thought, *If she keeps smiling at me like this, I'm not going to last...*

'You've done an amazing job. You must feel so proud to come here and know that you've helped the city in this way.'

His face was closed as he looked down at her and she could see his pulse jump at his temple. She wanted to reach up and touch it but she rapidly wiped the smile off her face. What was wrong with her? A few hours back in Greece and she was already falling back into the hole she'd dug herself seven years ago. She was beyond pathetic and hadn't even learnt one lesson. He had blackmailed her into marriage, for God's sake! Was planning on bedding her in a completely cold-blooded fashion. Her lips clamped together as Alexandros answered her, his eyes, as always, intent, assessing.

'I love it, too. Like you, I always used to see this area as...more than it was.'

Among the myriad, swirling emotions that threatened to rise up and strangle her completely, Kallie had to admit uncomfortably that her first impression that he had sold out to the rat race was undergoing a bit of a bashing. For a long moment they just looked at each other and then it was broken when an amorous couple who weren't looking where they were going bumped into them. Alexandros welcomed it.

'There's a restaurant around the corner. It's owned by a friend, one of the partners who redeveloped the area.'

Only trusting herself to nod, Kallie could feel herself starting to open up, despite her best efforts. She *had* to fight the shifting sands around her feet, around her feelings. She knew that Alexandros had a much more powerful weapon at his disposal for revenge. She knew she could not be hurt the same way again. Because this time she *wouldn't* survive.

Kallie looked around the restaurant again. Holding her back so straight, being on her guard was exhausting. Like her see-sawing emotions. One minute she'd feel herself start to open, like a flower turning towards the sun, the next she'd remember and close up. Alexandros was so much harder to handle when he was… Kallie had been about to say *nice* to herself, but he wasn't even being particularly nice, he was being polite, civil and she was like a pathetic mouse, picking up crumbs.

The dinner had been exquisite, the surroundings beautiful. They'd been treated like royalty since they'd arrived. But this see-sawing wouldn't stop. As if a force bigger than her was playing with her like a puppet on a string. What made it even harder was that their conversation hadn't strayed into any danger areas and she'd found herself genuinely enjoying talking to him. She felt herself relaxing, ever so slightly. Laughing even, albeit briefly, at one point and it felt so good after the weeks of tension and pressure.

Dessert had just been delivered. Kallie took a spoonful of ice cream and savoured the way it slipped down her throat. For some reason she'd never felt the experience of eating ice cream before as *sensual* but, sitting opposite Alexandros, she had to concede that she'd never ever been so aware of everything.

He brought her back to earth and showed her how he patently wasn't half as affected as her when he asked, 'You mentioned that your father took your mother's life in the crash?'

She put down her spoon and nodded warily. *She had?* Why had he remembered that? She looked at him for a long moment, focused on his eyes. There was no apparent malice there.

She shrugged lightly. 'You remember what he was like… always the *bon vivant*.' She avoided his eye now, playing with her spoon. 'After *ya ya* died, things got worse with the company. He never had time to go back to Athens and he just started drinking more and more.'

She sighed deeply, the grief not far from the surface as she remembered. 'That day…that day he'd accepted the fact that he had to get help. But he wanted one more drink…and he wouldn't let Mum drive…' Her mouth thinned when she thought of her father's typical macho Greek bluster. 'So she went, too, not wanting him to be alone.'

She finally lifted slightly defiant eyes to Alexandros and he was surprised. What had he expected? That she'd be looking for sympathy? He found himself responding from somewhere instinctive. 'I'm sorry, Kallie. I had no idea.'

She shrugged again, awkwardly. 'Well, you wouldn't would you…not after…'

'No,' he agreed. They both knew she didn't need to finish that sentence.

Kallie wanted to get the focus off her. 'What about your mother? Why wasn't she at the wedding?'

The change was stunning and immediate. His face shuttered, his eyes black pools. Kallie thought he wasn't going to answer until finally he said, 'She's never been one for travelling. She's happy as long as she knows that Kouros Shipping is making enough money to keep her in comfort.'

His voice was so cold and detached that Kallie sucked in a breath. She wasn't fooled. He spoke as though he didn't care but she could sense his pain, having been through intense grief herself, and could feel it as clear as day in him. But she knew he wouldn't appreciate her sympathy. She couldn't believe the well of emotion that rose up within her, making her want to go and take him in her arms. When she put down the spoon her hand was trembling and it clattered against the plate, making her start.

She excused herself to go to the ladies before he could read something in her expression and only came back when she felt composed. Coffee was waiting for her. She looked over. 'Thanks…but I didn't order coffee…'

'It's on the house…a treat from my friend Theo.'

She shrugged. 'OK…'

A silence stretched between them. Alexandros seemed to be brooding. They'd obviously used up the little conversation they had. Kallie's thoughts strayed as she sipped the coffee. Very soon they'd be back in the villa. Alone. Would he leave the door open tonight? Would he ask her to sleep with him? Would he kiss her into submission? Force her? *He wouldn't have to…*

Kallie's heart speeded up as she took a bigger gulp of coffee. She couldn't look across the table. She took some more coffee. Anything to distract her thoughts. It had a slightly funny taste that made her wrinkle her nose.

Half idly, belying the turmoil of her thoughts, she asked, 'What's in this coffee? It tastes different.'

Alexandros looked over, his hooded eyes making her pulse speed up, *again.*

'Some liqueur, I think the waiter said.'

Immediately Kallie could feel something slam into her. She hadn't touched alcohol in years. *Seven years.* And suddenly the only thing she could smell, or taste, or *feel* with a nauseous swimming in her head was the alcohol. And with shocking vividness, she was back there on the patio, her head swimming, feeling the acute mortification all over again. As if it were yesterday. Terror gripped her, squeezing around her heart, and she lifted a hand to her chest.

It was all hitting her at once. She was in Athens again. Greece. With Alexandros, who was looking over at her. She could see him frowning…was she looking funny? Kallie felt very strange…and she knew that for some reason she'd stopped breathing.

'What is it?' Alexandros's voice came from far away.

'Kallie, answer me…'

Her voice was raspy, she couldn't breathe. 'I don't know… must have been something…'

All she did know with some kind of miraculous self-protecting clarity was that he couldn't know why she was having this reaction. The room was spinning now and she felt herself drooping sideways, unable to sit up. Then she was being lifted up into strong arms, against a firm wall of something…muscle? She didn't care. She felt sick, but safe. Then she blacked out.

She came to in the most horrific, undignified fashion, hunched over a toilet bowl, her whole upper body dripping wet, retching. Alexandros was behind her, holding her hair back as life slammed back into her and she emptied her stomach. Finally it was over. She was shaking all over violently. She felt herself being pulled back up and a wet cloth over her face and neck. It felt wonderful. Then she was sitting on his lap and being held very firmly against a broad chest until the shaking started to subside. She finally managed faintly, 'Where…where are we?'

A rumble came from under her cheek. 'In the staff toilet of the restaurant.'

Kallie closed her eyes and clung to Alexandros. 'Oh, I'm so sorry…'

When she opened them again, she took in the shower and

realised that he must have had to put her underneath it to wake her up somehow. She pulled back.

'I'm so sorry…'

'Don't be. Kallie, what the hell was that?' His voice was harsh. 'For goodness' sake, woman, if you're allergic to liqueur or coffee, why didn't you tell me?'

But I'm not! Or, at least, she hadn't thought she was. But even as Kallie thought about the alcohol in the coffee, she could see the images flood her head again, the acute nausea close behind. She closed her eyes, gripped his shirt and breathed deeply. This was ridiculous. No way could this be affecting her so badly. It had to be the food…or something else. She couldn't still be so tied into what had happened. The thought that she *could* be made something in her head shut down.

She shook her head. 'No, it couldn't be…' *It couldn't be!*

'It must have been something I ate.'

'We had the same thing and I feel fine,' he pointed out grimly.

She was too weak to argue.

He stood, taking her with him, clasping her to his chest. She only saw then that his own hair was plastered to his head, his chest soaking. He'd got into the shower too? He answered her look. 'Well, I could hardly avoid getting wet, too, could I? I couldn't just dump you in there.'

'Sorry,' she said in a small voice. Again.

He elbowed his way out of the room and his friend Theo was there, the owner, looking awful and wringing his hands. 'I am so sorry, Alexandros. I have no idea how this could have happened.'

Kallie gave an involuntary shudder. Alexandros tightened his hold.

'Theo, it's fine. Forget it….we need to leave now, though, we're wet.'

His friend jumped around, clearly upset, and gave them towels. 'Your vehicle is right outside the door here, at the back…'

Kallie couldn't help another wave of mortification. She was sure the great Alexandros Kouros hated this embarrassment. When he climbed into the back of the vehicle, still keeping her tucked into his arms, she resolutely looked out the window, taking her arms away from his neck.

'I'm sorry,' she said stiffly yet again, her whole body rigid. 'I didn't mean to embarrass you in front of your friends...the people in the restaurant...'

Alexandros looked down at the bent head, her hair no less vibrant, even though it was wet. When she'd taken her arms down from his neck, he'd had the urge to bring them back up. And when she'd gone rigid, the loss of her soft curves nestled into him had been almost like a physical pain. And despite what she seemed to think, when she'd almost collapsed, the entire restaurant could have disappeared for all he'd cared. His only concern had been Kallie and getting her to safety. He'd even bellowed out for a doctor but none had been there.

'Don't be stupid, Kallie. We brought you out the back because it was quicker.'

'Oh...'

He took one of the towels and put Kallie away from him slightly, starting to undo her shirt. She slapped at his hand ineffectually. 'What do you think you're doing?'

He pushed her hands out of the way. 'Kallie, you're soaked, so am I. Unless you want to get hypothermia, you have to take off your shirt.'

He'd undone all the buttons and was slipping the shirt from her shoulders before she could do anything.

She let out a strangled whisper. *'The driver!'*

She was now in just her bra and Alexandros was pulling his own sodden shirt off. Totally unashamed, he ignored her concern. He drew her back against his bare chest and wrapped them both in a couple of towels, tucking her arms around his waist. Sensation flooded her belly, her breasts, making them tighten painfully. She bit her lip.

Alexandros looked down briefly and when he caught a glimpse of two perfect creamy half-mounds spilling from her bra, pressed against him, he felt desire rocket straight to his lap.

The inevitable response became more acute. His jaw clenched, the towel dropped slightly. She moved to get comfortable and he gritted out, 'Kallie, stop moving.'

She felt the hard ridge beneath her and heat flooded her body. The trip back up into the hills was excruciating and by the time they got out, Kallie's face was hectic with colour, her eyes so bright they looked feverish.

He carried her up to her room and gently stood her outside her bathroom door. She had pulled the towel tight around her upper body and looked anywhere but at the expanse of bare chest in front of her.

'Do you need help?'

'No,' she said quickly, and qualified it. 'No…thank you. I don't know what I would have done if—'

'You need to get out of those wet things before you get a chill.'

She just nodded and went inside, stripped off and had a hot shower. Putting on a voluminous toweling robe, she emerged to find an empty room. Disappointment gushed through her. Then Thea appeared at the door with a look of concern on her face. Which she quickly masked when she saw Kallie.

She bustled in and got Kallie into bed and Kallie's final thought before she fell into a dreamless sleep was that maybe Thea wasn't as cool towards her after all. Maybe she could try again. She refused to think of the dark angel who had saved her tonight, who had held her with such tenderness. Because it hadn't been. That had been her imagination. He had been functional, that's all.

* * *

When Kallie woke the next morning, her stomach muscles felt tender. She must have sensed something because just as she came fully awake, her door opened. Alexandros. Dressed and looking fresh and bright. Clean shaven. Her belly tightened and she pulled the sheet up around her neck.

He walked in and opened the curtains that covered the French doors leading onto her veranda. He stood looking out for a minute, hands stuck deep in his pockets, and then turned around. 'How are you feeling today?'

'Much better, thank you. I'm—'

He slashed a hand in the air. 'Don't say sorry, Kallie, you couldn't help it. You must have some kind of sensitivity to liqueurs. Maybe the shellfish.'

You mean a sensitivity to the past!

She watched warily as he came close to the bed. He looked so tall and imposing and masculine.

'I'm afraid I have to go to London for a couple of days. One of our ships has had a mutiny of sorts among the crew…' His mouth quirked. 'It would appear that only I can sort it out.'

Kallie could suddenly see very well that he would be a good negotiator. Tough but firm. Despite what had happened between them. With those people he'd have no bitterness. It was only with *her*.

She just nodded. His gaze slanted down at her, unfathomable. 'Don't miss me too much while I'm gone…'

She shook her head. 'I won't.'

But she would. The realisation mocked her.

'Oh, I'm sure you won't, Kallie.' He smiled briefly, tightly.

CHAPTER TEN

As ALEXANDROS drove away from the villa, he had to concede that being married to Kallie so far was nothing like he'd expected. And he had a feeling that things were only going to get more complicated. Again he had that funny sensation the perhaps somewhere along the line he'd made a monumental error of judgment. For the first time in his life, he hadn't bedded a woman he'd desired when *he'd* wanted. But how he wanted her. If she didn't come to him when he got back, her time was up. No more waiting. He'd had enough of her coy looks and game-playing.

Kallie went downstairs after a while and found some breakfast left over in the dining room. Feeling edgy and not wanting to look at why, she stacked the plates and made her way to the kitchen. She had finished washing them and had started putting them away when she heard a sound behind her. Thea stood there with a disgusted look on her face. 'Why do you do this? *Why?* He is not here now. He doesn't need to see you pretend to be something you're not!'

Kallie couldn't take her words in for a moment. Thea looked so hurt, and angry.

'Thea…'

The older woman huffed, ignoring Kallie, banging open

and closing cupboards randomly. Kallie could remember that she'd always done that when she'd got angry or upset when she'd been younger. It had made her laugh and she'd teased Thea about it at one time.

She went up and put her hand on Thea's arm. 'Thea... please. Can we talk?'

Thea finally let Kallie lead her over to the table. But she wouldn't look at her. So Kallie started anyway, and haltingly told Thea exactly what had happened that night. Right up to when Alexandros had thrown the newspaper at her feet the next morning.

She wasn't even really aware she'd stopped until Thea looked at her and said quietly, 'Eleni?'

Kallie nodded silently.

Thea sighed heavily. 'I think I do believe you. I knew that girl was a bad egg—'

Kallie dashed away wetness she hadn't noticed on her cheeks. 'But—'

Thea was indignant. 'Look! Even now you jump to defend her—what is wrong with you? You have to tell Alexandros.'

Kallie shook her head. 'I can't, Thea. I promised I wouldn't and he'll go after *her.*'

Thea snorted. '*Her?* Of course he wouldn't, that's just the problem. It was you he always cared about, not her, that's why she did it, and why he was so angry with you...'

Kallie didn't believe it. He hadn't really cared about her at all, that had been obvious in the way he'd been so quick to judge her.

'Thea, I can't tell him.' Kallie explained about Eleni's fragile mental and physical health.

Thea gave her a withering look. 'Please, that girl is just a manipulator.'

'But, Thea, can't you see? How can I take the risk of telling

Alexandros when he could very well decide to punish her…or her family?'

'That was always your problem, Kallie, you were too nice…and too naïve. It was always you he cared about…that was where the problem started. Eleni was jealous.'

Kallie winced. Was Thea right? Wouldn't he want to punish Eleni? She couldn't take the chance that he wouldn't. Some dark emotion was rearing its ugly head and she didn't want to look at it. No matter what Thea said, she had to protect Eleni.

Thea got up to make them both some coffee and changed it to green tea when she saw how Kallie paled at the smell. Her unconscious concern told Kallie she was on the way to being forgiven. The relief was immense. Thea came back.

'Child, you have no idea what happened to him after that…you think it was just the break-up of the engagement?'

Wasn't that bad enough?

Kallie shrugged awkwardly. 'I know he must have loved her…' Despite what he had told her before.

Thea laughed. 'Love? You can't still be that naïve surely? He didn't love her. He was being forced to marry her by his mother in order to save Kouros Shipping. He had no choice in the matter. When his father died and left him in control, the old cronies didn't have faith in him. They started to sell out, the company came close to bankruptcy. That merger was his only hope.' She looked at Kallie carefully. 'Didn't you know about this?'

Kallie knew she wasn't going to like what she was going to hear, and shook her head. 'No. He only told me a few times that he wasn't sure how he felt about taking over the business…' She smiled tightly. 'He used to tell me that he wanted to do a degree in fine arts.'

That was so far removed from the man today that Kallie couldn't even believe that he had said it once. Thea brought her back to earth with a crash.

'Which you confided in Eleni, and which she obviously then leaked to the papers, along with that photo…'

'Oh, God…' Kallie had never read the whole piece, she'd been too heart-sick.

'Yes. They vilified him, the golden boy of the shipping world who never wanted to go into the business, he wanted to go to art college! With the merger and engagement falling through, the company going down the tubes, Alexandros had to work twenty-four hours a day, seven days a week to bring things back… But he did. And no one would dare remind him of it today.'

Unmistakable pride shone from Thea's face. The past took on a different hue immediately. The person that Alexandros had become when his father had died had been born out of great responsibility and necessity. Not a greedy desire to make money. Kallie felt ill again. She looked at Thea with stricken eyes.

'My parents…they threw him out of the house. I'll never forget it.'

Thea nodded. 'I thought so.' She shook her head at Kallie's look. 'No, he didn't tell me, but I knew something bad had happened over there. He never mentioned your family again. And, in truth, you, your parents, your cousins were all the family he really had.'

Kallie felt numb. More than numb. She'd known they'd always been close, but he'd always seemed so…self-sufficient. He'd always held something back. He'd never talked about his own family. Not really. For the first time she could see how it could have been possible for her parents to judge him so harshly…if they'd felt they hadn't known him that well.

It was so much worse than she'd ever known. 'He must despise me.'

Thea got up to rinse her cup. 'In truth, Kallie, he was too busy to hate anyone. He just got on with it.' She came back and stood in front of her, tipping her face up with an old calloused hand, her eyes dark and bright with emotion. She looked pointedly at the ring on Kallie's finger, the simple platinum band. 'He's married you, Kallie, for a reason…'

Thea was right, but there were two reasons. Revenge and desire. Guilt burned into Kallie like a brand. There was no way she could tell him the truth, because there was no way she could betray Eleni, risk her fragile health. And right now Kallie felt like she didn't even deserve forgiveness. The facts were still the same. If she hadn't gone out there to kiss him that night, when her instinct had warned her against it, none of this would have happened. And she had. So she was the one who had to deal with it.

She had a lot to think about over the next twenty-four hours. She and Thea were tentatively re-establishing their friendship. By the following evening, after dinner and when Thea had gone to bed, Kallie sat up, determined to wait for Alexandros to come home. She wasn't sure what she was going to do, or say. She felt as if a protective layer of skin had been ripped off and she didn't know if she could hide it from him.

It got so late that Kallie felt herself falling asleep. Giving up, she went to bed. She'd see him in the morning, or perhaps he wouldn't be back for another few days. She felt hollow at the thought.

Kallie woke with a start. She'd been having a dream of some sort. Her heart was racing and she felt hot all over. Bleary-eyed, she got out of bed and went into the bathroom to get some water. Everywhere was quiet. She immediately thought of Alexandros. Had he come home? She knew she'd only been asleep at most for a couple of hours. About to go and get back into bed, Kallie stopped and looked at the knob of the adjoining door. In her fanciful imagination, it seemed to glow slightly in the moonlit room. She hadn't pulled the curtains earlier.

She felt herself walking towards the door as though compelled. He probably wouldn't even be there, she assured herself. She touched the knob. Her breath was coming in shallow bursts…and she hadn't even turned it yet! With a disgusted shake of her head at herself, she twisted it and the door fell back towards her, surprising her with how heavy it was.

The room was dark. She crept in. The bed was flat. No one there. In the half-light, like her own room, she could just make out shapes. It was stark and masculine. Fitting for someone like Alexandros. And yet there were paintings on the walls, not abstract, as she would have expected, but small exquisite studies, portraits…landscapes.

She suddenly felt like a voyeur and turned to go back to her own room, and in that very instant the bathroom door on the other side of the room opened, light spilled out and Alexandros walked out, rubbing his hair with a towel, stark naked.

She must have gasped, or something, because he stopped, every line in his body rigid, and looked up, seeing her instantly. He didn't drop the towel, just stood there, unashamed and magnificent. She didn't know how long they stared at each other. She was only aware of the drumbeat of her heart, the way her whole body seemed to be melting, igniting…

'Kallie…'

He was real, wasn't an apparition. Kallie finally moved. She turned and would have run back to her bedroom if she'd had the co-ordination, but she didn't. She stumbled at the door and it slammed shut in her face, keeping her inside the room. She could have stamped her foot in frustration. No doubt he was thinking that she had heard him come back and was fulfilling her wifely duty.

Her hand had gone sweaty in seconds, the knob wouldn't turn and she let out a small whimper of frustration. And then stopped. The carpet had muffled his approach but she could feel body heat behind her and she closed her eyes. And all she could see was *him*. Without even really looking, she'd made an imprint on her retinas of his body and it was all she could see now, every toned, muscled, perfectly formed part of him. Not an ounce of fat, not a blemish on that smooth, olive, silky skin.

Heavy hands dropped to the bare skin of her shoulders and she couldn't repress a shudder of reaction. He turned her to face him and she couldn't resist. She kept her eyes closed, knowing if she moved even slightly that she'd come into contact with that hard body.

'Kallie...' A thread of something laced his voice—was it amusement? Irritation? 'Open your eyes, dammit.'

She opened them. And was surprised to see that the room was lighter than she'd thought, the moonlight stronger. The lean lines of his face were starkly outlined, as was the need in his eyes. She couldn't look down to see if he'd put on the towel, the thought of him *naked* nearly made her legs buckle. That tiny movement had him pull her into him. She felt the towel, but it was a feeble barrier against the hot, hard erection underneath. Her legs were trembling in earnest now, his arms the only thing holding her up.

Her own silky vest and lace panties were no sort of barrier either. She felt the door against her back and his arms slackened, hands coming around her face. He was crowding her, nudging her thighs apart with his own hair-roughened one. Like a deadly inevitability it washed over her. This was it. No going back. This is what she was here for, what had sparked between them when they'd first looked at one another again.

And suddenly it didn't matter right at that moment why she was there, because all Kallie was aware of was his thigh between hers, and how she ached to feel more, experience him fully. She could have tried to run away but she might as well be running from herself. Maybe if he'd come out with clothes on…maybe this heated insanity wouldn't have taken her over body and soul… But to have seen him *naked*…

With a guttural, broken moan of something in Greek, he bent his head and took her mouth in an onslaught so savage, so passionate that Kallie's head almost exploded with the feeling. Electricity coursed through her body. Unable to resist the overwhelming need, she strained to meet him on tiptoe, wrapped her arms around his neck. She ached to be closer and welcomed his thigh between hers, trapping it. She could feel the moist expression of her lust between her thighs, moistening her panties, and moved subtly against him. The pulse between her legs beat for release.

He tore his mouth away and moved it down, trailing kisses along her jaw, down to her neck. Kallie's head fell back and hit the door but she didn't even notice the brief pain. All the muscles in her neck corded as she felt his hand move to cup one silk-covered breast, feeling, caressing through the fabric and then, with his thigh still holding her in place, his mouth touched her, surrounded the distended peak and suckled through the fabric. Her back arched and she could feel herself starting to splinter into tiny pieces. Nothing had ever prepared her for this wealth of feelings and sensations.

Before she could lose it completely he pulled back. Kallie opened glazed eyes and looked into his, which burnt with the glowing embers of his desire. *For her.* It was too huge a moment to take in. All she could do was…experience, feel.

She stretched up and took his face in her hands, bringing it down, and when his mouth touched hers again she sighed with deep satisfaction. Moving her hands down, she revelled in the feel of his skin, his broad shoulders, down over biceps, bunched from holding her waist, spanning it with his hands. Her hands moved all the way down until she came to the towel and she slid them around the back, underneath and snagged it off, her hands running over the taut globes of his bottom.

His big frame shuddered as his erection pressed against her

belly. 'Kallie, Kallie…this is all I've thought about…since seeing you… I want you so much…'

She kissed his neck, his shoulder, the words slipping out easily. She didn't even have to think about them. 'I want you too…'

'Then why did you try to leave?'

She was breathless, half-incoherent. 'I…I didn't know you were here… I didn't want you to think that I was giving in…'

Something about the way she said it, some kind of defiant independence, made her seem unbearably vulnerable. He had to drive it down. 'Well, you're here now. It's too late to go back.'

He lifted her up in a graceful movement and carried her over to the huge bed, laying her down with surprising care. She lay back and watched as he rested on strong arms over her. Like his namesake, one of the fabled Kouros statues. For a split second clarity and sanity rushed in. This man despised her…was bedding her as a form of punishment. Yet how could it feel so good? Going against her instincts to just say nothing, Kallie felt something inexorable rise up within her.

Alexandros felt himself close to exploding with how tightly this woman had him wound. But just then she came up on her elbows, her eyes darkened with passion but glittering with something else. Something he couldn't define.

'Alexandros…how can you…? How can we do this, when you hate me so much?'

CHAPTER ELEVEN

WHAT?

Something in his body went cold. Not his desire. Nothing could put that out now. His thoughts raced even though he didn't want to think. He had to admit that since he'd been gone, he'd found himself thinking of her, the past…wanting to come back to her with a hunger that had to be purely physical. It certainly felt that way now when she lay on his bed, in front of him, eyes darkened, lips plump from his kisses. Anything else, anything more, had to be their history, *that was all.*

That was complicated. But this wasn't. *This* was simple.

When he'd walked out of the shower and seen her there, every muscle had clenched in reaction. She looked like a young goddess. Pale and glowing in the moonlight, her firm breasts upthrust and enticingly visible under her flimsy vest. The shaded darkness that hid her sex a shadowy promise of paradise.

Enough thinking, enough talking!

'No, Kallie.' He was hoarse. 'I don't hate you. I told you once, love is the other side of that. For one, you must have the other. I desire you, I want you…that's all.'

And with a ruthlessness that made him feel on safer ground, he bent over her supine body, found her mouth and took it. Cruelly, to sate his hunger and to ignite hers. She lay rigid at first, as if in rejection of his words, but then slowly he could feel the tremor build until she was his again.

Kallie tried to hang onto his brutal words, tried to keep them in her head so that she'd stay rigid, stiff, unresponsive. But she couldn't. She was too weak. When he'd spoken them, coldness had flooded her, she'd seen the way his eyes had turned calculating. The passion still burned but when forced to think about it, when she'd *forced* him to think about it, his distaste for what he was doing was palpable.

But the wish to hang onto his words was beyond Kallie's weak grasp. At this moment only one thing was clear in her head. Only one thing she wanted more than his forgiveness, more than his acceptance, right now, was *him*.

Tearing his mouth from hers, he pulled her up, her hair tumbling over her shoulders, her long fringe covering her eyes. With one knee on the bed, he lifted her arms and pulled up her top, slipping it over her head. He pressed her back down. She looked away for a second as if she couldn't bring herself to look at him, and he brought her face back with a hand on her jaw. He looked deeply into her aquamarine eyes, that shone dark green now with her arousal.

'Kallie, don't turn away from me, you want me… Say it…'

As if the words were pulled from her. 'I…want you.'

He saw a glistening in her eyes and then she reached up and pulled him down on top of her, her hands on his shoulders, blindly searching for his mouth.

When he pulled back the brightness was gone from her eyes as though he'd imagined it. Length to length they touched. He was careful to keep his full weight off her. One thigh was a possessive heaviness between hers. He skimmed a hand down her chest, fingers circling her breasts. They thrust upwards, two perfect mounds, small pebble-hard tips. He could see her back arch, her stomach contract as his hand closed around one, fingers teasing, pulling at the peak. 'Alexandros…please…'

He bent down and his mouth and tongue laved and suckled. First one breast, then the other. Her hands clutched at his head, directed him, guided him. With his other hand he reached down over the soft mound of her belly, felt the flare of her hips and went under her knickers. The hair was soft and springy. He took her knickers with him and could feel her lift her legs to help him guide them off. They were wet with her arousal and his penis jumped in response. It ached he was so hard and he wanted to thrust in so far and so deep that he'd have immediate release. But he knew that slowly would bring the biggest, sweetest release of all, and she'd made him wait. Now it was her turn.

Pulling her into him, chest to chest with one strong arm, her breasts crushed against him, his hand cupped her bare bottom, the cheeks round and voluptuous. His thigh nudged her legs apart and his hand found its way, from the succulent cheeks, around her silky flank and to the soft curls. Fingers threaded through the softness and then he was stroking back and forth, back and forth. Her mouth was an open gasp that she pressed against his shoulder, teeth biting gently as she fought to keep her moans back.

She threw her leg over his thigh, opening herself up even more, and reached a hand down, searching for and finding his aching erection, which was so hard and full that she opened her eyes wide.

'All for you…' he whispered, and kissed her, his fingers still stroking, finding the small hard nub and relentlessly flicking, circling, before dipping back. Now he was moving three fingers in and out. Her head fell back, she moaned aloud and her hand on his shaft moved up and down, the satin skin slipping over and back. His hand stalled for a second as he had to contain a shudder of pure blinding arousal. She'd almost pushed him over the edge.

'Kallie…'

'Alexandros…'

'Stop…'

'But…I want you…I want more…'

He took his hand away and her sex throbbed. She burned to have him fill her completely. As tangled as everything between them was emotionally, as tangled as their histories were, and as inexperienced as Kallie was, this felt like a dance she'd choreographed a long time ago. She knew exactly what to do. And it felt amazing. Stupendous.

He pressed her down on her back and she felt him shift his weight. She kept her hand on his penis and he came off her slightly and on both arms was poised over her. She arched her back, her hips up towards his, until the head of his penis nudged her entrance, its length in her hand. She'd never felt anything so erotic, never been so focused on one thing, one moment. Here and now. Nothing else mattered. Not the past, not the future.

He was poised to move inside her. Kallie finally took her hand off and arched up even higher. Her hips off the bed, she tried to reach around to his behind but couldn't and put her hands on his waist, feeling the hollowed ridges that delineated the juncture to his thighs. Running soft hands, small fingers up and down. He pulsed and jumped between them.

She bit her lip, about to beg, and then, in one cataclysmic moment, he was *there,* sliding in…pushing into her moist welcoming heat. Her muscles clenched around him, drawing him in, all the way. Until they were completely joined, until she didn't know where he stopped and she began, and when he started to move that she lost all semblance of control and sanity.

Alexandros was in another universe. A place he'd never been. Entering Kallie was like entering a foreign kingdom. Yet somewhere he already *knew.* The way she rose up to meet him, the subtly innocent twitch of her thighs against his that rocked her against him made him press down and into her fully, deeper and deeper. Slowly, enjoying every moment of feeling himself enveloped in her lush warmth, he pulled out and then pushed back in again. And it felt like coming home.

Sweat beaded on his brow, his upper lip. Kallie's head was thrown back and as he thrust in again she looked up, reached hands up to his shoulders, then slid them down, reaching for and finding his buttocks, urging him deeper, longer, stronger, harder. One slim shapely leg caressed up and down the back of his thigh and he was losing it. All will for patience and finesse gone. He needed to have her *now*. Abandoning all control, he went with her urgings, incoherent mumbles, breathy whispers and thrust in, taking her hard and fast.

Her body arched up again, her hips rocked against his and with her breasts crushed against his chest, he felt her come apart in his arms, only managing to hold on himself until the last moment with a control he'd never had to call on before. And only then did he join her in his own blissful, incandescent climax.

Kallie woke with the first tentative light of dawn streaming into the room. She was on her side, facing Alexandros. Just a hair's breadth away from touching, they were so close that if she sucked in a deep breath, her breasts would touch his chest. She looked at his face, which looked so much younger and vulnerable in repose. None of the hard phenomenally successful businessman was in evidence and it reminded her so much of the young man she'd known that a lump formed in her throat. A completely unbidden, monumental wave of tenderness and something else washed over her and she went stiff with instant panic. No, she couldn't—*wouldn't*—allow it to rise. She knew if she did that it would be to admit something that would have the potential to devastate her life even beyond what she already knew to be possible.

She reasoned with herself that it was completely understandable that all these feelings would be emerging. How many people got to realise their dreams, long-held fantasies? And what a dream… She closed her eyes briefly as the memory of what had happened last night washed over her. He had been everything she could have ever fantasised about and then some. A lover beyond compare, a master of the art, more in tune with her body than even she had been. Eliciting a response that made her dizzy with desire all over again. He'd taken her to the brink and past it over and over again. She had been as insatiable as him.

She opened her eyes again and studiously avoided looking down that tempting body stretched alongside her. Thea's words came back into her head like poison. Insidious and spreading throughout her body, tainting what had happened. Things were so much worse than she could have ever imagined. What would his reaction be when he woke up? Perhaps a mocking, triumphant smile? She didn't want to wait and find out, as myriad scenarios flooded her brain, all of them leaving her feeling exposed and far too vulnerable.

She cringed when she thought of the pitiable fight she'd put up. She may as well have just been waiting on his bed, gift-wrapped. *That* finally gave her the impetus to move. With stealthy grace Kallie slid from the bed and paused to pick up her strewn bits of nightwear, a blush staining her cheeks as she did so and quietly let herself out of the room.

When Alexandros woke up, he let himself lie there without opening his eyes for a few moments. He was feeling… replete, complete. For the first time in his life. The memory of Kallie's body under his, so responsive, made a smile curve his lips. *Never* before had he had the experience of feeling like this afterwards. And as he woke a little more, the sated feeling was there but another feeling superseded it, which surprised him with its strength. A hunger. A craving, aching hunger of a body having tasted paradise and wanting more—*now*.

He smiled even wider as he thought of his instruction to his solicitor to have divorce papers ready for after the honeymoon. If he was feeling like this after one night, he anticipated the marriage lasting a little longer than a few weeks. This revenge was definitely sweet.

Where was she anyway? When they'd fallen asleep, exhausted, she'd been tucked into his chest, one lissome leg thrown over his. He stretched out an arm, the smile still on his face, expecting to find a warm, sexy body. Except he didn't. His eyes snapped open, awake immediately. He jerked up. The bed was empty. Sunlight streamed in the window. He looked at the clock.

'Theos!'

He never slept this late. Hadn't slept this late in years. And he'd never woken up after a night spent with a woman in his bed to find her gone. He was *always* the one who woke first, left first. The one in control. He leapt out of the bed and pulled on jeans and a T-shirt. It was only at the door, as he opened it, that he thought of something. A dark scowl marring his face, he quickly checked Kallie's room but it too was empty. His scowl got worse.

With his irritation growing and not really sure why he felt so annoyed, Alexandros came to the kitchen last. Sun was streaming in through the open door that led out to Thea's small patio, where she had her herb garden and a tiny olive grove. He could hear muted voices and the sound of laughter.

Was that Kallie?

He walked to the door and stood stunned at the sight, as a whole other host of reactions settled into his bloodstream on seeing Kallie again. She was dressed in long shorts, a peasant-style vest top, her hair tied back and a bright scarf protecting it from the sun. Bare feet. She and Thea had their heads close together over some pots they were replanting. Since when had Thea and Kallie become friends again? He'd seen the way

Thea had frozen Kallie out and had even felt a little sorry for her. But now…it reminded him so painfully of another time, so long ago that an inarticulate sound made both women start and turn around.

Kallie reacted quickly, her smile fading fast as she took in the dark mood that clung to Alexandros. He looked livid as he glared at her. Thankfully Thea provided a diversion, declaring in a flurry of movement that she would make him some breakfast. Alexandros never took his eyes off Kallie and stopped Thea going back inside with a curt 'No!'

To Kallie he seemed to wrestle with something and then he suddenly smiled at Thea, the mood gone. His smile took her breath away and he looked years younger. Like the young man she'd envisaged while lying beside him that morning. Her heart clenched painfully. She knew she was in serious trouble. He directed his words to Thea but looked at Kallie. 'I'm going to take Kallie out for a drive…would you prepare a picnic, please?'

Thea nodded enthusiastically and chattered on about where they should go. When she went back inside, Alexandros came close to Kallie. She had to tilt her head to look up, the sun harsh in her eyes. The look on his face, his whole demeanour screamed, *You aren't going to escape that easily.*

Kallie gulped. He saw the movement and touched a finger to her throat. 'We'll leave in an hour…'

And he turned and went back inside.

CHAPTER TWELVE

ALEXANDROS said nothing for a while on the drive to wherever he was taking her. Kallie was wary. She'd made her getaway from the bedroom that morning as an act of self-protection. Could he be angry because she hadn't been there when he'd woken up? But surely that's all he'd wanted? Sex. She wouldn't be surprised if he'd expected her to go back to her own room afterwards, to come to him only as some kind of concubine. And then she coloured as she remembered how tired she'd been afterwards, how she hadn't been able to move another muscle…

She looked over. His profile was grim. His jaw stern. She felt like reaching across and kissing that jaw, making him relax, teasing him to a smile. Like the one she'd seen earlier, which had been for Thea, not her. He hated her. She knew he did. Despite what he'd said, he *had* to. She represented such an awful time in his life, when everything had conspired against him and he'd been totally alone, against them all. She had to turn and look away again, feeling a sudden ache in her throat. She flipped her sunglasses down over her eyes so he wouldn't see the brightness.

'I thought we'd go to Kaisariani on Mt. Hymmetos.'

Kallie just nodded, couldn't trust herself to speak.

He flicked her a look because she didn't answer him. 'Kallie, did you hear me?'

It suddenly became too much, she couldn't hold it in any more, not after being so intimate with him last night. She turned in her seat as if galvanised by a bigger force—guilt. It rose up and threatened to strangle her unless she said *something*.

Tears made her voice distorted. 'Alexandros, I had no idea…I swear, I didn't do it…and I didn't know…about the other stuff…the merger…'

She gulped in a heaving breath, the tears running down her cheeks unchecked now. Self-protective arms coming around her belly. Alexandros cursed and swung the vehicle over into a layby. He had to indicate to the bodyguards following that everything was OK.

He turned and snatched Kallie's glasses off, putting his hands on her shoulders. Her face was red, her eyes streaming.

'What the hell are you talking about?'

'Thea… She told me…' Kallie made a huge effort to control herself and wiped the backs of her hands across her face. Alexandros was still just a blur in her vision.

'Thea what?' He was shaking his head, frowning.

A big shuddering breath. 'Thea… We spoke… She told me…what had been happening, what happened after…after…'

His hands tightened on her shoulders so tightly that she grimaced. Then he let her go and sat back. The paroxysm of tears was passing. She could see now, and his eyes were black, unreadable.

'I never read the article, Alexandros. I didn't know, I swear.'

His voice sounded funny and mechanical, as if he was repeating himself to a slow child. 'They printed conversations…private conversations that only *we* had…' His mouth twisted. 'You have no idea how much I regret that now…I *know*, Kallie. The evidence was there on their computer system…it was *your* e-mail, your password. Are you telling me you gave that to someone else?'

A physical pain struck her chest when he spoke about regretting the conversations, stunning her with its force. She had to shake her head miserably. Of course she hadn't *given* anyone her password.

They were back to square one. How had she let herself get this upset, so emotional? All she had to worry about was getting through this…experience in one piece. And when Alexandros had had enough, which she prayed would be soon, he'd let her go. That was the decision she'd come to in her long hours of contemplation the previous day. Why, oh, why did she have to be so impetuous? She may as well declare to him right now that she was very much afraid she was in love with him all over again, that she'd never *stopped* loving him.

And that had to make her the saddest woman in the world. She also knew, much to her dismay, part of the reason she couldn't launch into a proper confession. As much as she was still genuinely scared for Eleni and her family, after being with him last night she was very much afraid that a future, however brief, without him in it scared her even more. Was she really willing to plead guilty in order to snatch whatever this man might offer her? She took her sunglasses and put them back on, covering her eyes again.

A shiver ran through Alexandros as he saw the woman before him morph into some kind of a robot. *Why* was she so insistent on proclaiming her innocence? What was the point? Something struck him. And it seemed to make sense as he witnessed her lightning change. Sympathy. She was looking for a way to get to him…to play him, make him doubt his suspicions. What was she hoping for? A more permanent arrangement? To bring him to the point where he might possibly offer her something more out of the marriage? A heavy weight settled in his chest. She'd made him wait till she came to him, and now, after sleeping with him, she was pretending repentance. Innocence.

He conveniently ignored the voice reminding him that he

had insisted on her coming to him, told himself that she must have assumed their intimacy might have softened him up. How many countless women before her had done it? He crushed the concern, the confusing contradictions that had flooded his head on seeing her tears. She was even buttering up Thea, for goodness' sake!

He leant across and whipped off her sunglasses again. She shrank back, her eyes wary, which he read as calculating. Leaning across, he didn't allow her any escape. 'I don't want to hear you mention the past again. It has no relevance any more.'

Apart from the fact that you used it to get her where you want her…

He brutally crushed every contradiction. For the final time. Enough. And concentrated on the woman in front of him, the ache he could feel building in his groin as he took in the way her chest heaved with her breaths. She was as aware of him, this space around them as he was. She *was* lying, he'd prove it, right now.

'The only thing that matters is *this*…'

Kallie could feel the doorhandle digging into her back. Alexandros came closer and closer. She put up her hands but they only met a wall of hard muscle. And her insides lique-fied when she remembered touching it, feeling it last night. His whole body was like a statue brought to vibrant life. He was holding her head in his hands so she couldn't move, and Kallie clamped her mouth shut to deny him access. But instead of the brutal crushing kiss which she'd expected, it was soft, tender. His mouth moving across hers, like a whisper of things to come, an erotic invitation to join him. And, heaven help her, she wanted to, she wanted to so badly. He was re-lentless, patiently enticing, waiting. She couldn't withstand his sensual onslaught. Like last night, he managed to reduce her entire universe to here and now. Nothing else existed.

When he probed, she sighed, his tongue touched the seam

of her lips and she opened a little more. But still he didn't enter. Her nerve ends tingled, her blood hummed. She lifted her hands to his shoulders, trying to tell him silently that she was giving in, acquiescing…and then she knew exactly what he wanted. Tentatively at first, she darted her tongue forward in an erotically innocent foray, touched his mouth, traced his lips…and then delved in to that dark moistness of his mouth, feeling emboldened and heady when his tongue finally met and tangled with hers.

She felt a hand under her loose top cup one breast, a thumb pad running back and forth over her nipple. Her tongue thrust harder, she arched her back, pressing her breast into his palm. And then, as if a light switch had gone on, he pulled back, put his hands on her shoulders and looked deep into her shocked-glazed eyes.

'See? That's all we need to worry about…for as long as it lasts, we're going to be married.'

He lifted her hand and pressed a searing kiss to her palm. She couldn't move for a long moment as he looked at her. She felt her seat belt digging into her waist—she still had it on! They were at the side of the road with cars whizzing up and down outside.

Kallie shook herself free of his hands and sat up properly, mortified. She was as weak as a kitten where it came to him and she'd helped him achieve his aim. She wouldn't be so silly as to bring up the past again.

'I won't offer you wine…'

Kallie shook her head quickly. Her sunglasses covered her eyes. They had found a secluded glade, just down from the chapel which was higher up on the mountain than the Kaisariani monastery, which dated from the twelfth century. An uneasy truce seemed to have settled on them, and Kallie welcomed it.

Thea had prepared a veritable feast. Pity she'd lost her appetite, thought Kallie, which was very out of character for her. She couldn't stop her mind going back to the previous night. In anticipation of the coming night? And *nights?*

The only time reality had intruded last night, apart from her little outburst, had been when Alexandros had mentioned protection. The first time they hadn't used anything. His look of abject horror when he'd realised, she wouldn't forget in a hurry. She'd told him that she was on the Pill. She knew he'd probably taken that as a sign of promiscuity, in fact it was for her painful and irregular periods. And she reflected then that she'd just recently changed over to a new Pill. Maybe that's what was making her feel so emotional.

'What are you thinking?'

Kallie coloured. 'Nothing.' She grabbed some cheese and bread and searched for something—anything—to say to avoid his gaze, his assessing eyes.

'I was always surprised…'

He lifted a brow.

'Well, not surprised as much as intrigued when I heard of the huge success of Kouros Shipping…' She blushed. 'Even though Thea told me it was touch and go for a while…it's the opposite now.' She shrugged and suddenly wished she hadn't broached the subject. 'You just…you'd always said you didn't think you had the killer instinct…'

She stopped and could see the hole widen at her feet. What was she thinking? She was trying to avoid controversial topics, not bring them up. He'd no doubt be remembering the article, how he'd been made to look weak.

Alexandros was glad of his sunglasses as he watched Kallie squirm. He felt like she'd lifted up a protective layer of skin and looked underneath. He willed down the anger that threatened to rise as he thought of everything he'd been through, which she claimed not to have been aware of. Of course it had brought out the killer instinct, he'd had to fight for his very survival. And he had survived, spectacularly. But for the first time that thought didn't fill him with the satisfaction it normally did. What was this witch doing to him?

'Well,' he drawled, sitting back on one arm, long legs stretched out, 'as you can see, I found it from somewhere.'

He idly picked a grape from the bunch and Kallie flicked him a wary glance.

'Let's talk about you. Your business…it must be hard to keep it going with all that socialising…'

Kallie welcomed his attention being taken off her woeful attempt to be neutral. And registered his obvious attempt to rile her back. She dampened down the irritation and smiled sweetly. 'I just take copious amounts of drugs to keep going—isn't that what all people in PR do?'

He smiled and it nearly threw her off balance. 'I might have thought so before, but with your abstinence and aversion to alcohol I doubt it. I'd hate to see you try anything stronger.'

And then despite himself, he found that he was actually curious. 'Tell me about your job…really, I'd like to know.'

She shrugged, not trusting him. 'It's a job like any other. It's pressured, intense. When I'm working for someone, that's it for two or three months. I always have time to recuperate when it's over. But I do have to be available twenty-four seven.'

He looked at her but she couldn't see his eyes. He nodded. Something about his stillness told Kallie that she'd struck a chord somehow.

'But I can't imagine your kind of pressure. You have millions at stake…hundreds of people to think about, their livelihoods.'

Which was why it must have been so awful for him to have to fight for his company alone…

The gnawing guilt made Kallie falter for a second, and she forced a smile. 'My worst nightmare is a client's function being a disaster or that they might not make the papers…or *make* the papers, whichever they want at the time.'

It always amazed her, how one month one client would be doing everything to keep out of the papers and the next doing everything to get in.

Very quietly, Alexandros said, 'I know.' As if he'd heard her thoughts.

Kallie settled back into a comfortable cross-legged position. 'And as for the parties.' She shrugged and picked at small flowers. 'They're just a part of it. Usually I'm only there for a short time, just to make sure everything is OK, then I leave them to it and read about it the next day, like everyone else.'

'You could have had a bigger business…it's just you and Cécile?'

She nodded and frowned. 'How do you mean?'

'Your shares, of course, the ones you sold off…' His mouth tightened in obvious distaste. 'You didn't think it worth investing in the business? Wanted to spend it all on—?'

Kallie tensed, beyond incensed. Hands in fists by her sides, she spat, 'How dare you? I have worked my fingers to the bone getting that place off the ground. We made best new business through sheer graft. There were times I was so tired I couldn't see straight.'

He sat up and pushed his glasses up onto his head. She'd whipped hers off and cursed now. He'd seen too much, she was getting emotional again. She jumped up.

She could sense him get up behind her and turned back to face him. 'I'm not a bad person, Alexandros. I'm *not*.'

Despite her best efforts, she knew she was close to tears again, and she turned away again. Even though they were in a park in the middle of Athens, the city lay somewhere beneath them, silent. She willed him away, willed him not to touch her, and he must have felt it because he didn't. She found herself speaking quietly, quickly.

'After Mum and Dad died, I had no interest in the business. I never had. You *know* that. Even if you say you didn't. I gave my uncle those shares. I didn't sell them. I couldn't.' She turned around again and as he was closer than she'd anticipated, she backed away another step. 'What kind of person do you think I am?'

Stupid question, Kallie...

He felt at a loss, amazed at her passionate reaction. Her expressive eyes. Shining blue and green. And thought, *The kind of person most of us would be in that situation, who would demand every penny of their inheritance...*

'Kallie—'

'I'd already got a loan and Alexei gave me just enough to subsidise it. That's all. The only thing I regret is that my shares obviously weren't enough to help him turn the business around. If they had been, we mightn't be here now.'

Her words rang with bitterness and Alexandros felt something move in his chest. He couldn't analyse it. One of the biggest accusations he'd made in his own head about her was crumbling. He didn't even question the fact that he believed her. All he knew was that he wanted them to stop fighting, sniping...and do something else.

He pulled her into his arms. She stayed stiff against him. He tipped her chin up with one hand. 'Whatever has happened between us, that was uncalled for. I had no right to assume to know what you did with those shares. And I had no right to assume that you were some vacuous limpet on the social circuit.'

She searched his face, sure he was laughing at her somehow and shocked at this abrupt turnaround. How could he believe her about this but not *that?* He had to be doing it for some reason...she didn't think he meant it for a second.

'Are you making fun of me?'

He shifted his hips slightly and her eyes widened in silent eloquence when she felt what *he* was feeling. He shook his head. 'I've never been more serious in my life. Can we call a truce, Kallie? Make a pact not to talk about the past, just focus on this. And now.'

He was offering her a truce. A space to make things easier. For him? For her, too, she knew, if she accepted it. Although his ruthlessness could not be forgotten. He still had the power to ruin her family if he so wished. He'd keep her until she stopped pleasing him in bed. *Bed.* She felt weak. She'd tasted heaven now. The heaven she had longed for all those years ago. How could she go back? And she knew she wasn't strong enough to give it up. Just yet.

She nodded her head, saw the flare of something in his eyes and closed hers in mute supplication as he bent his head and all that did exist was *now*.

After that tacit agreement to a truce of sorts, the next days of their so-called honeymoon fled. Kallie and Alexandros circled each other warily. Careful of what they said. There seemed to be an unspoken agreement that all they had to focus on was the physical connection. And they couldn't get enough of one another.

The villa became a place outside reality. Kallie knew she was in danger of indulging in a fantasy that somehow this was real. That this existed. As if in some bizarre stroke of fate, her dreams as a seventeen-year-old had come true and she'd got her prince.

But that dream was quashed over and over again as it became all too clear that for Alexandros this was purely physical. Kallie had tried to start countless conversations, trying to get to know him better. Last night, Thea had served dinner on the terrace again. While Kallie had tried to find things to talk about, Alexandros had remained largely monosyllabic. In desperation at her own increasing sense of humiliation and futility, she'd jumped up in agitation.

'This is crazy…why can't you just talk to me? Why can't we have a conversation? Am I so boring—?'

Alexandros had jumped up, too, frightening Kallie with his barely leashed anger and the intensity on his face. He'd taken two quick steps, lifted her into his arms and brought her straight to bed, throwing her down. She'd scrambled backwards.

'You're…an animal,' she'd spluttered in indignation, and had watched with a traitorous and increasing excitement as he'd calmly proceeded to strip off. Completely.

He'd come down beside her, holding her an easy captive with his leanly muscled body, with the desires that made her quiver in his arms, even as she tried to pull away.

'Yes, Kallie. But you want me. That's all. We're not here to talk, or to get to know one another. I know all I need to know.'

And he'd subjected her to such an erotic attack that she'd been hard pushed to remember her own name afterwards, never mind hold a conversation. He'd made his point.

Kallie woke early, her head resting on Alexandros's chest, her leg thrown over his. She just lay there. Immediately awake. Emotion swirled around her head, in her chest, making it tight. She tried to keep her breathing even, closed her eyes tight. The ache built in her throat. She couldn't believe she'd done it again. Or rather, she had to acknowledge, things had never changed. She was still in love with Alexandros. The only thing different to when she'd been a child and a teenager was that back then she hadn't known the depth of that love, how all-permeating it was and how sleeping with him would crack her open and let her taste the extreme despair that would come from loving a man like him. A man beholden to none, least of all *her*.

The past few days he'd been looking at her with that heated gaze, stopping her in her tracks again and again. He'd brutally ignored her wish to talk last night, had effortlessly made her acquiesce to what he wanted… How could she be so weak? She could see very well what he was doing.

It was tantamount to a kidnapper not calling their victim by their name so they wouldn't identify with the captive.

How could she be in love with someone who was doing that to *her*?

Because she knew him. It was that simple. He was her soul mate. The part of him that she had once known, that he kept from her now, would never be hers. She might be his, but he was not hers. And never would be.

A large hand cupped her jaw, taking her by surprise. She hadn't noticed that he'd woken up. Her eyes stayed shut, the ache clogging her throat. Still no words, not even now…and yet her body was already humming, opening, moistening for his touch. The gratification that only he could bring her.

His hand smoothed its way down her collar-bone to the space between her breasts where her heart was beating steadily, and speeding up when he shifted them subtly and a leg came over hers, nudging them apart. The frisson of awareness, the hunger and need after a night of love-making scared her with its intensity. Today they were going back to Paris. Back to reality, back to the cruel, harsh world of media and photographers and *reminders* that all was not what it seemed.

She turned her head and opened her eyes. Her pain was buried deep and hidden inside her. He pressed a kiss to her lips, long and lingering, drew her up on top of him so that her breasts were crushed to his chest. His hands spanned her waist and moved her up and then down slightly where she could feel the powerful thrust of his erection.

She was already wet, ready for him. She slid her legs on either side of his hips and rocked back gently, coming up slightly, and sucked in a deep breath when she felt him thrust up and into her. Looking deep into his eyes, Kallie could feel the need rise up, the need to speak, to say something. The monumental realisation that she *still* loved him utterly was clawing at her insides to get out, even as he took them both on an ever-increasing spiral towards oblivion.

Approaching her climax, Kallie could feel the words tremble on her lips… She felt desperate but couldn't control it. Not when they were joined, literally. In desperation to avoid the ultimate act of self-destruction, she bent down and pressed her feverish lips against Alexandros's mouth, and her words were stifled as the wave broke over her, as he ruthlessly held her hips and his own release spilled into her body.

With Kallie resting on his chest, their bodies still joined, Alexandros couldn't believe the strength of his climax, every time, with this woman. She gave so freely, so generously. She was so responsive. With one touch…hell, without even a touch, with a *look,* she'd be his. He'd see her whole body start to quiver, like a bow, waiting for his touch. Those huge eyes would follow him, widen as he got closer, pupils dilating, making them look darker. And as he'd bend to kiss her, her mouth would open, soft lips waiting…

But last night…every night…ever since that day in the park, when she'd want to talk, he just couldn't. Something shut down inside him. He didn't want to. He wasn't interested. But even as he told himself that, he knew it was a lie. He knew it and hated it.

When he'd carried Kallie up to the bedroom last night, thrown her on the bed like some Neanderthal, he'd felt like a complete bastard. The truth was, he did want to talk to her. He did want to get to know her better. And that was not a part of the plan. Bed her, get her out of his system. She'd betrayed him before, she could do it again. It had taken a stronger will than he cared to admit to avoid talking to her.

She lifted her head at that moment and something in her eyes caught him. Something he didn't know, didn't recognise. Something he'd never seen in a woman's eyes. And he didn't want to know. He shifted his hips slightly and saw the flare of colour come into her cheeks when she could feel him still inside her, growing hard again. With the same ruthlessness as last night he watched with relief as whatever had been in Kallie's eyes faded, to be replaced by desire…as he took her with him again.

And when they were finished, he extricated himself from her embrace, got out of the bed, and as he went to shower, he coolly informed her that they'd leave in a couple of hours.

Under the spray he rested his hands on the wall, dropped his head and felt the crushing weight of something take residence in his chest. When he came out, Kallie had gone back to her own bedroom and Alexandros wanted to smash his fist into something very hard. He was at war with something… and he was very much afraid it was himself. And that he didn't know the terms of engagement.

CHAPTER THIRTEEN

KALLIE had walked around Alexandros's apartment, which was on the Rue du Faubourg Saint-Honoré. One of the most exclusive addresses in Paris. It was huge. It was her first time there. And now she stood in the main living room with her bags at her feet. When she'd returned home earlier that evening, her small apartment had been mobbed with the paparazzi who'd followed them from the airport. She'd been bombarded with questions. *Why are you here? Why aren't you living with Alexandros? Trouble in paradise already?*

Alexandros, behind her in the car, had stepped out and coolly informed them that they were merely picking up some things and that Kallie *was* moving in with him.

Too shocked to speak outside, she'd rounded on him in her tiny apartment, her voice high with tension. 'Since when was I going to move in with you?'

He'd merely shrugged, looking around with interest, making Kallie frightened. She'd wanted to kick and scream, tell him to get out of her sanctuary. It was too much. Her private space was the only place he *hadn't* invaded completely and now he was here, too, looking around like an inspector. This cool, aloof man scared her. He had the power to make her weak. To break her in two.

He'd fixed her with those eyes. Black and unreadable.

'Kallie, it makes sense. They'll be like dogs with a bone. Do you want that kind of attention? I certainly don't and I'd say your neighbours could do without it as well.'

Guilt had flooded her. A lot of old people lived in her building and she could only imagine what they'd make of having to step over photographers every day. They might even get hurt. But the thought of living with him terrified her. 'But surely it won't last?'

He'd shrugged again and she'd wanted to hit him. 'As long as they think there's a story, they'll hound you here. And by not moving in with me, that's a story.'

She'd closed her eyes briefly. The more time they spent together, the sooner he'd want to get rid of her. Maybe it *was* the best solution.

'I'll only do it out of respect for my area, for this building. I can't afford to be thrown out because I'm causing a disturbance.'

Kallie walked over to the window of his palatial living room now and looked out. They were between the Ritz Hotel and the Jardin des Tuileries. A truly spectacular address. And she couldn't have cared less. She could have been in the gritty suburbs for all she cared, as long as she was away from *him*. She sighed deeply. Because she knew that wasn't true.

Alexandros watched her back from the door. It was ramrod straight, her hands stuck into the back pockets of her jeans. Her cashmere cardigan buttoned down the back, making his fingers itch to go and unbutton it, run his hands around to her front and up to cup her breasts. He could feel their warmth and weight in his hands.

She was getting him hard just looking at her back!

She was the image of simplicity and natural beauty. Her hair was tied back in a ponytail, exposing her neck. He knew without looking that her skin had a glow from the Athenian sun, that more freckles had appeared on her nose. In a rare moment of lightness that had snuck up all too easily, he'd teased her and she'd become embarrassed. And then he'd taken her mind off it by insisting on checking the rest of her body for freckles.

His smile faded when he recalled her reaction to moving in with him. Especially when he hadn't even planned on asking her. He was meant to be saying goodbye, arranging for the divorce, having slaked his lust for this woman. And now she was here, living with him... But right now that lust still held him in its hot grip and he didn't feel like it was ever going to wane. A rebellious feeling rose up. He had her right where he wanted her. He didn't need to look into it any deeper than that.

Like an irritating itch, he remembered following her up to her apartment, which he'd only seen from the door before. He'd been pleasantly surprised by the chic, clean minimalism. The shelves filled with books. It had peace and tranquillity, inherent good taste that called to something inside him.

Kallie had paced up and down, agitated. Alexandros had felt a surge of dissatisfaction. What was so abhorrent about coming to live with him? He knew countless women who'd jump at the chance. He'd suddenly realised that, apart from paying for her tickets to Greece and covering meals out, he hadn't given Kallie any money or any gifts. It felt strange. He had to remind himself that he hadn't wanted to give her anything. And yet, why hadn't she asked? Why hadn't she cajoled something out of him by now? He just couldn't imagine her doing it.

She turned around now and saw him. His breath stopped. Her eyes that looked at him now so gravely were not the eyes of the Isabelle Zolanzes of the world. From what he'd seen in the past couple of weeks, she took too much delight in ordinary things. If he offered her a diamond bracelet right now, she'd probably wonder what he was up to and hand it back. It startled him how clearly he knew this, *felt* this. And how far removed it was from the woman he'd imagined her to be that night at the Ritz Hotel.

And how far removed it was from any woman he'd ever known.

That's why he couldn't trust it. He walked towards her, slowly and with intent. Catching her to him, he could feel that initial rigidity, as if she had to let him know she was fighting this, and as he took her mouth, feeling as though it was the first time again, he triumphed in the way with a little sigh she sank against him and became…his.

'Well, when is she going to be finished?'

'I'm not sure, Mr Kouros. It's a big function and Pierre Baudat has specifically requested that Kallie be here for the whole thing.'

Alexandros muttered something unintelligible and put down the phone. He stood up and strode over to his window, hands stuck deep in his pockets. When his secretary put her head around the door he told her to leave him alone for ten minutes. She scuttled back out.

In the past couple of weeks, since Kallie had moved into his apartment, he could count on his hands the amount of hours they'd spent together. The day after she'd moved in she'd got a contract to organise a last-minute function for one of France's top actor/directors.

Now, much to his chagrin, she was invariably up before him, home after him and so tired when she did get back that she didn't have the energy for much else. He'd actually found himself in the unique situation of living with a woman for the first time, yet *not* having a willing partner waiting for him every evening, and had to acknowledge the fact that she was possibly even busier than he was. This certainly wasn't part of the plan. She'd told him she worked hard but he hadn't expected her to do it while she was with him!

Alexandros frowned. The question niggled again. It had been haunting him for days now. Why didn't he just get the divorce? He'd only needed to get married for the minimum amount of time and that had been well served by now. He didn't need Kallie any more. She'd fulfilled her end of the agreement. *Agreement...don't you mean blackmail?*

He conveniently ignored the ever-present hum of desire in his body that told him exactly why he hadn't arranged for the divorce yet.

They'd exchanged a few terse words the previous evening, when he'd made a comment about how late she'd been working. 'You're not doing this just to avoid me, are you?'

When he'd walked towards her in the kitchen, she'd backed away, making a spike of anger spiral through him.

'Of course not. This is a huge job, Alexandros. I'm doing it because I was offered it, not just to annoy you. If you feel like you're not getting your money's worth then maybe—'

'Kallie...' he'd warned.

She'd swung away, towards the door, and he'd seen her hand in a white-knuckled grip on the handle. He'd wanted to go and prise her fingers free, make her relax...against him.

'Alexandros...unless you're going to take this revenge even further and sabotage my career somehow, then I will be doing this...'

He'd come close, trapping her before she could leave the room, and surprised himself by thinking, *Does she really think I would go that far?*

'Kallie, I have no problem with your work. As long as you're in my bed every night, you can do what you want.'

A dark frown marred his face as he looked unseeingly out the window, still back there with Kallie. With an abrupt movement he picked up his coat, walked out of his office and instructed his bemused secretary to hold all meetings for the rest of the evening. Kallie *was* avoiding him and he was tired of it.

Kallie's feet ached. She had visions of buckets of hot water and Epsom salts. She smiled and greeted the umpteenth person coming in through the heavily decorated damask-covered doors. The function for Pierre Baudat was a celebration of his life's work. A-listers from all over the world were there. This was the biggest event she'd been given so far and she'd been working night and day to get it organised. She hadn't failed to notice how Alexandros's bemusement over recent days had turned to irritation pretty quickly. No doubt, she thought bitterly, this wasn't part of the game plan. A wife who worked.

Well, tough, she told herself. And knew that she'd probably put more hours in than necessary. As avoidance tactics went, she was a master of the game. Extreme self-protection. Keep busy to avoid the pain of seeing Alexandros every day. She was sure it'd only be a matter of time now before she'd receive divorce papers and then she could start to pick up the pieces of her broken heart. Because every minute, every moment spent with Alexandros meant that her heart grew more and more heavy.

Cécile hurried up to her side. 'Kallie, Pierre is looking for you—something about the projector?'

Damn. Kallie's thoughts were pulled back to the evening. That was all she needed now, just when the producer of the latest Oscar-winning best film had arrived. She hurried in to see what the problem was.

Alexandros was tense, could feel it in every muscle. And didn't like it. The usual control he enjoyed seemingly at an ever-increasing distance. The car crawled along the Champs Elysées. He had his driver stop and jumped out. He started to walk to the art museum at the end of the boulevard, and as he walked the bizarre concern rose again, swiftly, like a dark cloud. He saw Kallie's face in his mind's eye. He stopped in his tracks. What if someone gave her something that could spark the same reaction she'd had in the restaurant in Athens?

Alexandros unconsciously speeded up, suddenly imagining Kallie vulnerable, weak, in trouble. He arrived at the door of the function, strode through and was stopped.

He looked down at the young woman who appeared to be in her early twenties, very lusciously half-dressed and looking up at him with big come-hither eyes that did absolutely nothing for him. She was caked in make-up.

'Excuse me?' she asked, fluttering her eyelashes at him.

Excuse me?

He couldn't remember the last time, if there'd ever been one, when he'd been stopped at the door of a party. Suddenly Cécile appeared and flushed prettily, like she normally did. 'Mr Kouros! Odette, this is Kallie's husband. He can come in.'

Odette gave Alexandros a simpering smile. 'So sorry, but we have a strict door policy.'

'No problem.' He'd already forgotten her. Looking at Cécile,' he asked, 'Where is she?'

'Is something wrong, Mr Kouros? You seem a little…'

He forced himself to calm. 'I'd like to see my wife, please.'

'Of course. I'll get her.' Cécile hurried away.

Alexandros finally saw her through the crowd and felt what seemed like a punch in his stomach. She was beautiful. Stunning. Wearing a cream satin dress, it fell Grecian-style to her knees. Off the shoulder on one side and held together on the other by a jewelled clip. Her hair was piled high and a slim golden band held her fringe back. A gold bracelet circled her toned upper arm and golden strappy sandals made him want to walk over, pick her up and carry her far away. She turned her head at that moment, just as Cécile reached her. He couldn't fail to see the shock and surprise register on her face and he didn't like it. They stared at each other for a long moment. Then someone said something to her and she smiled apologetically, indicating that she was busy, and gestured to the bar in the corner.

Alexandros felt a crushing feeling. She was OK. He felt a

little foolish and welcomed the respite for a moment. A short time later, he watched Kallie walk over with the man of the evening, Pierre Baudat. When she came close, he couldn't read the expression on her face and it made him nervous.

'Alexandros, I'd like you to meet Pierre Baudat. Pierre, my husband Alexandros Kouros.'

Kallie felt a bubble of hysteria rise up as she witnessed two very alpha males meeting. Even though Pierre was in his sixties, he was no less virile, exuding charisma. 'Kouros, pleased to meet you. Lovely wife you have here, quite the charmer. Don't know what I would have done without her.'

'I know…' Alexandros battened down his conflicting emotions and smiled lazily at Kallie. She recognised danger in the smile, and then he looked back at Pierre. 'She charmed me into marrying her.'

He could feel Kallie tense beside him and needed to touch her so badly that it was a physical pain and he pulled her into his side. They chatted for a few minutes more and Pierre left, wagging a finger. 'I'm going to need her back, Kouros…she's mine tonight.'

Alexandros couldn't help the reflex he had to smash a fist into the other man's face when he said that.

'Alexandros, you're hurting me.' Kallie pulled free and looked up at him. 'What are you doing here anyway?'

'I…'

What was he doing there? Had he really been afraid that she'd be in trouble? Or what? That she'd be flirting with other men? So far, from what he'd seen, she was working tirelessly, harder than anyone else in the room. An uncomfortable prickling skated over his skin.

Kallie still had butterflies in her tummy, which had sprung to life when she'd seen him across the room. Ridiculous. She'd known him practically all her life, and now she knew him even better. They were lovers. And she desperately wished they weren't. But right at that moment she felt as though she were seventeen all over again. The achingly sweet desire that he would have come like that, to see her, meet her at work because he missed her.

She'd gone through all the reasons as to why he might have come…had even dragged Pierre over to give her some time to collect herself. And now an awful thought struck her. Maybe he was going to serve her with the divorce papers here, now, tonight. She surreptitiously looked around him but couldn't see anything. Just him, leaning back against the glittering bar, nonchalant in his suit and open-necked shirt. Easily the best-looking man in the room.

She remembered his words to Pierre. 'How can you do that, say that?'

'What?'

'Let people think that this is a normal marriage. You said I *charmed* you into marrying you—'

'Kallie.' His face darkened. 'Would you prefer if I tell people how we came to be married? That you betrayed me and I took advantage of meeting you again to take a convenient wife?'

She shook her head miserably. An ache formed in her throat as he put two hands on her arms and pulled her close again.

She hated herself for reacting, even now. Her head felt heavy as she looked up.

He brushed the back of his hand across her cheek. 'We do have a real marriage, Kallie. As real as it can be in this day and age. We have great sex—'

His words tore at her. 'Yes, but that's all. If we didn't, you would have divorced me as soon as you could after the wedding, and I wish you had, believe me.'

Two bright spots had appeared on her cheeks and Alexandros could feel her chest heaving against his.

Kallie couldn't tear her gaze away from his. The room had disappeared, they could have been anywhere. Heat coiled in her belly like a live wire, her breasts tingled and pushed against the fabric of her dress. Alexandros's gaze grew dark and heavy-lidded.

'Just let me go, Alexandros.' *For good!* 'I have to get back to work. I'm busy.'

Alexandros felt off balance again, and felt like a fool for coming when he'd had no good reason. He'd acted on an instinct so strong he hadn't questioned it, and that made him very nervous.

His mouth twisted into a cynical smile. 'This *is* a normal marriage. When we get divorced we'll just be joining the statistics of thousands of others.'

She finally managed to jerk free from his hands and stalked away, determined not to show him how he affected her.

She could feel his eyes bore into her back. Tears threatened, blurring her vision as she walked back through the room, the crowd swallowing her up. Why couldn't he just leave her alone? Let her go? When would he stop desiring her? She bit her lip. That would be long before she stopped desiring him… and she knew she never would.

CHAPTER FOURTEEN

WHEN Kallie arrived back to the apartment that night, she crept in and slipped off her shoes, sagging back against the door with relief. Thank goodness that was over. She felt as if she'd been put through the wringer. She heard a noise and jerked upright, eyes wide, to see Alexandros standing at the door of the living room, in dark slacks, his shirt open at the throat, revealing the bronzed column. Tiredness vanished. Energy pulsed through her body and she felt desire, hot, low and immediate in her belly.

'What are you doing up? It's almost three in the morning…' She couldn't keep the breathy tone out of her voice.

He walked slowly towards her. 'I kept you some dinner.'

She gaped. 'You made dinner?'

He kept coming. She couldn't go anywhere, her back was to the door. Emotionally and physically. All she knew was that the man she *loved* was here, with her now, and she felt so weakly happy she could have burst. It must be the tiredness, she reassured herself, even though that had fled like a cowardly traitor.

He was now so close that she could feel his body heat, smell his particular scent, a hint of musk and citrus. Nothing cloying or artificial. All male, all him.

'Are you hungry?'

His arms came up on either side of her head. She looked up at him mutely and shook her head, thinking to herself, Only for you.

One hand came down and cupped her shoulder, feeling the smooth satin skin. 'The moment I saw you in this dress I wanted to do this…'

'What's that?'

'Take you out of it…'

'Oh…'

He bent his head, but didn't take her mouth. He pressed his lips to her shoulder, kissing, smoothing, his tongue flicking out to taste. Teeth nipping gently. A tiny shudder went through her. He turned his attention to the jewelled clip and with smooth finesse flicked it open. The dress fell down under its own weight, baring her lace-covered breasts to his hungry gaze, the nipples hard and pouting for his attention. When his mouth closed over one through the sheer material, Kallie sagged back even more, an electric wire of sensation connecting to her groin, making her breathe harshly. An unstoppable force was building up, an urgency that only this man could assuage.

She pulled his head back up and clasped it in her hands, kissing him deeply. Her tongue making a sensual foray, searching for his…tangling in a heated dance. The sense of urgency drove her. She blindly searched for buttons, popping them open with scant regard for care, wanting to feel his broad chest, the smooth skin, the light smattering of hair which led in a silky line all the way down to his trousers. Her hand traced this line as they kissed. Her fingers met the buckle and all without looking, or thinking, only feeling, she opened the buckle, then his trousers and slid her hands around and under, reaching around to pull him towards her and caress his bottom.

He groaned against her mouth, 'Kallie, Kallie…'

She whispered against his mouth, 'I want you, Alexandros…'

Here, like this, when nothing existed but the heat between them, she could be honest. Indulge her weakness.

Taking her mouth again with a fevered urgency that made her exultant, Kallie felt him reach under her dress, pulling it up, fingers finding the sides of her panties and sliding them down over her hips. She helped when they fell and stepped out of them. And in turn she pushed down his trousers and briefs, which snagged on his erection for a moment. He kicked his clothes aside impatiently.

She tore her mouth away from his and reached for him, holding him. Alexandros braced two hands on the door behind her. His eyes glittered fiercely as she looked up at him, her hands sliding up and down the shaft.

Two slashes of colour raced across his cheekbones, and she saw him swallow, fight for control. She couldn't help but exult in the power she had over him in these all too brief moments. He stopped her hands with one of his.

'Stop…unless you want to make me lose it…'

With easy strength, he lifted her up, her legs automatically coming around his waist, and with her back resting against the door, with one smooth movement he surged up and into her, piercing her moist silken flesh with his. She gripped his neck and stifled her gasp of pure pleasure against his heated skin, against the corded muscles that spoke of his effort to control himself.

Time and time again he thrust up into the heart of her, taking them both on a roller-coaster ride, more intense than ever before. When he thrust upwards for the final time, Kallie's whole body shook with the violence of her orgasm, and shook still as he threw back his head and allowed himself to spill into her, his release unending. It took a long time for the room to right itself or for either of them to have the strength to extricate themselves. Alexandros lowered her gently back down and Kallie's legs couldn't hold her up.

They buckled and she would have fallen if he hadn't caught her and swung her into his arms. She buried her head in his shoulder and he brought her into the bedroom, kicking open the door of the bathroom.

The bath was full, the water lukewarm. Kallie lifted her head in surprise. 'You were going to have a bath?'

He set her down and shook his head, avoiding her eye. 'No. It was for you. I told Cécile to call me when you'd be leaving…' *And the minute she came in the door you fell on her like a lust-crazed teenager.*

Self-derision made his movements jerky, but Kallie was too stunned to notice. He'd done this for her? She could feel the shaking set in again. She just couldn't fathom this…or the strength of her climax, which still left her feeling slightly shell-shocked and sensitive to the touch all over.

She watched as Alexandros briskly turned on the tap, emptying in more hot water. Then he helped her out of her clothes and into the bath, where she sank down into foam and bubbles so exquisite she had to catch her breath.

'I'll go and heat up the dinner.'

She looked up at him. He should have looked ridiculous, standing there naked in nothing but his open shirt…but he didn't. He looked virile and masculine. Her eyes travelled down. Already one part of him was making a comeback. She hurriedly averted her gaze. After the last climax she didn't think she could survive another like it any time soon.

'OK, that'd be lovely, I'm starving now,' she babbled inanely.

He left and Kallie breathed out. And then felt tears threaten. What was wrong with her? And what was wrong with *him?* And how much longer could she endure this exquisite punishment? She let the water calm and soothe her but couldn't relax fully, his behaviour was confusing her. She was out and wrapped in a voluminous toweling robe when he came back to tell her the food was ready.

He'd prepared a delicious meal of pastitsio, a Greek form of lasagne, with lots of crusty bread. Kallie fell on the food, feeling like she hadn't eaten in weeks. Which, she realised, she hadn't really.

He watched her eat, shaking his head. 'You really are unbelievable. Any other woman I know would run screaming into the hills if faced with a plate of food like that, but you can polish it off in minutes.'

Kallie blushed, feeling like the overweight teenager she'd been all over again. He reached across and grabbed her hand. 'It's a good thing, Kallie. Just because you had a little bit of puppy fat growing up…'

She took her hand away and said lightly, 'It must be a refreshing change. You'll be back to watching women chase a lettuce leaf around their plates in no time.'

Before he could say anything else, she took the plates over to the dishwasher. She was unaware of the spasm of emotion that had crossed his face for a split second. He was silent behind her and when she finally turned around, his expression was cool, blank. She felt awkward.

'Thanks for making dinner…'

She quipped lightly, 'If the shipping business fell through in the morning, you'd get a job as a chef no problem. I could even turn it into a reality show…'

Her words fell flat as she watched him come back from a long distance. His eyes focused on her again. 'What did you say?'

She shook her head, 'Nothing, just thanks for dinner. I appreciate it.'

He stood and pulled her close, speaking without thinking. 'You work too hard.'

'This from someone who thinks PR is full of drug-crazed lunatics running around partying?' She wanted to smile teasingly but couldn't. There was a still, heavy energy surrounding them that confused her.

'I can see that I'm just going to have to get—' He broke off suddenly and Kallie saw him go pale. She frowned but he'd gone inwards, disappeared. Shut down. He took her by the hand.

'Let's go to bed.'

With dawn coming up outside the bedroom window, Alexandros slid the robe from Kallie's shoulders. Carefully took the pins and band out of her hair, until it fell around her shoulders. Shrugging off his own top and jeans, naked, he led her over to the bed and curled her back into his front, his strong powerful thighs cupping her bottom. She gave up trying to figure out what he'd been going to say.

For a long time Alexandros's eyes stayed open, looking into the middle distance. He could hear Kallie's breath deepen and feel her curl even closer to his chest. The shock that had rippled through him when he'd realised what he'd been about to say still made him feel queasy. He'd been about to say, without any preamble, without the slightest hint of any warning, *I'm just going to have to get you pregnant...*

The whole night made him feel queasy. The way he'd found himself going to the function...drawn her a bath, *made dinner.* He'd been led by impulse and instinct. And he did not want to look at what might have prompted those instincts or impulses.

He knew what he had to do.

When Kallie woke up it was nearly lunchtime. She didn't panic, she knew she and Cécile had a day off today to recover. Needless to say, the bed was empty beside her. She sank deeper. The glorious feeling of knowing she had finished a job and that it had been well done made her smile. But it wasn't long before her thoughts turned back to Alexandros. She groaned and rolled over, burying her head under a pillow.

After a few minutes she sat up on the edge of the bed and, finding her robe to pull on, stood up. The intense wave of dizziness that struck her made her sit back down again quickly.

What was that? On an instinctive reflex her hand went to her belly. And then, just as quickly as the dizziness had struck, she felt nausea surge, fast and urgent. She just made it to the bathroom in time.

When she had finished retching into the toilet she stood up and washed her face. She had an awful certainty about what was wrong. And she didn't even question that it could be something else. The past few days, the intense tiredness, increased sensitivity, the emotional roller-coaster she seemed to be on…

It must be down to the change in her Pill, just before she'd met Alexandros again. As if moving on autopilot, she showered, got dressed and left the apartment.

Alexandros was curt. 'You have the papers ready?'

'Of course.' His solicitor laughed briefly, his curiosity evident. 'I was expecting you to call a few weeks ago…'

'Yes, well, I'm calling now.'

His solicitor knew better than to test Alexandros's patience. 'Of course. Leave it with me. It'll only take a few days to process the paperwork.'

'Good. I'll be in Athens this weekend if you need me.'

'I don't foresee any problems. This'll be quick and easy.'

Alexandros put down the phone and rested his chin on steepled fingers. *Quick and easy.*

Exactly how he'd envisaged this marriage of convenience and revenge. But it hadn't been quick and easy. For one thing, it had lasted a lot longer than he'd expected, and Kallie had been anything but easy, fighting him every step of the way. But when they didn't fight…he felt his stomach contract in a clutch of something he didn't understand.

That was the problem. His whole life he'd understood. Everything. Understood that he had obligations and responsibilities, that in many respects his life was not his own. Understood that life could be different for others, but not for him. He'd understood that the minute his mother had informed him he had to marry Pia Kyriapolous.

A shudder of revulsion spiralled through him as the memory came back. He shut it down. But despite his best efforts he couldn't shut down where it led him…to that night. The contrast between what he'd seen and then…Kallie.

When he'd felt her soft body against his, her warm sweet mouth pressed against his, it had called to him on a deep level so hidden, so untouched that he hadn't been able to move. He'd been shocked to find himself almost reacting to her un-tutored caresses, which had been so innocent when compared to what he'd witnessed earlier.

His mouth twisted. Or so he'd thought. He needed to remember that now. To call on that sense of anger, betrayal. In the past few weeks it had faded far too much into the distance, the past…even calling it up was a struggle, as if it was becoming blurred. Kallie Demarchis was dangerous. She had the ability to trick him all over again and he wouldn't let her.

'But why do you want us to go to Athens for the weekend?'

Kallie felt panicky and didn't know why. Well, yes, she knew exactly why. She needed time to think, to be alone, to sort things out. She'd been about to tell Alexandros that she wanted to move back into her apartment, put it to him that it would look better for when he broke the news of the divorce, as if problems were brewing. And *why* hadn't he mentioned a divorce yet? That was a special form of torture in itself, the constant not knowing…

His face was closed, remote, shuttered. A million miles from the Alexandros of last night.

He shrugged. 'You've been working hard, you could do with a break…'

She turned away from him and wrapped her arms around herself. Even though he hadn't mentioned divorce, she knew it hung in the air around them. Was this weekend it? As much as she wanted to bring it up, to be brave enough to confront him about it, especially *now,* she couldn't. And hated herself for it. And he still had the power to do serious damage to her family. But she knew that as reasons went, if she was honest, she hadn't thought about her family much since the day of the wedding.

She turned back. If this was the last time she'd have with him then she'd take it. And when it was over, she'd insist on the divorce. And then think about what she had to do. 'Very well…'

Alexandros shut himself off from the vulnerability in her eyes, flashing blue and green. This weekend in Athens was going to be it. And with it, he'd get her out of his system for good. He should mention the divorce…but for some perverse reason, he didn't want to at that moment.

He smiled. 'Good. We leave in the morning.'

Getting out of the four-wheel-drive at the villa the next day and watching Thea come down the steps made a vivid sense of déjà vu wash over Kallie. She held onto the vehicle door to steady herself. She had felt nauseous again that morning but had managed to make it to the bathroom and avoid Alexandros hearing her. She had to keep her secret. Had to. If he found out before the divorce, he'd insist she stay married to him. She knew him too well now.

At least if they were already divorced, he couldn't march her back up the aisle, and as for her uncle… She could feel the blood leave her face. She couldn't think now about what she'd do if he threatened them again.

Thea came and embraced Kallie, looking at her closely. Kallie felt a quiver of panic. Could Thea see her secret? But the moment was gone as Thea led them inside. This time there were no questions about bedrooms and both their bags were left in his bedroom.

That night Kallie made a pact with herself as she lay in

Alexandros's arms. After the weekend she would do whatever
it took to get the divorce. Insist on moving back into her own
apartment. He'd have to lock her up if he wanted to stop her.
She couldn't take it any more. She felt panicky. She'd even
call the police if she had to. She forced herself to be calm, confident that she could make him let her go. So that meant there
were two days left, two days sharing Alexandros's bed. Then
a lifetime without it.

Sudden desperation made her seek his embrace again, even
though they'd only shortly come down from a high plateau.
Alexandros was all too eager to comply and for a blissful
while Kallie didn't have to think about anything else.

All the following day, Kallie felt like a cat on a hot tin roof.
She tried to avoid being anywhere near Alexandros, but in the
evening he insisted they go for dinner in Athens. Their conversation was desultory and forced. Kallie miserably had to
concede that this was obviously the precursor to the divorce,
even though he hadn't said so.

She sipped at coffee. And finally they were ready to go.
Silently they made the journey back to the villa. All the way
up the hill Kallie could feel something in her stirring,
moving. A sense of growing doom, panic. How could she
be so complacent? Allow him to bring her here, like some
mute sheep. She now had a life growing in her, she wasn't
just responsible for herself any more.

By the time they got to the villa she felt jerky and anxious
as she followed him inside. Alexandros sensed her mood and
turned to her, one step on the bottom of the stairs. Brows
drawn together. 'What is it?'

See? Kallie thought, slightly hysterically, I'm not perform-
ing exactly how he wants, not following instructions.

'I can't do this any more, Alexandros. You've had your

pound of flesh. I want to go home. Now. And I want us to be divorced as soon as possible.'

He came towards her and she backed away towards the main living room. She put out her hands. 'Stay away, Alexandros. I'm not some puppet on a string. I've had enough.'

She'd had enough? He'd tell her when she'd had enough. That'd be when *he'd* had enough and this weekend was it. No way was she going to deny him this, not when she was patently lying, her whole body reacting and quivering for his touch. The fact that she'd mentioned divorce didn't even impinge on his consciousness. The only thing he could think about was that she was denying herself to him.

She turned before he could reach her and had run across the living room to the patio doors. She opened them and went outside. When he stepped out, the moonlight gave a glow that seemed to circle around her form. The strands of her golden hair glistened. She was backed against the wall, facing him, breathing harshly. His arousal levels skyrocketed. He didn't know what she was up to, or what was going on, but all he did know was that he had to have her. The hunger in his blood obliterated any other concern.

He strode over and caught her to him. 'Kallie, what is wrong with you?'

She shook her head fiercely. 'Don't… Please, Alexandros, you know I can't…can't resist…'

He bent his head and took her mouth. Hauling her even closer. The familiar battle was fought and somewhere he knew he yearned for a time when Kallie would come to him willingly, without having to fight him, even for a moment. But it was lost in the whirlwind of passion that took them over.

It was only after a long moment, when he pulled back and looked down, that he became aware of his surroundings, where they were. It touched something deep inside him.

Primeval…visceral and extreme. Something he had to lash out against instinctively. So many threads in his head… tangled and knotted, and in the middle of it all, this woman. Kallie. History was being repeated and she *had* to know what she was doing to him. He cupped her jaw and laughed softly into her face.

'Very good. I didn't even notice where we were.'

She was leaning back against the wall, hands against his chest, her pelvis tight against his, his arousal insistent against her.

She frowned. He could see a wary light cut through the desire in her eyes. 'What are you talking about?'

He turned her chin with his thumb and forefinger.

Kallie felt shock rush through her entire body when Alexandros turned her head and she saw what he wanted her to see. Where she'd unwittingly led them. To the patio. There was the tree. The place where she had come to find him seven years ago. The place of her youthful folly and utter humiliation. The pain came back so intensely she felt faint, then for a moment she just felt still. Incredibly calm.

And then the reaction set in. The same one that had hit her that night in the restaurant. Her tongue felt heavy, the clamminess, nausea and that awful tightening in her chest.

CHAPTER FIFTEEN

KALLIE was struggling to breathe through the intense pain. 'I can't… Alex… I can't breathe…can't move…'

For a moment when Kallie pushed weakly at Alexandros's chest, he thought she was still fighting him. He looked down. She was pasty. That same colour as the night in the restaurant. Panic slammed into his body, even as he tried to rationalise what could be causing the same reaction.

He lifted her up into his arms and strode through the house, an unbidden and constricting fear making him feel uncoordinated. He bellowed for Thea and when she appeared at the top of the stairs he instructed her to call the doctor.

After Kallie had thrown up, he brought her over to the bed and sat there, cradling her in his lap, until the intense, violent shaking calmed somewhat, until the storm had passed and she could breathe again. She was so limp that he felt a shard of ice slice through his chest. He was about to shout for Thea again when the doctor appeared at the door. The relief he felt was intense.

He paced up and down outside while the doctor examined Kallie. Thea was wringing her hands. Finally the doctor came out and told Thea to make Kallie a hot, sweet cup of tea. Thea left. Alexandros looked at the doctor, barely able to stay civil.

'Well?'

The doctor took off his glasses and put them away. He looked at Alexandros, and led him away from the door. 'From what I can see, and I've given her a thorough check-up, your wife has just suffered a severe panic attack. They're not serious but can be very frightening to the person undergoing it, and to the people with them. The common symptoms are shortness of breath, rising fear, shaking, nausea, feeling like they can't breathe, intense chest pain… She has all those—a classic case.'

Alexandros reeled. A panic attack?

'It happened out on the patio…is there any reason why it might have happened there?'

Alexandros felt a grim suspicion settle into him. 'Maybe… I'm not sure.'

The doctor continued, 'She told me the same thing happened one night when she had alcohol—she said until then she hadn't had a drink since she was in her teens. It's extreme but possible she could have reacted like that. It would seem to me that it's all linked. Something happened and ever since then something triggers the reaction. It's a lot more common than you'd think…' The doctor frowned slightly and shrugged. 'Only she knows the answer.'

Alexandros was grim, things that he didn't want to face becoming illuminated, begging for his attention. 'Thank you for coming at such short notice.'

The doctor shrugged. 'No problem. Any time.'

As he watched the doctor walk away, Alexandros couldn't halt the image coming into his head of Kallie that night, aged seventeen, taking the bottle of ouzo out of his hands and drinking. Yet she'd never touched a drop since he'd seen her again, except that night at the restaurant. If the doctor was right and she'd stopped drinking years ago… He rubbed a weary hand over his face.

Thea came back up and he took the cup of tea she'd

prepared, bringing it into the bedroom. Kallie looked at him from under the covers with big scared eyes. He made her drink the tea and watched as the colour came back into her face.

'Alexandros…' she said finally.

'Shh.' He put a finger to her lips. 'We'll talk tomorrow. Get some rest.'

They had a lot to talk about. He left the room only when she fell asleep, then he went back downstairs to the patio. He didn't sleep that night.

And very early he got into his vehicle and left the villa.

Kallie woke and sank back against the pillows, groaning. She couldn't believe she'd had that reaction again. And could it really just have been a panic attack, as the doctor had suggested? Yet it seemed to make sense, as she remembered her shock on realising where they were last night.

Could it really be because of that night? Could she have been so upset—and hurt—by what had happened that she'd somehow, in her head, placed her fears and guilt onto something random like alcohol that night in the restaurant? Used it as a trigger? How else would she have had exactly the same reaction just from being on the patio?

She felt a weight lift off her shoulders, even as she felt absurdly embarrassed and mortified. What must Alexandros think? A hysterical female. She swung out of bed, relieved not to feel the familiar morning nausea. She cringed again. He'd already witnessed her emptying the contents of her stomach into a toilet bowl. Not exactly the most romantic thing in the world. But, then, what did romance have to do with any of this anyway?

She got dressed into casual trousers and a sweater, tied her hair back and went downstairs with a leaden feeling in her chest. If anything was likely to make Alexandros run to arrange a divorce, this was it. He'd go back into the smooth, coiffed arms of Isabelle Zolanz in a heartbeat rather than watch Kallie throw up again. She didn't even have the energy to castigate herself for that thought not making her happy.

Thea met her and Kallie gave up silent thanks that they were friends again. She couldn't have borne Thea's condemnation any more. Thea fussed around Kallie and made her breakfast, sitting down beside her at the kitchen table where Kallie had insisted on eating.

'When are you going to tell him?'

Kallie nearly choked on her toast. 'Excuse me?'

Thea looked stern. 'You know very well what I'm talking about…'

Kallie's stomach fell and she said brightly, 'Oh, that? It was just a panic attack, can you believe that? I'm fine now. The doctor even said that once you know what it is, it can stop happening.'

Thea snorted. 'Doctors! What do they know? I could have told you weeks ago what that was if I'd known what was happening. I'm not talking about that, and you won't have one of them again, Kallie. You know what I'm talking about.' And she placed her hand on Kallie's belly.

So she had known…

Kallie went pink and shrugged awkwardly, too bemused to even be surprised at Thea's intuition. 'I don't know, Thea. I don't know that I can…until…until…'

Just then the main door slammed. Alexandros. Kallie tensed. Thea stood up and looked at her. 'You have to tell him. Everything. Now.'

Kallie got up and walked up into the hall from the kitchen. Alexandros was coming down the stairs.

'I was looking for you…'

She nodded jerkily. 'I think we need to talk.'

'Yes.' He was grim. 'We do.'

This is it. He's going to tell me about the divorce and I know I should tell him about the pregnancy now but if I do…

'Kallie?' He was looking at her intently.

She faced him squarely and drew up reserves of strength from somewhere.

'Yes?'

'Let's sit down.'

He took her hand and led her over to the sofa, sitting down beside her. Putting a little distance between them.

Oh, God, he's going to be nice about it… This is so much worse…

Kallie felt bile rise and had to take deep breaths to will it down.

'Kallie. The doctor told me what he thinks happened last night, that it was some form of a panic attack…'

The abject and pitiful relief that flooded Kallie when he didn't mention divorce straight off made her feel like laughing out loud. She nodded her head and focused on his face. His strong, hard-boned face. Lovingly took in every feature as if she had to imprint it on her memory.

'Last night…you were thinking about what happened seven years ago, weren't you?'

She stopped breathing and started again painfully. His hand tightened on hers. Eventually she nodded. Something intense flashed across his face but then it was gone.

'Kallie, I've been thinking. A lot. I suspect that your reaction in the restaurant came from what happened that night, too, that somehow the alcohol triggered it, especially after not drinking for so long…'

How could he intuit what she'd only just figured out for herself? Her mouth opened. 'The doctor… But how…?'

'Because I know you now, Kallie.' He gave a small smile. 'I knew you then, too, and I think that's why I was so shocked when you came on to me…'

Her cheeks went hot with embarrassment. Her voice was strangled. 'I was only seventeen… It was a crush, Alexandros. That's *all*. No hidden agenda. I *was* the same person you knew.' She shrugged, dying somewhere inside at having to explain herself. 'I was just growing up and wanted you to see me…as a grown-up…'

'Kallie, the last time we really would have talked was before my father died…you were fifteen. Can you see what it must have been like for me? To suddenly have you kiss me? Especially when I'd been so distracted, busy. We hadn't seen each other in so long and…I just…I thought you had changed beyond all recognition.'

He drew in a breath. 'But I know you didn't do it, Kallie. When I really thought about it and remembered your reaction that day…when I showed you the paper, it was the first you knew of it, wasn't it?'

She nodded vaguely, couldn't believe what she was hearing.

'And you got so upset when Thea told you what had happened afterwards. You said you hadn't read the article. I just chose not to believe you. It was easier…' *Easier than facing uncomfortable feelings…* But he couldn't get into that yet, they still had more to discuss.

'I think it's time you told me what really happened.'

Kallie took a deep breath and searched his eyes. They were so far off course from where she'd thought they were going that she felt disoriented. She felt the inevitability of the moment. Thea was right. No matter how or why she'd rationalised it to herself…she knew he wouldn't do anything to Eleni. So she told him. Everything, right down to how she'd confided their private conversations to her cousin.

Her eyes beseeched him. 'I trusted her, Alexandros… We told each other everything…' Her mouth twisted. 'At least *I* thought we did.'

And then she told him that she couldn't tell him before now

because she'd promised not to out of concern for Eleni's delicate health. That last piece caused a savage expression to cross Alexandros's face.

He stood abruptly and paced away from Kallie, running a hand through his hair.

'What is it…?' She was hesitant, afraid she'd just imagined his wish to hear her side of things for the first time. Was he going to turn around and laugh? Tell her she was lying again? She could feel herself tensing.

But then he turned back and there was such a bleak look on his suddenly drawn face that she was shocked.

'Kallie…' He stayed on his feet, pacing. 'Something else happened years ago…something I never told you because… so much was going on then…and I think I assumed you knew about it.'

'What?' She was feeling scared.

'Eleni…'

'Eleni…' repeated Kallie blankly.

'A few days before the party…we were in the same night-club in Athens…'

Kallie didn't move. She hadn't known this.

Alexandros grimaced. 'She was dressed up. Make-up, the works. Before I knew it she was coming on to me, trying to kiss me.'

He came back and sat down, taking her hand again but it was cold in his. 'She was like someone deranged, kept going on about my engagement to Pia, and *how* she found out about that I don't even know because it was top secret. She kept insisting that *she* could marry me, that her father could give me the same merger deal…' He shook his head. 'In the end, I had to get her thrown out of the club. And then just a couple of days later when you did almost the same thing… apart from anything else, I assumed it was some campaign by your family to sabotage my engagement.'

He cursed himself for not remembering this before.

Kallie's mind travelled inwards, back. She could see Eleni's face close to hers, the way she'd practically frog-marched Kallie out to the patio. She looked back at Alexandros. It all made sickening sense. Eleni *had* known about the marriage announcement… The magnitude of how little she'd known her own cousin hit her. And how much she'd still kept from her, despite the confession. Petty teenage jealousy and spite had done this. She felt stiff inside. He was shaking his head.

'I can't believe you defended her so staunchly, especially when you knew what she'd done…'

'I'm so sorry, Alexandros. I truly had no idea what her agenda was. She must have been so angry. If I had known about your engagement, there's no way—'

He cupped her cheek lightly, the look in his eyes, his tenderness making something melt inside her. She tried to fight it. 'I know…I know that now.'

'I'm so sorry, Pia was so beautiful…' He *had* to have loved her. Perhaps still…

Something twisted in his face and a hard look came into his eyes, making Kallie shiver inwardly. 'She was *not* beautiful, Kallie. The day before the announcement, I went to her apartment and witnessed something…awful. She was there with a group…' He shook his head. 'Believe me, you don't want to know. My only regret about that marriage falling through was the collapse of the merger…'

The guilt washed through her again. 'If I hadn't followed you that night, tried to kiss you…none of this would have happened. You wouldn't have had to work so hard to rebuild the company, my parents wouldn't have been so cruel.'

She shuddered and wanted to hold a hand up to his cheek. 'When my parents sent you out of the house…' Her voice died away. The tears in her eyes told Alexandros all he needed to know. He lifted her hand, as if he'd somehow known what she wanted to do, and kissed it. Gently. Reverently.

'If you hadn't followed me out there, we wouldn't be sitting here now…'

Kallie's breath stopped. What was going on? He was almost looking at her as if—

'Kallie, I—'

Just then the phone rang in his pocket. Kallie jumped. She'd been close to drowning in Alexandros's eyes, close to saying something, believing something…so close to revealing herself again as she had done before. She pulled back, searching for some distance. Space.

'Shouldn't you get that?'

He looked at her so intently for a second that she felt something alien quiver through her. Could it be *hope?*

He took the phone out and flipped it open. *'Ne?'*

After a quick brief conversation, so quick that Kallie couldn't follow it, he closed the phone again.

'There's something I have to do. But I don't want you to move. Kallie, promise me, just stay here, exactly as you are. I'll be back in half an hour—we've not finished talking yet.'

She nodded slowly and felt something momentous move between them. But she didn't dare try and fathom what it could possibly be.

When he had gone, she stayed on the sofa, exactly where she was. Not moving. *How* had he guessed so much? She didn't even feel relief. She just felt curiously at peace and a bit numb. As if something huge had shifted.

The phone rang shrilly in the hall, making Kallie jump. She left it for a minute, thinking Thea would appear to answer it, but she didn't. Kallie figured she must be out in the garden. She went and picked it up. A curt, officious voice on the other end asked abruptly for Alexandros.

'He's not here. He's gone into Athens.'

'Damn! I tried him on his mobile.'

'Sometimes the signal goes on the way down the hill.'

'Look, it's very important I speak with him.'

Kallie felt a little awkward now. 'Well, I'm his wife. He'll be back—'

The man sounded distracted. 'I'm out of my office. You said you're his wife…so you're Kallie Demarchis?'

'Yes.' She felt a prickle of foreboding come over her skin.

'Well, this involves you, too. I'm sure you know anyway. It's about the divorce. He said he wanted it to happen as soon as possible…'

Kallie nearly dropped the phone. And found herself saying in a thin voice, 'I'm sorry, who did you say you were?'

'I'm his solicitor. Look, I'm sorry to be so rushed, I didn't think I'd have to call. Just tell him to call me on my mobile when he gets back, if he wants this to happen as quickly as he said he did then I need some papers signed immediately. Oh, and, Miss Demarchis?' He didn't wait for a reply. 'You'll probably be hearing from your solicitor next week. Have a nice day.'

CHAPTER SIXTEEN

KALLIE dropped the phone back into its cradle. Thea rounded the corner. 'Did I hear the phone?'

Kallie nodded briefly, didn't look at her except fleetingly. 'Wrong number.'

Thankfully Thea went off again, muttering about her hearing. Without feeling her legs move, Kallie went upstairs to the bedroom and very calmly started to pack her things. Every now and then, as if trying to break into her consciousness, she'd get flashes of pain so intense she had to close her eyes and focus on breathing. She would not let this turn into another panic attack. All she needed was to get away from here. Right now. Before Alexandros came back. She'd get a flight back to Paris. Maybe even get the train to London for a few days, somewhere he wouldn't be able to find her.

She sat on the bed and looked blankly at her packed case. She couldn't believe that she'd come so close to telling him…to almost telling him everything. To think that she'd thought for one second that something momentous had happened downstairs between them. Of course he'd figured it out. He was an intelligent man, and when emotions weren't in the way, he'd been able to see the facts for what they were.

All this showed now was that he wasn't angry any more.

She put a shaking hand on her belly. Thank God she hadn't told him she was pregnant.

The door opened. Alexandros. 'Kallie, why didn't you stay downstairs?'

He came in and answered himself. 'It doesn't matter. I can say what I have to say—'

He stopped abruptly when he saw her face properly. It was white, the freckles standing out starkly against the unnatural hue.

His concern was immediate. He came in further but something held him back from touching her. She was so unnaturally still.

'What is it, Kallie? Did you have another attack? Did you—?'

He broke off as he saw the packed case on the bed behind her, looked around and saw the other case on the floor. He felt cold inside.

'What's going on?'

Kallie shrugged and stood up, forcing him to move back slightly. 'I want to go home, Alexandros. Like I told you last night. I've had enough.'

He gripped her arms. 'Kallie…downstairs just now…' He frowned. 'Why didn't you stay there? What the hell is going on?'

She laughed harshly, and when he looked now her eyes were dead. Dread moved through him.

'Alexandros, you know what happened now. We can both move on.'

Something flashed in her eyes, brief but intense. She quickly masked it but not before he saw it.

'Please.' She tried to pull free of his arms. 'Just let me go.'

'Not until you tell me what's happened. When I left you were sitting on that couch, not moving a muscle.' A different Kallie. With *warm* eyes. Not this cold stranger in front of him.

Kallie quailed under his look. *But if I tell him then he'll know…*

But he'll know anyway, a little voice reasoned, when the solicitor calls back when he doesn't hear from Aexandros. *All you have to do is pass on the message...*

Kallie shrugged again and averted her gaze. 'Your solicitor rang.'

Alexandros was confused. How could that have had *this* effect? Then he closed his eyes and groaned inwardly.

He opened them again and clutched Kallie's arms even harder. 'What did he say?'

She looked back up. 'Just that he wants you to call.'

'I don't believe you.'

Anger rushed through her. She shook in his arms. 'Fine. He said that if you want your quickie divorce then you'll have to sign some papers as soon as you get back.'

Alexandros was very calm, didn't react, apart from a muscle twitching in his jaw.

'And why is this making you so upset, Kallie?'

'It's not,' she denied pathetically, even as she trembled and shook under his hands.

'Isn't this what you want, too? What you begged for last night?'

'Of course it is. There's nothing I want more in the whole world.'

He quirked a brow. 'Really?'

'Yes. Please, Alexandros.' That little flash of something in her eyes caught him again. Giving him hope. Even as she said again, 'Just let me go.'

He let her go and she stumbled back slightly. He opened his hands, palms out, and backed towards the door, closing it.

'What are you doing?' she asked painfully.

'I'll let you go, Kallie. But only when you've heard me out. I'm going to ask you something and if you still want to go after than, *then* I'll let you go...'

He was a huge, steely immovable force. As if she could

even get past him. She just shrugged and sat on the bed behind her, her legs feeling wobbly. Soon, she reassured herself, soon I can go and be on my own.

He surprised her by coming back and kneeling down before her. She went to stand up and his hands on her knees forced her back down.

'Kallie, dammit, stay still. Stop fighting me for one second.'

She opened her mouth and closed it again. And couldn't believe what she was seeing. Alexandros's hands on her knees were shaking—ever so slightly, but definitely shaking. And when he looked up, her breath caught at the nervousness that flashed across his face. *It couldn't be…*

'Kallie, I've never done this before. It's new territory for me and it's taken me a while to figure out what's been happening…'

He looked up, his hands still on her knees, burning her through the fabric.

'Ever since I saw you that night at the Ritz…I wanted you with a passion that I've never felt before. *Before* I realised who you were. And then when you bumped into me and I saw you up close…you took my breath away. You take my breath away every time I look at you, Kallie…'

The way he was looking at her…it couldn't be…he was playing some cruel joke.

'Alexandros—'

He closed his eyes. 'Kallie, I'm in the middle of the hardest thing I've ever done.'

Opening them again, they blazed with something that shut her up. 'Using you, making you marry me were knee-jerk re-actions to the desire that took me over. It just so happened that I did need to marry. But I could have married anyone. I could have got my solicitor to arrange a civil wedding, and got the divorce the following week, protected my fortune. But I didn't. I wanted you: And I had a hold over you.' His mouth twisted. 'Which your uncle unwittingly supplied.'

He shook his head, not taking his eyes off hers. 'From day one you didn't conform to what I thought, what I'd expected. And when we slept together…' Dark colour flooded his cheeks. 'I've never, ever experienced something so intense, and it wasn't just that time, it's every time.'

Kallie blushed.

He looked at her and she could see a glint of something in his eyes, almost defiant, as if he was gathering his strength for something monumental. Determined. She could feel something move through his huge frame as he knelt before her.

'The reason I left just now is because I went to get something. After sitting up all night, thinking, I went into Athens this morning to get this…'

He didn't take his eyes off hers, and reached into his trouser pocket to pull out a small box. He opened it up and Kallie tore her eyes away and looked down. There, nestled in a bed of velvet, was a ring, an aquamarine surrounded by tiny diamonds. It was stunning, taking her breath away and yet so discreet that its simple beauty turned her heart over. She watched with shocked disbelief and bewilderment as he took it out of the box and with a visibly shaking hand placed it at the top of her ring finger.

He looked at her and she could see, feel his chest move as he sucked in a deep breath.

'Kallie Demarchis. Will you marry me?'

Her mouth opened and closed like that of a fish. She could feel the ring slip onto her finger even without him pushing it, as if it belonged. She looked from it to him.

'But…but…'

He looked pale again. 'Kallie, please. Say yes.'

'But you don't… You…hate… You don't love me.'

She was beginning to feel like she was about to hyperventilate. Alexandros pushed her legs apart to come between them, taking her face in his hands. She could already feel her lower body respond to his proximity.

'Did I forget to mention that I love you?'

She couldn't move. She was in shock. His hands were warm and heavy on her face, his eyes intense, on *her*.

'Kallie, I love you.' He kissed her forehead. 'I love you.' He kissed her cheek. 'I love you.' He kissed her other cheek. 'I love you…' He looked into her eyes for an eternity until she could read the truth there. Then he took her lips, her mouth, her soul and kissed her so sweetly, so passionately that she felt drugged. Could she believe? Or was this the ultimate revenge? A cruel play on how she'd offered herself to him…

When he finally pulled back, Kallie opened dazed eyes.

He was intent, his voice hoarse. 'Say something…'

She could feel tears well. And shook her head. 'I don't… How can I believe you? After everything that's happened, you don't…'

She gulped in huge fractured breaths, the magnitude of the moment, the feeling of standing on a precipice too huge. He was asking her to do it again. To hand him her heart. And she really didn't know if she could…

His hand smoothed her face, lovingly tucked her fringe behind one ear.

'I knew I was in trouble when I was running you baths and making you eat at three in the morning. Not to mention following you to work just to *see* you. I was enraged that you were so unavailable. My love…you're just going to have to trust me. I don't want to hurt you. I don't ever want you to be hurt again. Trust me. Please.'

She searched his face, his eyes. Tears slipped down her cheeks. Finally she spoke with a husky catch that made Alexandros feel weak inside. Weak with love for this woman he knelt in front of.

'I fell in love with you a long time ago… When I went

to you that night, I truly believed I loved you with all my heart and soul…'

'And I rejected you.' Alexandros's heart clenched painfully. Had he hurt her so badly that she couldn't love him now?

'Kallie—'

She shook her head. 'Wait.' Her voice was suddenly stronger. Even if this was some kind of cruel punishment, she couldn't deny the truth to him, or herself. She had to trust him.

'I was young, very naïve…but I don't regret it. It was a brave thing to do even if it had drastic consequences.' She took a deep, shaky breath. 'I'd do it again if I had the chance, and I'll do it again now.' She stopped for a long second and then said with simple truth, 'Alexandros, I love you.'

She lifted his hand and kissed the palm. 'I love you.' She drew his head to hers, pressing a kiss to his lips. 'I love you, Alexandros Kouros, and nothing in the world would make me happier than to be your wife…'

His hands went to her waist. She could feel them shaking and it made an exultant force move through her. She had taken the leap. His uncertainty made her ache.

'Are you…? I mean, you're not just saying it? Kallie…'

She nodded. 'I mean it.'

He stood and pulled her up with him, drawing her so tightly into his arms that Kallie never wanted the moment to end. The ring twinkled on her finger and she looked up. 'But…we're already married. How can we…?'

His voice was husky. 'I want us to walk around an altar three times, in a church. To symbolise our journey together, from when we first met to when we will end our days…together.'

She just nodded tearily and reached up again, meeting his hungry mouth with hers.

Much later, when they lay in each other's arms among tousled sheets, Kallie looked at Alexandros. He kissed her and slid a hand over the curve of her hip, across her belly. She stopped his hand and held it there. For a long moment she revelled in the silent communication that flowed between them.

It was time… 'There's something…I have to tell you…'

'What is it?' He shifted slightly so that his hand stayed on her belly, but he came up on one elbow to look down at her.

She opened her mouth and stopped again, suddenly scared that it was too soon, that he wouldn't be ready. That what they had between them was too fragile. She didn't want that love to fade from his eyes.

'Kallie?' He looked worried.

She had to trust again. She took a deep breath. 'I'm… pregnant. I was on the Pill but I changed over just before we met…' She was starting to babble and she knew it. 'That's why…I was so adamant about a divorce last night. I couldn't stand the thought of you tying me to you in a loveless marriage if you found out…'

For a moment he didn't move, and then a surge of something powerful moved through him. His hand tightened on her belly. He looked up for a second and Kallie felt unbelievably nervous. It was too soon, it was too—

He looked back down at her and she could see the glint of tears in his eyes. She looked up with worried ones.

'Are you…? Is it too soon?'

He shook his head, unable to speak for a moment. The thought of Kallie loving him, marrying him had been all he'd thought he could handle, but now *this*?

'Us…' His voice was reverent. 'Having a baby…'

He dipped his head and told her everything she needed to know with his kiss.

EPILOGUE

THE moonlight lit the patio with a magical glow. On a seat with huge cushions, Alexandros kissed Kallie's neck and she leant back against his big body with a blissful sigh.

His hands were around her, on her distended belly. Her hands were over his, their fingers intertwined.

'Anything?' he whispered in her ear.

She shook her head against him. The lights of Athens twinkled in the distance.

'Are you sure?'

She turned sideways in his lap, lacing her hands behind his neck, feeling her belly pressing into him. He pulled her even closer. Her heart was so full of love for him she thought she might burst. And she could see it reflected in his eyes.

'The only thing I'm feeling, Mr Kouros, is your son or daughter playing football in my insides…and how in love with you I am.'

She moved experimentally in his lap and smiled at her husband's low appreciative groan. 'Hmm, and something hard…'

He bent his head to hers and she tingled all over, his lips hovering. Thea came onto the patio at that moment with a squirming body in her arms, a mock angry look on her face.

'A certain someone refuses to go to sleep unless Daddy reads him another story.'

Alexandros groaned and gave Kallie a kiss that promised his swift return. She stood with a bit of effort to let him out of the seat. He took their son Nikos from Thea, holding him high. 'We're going to have to work on your timing, young man.'

'What's timing, Daddy? Night, Mummy!' the little boy called as his father carried him back through the doors.

Kallie blew him a kiss and smiled dryly. She'd said good-night twice already. She watched her family—*her life*—go back into the house. Placing a hand back on her belly, she walked over to the low wall and took in the magical view. She felt tears slip down her cheeks. But she knew that they were tears of joy…

* * * * *

CHOSEN AS THE FRENCHMAN'S BRIDE

PROLOGUE

The poolside, Hotel Lézille, 8.30pm

HE NOTICED her as soon as she appeared in the archway between the lobby and the pool, his eyes drawn there as if pulled by a magnetic force. A rare excitement stirred his pulse. He told himself that he hadn't come especially to seek her out. She seemed slightly hesitant, unsure. She wasn't the most beautiful woman he'd ever seen, but she had a stunningly natural quality about her, which in his world was rare, compelling. In a simple black dress that outlined every slender curve and a generous bosom, she caught his eye *again*, and he couldn't look away. Didn't want to.

The soft waves of her dark hair framed her face. Intriguingly, she seemed to be slightly self-conscious. Or perhaps, he thought with a hardened cynicism that had been honed over years, she carefully projected that vulnerable fragility. God knew she had managed to capture his attention in the street yesterday. Her huge, striking blue eyes had momentarily stunned him, rendering him speechless. And he was never stunned, or speechless. Something in their depths had caught him, combined with that lush mouth, looking up at him so innocently, full of a shocked kind of awe.

Then, amazingly, when he had seen her on the island earlier today, he had followed some base instinct to see her up close again… She was everything he remembered, and more. He recalled how she had trembled under his hands in the street yesterday, and under his look earlier today on the island. He couldn't ever remember a woman being so blatantly responsive.

His mouth compressed when he thought of her refusal to have dinner with him. That certainly hadn't happened in a while, if ever. Was she playing some game? He wouldn't be surprised… He was constantly amazed at the lengths some women went to just to get his attention. Playing hard to get wasn't a new trick…

He mentally dismissed the bottle redhead to his left, who was chattering incessantly, oblivious of the fact that his attention had long wandered from her far too obviously surgically enhanced assets.

With a barely perceptible flick of his wrist a man materialised at his side, bending low.

'Yes, sir?'

'Who is that woman?' He indicated to where she stood.

'She's not a guest with us, sir, but I can find out if you like…'

He just shook his head and dismissed him.

The ennui that had settled over him recently was definitely fading as he took in her graceful progress through the tables to reach her companions. With a skill based on years of reading people and body language, a skill that had tripled his fortune many times over, he assessed them in seconds, focusing on the man he guessed was her date. No competition. His heart-rate speeded up pleasantly as he contemplated them from under hooded lids. He decided now that he would conveniently forget the blow to his pride when she had refused him earlier. She was definitely worth pursuing. A surge of anticipation and desire made him feel alive in a way he hadn't in months…

CHAPTER ONE

Earlier that day...

JANE VAUGHAN wandered up and down the bustling jetty with a frown appearing over the ridge of her sunglasses. She couldn't remember exactly which gate she'd been at yesterday; now there were lots of bobbing boats and people lining up to get on board. The man she'd approached had taken no deposit, nor given her a ticket, but instead had reassured her that if she came back to him he would make sure she got on the right boat...the only problem now was that she couldn't spot him anywhere.

Bumping into that stranger in the street just afterwards must have scrambled her brain more than she'd thought. She shook her head wryly. She'd never thought herself to be the kind of woman that would spend a night fantasising about someone she had bumped into for mere moments. A newly familiar heat flooded her belly, however, as his tall, powerful body and hard-boned face swam into her mind's eye, his image still as vivid as if he were standing right in front of her. She shook her head again, this time to shake free of the memory. Honestly, this was so unlike her.

She went towards a gate that looked familiar, tagging onto the end of a queue. When she got to the man at the top he seemed a little harassed. At her query of, *'Excusez-moi. C'est le bâteau pour les îles?'* he just gestured impatiently into the boat. She hesitated for a moment, before figuring what was the worst that could happen? So if she didn't end up exactly where she'd expected to then it would be an adventure. They were going somewhere, and she was on holiday, not everything had to be strictly organised. She needed to relax more.

Once they were underway she had to admit grudgingly that she was enjoying the breeze and the sun across her shoulders and bare legs. The brightly patterned halterneck dress she wore was a present from her friend Lisa, given with an order to make herself more visible.

She pushed her sunglasses onto her head, tipping her face up to the sun, and for the first time since landing on the Côte D'Azur a week ago felt a rush of wellbeing and freedom. She didn't even really miss her friend's presence. Lisa was meant to have travelled with her—after all, it was *her* family's villa that Jane was staying in. But at the last minute Lisa's father had been rushed into hospital with a suspected heart attack, and this very week was undergoing a delicate operation. The conversation she'd had with Lisa the night before her departure had been rushed, but her friend had been insistent.

'Janey, if you don't go then I'll feel guilty on top of everything else. Anyway, you'll be doing us a favour. No one has been at the house for months, and it needs to be aired, so look at it like that.'

'But I can't just leave when you might need me most…'

'Look,' Lisa pointed out, 'you know my family. It'll be like Picadilly Circus in the hospital, and we've been assured Dad is going to be fine… Seeing your little face here would only upset me, and I mean that in a good way.'

She knew Lisa was just being brave, that the outcome was anything but assured, and didn't want to put her under any more pressure.

'OK, OK.'

Jane had given in. Lisa was right; there wasn't anything she could do. With a formidable mother, four sisters and three brothers she would only get in the way. And of the three brothers one in particular was intent on pursuing Jane. Not sure how she felt about Dominic, who was lovely, if a little dull, Jane was well aware that the campaign would have been taken up with enthusiasm by Lisa had she had the opportunity.

She got up and wandered over to the railing, shades back on against the glare of the sun, the sea spray catching her every now and then.

She still couldn't help a little pang of guilt at enjoying her solitude so much. She really hadn't expected to embrace it, but for the first time in her twenty-six years she was truly alone, without the crushing responsibility she'd carried for so long.

And it felt good!

Looking up from her contemplation of the foaming sea, she saw that they were approaching an island. Something about it, rising majestically from the water, made her shiver—as if someone had just run a finger down her spine. It was a forbidding rock, softened only by the sandy beach and picturesque houses that surrounded the small harbour. The sun glinted off the water as the boat docked and they disembarked. On the jetty, as she waited with the other passengers to be told where to go, her mind wandered back to danger territory, as if it had been waiting patiently in the wings until she'd stopped thinking of other things. She tried to resist, but it was too strong, yet again she re-lived the events of yesterday…that burning moment in the streets near the harbour came flooding back.

She'd escaped the crowded pedestrian area, feeling somewhat claustrophobic, and stumbled into a charming winding street that had been blessedly quiet, with no sign of any tourists. She had looked for a street name to figure out where she was; she wanted to explore more of this sleepy part of the town.

With her map open, trying to walk and read at the same

time, she'd been unaware of the approaching corner. She had looked up briefly, there had been a flash of something, and she'd crashed into a wall.

Except it hadn't been a wall, because a wall wouldn't have reached out and clamped hard hands on her upper arms. Winded and stunned, the map slipping from her fingers, she'd realised that she'd bumped into a man. Her gaze, on a level with a T-shirt-clad broad chest, had moved up, and up again, before coming face to face with the most beautiful pair of green eyes she'd ever seen—like the green of a distant oasis in the desert—in a dark olive-skinned face, with black brows drawn together forbiddingly. Her jaw had dropped.

It had been only then that she'd become aware of her own hands, curled around his biceps, where they had gone automatically to steady herself. And with that awareness had come the feel of bunched muscle beneath his warm, silky skin. They had flexed lightly under her fingertips as his arms held her, and out of nowhere came a spiking of pleasure so intense and alien through her entire body that she'd felt her eyes open wide in shock. His gaze had moved down to her mouth, and she'd had a weightless, almost out-of-body feeling, as if they hadn't been in a side street, as if this hadn't really been happening.

The spell had been jarringly broken when a shrill voice had sounded. Jane's gaze had shifted with effort to take in a stunning blonde woman rounding the corner, her stream of incomprehensible French directed at the man. His hands had tightened momentarily before he'd dipped from view and come back up with her map in his hand. He'd held it out to her wordlessly, a slightly mocking smile on his mouth. She'd taken it, and before she had even been able to say sorry, or thank you, the blonde had grabbed the man's attention and with a scant glance at Jane had urged him away, looking at her watch with exaggerated motions. And he had disappeared.

Jane had stood, still stunned, her body energised to a

point of awareness just short of pain. She had still been able to feel the imprint of his hands on her arms. She'd lifted fingers to her lips, which had tingled…as if he had actually touched them. It had been just seconds, a mere moment, but she'd felt as though she'd stood there with him for hours. The most bizarre and disturbing feeling. And then she had remembered his enigmatic smile, as if he'd known exactly what effect he was having on her. Arrogant, as if it was expected.

Jane's reverie ended abruptly as she found that she was following the other tourists onto a small air-conditioned bus. She vowed that that was the last time she would indulge herself in thinking about that man. The last time she would indulge the fantasy she'd had of sitting across a table from him, sharing an intimate dinner, candlelight flickering, picking up the silverware and sparkling glasses. Those green eyes holding hers, not letting her look away. She quashed the silly flutter in her belly and took in the other people on the bus, leaning over to a young couple about her age across the aisle.

'Excuse me, do you know where we are?'

The woman leant across her boyfriend, replying with a strong American accent. 'Honey, this is Lézille Island—but you'd know that, coming from the hotel…aren't you a guest?'

'No!' Jane clapped a hand to her mouth. 'I'm not in a hotel…I thought this was just a general trip…'

Dismayed, she wondered what she should do, she hadn't paid for this trip… She belatedly remembered asking the man if this was the boat to *les îles*—the islands, in French, which sounded exactly like the name of this island. Lézille. No wonder he had just ushered her on board.

The other woman waved a hand. 'Oh, don't worry. I won't say anything, and no one will notice…you just bagged yourself a free trip!'

Jane smiled weakly. She hated any sort of subterfuge. But maybe it wasn't such a big deal. She could always follow them back to their hotel afterwards and offer to pay for the trip. She felt a little better with that thought.

The woman told her that they were due to visit a vineyard for some wine-tasting, and afterwards to take in an aerial display. Jane gave in and relaxed, and started to enjoy the mystery tour nature of the trip…this was exactly what she needed.

The vineyard was enormous, with beautifully kept rows of vines. They were shown every part of the winemaking process—which Jane had to admit was more interesting than she would have expected. The name on the bottles sounded familiar—as had the name of the island.

When they emerged at the other end of the buildings, they could see what looked like a medieval castle in the distance. Again she felt that funny sensation…almost like déjà vu.

'You know this island is owned by a billionaire who lives in that castle?'

Jane looked around the see the friendly woman from the bus. 'No…no, I don't know anything about it.'

Her voice lowered dramatically. 'Well, apparently he owns half the coast too—his family go back centuries… He's so private, he only allows people to visit a few times a year. There's all sorts of stories about—' She broke off when her boyfriend came and dragged her away to see something.

Jane looked back to the castle. It certainly looked as if it could have been around in the Middle Ages. On a small island like this, she guessed it could have been some kind of protective fortress.

After another short trip in the bus, along a picturesque strip of coastline, they were deposited in a big green field, full of wild flowers, with an airstrip at the far end. A dozen planes were lined up in readiness. There was a fiesta-like atmosphere, with families stretched out around the ground with picnics, stalls set up with drinks, food and handicrafts. A small stone building to the side looked like some kind of museum, and on closer inspection Jane discovered that it was. She just gave it a brief look, before wandering over to see the stalls, where she bought some bread and cheese for a light lunch, noticing that everyone else seemed to have brought picnics.

Suddenly her arm was grabbed. 'We haven't introduced ourselves. I'm Sherry, and this is Brad. We're on honeymoon from New York. You should stick with us if you're on your own.'

The woman from the bus barely allowed Jane to get a word in edgeways to introduce herself as they led her away to a spot they had picked out on the grass. It was nice to have the company as she ate her meagre lunch, and they turned out to be very friendly, insisting on sharing their wine and fruit.

After lunch Jane noticed men in flight suits walking towards the small planes from a hangar area, and the crowd got up and started to cheer. Soon there was one last pilot walking to his plane. With the sun in her eyes, he just was a shape in the distance.

A hush went around the field and, wondering at the strange reaction, Jane lifted a hand to shade her eyes—and stiffened when she saw more clearly who it was. It was the man from the street; she was sure of it. He was unmistakable. His impressive build and height set him apart.

Before she knew what she was doing she was on her feet with the rest of the crowd. He had an innately powerful grace, commanding attention as he strode towards the plane. Clearly the leader. On a gesture from him, the other pilots started up.

When he got into the plane, something in Jane's stomach fell, and she found she couldn't sit down again and relax. As they took off one by one, he being the last, she unconsciously clenched her fists. The display probably only took fifteen minutes but to Jane it seemed to go on for ever. Her eyes never left his plane, a ball lodging in her gut. She couldn't explain or fathom the completely irrational fear she felt; she just knew that nothing could move her from the spot until that plane was back on the ground and he walked out, safe.

He flew as though he had a death wish. Dizzying turns and ever increasingly daring stunts had the crowd gasping in unison and clapping. He was the last to land, watched by the other pilots, their respect obvious.

When he stepped out of the plane to thunderous applause, Jane unclenched her fists, noticing that her nails had carved half moons into her palms. Unbelievably she felt anger towards him—this complete stranger!

The sun must be getting to her, she thought, unable to tear her eyes away. As the crowd surged towards the planes, his head turned, and even though at least fifty metres separated them, his gaze caught hers. She had a freefall feeling, couldn't move. She felt as if he had reached out and touched her with those amazing eyes. With a supremely difficult struggle she turned away, and almost fell to the ground beside the American couple, who were chattering happily, oblivious to her inner turmoil. Maybe she *had* actually become delusional…conjured him up out of her rampant imagination.

When Brad and Sherry got up to check out the small museum she followed gratefully, feeling inexplicably as if she was escaping something…

She cast a quick glance back towards the planes, unable to help herself. She could just see the top of his dark head, surrounded by people—mainly adoring women from the looks of it.

She turned away resolutely and ducked inside, reassuring herself that by the time they came out all the pilots would be gone. After a few minutes she was feeling somewhat calmer, and walked around taking in the information with genuine interest. From a small plaque that was tucked into a corner she learned about a devastating earthquake at the turn of the century, which had reduced the population of nearly a thousand to a few hundred. It was only in recent decades that the island had begun to thrive again.

Apparently it had been in the hands of one family since

the time of the crusades. They were called Salgado-Lézille, and had come originally from Spain. That would explain the hacienda-like houses Jane thought, remembering seeing them dotted around the harbour and elsewhere. And in retrospect there was something vaguely Moorish about the shape of the majestic castle.

She had turned to follow the crush out the door when the light was blocked momentarily and someone came in.

It was him. Even before she saw his face she knew. He scanned the room as people passed by him, and Jane held her breath. Slowly his gaze came to rest on her and stopped. Immediately her heart started to thump and her legs turned to jelly.

He stared at her.

Jane shook herself mentally. This was crazy. How could she be reacting like this *again*? She turned away and looked back at a document behind the glass, but she could see his shape reflected. He wasn't moving. She forced herself to walk around the exhibit again and admonished herself. She was going to have to leave sooner or later, and there was no way he would have come in just to stare at her.

But he was. She could feel it.

All she had to do was walk past him. Easy.

She followed the chattering line of other tourists heading out, drawing ever closer to the door, looking anywhere but at the disturbing man and his large, broad-shouldered body leaning insouciantly against the wall. She sensed his dark gaze, hot and heavy upon her, like a physical caress, and trembled.

Now there were only two people in front of her. Why had they stopped? She dampened down her irritation. Her reaction was completely over the top. She just needed to get back out into the fresh air. That must be it, she comforted herself—the heat. As if to prove her point, she felt a trickle of sweat between her breasts.

She could see his long legs crossed at the ankles. She focused on the back of the heavy loud man in front of her. Maybe she could pretend she was with him, ensuring a smooth passage past. She had no idea why it was so important; she just felt it deep in the core of her being.

She was almost beside him now, the breath hitching in her throat. He took up her peripheral vision. She didn't have to be looking at him to know what he was like. Despite only the brief moment the day before, and her distant view earlier today, she knew she would be able to describe him in detail.

Thick dark hair, swept high off a strong broad forehead. Harsh, vitally masculine face, lines broken only by an aquiline nose, sensually sculpted lips. And those mesmerising eyes, the eyelashes visible even from a distance. His flight suit enhanced his commanding physique.

'Oh, my God, he is gorgeous.'

You don't say, Jane thought wryly at Sherry's indiscreetly loud whisper behind her. Without looking she could feel his sardonic smile. He had heard and understood; he must speak English.

She was almost at the door, almost home free, when her wrist was captured in an electrifying grip by a familiarly strong lean hand. The people behind her jostled, and to avoid a crush she had to move closer, go with the pull of the hand. Her blue eyes huge, she looked up at him.

He drew her in, close to his body, the people pushing past her inadvertently moving her in even closer. She could feel the heat of his thigh, hard against her own through the thin material of her dress.

What was happening?

She looked up, the question on her face, captivated by his gaze, which looked back down at her, lazily assessing. This man who had dominated nearly her every thought since yesterday.

'What are you looking at?' she croaked.

'You,' he answered with deceptive simplicity, and the word rocked through Jane's body.

'Who…who are you?'

He didn't answer, just kept a loose, yet immovable grip on her wrist. She could feel her pulse thumping against the warm skin of his hand like a captured bird. Something in her blood leapt, and excited anticipation built in her belly. The part of her that he had reached yesterday, unknown and alien, was coming to life again…just under his look. He smiled indolently, before his eyes left hers to look her up and down so thoroughly that she felt naked, exposed. A flush spread from her belly all the way up to her neck. She tried to yank her wrist away to no avail; his grip only tightened. He couldn't possibly remember her, could he?

Nerves made her blurt out, 'Who do you think you are? How dare you look at me like that…?'

His eyes bored into hers, the green becoming darker, making him look dangerous, 'You pretend to not recognise me?'

He remembered.

'No…well, that is, yes. I saw you yesterday in the street… when you bumped into me.'

'As I recall it was the other way around, *n'est ce pas?*'

His voice sounded as though it had been dipped in honey treacle, deep and dark, with only the barest hint of an accent, his English flawless. She was finding it hard to concentrate.

'I was just reading a map. Surely you saw me…' She cursed the breathless tone in her voice.

He ran a quick glance up and down again. 'Oh, I saw you all right.'

She saw the amusement lurking in his eyes and she tried to pull away again. This time he let her go, and she felt inexplicably bereft.

'You should have been looking where you were going. You could have collided with a more…immovable object.'

From what she could remember, all too well, *he* had been

like a wall…a wall of hard-packed muscle. She felt her legs weaken. More than disturbed by the effect he was having on her, she looked at him incensed,

'The street was empty…it's hardly a crime to divert one's attention for a moment.'

He inclined his head in a surprisingly old-fashioned gesture. 'Maybe we can agree that we were equally to blame.'

She huffed slightly. 'It's no big deal.'

'Yet you are the one who seems to be upset about it,' he pointed out, picking up on her discomfort.

Jane looked around then, and saw that they were alone in the building. Everyone else had disappeared. When had that happened?

She looked out through the door and sighed with relief when she saw the bus, where the others were embarking. She turned to find him right behind her, and stepped back hurriedly.

'I have to go…that's my bus leaving now.'

He caught her hand just as she turned away. Her pulse leapt again.

'Would you do me the honour of being my dinner guest tonight? To…foster a truce and allow me to make amends for my part in our collision.'

He was smooth, and practised, and too, too seductive. Jane shook her head, slightly dazed. He was asking her out for dinner? Her eyes met his. *No way, no way*, went through her mind. This man was so out of her league that he might as well be from another planet. She didn't have the wherewithal to sit across a table from him! She'd dissolve in a puddle within minutes. And the way he was looking at her…as though he wanted to have *her* for dinner!

'I'm sorry,' she said stiffly, pulling her hand free. 'I…I have arrangements made already, but thank you for asking.'

His eyes probed hers for an uncomfortably long moment, and then he shrugged lightly, a shuttered look descending over his face. 'Very well.'

Now she had offended him, she thought miserably. Without knowing what to say or do, she stepped away and half ran, half walked back to the bus.

She sank into her seat breathing heavily. She felt hot and bothered, her hand still tingling where he had caught it. Jane evaded Sherry's very pointed look and stared out of the window.

All the way back to the mainland she veered between feeling as if she had made a lucky escape and extreme self-recrimination. Since bumping into him she had thought of little else, even fantasised about having dinner with him, but when she was offered the opportunity what did she do? Refused point-blank.

She didn't deserve a date with such a man if she couldn't even handle being asked out. And *why* had he asked her out? She couldn't fathom it. She could tell that he was mannerly—perhaps it was a pilot thing, a code of conduct? Although somehow he didn't look like just a pilot. Her brain began to throb. She couldn't help but feel as though she had let herself down in some way. She could well imagine Lisa's reaction.

Back on land, she sighed to herself, trying to catch a glimpse of the island which was too far away to view in the late-afternoon haze. She would just have to put it down to experience. A man like Lisa's brother Dominic was obviously all she could handle…maybe this was a sign.

When she saw the others get on the bus for their hotel she followed them on board.

Fifteen minutes later they pulled off the road and into a resort. It screamed extreme wealth. Immaculate lawns and manicured gardens led up to a beautiful hacienda-style building, all in white. In the early dusk lights shone from the windows, gauzy curtains fluttering in the breeze. She read the name of the hotel carved discreetly into a low stone wall, and only registered then how well dressed her companions were.

She had tagged on to a day trip from one of the Lézille Hotels. No wonder the name had sounded familiar. The owner of the island obviously also owned this very well-known string of resorts dotted all over the world in prime locations and renowned for their discretion, luxuriousness, exclusivity.

She followed the others into the lobby and they split off in different directions. Just as she went to look for the tourist office Sherry stopped her. 'Hey, Jane, why don't you come back here for dinner tonight? You said you were on your own, and we've made friends with a guy from Washington DC who works in town… We could make a foursome; he'd love your accent.'

Jane opened her mouth on reflex to say no, and stopped herself. Had she learnt nothing from her recent experience? Here she was, being offered another chance. She smiled at Sherry. 'I'd love to.'

'Plus, I want to hear all about your conversation with Mr Gorgeous!'

Jane's smile faded. They would most certainly *not* be discussing that. She made a mental note to make sure the conversation never strayed into that area.

Once she had sorted out payment for the trip with a very bemused tour manager she made her way back to the villa.

A few hours later Jane was in a taxi on her way back to the hotel. She hoped that her mystery date was tall. She was five foot nine herself in flats, and if he wasn't they would look ridiculous. Unlike *him*—she knew she could wear the highest heels and would still have to look up. Her heart started to thump, just thinking of what it would be like to be on the way to meet *him… But you were a chicken and turned him down.* As if she needed to be reminded…

The taxi pulled into the front courtyard and Jane made a last-ditch effort to erase his image. She made her way out to the poolside buffet, where she had arranged to meet the others, and Sherry's madly waving arm caught her attention easily enough—along with the sparkly half-dress she was wearing. She weaved through the tables to get to them, completely oblivious of several admiring glances on the way. And one in particular from the other side of the pool.

CHAPTER TWO

'JANE! Meet Pete—he split up with his fiancée back home a few months ago and moved here to lick his wounds.'

Jane had to hold back a smile at Sherry's effervescent indiscretion, and stuck out her hand to the other man. 'Pleased to meet you. I'm Jane Vaughan.'

He was pleasantly attractive, with nothing overpowering about him—brown hair, brown eyes, nice smile. No chemistry whatsoever. Jane relaxed, and they settled into a light easy conversation. When the band struck up a slow jazzy tune Pete stood and asked her to dance. As she went into his arms on the dance floor she had to admit that it was all very agreeable. This was much more her scene than the messily overwhelming attraction she had felt for the stranger. Heat induced lust. This she could handle. That... She shivered at the thought.

Pete tightened his arms around her. 'Hey, are you cold?'

Jane immediately recoiled, surprised at the strength of her reaction. 'No!' she said, far too quickly, amending it with a smile. 'No...just a little tired. Maybe if we could sit down again...'

As they approached the table another woman was leaving and waving gaily at Sherry, who turned gleaming eyes on Jane as she sat down. 'You'll never guess what I just found out.'

Jane obediently supplied, 'What?'

The men took themselves off to the bar, muttering something about women and gossip. It made Jane cringe a little, but Sherry was leaning over the table, saying with a loud whisper, 'That guy…the gorgeous hunk from earlier…well, don't look now, but he's behind you on the other side of the pool, and he's been looking this way.'

Immediately Jane's back straightened, and she started breathing faster. She just managed to stop herself from turning around, but Sherry was doing it for her, looking over Jane's shoulder. A frown marred her pretty features,

'Shoot—he's gone. Oh, well…anyway, wait till you hear what I found out from Tilly Brown. He's Mr Island!' She looked at Jane as if to say, *Don't you get it?* Jane just looked back blankly. What on earth did she mean?

Sherry sighed exaggeratedly. 'He owns the island we were on today. *He's* the billionaire. His name is—get this for a mouthful—Xavier Salgado-Lézille, and he owns this whole complex too. Can you believe that? To think that we saw him and didn't know. I'm so dumb…'

Jane sat there stunned as Sherry chattered on. It made sense now—his presence, the authority he commanded. She recognised that he must have assumed she was a guest at the hotel. His reaction to her refusal earlier didn't surprise her now. She doubted that many women would turn down someone like him.

'And the best thing is,' Sherry continued, pausing for dramatic effect, 'he's a bachelor. Well, actually a notorious playboy, incapable of commitment some say—they call him the Prince of Darkness because he's so dark and brooding and—'

'You really shouldn't listen to idle gossip you know.'

The deep voice beside them could have cut through steel. They both looked up to find the object of their conversation beside the table. The epitome of wealth and sophistication in an impeccable tuxedo. The man who had loomed large in

Jane's imagination for two days now had a name—and an island, a hotel chain, a wine label, a reputation. Her head swirled. Sherry didn't even have the grace to blush, but Jane did, horribly aware of how they must have looked, their heads close together like conspirators.

'Why, Mr Salgado-Lézille—why don't you join us?'

'Please, Mr Salgado will do. The full name is such a… *mouthful*…if that's the right term.'

Jane cringed, going even pinker with embarrassment, and she marvelled at Sherry's hide, which was as thick as a rhinoceros. He flicked Sherry a dismissive glance and turned his attention to Jane, holding out a hand in a clear invitation to dance. She couldn't refuse. Especially after what had just happened. Wordlessly she put her hand in his much larger one and felt a tingle go up her arm as he lightly guided her onto the dance floor.

Drawing into his arms, Jane fought for composure. The difference between this man and Pete from only a few moments ago was laughable. This was what she had been afraid of—this melting feeling, a hyper-awareness of every part of her skin, an acute consciousness of the way her body seemed to want to fuse with his. His scent was clean and crisp, with a hint of some indefinably erotic element. The man himself, she guessed.

One arm held her securely, high across her back, his hand curving around to just beside her breast. His other hand held hers lightly against his chest. They said nothing, swaying together in perfect unison. When the song ended he held her fast when she would have pulled away until another number started up.

'Don't you think you owe me at least one more dance?'

Jane lifted her head and looked up into his eyes. 'Of…of course.'

His eyes glinted in the flickering light of the candles all around them, a small hard smile playing around his mouth.

As they started to move again she felt she had to say something, blurting out, 'I'm sorry about Sherry… That is, I don't even really know her. I'd hate for you to think that you were the subject of our…' She trailed off, reminding herself that she *had* been listening to Sherry with bated breath. 'I thought you were just one of the pilots…'

Even as the words came out she wanted to grab them back. But it was too late. She couldn't mistake the cynical edge to his voice,

'Ah…I should have known. It is much easier to accept a dance, or dinner for that matter, from the owner of a hotel rather than just a pilot.'

She pulled back as far as he would allow, every line in her body indignant. 'I didn't mean it like that…that had nothing to do with anything, Mr Salgado. The reason I declined your invitation earlier was because—' She broke off. As if she could tell him that the reason she'd turned him down was because her reaction to him had scared the life out of her.

'Well?' he prompted softly, one dark brow lifted.

'I…I, well, as you can see I had made arrangements with Sherry and Brad.' She crossed her fingers, hating the lie, but self-preservation was more important. 'I'm not actually staying here…I'm alone, staying at a friend's villa on the hill. I ended up on the day trip by mistake earlier, and they invited me for dinner.'

It wasn't a complete lie, she reassured herself. Their invitation had just come after his.

He frowned slightly. 'The tour manager told me about someone who had inadvertently ended up on a trip coming in afterwards to pay…was that you?'

'I guess so…unless there was someone else.'

'Quite an enigma, aren't you? Miss…?'

'Vaughan. Jane Vaughan.'

He stepped back for a moment and made a courteous bow, taking her hand. 'Pleased to meet you, Miss Vaughan.'

And then he kissed her hand. She could feel his lips firm and yet soft against her skin, and the fluttering excitement grew stronger in her belly.

'Let's start again,' he said, in a low seductive voice, tucking her into him even closer than before.

Jane fought an internal battle for a few seconds and then gave in. It was too strong…this…whatever it was that she was feeling. She allowed her head to fall into the crook of his neck and shoulder, closing her eyes. A perfect fit.

His hand on her back was moving in slow sensuous circles, grazing her bare skin. She could feel her breasts grow heavier, sensitive against the material of her dress. When he shifted subtly she could feel the thrust of his arousal low against her belly. She pulled back for a second, but Xavier felt it and caught her even closer, growling into her ear, 'You can't move now. Everyone will see what you're doing to me.'

Jane blushed scarlet to the roots of her hair. The next few minutes were an exercise in erotic torture. She had never felt anything like this in her life. Completely unaware of everyone around them. Burning up.

Finally, when she feared her very legs weren't capable of holding her up any more, he pulled back, but held onto her hand. Dark green eyes glittered into blue ones.

'Let's get out of here.'

She nodded mutely. She was being swept away on a tidal wave of feelings and sensations. Sanity tried to break through her consciousness but she pushed it aside. She couldn't let this second chance slip away.

They were in the alcove that led outside to the front of the building and the gardens. Muslin drapes fluttered around them, acting as a shield between the lobby and the main entrance. Jane stopped suddenly. 'Wait!' She turned horrified eyes to his. 'I can't just leave…I'm with people…Pete.'

How could she have forgotten and be so unquestionably rude? No matter what wild spirit seemed to have taken her over, there was no excuse for leaving so abruptly. And, more to the point, the fact that this man had made her take leave of her senses so easily caused a panicky sensation in her belly.

Xavier's eyes narrowed as he looked down at her and took in her expressive face. He had forgotten about her companions too…all he had been aware of was getting her out of there to some private place where he could explore that lush mouth and—

'I'm sorry, Mr Salgado—'

'Xavier, please…'

She couldn't bring herself to say his name. 'I'll have to go back to the others. I really can't just run out on them like this.'

She hoped that the regret in her voice didn't sound too obvious. But the heavy disappointment in her chest dispelled any panic. He'd wouldn't indulge her again. No doubt he thought she must be playing some game with him. She watched with dismay as he seemed to concur.

'You are right. It would be remiss of me to take you away. But be under no illusion that if you weren't obliged to return then right now I would be doing this…'

Before she knew what was happening he had pulled her close, one arm around her back, the other cradling her head, covering her mouth with his. Taking advantage of her startled sigh, he expertly plundered the moist interior, exploring, tracing her lips. When his tongue sought and found hers, stroking with sure mastery, a white-hot flame of desire raced through her body. Her hands clenched on his shoulders in reaction. She was lost in the moment…and in him.

Reluctantly Xavier lifted his head to look down. She took a second to open glazed eyes, lashes long against her cheeks, her lips swollen and parted slightly. He felt the tremor in the body held tightly against his. She would be his, of that he had no doubt. He had branded her.

Jane stepped back and tried to control her breathing, just

managing to stop herself from bringing a hand up to feel her lips. Crazily, she felt as if he had just marked her in some way. She had heard about kisses like that, and thought it was some pathetic fantasy, or Lisa waxing lyrical about her latest obsession…but it wasn't. If he hadn't stopped when he had…

She had been reduced to mush by little more than a kiss.

'Yes…well…I…have to…'

'Have lunch with me tomorrow.'

He still wanted to see her?

She looked at him helplessly. She felt like a moth that was being attracted to a flame with danger written all over it, but the pull was so inexorable that she couldn't help herself. She took a deep breath. The new Jane. Quash the panic. She felt shaky.

'I'd like that.'

'Which villa are you staying at?'

She told him the address.

'*Bien.* I will pick you up at midday…till then.'

He strode back into the lobby and got into the lift without a backward glance.

Jane wandered back out to the poolside table in a daze. Sherry squealed when she saw her arrive. Remarkably, the men still hadn't returned from the bar. Jane felt as though whole lifetimes had passed since Xavier had asked her to dance.

She fielded Sherry's questions, being as vague as possible. When the men arrived back poor Pete didn't stand a chance. He tried to press a kiss to her lips before she left at the end of the evening, but she gave him her cheek. Somehow the thought of anyone else kissing her where Xavier had was anathema.

She didn't see the look of triumph on the face of the man watching from his penthouse suite overlooking the pool.

Back in the villa, Jane couldn't settle and went up to the terrace which overlooked the twinkling lights of the town below, still feeling slightly dazed. Her thoughts drifted to her mother, who she hoped was enjoying much the same view. She was on her honeymoon in Cyprus, with Arthur, the man she'd met a year previously. Jane thought of the recent wedding day with a smile. How proud she had been to give her mother away to such a kind, gentle man. If anyone deserved another stab at happiness it was she.

Since her father had died at just thirty, leaving her mother penniless, with Jane still a baby, it had been a monumental struggle. Her mother had changed overnight from a relatively carefree newlywed to a woman who had had to seek work to make ends meet. Sometimes she worked three jobs at once, just to put food on the table and get Jane through school and then college, despite Jane working too to help out.

Even when Jane had finished her degree and had begun working as a teacher her mother had refused money, insisting that she build up a nest egg for herself.

Years of worry and work had sapped her mother's joy and increased Jane's concern. But now…now she was allowing herself to feel love and happiness again, and if she could embrace a new lease on life then so could Jane.

Starting tomorrow.

With a shiver of anticipation snaking down her spine she finally left the view.

CHAPTER THREE

WHEN she woke the next morning Jane couldn't believe she had slept at all—much less for… She consulted her watch in disbelief—ten hours straight. Which meant, she realised with a lurch of panic, that she had exactly one hour before Xavier was due to pick her up for lunch.

She sprang out of bed and after a quick shower regarded her wardrobe, plucking a pair of white culottes from the messy pile, and a striped white and black halterneck top. She smoothed her hair behind her ears, and with espadrilles and a pair of hoop earrings was just about ready to go downstairs when the doorbell rang.

Already!

She took a few deep breaths and walked to the front door, trying to calm the butterflies in her belly.

Be cool, be calm, be sophisticated.

She opened the door, the smile on her face fading and her mouth going dry when she took in the man in front of her. Pure devastation. He was leaning against the doorframe, arms folded across his broad chest, showing his muscles off to perfection. He wore a casually faded black T-shirt and jeans, scuffed deck shoes on his bare feet. She could feel her face colour as she brought her eyes back up. She had just examined him…and blatantly!

She couldn't see his eyes, as they were hidden behind

dark shades, but she saw all too well the way his mouth quirked.

'I hope I pass inspection?'

What could she do? She had been caught out beautifully. She had to smile, revealing small, even white teeth and a dimple in her cheek.

'You'll do.'

She bent down to pick up her bag, where she'd stuffed her bikini and a sarong among other bits and pieces, not sure what he had planned, and pulled the door behind her, careful to lock it securely. He took the bag from her and led the way to his car. She was glad to see that although it was a convertible it wasn't one of those tiny low-slung things that she privately thought looked ridiculous.

As he negotiated his way down the small winding streets with casual expertise she started to relax and look around. She was very aware of his tanned hands on the wheel, moving to the gear-stick near her leg, and of the long fingers with short square nails. She swallowed and quickly put on the shades that had been resting on her head in case he caught her staring again.

'How long are you here for?' he asked idly.

'Just another week; I've already been here for one. This is such a treat.'

'What is?'

Nerves made her babble. 'To be taken out…driven around. I have a hire car, but this place is like a labyrinth… The first day it took me an hour to find my way back up the hill from the town.'

'I know…it is getting crazier, with more and more tourists… We're hoping that they'll make the centre of the town entirely for pedestrians only; it's small enough, so it could work.'

His comment reminded her who she was dealing with. He wasn't just a local, he was *the* local. She felt intimidated all of a sudden.

He cast a curious glance her way. 'Cat got your tongue?'

She shrugged lightly, honesty prevailing. 'I know this might sound silly, but I keep forgetting that you are…who you are. You own that entire island…that hotel chain. I guess it's just a little overwhelming. I bump into you in the street two days ago and now here I am in your car.' She gave a nervous laugh.

Xavier looked over at her sharply, but she had her face averted. Well, this was a new approach—and one that he hadn't encountered before. Was she for real? More or less hinting that she'd be more comfortable with him if he were just a pilot? He'd never had to reassure a woman before by playing his status down…normally they wanted him to play it up! Well, if this was a game that she was playing then he would play along. She was intriguingly different from any other woman he'd ever known. Whether it was artifice or not he didn't much care. He wasn't planning on getting to know her too well…just well enough.

His glance took in the long shapely legs beside him. He could imagine how they might feel wrapped around his naked back. He grew hard there and then, much to his chagrin. He wasn't used to being at the mercy of hormones he had long ago learnt to control. A woman hadn't had the power to ignite his desire so forcibly since…*ever*, he realised. He focused on the road, hands gripping the wheel. Only one way to exorcise this hunger raging in his blood.

He forced himself to say lightly, 'Ah, so you admit now that you were the one who bumped into me?'

Jane cast him a quick glance, relieved to see him flash her a teasing smile.

Lord, but he was gorgeous. She couldn't answer, nervously touching her tongue to dry lips.

'I thought we'd take a little trip on my boat. I know a cove near here that's usually deserted. We can swim and have a picnic.'

She was going to forget everything and enjoy this moment

for what it was. She was being given a second chance…her fantasy was coming true…and she was smart enough not to sabotage it again. She hoped.

'That sounds lovely.'

After he had parked the car and lifted out a hamper, he led her into a private marina, where yacht after yacht was lined up, bobbing on the water. His was a small sleek speed boat, with a tiny cabin down below.

'This is how you get to and from the island?'

'Yes…or I use the helicopter. This takes fifteen minutes.'

Of course…the helicopter!

It was hard to keep her intimidation at bay when he threw out such admissions of extreme wealth. She forgot everything, though, as he helped her into the boat, big hands curling around her waist to steady her, just under her breasts. Suddenly breathless, she moved away quickly to the other end and looked anywhere but at him. She could see the tourists in the distance, lining up for their day trips. That had been her yesterday, and if she hadn't tagged onto that particular queue…

He showed her where to sit back and relax as he started up the engine and they pulled out into the open water. The breeze felt wonderfully cool on Jane's skin, and she closed her eyes, lifting her face to the sun.

When she opened them again she found Xavier staring at her from behind the wheel, shades on his head. He didn't look away. The gleam in his eyes was explicit, and Jane's pulse started to speed up and throb through her veins. That kiss last night came back in vivid Technicolor, the feel of his chest against hers… She was the one to break contact first, putting on her sunglasses again. His mouth quirked in a mocking smile, the same one he had smiled in the street, aware of his effect. She tried not to let it unsettle her.

Leaving the harbour and marina behind, Xavier hugged the coast for a while. Jane was enthralled by the view of all the huge estates visible from their vantage point. They couldn't really talk over the sound of the engine, but she was happy to drink in the sight of him when she was sure she couldn't be caught. She'd never been reduced to this level of carnal feeling before. Didn't know how to handle it.

She could see a small cove come into view, and Xavier negotiated the boat towards it. It looked empty. She was bizarrely both disappointed and excited not to have company, but if she was honest with herself she knew which feeling won out.

When he had anchored a short way from the shore he indicated the cabin below. 'Why don't you change into your swimsuit here? That way you can leave your things on board.'

'Sure.' Jane feigned a nonchalance that she was far from feeling.

Down below in the small cabin, she changed with awkward haste, half terrified that he'd come down the ladder. Her bikini had felt perfectly adequate up until today, but now she pulled at it ineffectually and tried to stretch it out. Had it shrunk? Somehow it felt as if it had become the skimpiest two-piece on earth since she had last worn it, and she was very conscious of her skin, still pale despite a slight tan. She chastised herself. He was no doubt used to seeing women baring a lot more, especially in this part of the world.

When she emerged from the cabin her skin was still gleaming from an application of suncream. Xavier's breath stopped in his throat as she was revealed bit by bit. Like a lust-controlled youth, he couldn't take his eyes off her chest, full and generous, yet perfectly shaped. She had tied a sarong around hips that flared out gently from a small waist. She looked shy and uncertain, as if she couldn't bring herself to meet his eyes, which were hidden behind his dark lenses. Unbidden, and as swift as his physical response, came a desire to reassure and protect. Alien and unwelcome emotions when it came to him and women. Especially ones he'd known for less than forty-eight hours.

He masked it speaking more brusquely than he'd intended. 'The water should only be waist-deep here, so you can wade ashore.'

He had to stop himself staring when she took off her sarong to reveal a curvy bottom and those never-ending legs… Her self-consciousness was at odds with her body. A body made for pleasure. *His* pleasure.

When Jane hit the water she welcomed the distraction from the fever racing in her blood. Tried to block out the potent image of the man leaning over the edge.

'OK?'

'Yes…fine.'

She half-swam, half-waded to the shore, grateful for the moment to herself. However impressive she had thought his physique while under clothes, it hadn't prepared her for seeing him half naked. He should come with a health warning. He was the most perfect man she had ever seen. She'd tried to avoid looking, but it was impossible not to take in that expanse of bare, toned, exquisitely muscled chest. A light smattering of dark hair led down in a silky line to where his shorts… She gulped as she rested on the sand.

He was wading towards her, with the hamper held aloft in his arms, dark hair gleaming wetly against his head. Strong-muscled legs strode out of the water towards her. She had spread her sarong out on the sand, and was glad of the need for sunglasses and the protection, however slight, they afforded her. She brought her knees up to her chest, wrapping her arms around them in another unconscious gesture of protection.

To her relief, he was businesslike. Coming to rest beside her on the sand, he opened up the basket, taking out a light blanket. He spread it out and started to take out a mouthwatering array of food. Olives, bread, cheese, houmous…sliced ham, chicken wings, pâté.

'There's enough food here to feed an army.'

'Well, I don't know about you, but I'm starving.'

'I wouldn't know where to start.'

'Why don't we start here?' he said, uncorking a bottle of champagne that came in its own encasing to ensure it stayed chilled. He filled two glasses and handed one to her.

'To…meeting you.'

'To meeting you.' She echoed his words, not sure what to say.

A funny feeling lodged in her chest as she took a sip, the bubbles tickling her nostrils. As he busied himself preparing her a selection of food to pick from on a plate, she couldn't help but shake the feeling that this was all a little too smooth…practiced, even—as if he had done it a thousand times before.

'Do you come here often?' she asked lightly, trying to make it sound like a joke.

He stopped what he was doing and looked at her sharply. 'Do you mean have I brought women here before? Then the answer is yes.'

She was taken aback by his honesty. He hadn't tried to temper his words, or make her feel better. Somehow it comforted her. Although the thought of being the latest in a long line of undoubtedly more beautiful women caused some dark emotion to threaten her equilibrium, which she was barely clinging on to as it was.

'I can tell you, though, that it hasn't been for some time. And there probably haven't been half as many as you seem to be imagining. I've come here since my teens, and it's a favourite hang-out for friends of both sexes…not some place purely to seduce women.'

'Oh…well, of course. I never thought for a second—'

'Yes, you did—but I suppose I can't blame you.'

A blush crept up over her face and she turned her attention to the food, hoping to distract him and get off the subject. She could envisage a neon sign above her head with an arrow pointing downwards saying—*Gauche!*

She crossed her legs and helped him to put out the food.

If anything had ever helped her to take her mind off things then it was food. She tucked in healthily. After the first few mouthfuls she looked up to find him staring.

'What?' She wiped her mouth with a napkin. 'Have I got some food somewhere?'

He shook his head, taking his glasses off. 'I don't think I've ever seen a woman eat the way you do. You look like you could keep going until everything is gone.'

She smiled wryly. 'My appetite is legendary, I'm afraid. You've probably met your match. I've never been a delicate eater…'

He nodded towards her. 'Keep going, please—I'm enjoying the novelty of watching a woman relish her food.'

Suddenly self-conscious, she took a sip of champagne to wet her throat and forced herself to keep eating as nonchalantly as possible. But now his attention was focused on her it was impossible. He seemed to be fixated by her mouth. She swallowed a piece of cheese with difficulty.

'The history of your island seems fascinating…what I read of it in the exhibit space. Has your family really been there for centuries?'

Thankfully he finally took his gaze away. 'Yes. They were given the island as a gift by the French royal family in the twelfth century. We originally came from Aragon, in Spain. The royals in the north wanted to establish allies in the south. We took the name of the island and added it to Salgado… hence my name today.'

'And are there many in your family now?'

His voice was curiously unemotional. 'No, just me left… Hard to believe that the line could very well die out with me. I was the first born, and my mother passed away when I was five…my father never married again, and he died when I was in my early twenties.'

Jane pushed her glasses up onto her head, her eyes wide and sympathetic. 'I'm sorry…he must have loved her a great deal…and to lose both parents so young… My father died when I was small too—a baby. But at least I still have my mother.'

Xavier looked into her eyes and felt an unfamiliar sensation, almost like losing his footing. How had they got onto this subject?

She gazed out to the sea and shook her head.

'I just remembered what I read about the earthquake…it must have affected your family?'

He followed her look. 'Yes, it did…all of them perished apart from my great-grandparents…not to mention many of the islanders. Whole families were wiped out.'

'That's awful. It must have taken generations to begin to forget, rebuild lives…'

He nodded. 'We built a commemorative grotto to their memory on the island some years ago. There are hundreds of names inscribed.'

She turned shining eyes on him, stunning him again momentarily. 'That sounds like a lovely thing to do. I wish I'd seen it…how come the tour didn't go there?'

He shrugged. 'It's small, and wouldn't mean much to anyone else. It's a very personal space for the islanders.'

He regarded her profile. 'If you want you could come back there with me tomorrow and I'll show it to you.'

'Would you really?'

She couldn't control the surge of excitement that took hold at the thought of seeing him again the next day.

He nodded. They didn't speak for a few moments, and then he started to pack away some food but refilled her glass. He avoided her eye.

'I'm going for a quick swim, but you should let your food settle for a while.'

She had to smile inwardly at his arrogant assumption that he was somehow immune to cramp after eating. Which, she had to admit as she watched his powerful back and legs walk away from her, he probably was. Immune to banal mortal complaints.

She lay back on her sarong, feeling deliciously relaxed and replete. The sky was hazy, the sun blissfully not beating down with full force. The lapping of the waves lulled her into a light sleep.

A while later she woke with a start… She looked to her side, to see Xavier stretched out beside her. The basket was gone and there was nothing between them. His eyes were closed, lashes long and dark against high cheekbones. He really was beautiful.

'Do I pass inspection again?' he asked, opening one eye, fixing her.

She sat up quickly to hide her mortification. 'I think I'll go for a swim now…'

'I'll join you.' And with lithe grace he stood up beside her and held out a hand. She looked at it warily for a moment before taking it.

The initial cool of the waves lapping against her feet woke her up better than a pail of water over her head.

She extricated her hand from his, and once in far enough dived headlong into the first big wave, swimming underwater for as long as her breath held out.

She popped up to the surface some way off and shook her head. The sun glinting off the water was dazzling. She looked around and could see Xavier's sleek head, arms gracefully scissoring through the water as he swam powerfully towards her. She trod water, breathing far more heavily than was normal after what she had just done.

He came within a couple of feet of her. They just looked at each other. Simultaneously his arms reached for her, and she felt herself gravitate towards him as if being pulled by a magnetic force until she was in his arms. It felt completely right…inevitable.

He brought her arms around his neck and instinctively she wrapped her legs around his waist to steady herself. She was out of her depth…in more ways than one.

Seduced by the place, by him, and her resolve to embrace the moment, she gave in to a powerful desire. Slowly she dipped her head towards his, eyes closing as she felt the hard, sensual contours of his lips. His arms were like a steel band around her waist.

With naive boldness she explored his lips, feeling their shape and texture. One of his hands moved up to the back of her head and he angled it, his tongue sliding between her lips to taste and explore. Hesitantly she allowed him access.

A molten urgent feeling was building between her legs, the centre of her desire. She could feel the friction against his chest, and just below her bottom she could feel a hard ridge. Realizing what it was made her gasp.

He tore his lips from hers and looked down. Her nipples were two hard points thrusting against the wet material of her bikini.

He brought smoky green eyes up to hers and shifted her subtly, so that now he carried her in his arms and out of the water.

Jane knew that if he had put her down her legs would have given way, and was thankful he didn't as he walked up the beach and laid her down on the sarong, stretching out his long length beside her. He looked down her body, a hand resting possessively on her stomach, its gentle feminine swell.

'So beautiful…'

'So are you,' she said shyly.

The sun was blocked as his head dipped again to take her mouth, slowly, languorously. As if they had all the time in the world to touch, explore. She arched herself towards him slightly, a hand reaching out blindly to rest against his chest, revelling in the feel of the surprisingly silky hair, finding a hard nipple, circling it experimentally before flicking it accidentally with a nail.

He tore his mouth away with a moan. 'Let's see how *you* like that.'

Before she could question what he was doing, he had lowered his mouth to one jutting peak, sucking through the wet material of her top. An exquisite burst of pleasure made her cry out. He was relentless, and she gasped when he finally pulled the material aside to reveal the dark peak, raw and aroused. The feel of his tongue on her bare skin made her almost pass out with pleasure, and then he moved to the other side.

Jane barely recognised this wanton version of herself. Her hands tangled in his hair, holding his head in case he might pull away. She was caught up…caught up in uncharted territory…powerless to do anything but feel…respond.

She could feel him drifting a hand down over her belly, to rest near the top of her briefs. Toying with her, moving in slow sensuous circles, before his fingers moved down…under the elastic, over the mound of soft hair…down further, until…

She held her breath, her body tensing as his fingers dipped into her most secret place, exploring, rubbing back and forth over the most sensitive part, which she could feel getting slicker, harder. It was too much. No one had ever touched her there.

Her legs came together, trapping his hand, but he gently manoeuvred them apart again.

A very strident child-like squeal made them both tense.

In a haze of pleasure that was fast receding Jane became aware of Xavier reacting quicker than her, adjusting her bikini back over her body, which felt acutely sensitised.

'We have company…pity,' he drawled, making sure she was decent again, and then he looked down into her shocked eyes.

Sure enough another boat was pulling into the small cove, and a gang of children were starting to jump down from a yacht into the water, splashing and swimming towards the beach. Thankfully they were far enough out not to have seen anything…she hoped.

She wanted the sand to rise up around her and suck her

down. A mortified flush burned her skin as she thought of what would have happened if they hadn't arrived. He must think her so…easy. Bring her to a deserted stretch of beach, ply her with a little champagne and food, and she was a possessed woman in his arms, with little or no encouragement. The worst cliché of a tourist looking for a quick holiday fling.

She thrust herself away from him and sat up, gathering her sarong around her waist and tying it in a knot.

'This has been…lovely…but we probably should be getting back. I'm sure you have lots of important things to be doing.'

She couldn't even look at him. She stood up awkwardly and a soft gasp escaped her lips as she felt him whirl her around to face him. She couldn't escape his eyes, which probed far deeper than the surface. They were oblivious to the people arriving onto the beach only feet away from them.

'Lovely…?' He shook his head incredulously. 'Correct me if I'm wrong, but if we hadn't been interrupted, right about now I think you would be fast approaching a climax.'

She blanched at the starkness of his words.

'*Lovely* is a little bit of an understatement, don't you think, for what two people seem to be able to ignite in each other within seconds or with just a look?'

'I…I…well, maybe…'

His eyes were hypnotic. 'The most important thing on my mind at the moment is exploring this attraction between us.'

'It is?'

'Yes.'

'Look…Xavier…we hardly know each other, and I'm not normally—'

'So responsive? Well, neither am I.' His voice sounded harsh.

She had been about to say *easy*, and amended her words. 'That is…I mean…I want you to know that it wasn't my intention to come here just for some kind of holiday…thing.'

He moved her closer to him, looping deceptively loose

arms around her waist, ignoring the chatter around them. She came in contact with the still semi-hard evidence of his arousal. Immediately an answering liquid heat pooled in her groin.

'And, contrary to what you may think, I'm not in the habit of pursuing random tourists…I'm not sure what this is either, but don't you think it might be fun to explore?'

Fun. Explore. The words resounded in her head.

He stepped back, putting her away from him gently. 'I'll take you back now, but I have a proposition…' He trailed a long finger down one cheek. 'I promised to bring you to the island tomorrow to show you the memorial.'

He lifted a brow as if to ask if she still wanted to do that.

She felt herself nodding slowly, trying to focus just on his words, not on the finger caressing her heated skin.

'I'd like you to come and stay there as my guest for the rest of the week… We could get to know one another… explore this…attraction.' His finger left her cheek. 'It's up to you.'

He looked at her for a long moment, before shading his eyes again with the dark glasses and starting back towards the boat. He hadn't meant to ask her to stay, the words had surprised him, but now, having asked, it felt right. One thing was for sure. An afternoon picnic wasn't enough.

A few seconds later Jane followed blindly, her mind churning furiously. She would never see him again after this week. She would have it to hug to herself for ever. What did she have to lose? Could she really be contemplating this? Could she indulge the fantasy?

They were silent on the boat back, and during the car journey up to the villa. He was detached and polite. At her front door they looked at one another for the first time since they had left the beach. He tipped up her face with a finger under her chin.

'So, Jane Vaughan…I'll be here to pick you up at ten a.m. It can be a simple day trip to see the grotto, or you can come and stay for the next few days… Like I said, the choice is yours.'

And then he was in his car, the purring sound of the engine growing fainter before she drew in another breath, still looking at the spot where he had stood. She knew without a doubt that he would let her go at the end of the next day if she so desired. He was far too proud to push her. It was, as he'd said, up to her.

She mechanically went into the house, and before she knew what she was doing she realised that she was packing her things, tidying up in readiness to leave for a few days. Her body was ahead of her brain. She sat on the couch in the living room, an excited, nervous, shivery feeling in her belly.

Be careful what you wish for because you just might get it. The words popped into her head. Well, this was what she had wished for, wasn't it? The start of something new. Letting go of the old reliable, sensible, mature Jane. It was time for her to have some fun for a change. And when someone like Xavier Salgado-Lézille wanted you…then surely it went against the flow of the universe to say no? She was being offered a taste of something that she knew many women would not hesitate for a second to experience.

The only thing was…she had a sneaking suspicion that more than her body was in danger of falling under his spell. Was it a risk she was prepared to take? A resounding voice in her head said *yes*. Throw caution to the wind. She caught sight of her reflection in a mirror. I mean really, she asked herself, how involved could she get in one week? She turned away before she could see the mocking glint in her eye.

CHAPTER FOUR

BY NINE forty-five the next morning Jane was having second, third and fourth thoughts. In the cold light of day things were more stark. She would get burned. And not from the sun. She knew it. She heard an engine outside. He was early. As if he could hear the doubts that were in her private thoughts. Which was ridiculous.

She took a deep breath and waited for the doorbell to sound. She was wearing simple shorts, flip-flops and a plain T-shirt. If he wanted her then he could have her as she was, unadorned.

She lifted the small weekend bag that she had brought to carry home gifts, and suddenly it felt as if it held rocks instead of clothes and toiletries for the next few days.

The doorbell rang. Her heart stopped. She could see his tall dark shape against the glass. The Prince of Darkness. The name made her shiver.

When she opened the door his sharp eyes took in her slender figure in the plain clothes, and the bag clutched in one hand with her knuckles showing white. Instinctively he schooled his features, not allowing the surge of triumph he felt to show on his face. For once in his life he actually hadn't been sure which way a woman was going to react, and had been prepared for her to reject his offer. But the bag told him that she was saying yes. He needed to tread carefully. She was as skittish as a colt. He bent to take the bag from her grip, and left her to lock up.

Jane had sent a text to Lisa that morning, wishing her all the best for her dad's operation and saying she was taking a small trip. Just in case Lisa rang and got no answer from the house. She wasn't going to go into any details about Xavier yet. If her friend thought for a second there was a man in the picture she'd be like a dog with a bone.

And, as Jane could barely quantify to herself what was happening, she could hardly begin to explain herself to someone else.

By the time they reached the island, and Xavier had guided her to a waiting Jeep, she had pushed any last dissenting voices out of her head. He was being a complete gentleman. Charming, funny, insightful. She hadn't felt this kind of connection with anyone before—almost as though they'd known each other for years.

A couple of times when they'd locked eyes the heat had flared, swift and intense, reminding her of what was not so far from the surface.

He paused in the Jeep, turning towards her in his seat. 'We'll have to go to my home first…an unavoidable conference call I need to take. My penance for taking some time off…I'm sorry.'

'That's OK…I don't mind.'

'So, what I was going to suggest was this…as it's nearly lunch, why don't we eat, you can get settled, and we see the memorial tomorrow?'

This was it. Even though he was assuming that she wanted to stay, he was giving her the opportunity to back out now. But she didn't want to. She had to take the chance, knowing that in her acceptance, should she choose it, he would read her total acquiescence. She took a deep breath, feeling as though she were stepping over an invisible line drawn in the sand.

'All right. That sounds good.'

He looked at her for a long moment before leaning over and placing a feather-light kiss on her lips. 'It will be, Jane…are you sure?'

She looked at him steadily. 'Yes, I'm sure.'

With a spurt of dry earth, he turned the Jeep towards the castle in the distance. After they came to a stop in the courtyard outside, Jane couldn't hide her reaction. It didn't look like a castle, in the sense of turrets and moats. It had two higher wings on either side, huge, imposing archways, and intricate carvings on every stone. She had never seen anything like it before.

'It's amazing… Sorry—I'm sure you get that all the time. But really it is beautiful.'

Xavier had stepped out of the Jeep and looked up, hands on hips. 'Yes, I guess it is…the Moorish influence probably makes it a little less austere.'

'I thought that was what it was, when I saw it from the distance the other day, but I wasn't sure.'

He lifted out her bag and took her hand, leading her into a huge open-plan flagstoned hall covered in complicated mosaics. Numerous green plants stood against the walls, and the open spaces were light-filled and indescribably foreign and exotic. Tall pillars led to an inner roofless courtyard.

Jane looked around in awe, taking it all in. She could almost imagine an ancestor of Xavier's reclining darkly on a divan, voluminous folds of silk covering his body, being attended to by lustrous haired beauties. She blushed at her imagination. Xavier reached out a finger and trailed it down her cheek, leaving a line of fire in its wake.

'You blush so easily…a rare phenomenon these days.'

'An embarrassing one, you mean…it tends to come at the most awkward moments, when the last thing I want is for someone to guess I might be unnerved.'

'And are you…unnerved…here, now, with me?'

'Well…a little.'

'Your honesty is refreshing. How have you managed not to lose it yet?'

'That's a very cynical thing to say.'

'I've come to learn it's a very cynical world we live in…but you might prove me wrong.'

Her eyes widened, a vulnerable light in their depths. That and any other thought flew from her mind as his large body closed the distance between them and he claimed her mouth with a kiss full of pent-up passion, his hands moving over her back. She found herself responding, instinctively matching his passion with her own.

Before she knew what was what, she felt herself being lifted into strong arms, and hers automatically went around his neck as he walked back into the hall and up some stairs which were obscured behind material moving gently in the breeze.

She took in an upper level, corridors, more open spaces, before Xavier shouldered his way through an imposing oak door and into a vast room, with a huge king-size bed in the centre. She barely had time to take in the rest of the room before he put her on her feet. Sudden panic gripped her. This was happening too quickly. She backed away, breath coming hard and fast.

'Wait…do you think we could just…take things slowly for now?'

He stood back from her and ran a hand through his hair. When he saw the look on her face he said quickly, 'I never planned on dragging you up here like some teenager…I just lost control…which seems to happen more and more frequently since I saw you.'

He gave her a rueful smile. He held out a hand and she took it.

'Come on. Let's have some lunch, and I promise not to manhandle you again.'

'That's OK. It's not that I don't *want* to be manhandled by you. I'm sure that'd be perfectly nice—'

'Jane.'

'Yes?'

'Stop talking. It's fine, you don't have to say anything.'

'OK.'

He paused at a door almost opposite his bedroom, opening it to reveal another equally stunning room.

'This is your room. I'll bring your bag up after we've eaten and you can get settled.' He turned towards her. 'I'm sorry again, Jane. Believe me, I didn't just assume that because you're staying falling into my bed is a foregone conclusion, but I won't lie to you...I want you. I'm perfectly happy for us to take it slowly, get to know each other...I'll wait until you're ready'

Her heart flipped over. Danger. She looked up into his eyes, feeling a drowning sensation, 'Thank you...'

He needed the space as much as she did. The truth was that he had never before felt such an overwhelming urge to take a woman to his bed... His plan, as he had told her, had been that they would have lunch, get to know one another a little better, have dinner in the evening and then...who knew? But within mere minutes of coming in the front door he had been overtaken by his hormones.

People called him the Prince of Darkness. Because in business he was ruthless and brilliant—even cold, some would say, but always fair. He had that necessary detachment. It was the same with women. He was the one in control. Always. Without exception. Until now.

Jane sat back a while later, in her chair at the lunch table Xavier had set up in the inner courtyard. He had made a light meal of gazpacho soup with a summer salad and crusty bread, all washed down with a crisp white wine.

'That was delicious...I don't think I've eaten as well in months.'

'Like I said yesterday, it's a pleasure to see a woman enjoy her food, and I like cooking.'

'You'd better be careful or you might be rolling me out of here in a few days.'

She smiled easily, but the words reminded her that this *was* only for a few days. A mere interlude. Xavier would never remember someone like her when this was over. He would be moving on to the next exquisite beauty. Someone much more his equal, in every way.

'You have such an expressive face…'

She groaned with a lightness she suddenly didn't feel. 'That along with the blushing…it must be an intoxicating mix for someone used to a more sophist—'

He shook his head, cutting her off. 'Don't even say it…you have more innate grace in you than half the people I deal with every day.'

'Th…thank you.' Her tongue felt heavy in her mouth. She wasn't used to compliments. Wanting to change to subject, she asked, 'Do you have any staff? Surely you can't look after this place by yourself.'

'Yes, I do but they're on a few days' break.'

She couldn't help a silly flutter of fear.

Xavier read the look on her face effortlessly. 'They go on holiday this time every year. It's pure coincidence that it happens to be this week.'

'Oh…of course.'

The fact that he seemed to be able to read her better than anyone she knew made the flutter come back. That was nearly more disturbing than the thought of being alone with him in this huge castle.

'Come on, I'll show you around.'

He stood and held out a hand again, and she found herself taking it without thinking.

Every corner they turned made her exclaim anew. It was full of nooks and crannies, and secret courtyards overflowing with plants and eclectic furniture. She could imagine it being a children's paradise…and immediately stopped her wayward mind. What on earth had made her think of that?

He brought her to a swimming pool at the back. It was surrounded by trees and flowering bushes, in idyllic seclusion from the rest of the house.

'Why don't you go for a swim and relax for a bit? I've got that call to take.'

'OK…why not? If I can ever find my way back here.'

'There are cabins just behind the trees.' He indicated to the other side of the pool. 'Help yourself to a bathing suit and towels; there are robes as well.'

She should have guessed.

She chose a modest one-piece in dark blue, and went back to the pool to choose a lounger. After a quick dip and drying off she succumbed to the peace, which was broken only by the sound of birds and crickets.

A couple of hours later there was still no sign of him, and Jane felt she wanted to wash and get rid of the stickiness of the day. She gathered up her things and tied a robe securely around herself, wandering back through the house until she eventually found the stairs. She whirled around at the sound of a door opening. Xavier stood framed in the doorway. She could see a vast room behind him, with all manner of hi-tech office equipment.

'I'm sorry, but I'm still caught up with this call… Make yourself at home. I shouldn't be much longer.'

'Oh, don't worry about me,' Jane declared airily.

Up in the bedroom, she found her bag and padded barefoot to the *en suite* bathroom. She looked at the huge bath. The bath of her dreams. Filling it almost to the top, and adding copious amounts of the oils and scents that she'd found in a cupboard, she sank blissfully into the bubbles. Along with food, baths were her only other fatal weakness. This one was so huge she could have almost done a length.

But before she could turn into a prune—or, more disturbingly, have Xavier come looking for her—she stepped out. She smoothed on some body lotion and wrapped a towel around herself. Despite it being her own room, she went out cautiously. She couldn't hear any sounds…he must be busy still.

She caught sight of her reflection in a mirror and stopped for a second. She nearly didn't recognise herself. Skin glowing a light golden, her hair drifting around her face in waves, softening the harsh bob it had been when she'd first got it cut. Her eyes shone and sparkled, and her cheeks were flushed rosy from the bath.

In the mirror behind her a figure materialised in the doorway. Her eyes lifted, and she froze and watched as Xavier crossed the room to stand behind her.

Their eyes met in the mirror. There was only the sound of their breathing in the room. His hands were on her shoulders, dark against her skin. She watched, barely able to breathe, as they moved down her arms. She brought her eyes back up to his. Her whole body seemed to be pulsating in time with her heart, goosebumps making her skin prickle in anticipation. Right at that moment she wanted nothing more than for him to read her mind, undo her towel, let it drop to the floor, baring her to his gaze. She wanted him to take her breasts in his dark hands, weigh them, feel their heaviness, she wanted him to take off his clothes so she could lean back against the naked length of him…

But he didn't. His hands came up to her shoulders and rested there heavily.

'I'm sorry it took so long… When you're dressed come back downstairs and I'll cook us some dinner.'

She nodded at his reflection in the mirror, wordlessly watched as he stepped back and away. Thank God he *couldn't* read her mind, she thought shakily as he disappeared. Talk about waking a hitherto dormant sexual desire. Where had those images come from?

She went to close the door and whisked off the towel abruptly, studiously avoiding her own reflection again. In the space of a few hours she had morphed from shrinking virgin to mentally stripping him…but he was taking her at her word, holding back, letting her get comfortable. Well, she'd asked for it. She just hoped that he would take the initiative again, before she had to drum up the courage to let him know that she was ready!

A while later Jane sipped from a glass of deep red wine in the open-plan kitchen as she watched Xavier prepare a simple pasta dish. He was dressed casually, in jeans and a loose shirt, and she was equally casual, in a loose pair of linen trousers and a crossover short-sleeved top. She enjoyed watching him move dexterously around the kitchen.

'Where did you learn to cook?'

He glanced up briefly. 'In my teens I rebelled against the role my father wanted me to take up in the family business—namely the island—and ran away to the flight school on the mainland…I worked as a cook in a restaurant to help pay my way.'

'That's why you took part in the display?'

'Yes…I allow the pilots to do it here every year. Since my father died, we've incorporated it into a summer fête. It's a day out for everyone, and it's good for morale—and it allows me to indulge my love for flying.'

Jane had to suppress a slight shudder when she remembered his death-defying stunts.

'You were better then any of the others…you had some edge that they don't.'

He looked at her, but instead of finding a look of false flattery on her face saw she was busily picking at a salad. She had merely stated a fact.

'Thank you… I do miss it, but it was never going to be my destiny. Once my father died, I had to come back and take over the reins here. It used to be just the vineyard, but I developed abroad into the hotel chain and various other investments…mainly property.'

'Did you see your father before he died?' she asked softly.

'No.' It was curt, and Jane knew she'd hit a nerve. She deflected his attention.

'Well, this all looks more than fabulous—if that's possible. You'll have to let me cook for you, maybe tomorrow…'

He placed a swift kiss on her lips. 'For now, I'm quite happy to cook and enjoy watching you eat.'

For a moment he seemed as shocked as she was at the impulsive kiss that had come so naturally, but he recovered himself quickly.

Jane coloured as he had known she would. How was it that he felt as though he could read her like a book?

They sat out on a veranda at the back of the house. Soft jazz was coming from a speaker that was artfully hidden. Low lights from the house and candles illuminated the scene outside. Steps led down to a beautifully manicured lawn, teeming with exotic flowers. A clear sky glittered with stars and a full moon hung low in the horizon. It was magical.

The conversation flowed as Jane told him about her mother, the marriage, her job…her life. Instead of a glazed look of boredom passing over his face, as she had feared, he seemed genuinely interested.

He cradled his glass of wine. 'It's a strange connection to have…'

When she lifted a quizzical brow he elaborated.

'You growing up without a father, me without a mother.'

Jane nodded and shrugged lightly. 'I know…I wish I'd known him. But you can't really miss what you never had. I think for years Mum immortalised him as the perfect husband, but the truth was that he left us with nothing, and that…that was hard.'

'The truth usually is…'

She was surprised by the bleak look that crossed his face but then it was gone.

He leant forward to top up her glass of wine. 'Enough of this maudlin talk…'

He deftly changed the subject and she found herself forgetting about his enigmatic look as he effortlessly charmed her. After they had exhausted several topics, she couldn't remember when she had enjoyed talking to anyone as much. When she could forget for a moment the intense attraction that was always humming between them…

Later, when he stood and held out a hand to lead her inside, she took it easily. She followed him upstairs to her bedroom door. In the moonlit hallway she could just make out his eyes, feeling them rove over her face. Surely he would…?

She wanted him to take her, mould her to him, kiss her senseless. Her hands itched to pull his head down to hers. But she was too shy to show him. He bent his head and pressed a friendly kiss to her forehead…she felt a crushing disappointment.

'Goodnight, sweet Jane… I'll see you in the morning.' And he firmly turned her towards the bedroom and pushed her gently in.

Hours later Jane lay in sheets that were a tangled mess around her overheated body. Overheated because of all the images that wouldn't abate. Because of the knowledge that that man was mere feet away, probably naked, just lying there… All she had to do was get up, walk over…

She veered between just about getting up and sinking back into the pillows. At one point she cursed him. He probably knew exactly what he was doing, was so tuned in to the female psyche that this was a tried and tested technique… He was probably sleeping like a baby. As the first fingers of dawn crept into the sky she gave up and admitted defeat. She was a coward. Tomorrow, after all, was another day. And it was her own fault. She finally fell into a deep, dreamless sleep of exhaustion.

* * *

Jane woke to a gentle prodding, opening up one eye to see a cleanshaven and impeccable Xavier looking down at her. Both eyes snapped open.

'What time is it?'

'Almost midday…couldn't you sleep last night?'

She eyed him suspiciously from under her lashes, was that a mocking smile? She as good as had *sexual frustration* tattooed on her forehead.

'Fine, thank you, actually…and you?' she asked sweetly, making sure the sheet was pulled all the way up to her neck. Did he *have* to stand so close to the bed?

'Oh…like the proverbial log. I've made a picnic. There's a nice route we can take on the boat to get around to the memorial. We can take a gentle hike up to see it. It's a little more demanding, but ultimately rewarding.'

With a glint in his eye and his lip twitching he took his leave to let her get ready, before she could make a smart comeback to his none too subtle *double entendre*.

Gentle hike…? Some gentle hike, she thought about two hours later, when her legs were aching and sweat was running in rivulets down her brow, between her breasts and down her back. Her shorts and vest clung to her body like an indecent second skin, and all she could do was focus on Xavier's feet ahead of her, making sure to take exactly the same steps as him.

They had come around to the other end of the island, with Xavier pointing out landmarks, interesting birds and fauna along the way. There was so much more than she had seen at first. It was vibrant with the colour of thousands of wild flowers, cared for laboriously by the islanders who grew them to sell on the mainland.

They had docked the boat at a small cove, not dissimilar to the one he had taken her to the other day. He'd pointed up at what looked a perilously long way away to an overhanging rock. She hadn't been able to see the memorial, but he'd assured her that it was up there.

They had left their picnic in the shade on the beach, and now she was following Xavier up the hill, which was fast becoming her personal Everest.

Finally, just when she was about to beg for a break, his feet disappeared. She lifted her head to see his outstretched hand and took it gratefully, allowing him to haul her up the last couple of feet. He didn't let go of her hand, waiting until she had her breath under control, but the view was threatening to take it away again. They had emerged at the highest point of the island, the southernmost tip, and falling away from them and to the north they could see everything…the mainland shimmering faintly in the distance and the castle a small speck up at the other tip.

'This is…words fail me,' she breathed when she had enough to spare.

'I know…it's beautiful, isn't it?'

'Beautiful doesn't do it justice. It's epic…and it's yours.' She shook her head. 'How must it feel to come up here and know that all you survey is yours and yours alone?'

'Not everything…'

She turned her head to see him looking at her. Words crammed her mouth, wanting to come out, but she couldn't say them. She was tongue-tied, wanting to make some flip comment…but it just wasn't her.

He drew her attention to the grotto-like shrine a few feet to their left. It was a simple altar, with some candles, and vases with flowers that looked a few days old. It was sheltered on three sides by walls and a roof, facing out to the sea. She felt immeasurably honoured to be shown this special place. She took the small backpack off her shoulders and reached in, pulling out some flowers she had picked on their way up the hill, placing them in one of the vases. Around at the back, Xavier pointed out where the names were inscribed in clear and simple black paint.

'Thank you for showing me this…it's very special.' Her voice was husky.

'My pleasure.'

He made sure she drank some water, and after a few minutes of companionable silence he took her hand again and started to lead her back down the rocky path.

When they reached the beach Jane saw the water glinting and shimmering, and it was the best thing she'd ever seen. She tore off her shorts and vest, thankful that she had thought to put her bikini on before they left, and ran into the water, relishing the first cool sting and freshness over her sticky body.

Xavier did the same, and she squealed with delight when he emerged from underneath the water only inches away, pulling her down playfully. She silently urged him to kiss her, as he had done that first day, but he was still being the consummate gentleman—much to her growing frustration.

When they were cooled down, he led her back to the beach and spread out a delicious feast. Jane relaxed back and watched him talk…not even hearing his words. She couldn't remember a time when she had felt so full of delighted expectation. She was aware of every part of him—his hands, his mouth, legs…that chest. She was burning up just thinking about touching him, having him touch her. Her skin itched to be next to his. She wanted to reach over, stop his mouth with hers, run her hands over his muscles. But she didn't.

It was as if there was a silent communication going on between them on a subliminal level:

Come on, touch me if you dare…you're the one who wanted to go slowly…

I know! I just don't know what to do…how to make the move.

The atmosphere that surrounded them was thick with it.

That evening her skin felt hot after the sun…or else her imagination was just keeping it overheated. In bare feet and a plain shift dress, she padded down to the kitchen where she could hear Xavier making dinner. She paused at the door, drinking him in as he worked. He wore a white T-shirt and faded jeans, feet bare like hers. His hair was still wet from the shower, like hers, and a crisp fresh scent intoxicated her nostrils as he moved. He looked up then, and caught her staring. She didn't even blush…she was beyond that…just smiled.

His eyes boldly appraised her as she came towards him. She was completely unconscious of the provocatively innocent sway to her hips. He poured her a glass of wine and lifted his to hers. They clinked glasses.

'*À nous.*'

She nodded jerkily in response.

All through dinner they talked, but it had a hushed, frantic quality. A breathless anticipation was building in Jane's belly.

When he stood to take her hand under the stars at the end of the evening she was trembling, unable to speak. They stopped once again outside her door. She turned her face up to his. Wordlessly she tried to communicate with him. Couldn't he tell? Surely he had to know how ready she was? She watched as he brought her hand to his mouth and pressed a kiss to the delicate underside of her wrist. She closed her eyes and felt a weakening in her body, her blood slowing to a deep throbbing pulse.

'Goodnight, Jane. Sleep tight.'

CHAPTER FIVE

GOODNIGHT, Jane…Sleep tight?

Her eyes flew open. *No!* her mind screamed…he had let her hand go. A dark, bottomless pit threatened to suck her down. She had to do something. But even as she thought this, she could feel herself turning away, sudden doubts assailing her. Maybe he didn't find her attractive any more? Maybe he was regretting having asked her to stay? Surely he would have tried to make love to her again?

Then she stopped. She realised that she hadn't heard him move behind her. She turned around slowly and saw his face. It told her everything she needed to know. Raw masculine arousal was stamped into every line. She felt every cell in her body jump in response.

'Xavier—' Her words were stopped as he hauled her into his arms. The relief made her dizzy as she locked her arms around his neck.

'I swear if you had gone into that room I was going to come after you, ready or not…'

'Thank God…because I nearly did…'

'I couldn't have spent another night in that bed, knowing you were only feet away.'

'I nearly went to you last night, but couldn't work up the nerve…'

'What? Do you know how hard it's been for me to keep from touching you all day?'

He groaned and bent his head to hers, finding and taking her lips, tasting them as if they were succulent fruits. His control was fast slipping as his hands smoothed down her back, down to her buttocks, moulding their peachy firmness, cupping them and drawing her up into the cradle of his lap, where he felt her gasp against his mouth when she felt his arousal.

In one graceful move he lifted her against his chest and kicked open his bedroom door, bringing her inside. He brought her over to the mirror, where he stood her in front of him. She looked at him in the reflection, a question on her face.

'This is what I thought of last night, the image that kept me awake.'

She felt his hands at the top of her dress, fingers grazing her skin as he slowly started to pull the zip down. Immediately she knew what he meant, and the thought of him imagining the same scenario made her knees weak.

She felt the slight night breeze on her skin, and shivered in reaction as he gently but firmly pulled the dress from her shoulders and down, past her breasts, past her waist, over the swell of her hips, until it hit the floor with a muted swish. Her bra quickly followed, and she was standing there naked but for a pair of very brief briefs. She brought her hands up to cover her breasts, feeling shy, but he came close behind her and brought them back down.

'Look at how beautiful you are.'

His head lowered and he pressed a hot kiss to where her neck and shoulder met, causing a shudder to run through her body…and then began to shed his own clothes behind her. She could hear the whisper of his T-shirt dropping to the floor, a button being snapped, jeans falling. An unbearable tightness began to build in her abdomen as she continued to watch through their reflection, until he stood behind her completely naked, his dark form a contrast to her much paler one.

Her head felt light. She watched in the mirror as his hands came around her to cup her breasts. They looked full and heavy in his palms. Her eyes widened as she saw her nipples growing harder, puckering, felt the ache that escaped as a guttural moan when his hands closed over them, her nipples caught between his fingers. She could feel his arousal against her bottom and instinctively moved back and leant against him, delighting in his own low moan.

He turned her to face him, bringing her into intimate contact with his whole length, taking her mouth with his. His hands were under her panties, slowly tugging them down until they fell at her feet.

She started to shake uncontrollably with reaction as he lifted her into his arms and walked over to the bed.

He gently laid her down, following her, leaning over her with strong arms. He bent to take her lips, the kiss starting out gentle, rapidly becoming more heated and passionate. Jane's hands stretched out blindly, searching for and finding his chest, his shoulders, smoothing, touching every part she could reach.

He groaned softly as her hands reached lower, coming dangerously close to his rock-hard erection. He couldn't remember ever being so aroused. He shifted to lie down beside her, lifting his head for a moment, watching her reaction as his fingertips closed over one nipple, how her back arched, her eyes closed and her breathing became fractured. Noticing how her skin had flushed to a dull red. He bent and took the jewel-hard peak into this mouth, his own control fast slipping as he suckled and nipped gently, first at one, then the other.

'Xavier… I can't… God!'

Her hands clutched at his shoulders, and her body writhed as he moved a hand down over her belly to feel how ready she was. The wetness he felt at the apex of her thighs almost pushed him over the edge, and he'd hardly touched her! Or she him…

As his hand explored, stroked, Jane felt herself bucking.

She'd had no idea it could be like this. Had had no expectation…certainly hadn't expected this hunger in her blood that was consuming her to the point where she was no longer herself. She had become…someone else? Or perhaps the person she was meant to be… All these incoherent fevered thoughts raced through her head at the same time.

Xavier's fingers were pushing her to a point of no return, his mouth was on hers, then on her breast. It was too much…her whole body stilled for a moment before she felt herself crashing over the edge and tumbling down, her body contracting and pulsating in the aftermath. His hand cupped her mound, waiting until her tremors had stopped. She looked up into his face, her eyes wide with shock… Words trembled on her lips, but then he claimed her mouth once more, with a hot, drugging kiss, and she felt him move over her body. He lifted his head, his eyes glittering in the half-light, pupils dilated with barely contained passion. She sucked in a breath of anticipation as she took in the daunting size of him, moisture beading at the tip.

His voice was hoarse with need and restraint. 'Jane…I can't wait.'

Moving instinctively, she nudged her hips up towards him, silently encouraging him. A sheen of light sweat covered their bodies. Slowly, so slowly, he started to enter her. Jane felt no pain. Her body seemed to recognise him and welcomed him in deeper and deeper.

'Oh…that feels so good.'

Was that low, husky voice hers?

When he drew out again she whimpered, until he thrust back in all the way. She wrapped her legs around his back, as if to draw him in even deeper, tighter. His strokes were long and hard and assured. She felt the anticipation build once again. After what seemed like an eternity of sensation, building and building until she thought she'd expire, his pace quickened and his movements became less controlled, as if he couldn't hold on. And she couldn't either.

She felt herself tense. Xavier was thrusting so deep that she bit her lips to stop from crying out at the exquisite pleasure of it… And then she came, fast and strong, only dimly registering Xavier's final thrust as his whole body went taut and she felt his own orgasm deep inside her.

They lay locked together for some time. Xavier shifted slightly so that his heavy weight was off her, his hand drifting idly up and down her back. Jane couldn't help a feeling of serene completion from stealing over her. As if she was now whole. He was still part of her, hadn't pulled away yet from her body's tight embrace.

He opened his eyes, that brilliant green pinning her to the spot.

'Are you OK?'

She nodded her head, incapable of speech, her eyes drawn helplessly to his. They lay face to face, her hands captured against his chest, his arms around her. She was mesmerised by every part of him—his eyes, nose, mouth. She reached a finger up to trace his lips wonderingly. He gently pulled himself from her body and she blushed.

He shook his head wryly. 'You're the first virgin I've slept with since my teens…I suspected, but wasn't sure, and when you didn't say anything—'

Jane coloured, wanting to hide. Her virginity had been the last thing on her mind.

'If I'd known…'

She felt herself tense slightly. 'If…if you'd known, what?'

He wouldn't have pursued her? He preferred his women more experienced?

His hand drifted up and down her back, relaxing her again. 'It doesn't matter now. To think I'm your first lover is actually the most erotic thing I've experienced in…'

He didn't finish, just bent and kissed her mouth with aching tenderness. What had she expected after all? The man was sinfully gorgeous, powerful and rich. Of course he was experienced, used to women falling at his feet. She locked her misgivings away somewhere deep inside her.

He curled her into him more tightly, and finally she drifted off to sleep, enclosed in his arms, his strong heart beating under her cheek.

Jane woke the next morning to face an expanse of naked chest. Lifted her eyes slowly to meet green ones looking back. A heavy, possessive arm lay across her hip, the hand moving in slow circles.

'Morning,' she said shyly, wanting to duck her head as the previous night came back into her consciousness. She felt a pleasurable ache in every muscle.

'Morning.' He pressed a kiss to her mouth.

She could feel some tension in the air, and his eyes took on a serious light, making a finger of something skate up and down her spine.

'I didn't use protection last night. I never usually forget, but…' A strange expression came over his face, but it was bland again in a second, making her think she'd imagined it.

'I'm guessing you're probably not on the Pill?'

Reality crashed in on Jane, waking her sleep-muddled brain up in a second. Of course he wouldn't want any complications from this…holiday fling. Because that was all it was. She tried to remain unaware of his naked body stretched close against hers, where she could already feel the stirrings of his arousal, and felt herself responding, with heat unfurling in her lower body. She struggled to focus on his words, not the response of her body.

'No, I'm not…but it's a safe time of the month for me…'

It wasn't strictly accurate, but she did a quick calculation in her head. She was sure it would be fine. Seemingly content with her assurance, he relaxed and drew her in tighter against his body, where she could feel the full strength of his hardness as it pressed against her.

'I think you owe me at least a day in bed…to make up for making me wait…'

All previous thoughts fled as her pulse threatened to strangle her words. She was already breathing faster as his hand caressed the globe of her bottom. 'You knew better than me…you must have known the torture I was going through.'

'No…I was going through my own… In fact it's happening again—something you can help me remedy…'

He drew her on top of him, running his hands down her smooth back, cupping her bottom, bringing up her legs to either side of him. He drew her head down to his, and as she closed her eyes she thought that she'd never get enough of him.

Over the next two days they made love, talked, ate. Xavier revelled in teaching her how much her body could respond to his touch…and how he could respond to hers.

Jane shut out the outside world. Even when they went beyond the confines of the castle and he took her on a sight-seeing tour of the rest of the island, it felt as though the island itself was the perimeter of this world, that nothing could intrude. He brought her to the small village, with exactly two hundred and seven inhabitants. It was a bustling, thriving community—largely thanks to him. The people considered themselves markedly different from the mainland, with their Spanish heritage, and it was reflected everywhere. The locals welcomed him as if he was their king…the children shy, men respectful, young women blushing.

Jane knew that without his presence there was no way the island would have retained its unique heritage.

Xavier had promised to show her his favourite childhood spot for swimming, and as they drove there another Jeep approached them on the small narrow road. When it drew alongside the driver was gesturing. Xavier stopped and got out. Jane followed. A stunning brunette, clad in an exquisite suit, was embracing Xavier energetically, speaking fast and furiously.

Jane walked around to join them, feeling very mussed-up and plain next to this vision of chic. Xavier pulled her close and cut through the other woman's stream of words. 'Sophie Vercors…meet Jane Vaughan.'

The woman halted with comic surprise as Jane was revealed, her eyes widening, and then a mischievous look dawned, an undeniable warmth in her face.

She replied in English, 'Xavier, you dark horse…entertaining on the island? Why, I thought you never—'

He cut her off with a warning look in his eye. 'Sophie, Jane is on holiday from England. She goes home in two days.'

Jane felt the brusque comment like a physical slap. He was very tacitly stating the extent of their involvement…

She held out a hand and smiled, ignoring an ache somewhere deep inside. 'Nice to meet you.'

'You too, Jane.' Sophie's smile was wide and unaffected. She had obviously decided to drop any further probing, and launched into a long and hilarious explanation of how she had to race to the mainland to meet her husband, who had forgotten something. She left after a few minutes with a friendly wink to Jane, a flurry of kisses and a cloud of dust in her wake.

Xavier didn't elaborate, beyond telling Jane that she was a Parisienne who had married one of his oldest friends. He, like Xavier, worked primarily on the mainland. It was obvious that she and Xavier were very good friends, easily affectionate with each other.

After a short drive, they pulled in off the track and made their way on foot to the secluded cove. They left the picnic Jane had prepared under a tree on the edge of the beach and raced each other into the water. All thoughts of the future, and her looming departure, were gone, and Jane strenuously focused on the present moment.

In the water, their horseplay quickly turned into something more serious, and afterwards, under the shade of the tree,

Xavier laid out the blanket and stood before her. Hair slicked against his head, the tang of the salty water on his skin, Xavier removed her bikini, kissing every exposed piece of flesh until he came to kneel before her. Her hands were on his shoulders, and her legs were threatening to buckle under waves of intense pleasure as he held her bottom. He wouldn't allow her to fall as his mouth and tongue did wicked things between her legs. Finally, when she thought she couldn't bear it any more, with words pleading for release on her lips, he laid her down and stretched over her, his body long and lean, every muscle clearly delineated, his erection jutting proudly, majestically between their bodies.

Jane felt a primal possessiveness as she looked into his eyes. *This man is mine…*

And it scared her to death. She drove it away, reaching up, her lips seeking and finding his, saying his name on a moan. 'Xavier…now, please now.'

'What…what do you want?'

She urged her hips to his, but he went with her, thwarting her efforts. She bit her lip in frustration.

He took a second to slip on protection, and the knowledge that he hadn't failed to do so since that first time was all too clear in Jane's head. But the throbbing of her body drowned that thought out as she felt him position himself between her legs in one fluid move.

'Tell me what you want…is it this?'

He started to enter the heart of her, just with the tip, and pulled out again.

Jane was nearly mindless with need, barely coherent. 'Yes…yes! Please, Xavier, I can't…hold on…'

He continued to torture her, focusing his attention on her breasts, taking each peak with a hot mouth and stimulating them unbearably, and then his mouth found hers, tongue stroking hers, igniting an ever-climbing fire of need that raced along every vein and cell.

Finally he entered her again, a little deeper, but this time Jane wanted to frustrate *him* and she pulled back. Much as it pained her, it excited her unbearably, this erotic dance.

'Two can play that game…' she breathed with a new confidence.

'Oh, really…?' Xavier growled low in his throat. 'We'll see about that.'

He cupped her bottom, tilting it upwards, laying her bare to his gaze, not allowing her to move, and with one deep thrust entered her so completely that she cried out with pleasure. He didn't allow her any quarter as he drove in and out with a relentless rhythm, sometimes shallow, sometimes deep, until at last they tipped over the precipice of extreme pleasure together, and down into a state of such bliss that it was some time before either one could move.

For the rest of the afternoon, as the light fell, they ate and watched the sun set over the horizon. Jane couldn't help but feel that this was possibly the happiest she had ever been in her life, and she tried to keep it from her eyes, fearing it must be blatantly obvious every time he looked at her.

The next morning she woke in the bed to find Xavier already up. She rolled over onto her side and tucked her head into her arm. Her last day on the island.

With a heavy heart she got up and dressed. She went downstairs and found him in the kitchen, sipping from a cup of coffee. She tried to project a light front, when inside she felt as though she was shrivelling up.

He looked up, a dazzling smile illuminating his face when he saw her in the doorway.

'I have to go to the mainland for a couple of hours today…you could stay here, or come with me if you like?'

Jane poured herself a cup of coffee, praying that he wouldn't notice the tremor in her hands. Delay the inevitable? One more night? Was is so self-indulgent to want to hang on to the fantasy?

A rogue dark part of her answered, 'I'll stay here, if you don't mind…'

He frowned for a second. 'When did you say your flight was?'

'Tomorrow night…I'll have to get back to the villa first thing in the morning, to clean it up and make sure everything is tidied away…pack my things.'

He thought for a second. 'Well, look, why don't you come back to the mainland with me today? You can do your things at the villa, pack and lock it up while I'm busy, and then we could spend the night at the hotel. You could leave from there tomorrow.'

Her heart twisted at his matter-of-fact tone. He was obviously having no qualms at the thought of her leaving. She had an irrational fear that once they stepped off the island, all this would fade as if it never happened.

But what he was saying made perfect sense. Perfect practical sense. He wouldn't understand if she said she'd prefer their last night to be here…to hang on to the dream for as long as possible. No, it was for the best. The break would be easier surrounded by the hustle and bustle of the real world.

Maybe he wanted them to be surrounded by people, the town, in case she became clingy, refused to go. Was he used to women acting that way? She wouldn't be one of those women—couldn't have him suspect for a moment how deeply involved she'd become.

'Yes…yes, of course you're right…'

CHAPTER SIX

AN HOUR later, bag packed and ready to go, Jane waited by the front entrance of the castle. She turned around and drank in the view, committing it all to memory, sucked in the air deeply. The morning sun was gathering more and more heat. In late June its potency was powerful, and the distinctive smell of sun-baked earth wafted over her. The cicadas' incessant chatter stopped, and then started further away every time she moved to try and catch them out.

In the space of just one week she had come to really love this island. That first forbidding view had hidden something much more complex. It had a heart and a vitality that was artfully disguised by its appearance. Completely unique. Much like the man who was striding through the doors towards her now. Every line of his physique screamed dynamic…independent…successful. He reminded her of a lone wolf. Who would get to tame him in the end? Could any one woman do it?

She schooled her features as he approached, and let him take her bag to swing it into the back of his car, which would take them to the boat.

As they got close to the private marina at the harbour on the mainland, Jane could see someone waiting for them. It was the beautiful blonde woman she had noticed that first time she had seen him in the street.

She was waving gaily as the boat approached, but Jane could see her arm falter slightly when she noticed Xavier had a companion.

As they climbed out Jane took Xavier's helping hand, a familiar tingle travelling up her arm, slightly breathless when she came to stand beside him. The other woman didn't even glance Jane's way as she unleashed a torrent of French at Xavier. She was stunning, her perfectly proportioned petite figure and deep tan set off by white jeans and a tight white shirt, artfully tousled blonde hair cascaded down her back.

Xavier drew Jane in to his side with a possessive arm, and when he could get a word in edgeways interjected in English. 'Sasha, don't be so rude. I'd like you to meet Jane. She's been my guest for the past week. You haven't been able to get me because I made sure I was unavailable. Jane, this is Sasha— one of my assistants.'

His tone, while light, held a steely undertone. Jane shivered, and felt a little sorry for Sasha. Any hint of which was swiftly gone when the girl turned her exacting gaze on Jane. Pure venom. She sneaked a look at Xavier, to see if he had noticed, but he had let go of her to rope off the boat, and had moved away a few feet. Jane was acutely conscious of her added inches and bigger frame as the woman sent a scathing glance up and down, summarily dismissing her. Her accent when she spoke was captivating, her English impeccable.

'So nice to meet you…thank you for entertaining Xavi for me…he works far too hard. Tell me, England, is it? You're a tourist?'

Jane nodded warily, feeling hackles that she'd never known she possessed rise.

'Ah, I thought so… Xavi is incorrigible—such a weakness for the—'

But whatever she'd been going to say was halted when Xavier came back to stand beside them.

'Jane, I'll give you a lift to the villa. Sasha, will you arrange for a car to pick Jane up this afternoon? Say around four p.m.'

Jane was still slightly stunned from Sasha's words, not sure where she had been going and not sure if she wanted to know. She looked at her uneasily. Her beautiful smile didn't go near her chocolate-brown eyes. Jane didn't want anything to do with this woman, and remembered belatedly with relief, 'I still have my hire car. I have to get it back anyway, so I'll make my own way to the hotel later.'

These words earned positive waves of radioactivity from the other woman. Jane avoided her eye, relieved when Xavier said, 'Fine. Sasha, I'll see you in the office in about an hour.'

Back in the villa, after Xavier had dropped her off, Jane wandered around disconsolately. She went through the motions of cleaning up and packing. She felt as though she were empty inside, and tried to shake the feeling off.

She made a light lunch for herself, and carried it up to the terrace, remembering back to the night she had stood there, dreaming about him—the night after she had bumped into him in the street. Wandering back to take in the view, she had to smile a little sad smile to herself.

Well, her fantasy had come true. Spectacularly. It had come to life…*he* had come to life…brought *her* to life in ways she would have never envisaged. He had awakened her. Been her first lover. Opened her eyes to a sensuality she had never imagined herself to possess. Helped her to own that sensuality. He had been her gift for the past week…and tonight would be their last night.

She would have to let him go. Be strong. She wouldn't fall at his feet, weeping and wailing. He belonged in this world of unimaginable wealth and beauty. Every day blessed by the benediction of the sun. And she belonged… She didn't belong here.

God knew what it was that attracted him to her…but he

was offering her one more night. And she would take it. Savour it. And somehow find the strength to walk away tomorrow with her head held high.

Later, when Jane walked into the hotel lobby after dropping the car off, she felt a little more in control of her emotions. Xavier had told her to give her name to the receptionist, who would be expecting her. She did so, and a bellboy came to take her luggage and show her up to the penthouse suite.

When she got up there she couldn't see any sign of him, and her heart slowed to a regular beat again. She spied a bottle of champagne in an ice bucket, with a note and pristine white rose resting against its side. With trembling fingers she opened the note after smelling the rose. The handwriting was big and curt. She smiled, imagining his impatience.

I'm sorry I'm not here to meet you. Have a glass of champagne while you are waited on hand and foot, and I will be there to pick you up at 7.30. *A bientôt.* X

For a minute she wondered if the X meant a kiss or was just his initial, before trying to figure out the rest of the message. A knock came and she went to answer it, still puzzling over his note.

At the door were three women, all carrying various accoutrements. The light dawned when they came in and told Jane they were there to do a massage, pedicure, manicure, facial, her hair…in no special order. Her mouth dropped open, but they were too well trained to make any comment when it became apparent that they were dealing with a novice. Having never indulged herself like this before, Jane, after a moment of trepidation and the old haunting guilt, gave herself over to the experience. And went to heaven and back.

A couple of hours later, when they'd left, she went to one of the mirrors and stared incredulously. Another creature looked back. A relaxed, buffed, shining version of herself, with sleek hair that fell in a smooth wave to just below her jaw. They had tinted her eyelashes, which she had never had done before, and now her eyes seemed huge in her face, framed by thick luxurious lashes.

Before she could lose herself in uncustomary narcissistic bliss, she spied the clock out of the corner of her eye and saw that it was almost seven-fifteen. In a panic, she realised that she hadn't even unpacked—and what could she possibly wear that he hadn't already seen by now? With dismay, she pulled her bag into the bedroom and stopped when she saw the bed. A huge white box lay there, with another note and a red rose this time.

Just in case. X

She opened the box with clumsy fingers and pulled out a dress from the folds of tissue paper. And what a dress. It slid through her fingers when she tried to hold it. She gathered it back again, and stared in shock. It screamed *designer*. Sure enough, the label confirmed her suspicion. She mightn't be a fount of knowledge when it came to celebrity and celebrity lifestyles, but even she recognised the famous name. It must be worth a fortune. She spied more in the box, and opened up the paper to reveal a matching set of silk and lace underwear. Silk stockings. Even shoes.

Against every penny-scrimping sensibility that had been drummed into her, she couldn't resist. She allowed the hotel robe to drop from her shoulders and she pulled on the underwear before stepping into the dress. It was strapless and tight-fitting. She looked at herself in the mirror. Was it meant to cling like that? Especially around her breasts? She looked behind…her bottom looked so…round.

She heard the door and her heart thudded to a stop, before starting up again at twice the speed.

'Jane? Where are you?'

'In…in here… Wait! I'll come out.'

She felt suddenly panicked at the thought of him coming into the bedroom. With a deep breath, and squaring her shoulders, she opened the door and went into the suite.

Xavier was pouring himself a glass of champagne, and he looked up, his hand stilling in the action. He put the bottle down slowly as his gaze raked her up and down from under his lashes. He had to put his hands into his pockets in a reflex action, to stop himself from reaching out and hauling her against his chest and crushing that soft kissable mouth under his.

She looked…stunning. The dress showed off her figure to perfection, emphasising her hourglass shape, exactly as he had imagined. And her eyes… Lord, those eyes…with their innocently sensual promise—they made him want to lock all the doors, take her and bury himself so deep inside her that she'd never want another man again.

He shook himself mentally. It was a nice dress. No need to go over the top about it. He'd seen plenty of women in far more revealing dresses. Taken them off too. And he would again in the future. Jane Vaughan was going home tomorrow, and it was a good thing… He'd been far too uncomfortably aware of alien emotions all week. Time to say goodbye and get back to normal. He had one more night. To get her out of his system for good.

He dropped heavy lids over his eyes and bent to pour another glass of champagne before strolling over and passing it to her.

Jane still hadn't moved—had been rendered immobile under his very thorough inspection. She covered up her insecurity by taking a gulp of the sparkling vintage wine. The bubbles made her nose screw up, and she immediately felt silly for worrying. She was going to enjoy this last night, be free and easy.

Xavier said throatily, 'To you…you look beautiful tonight.'

'Thank you…so do you.' And he did. Darkly handsome in a black tuxedo. The snowy white shirt making his eyes stand out, that glittering phenomenal green.

'Thank you for…laying on the massage and things today and this…' She indicated the dress shyly.

'My pleasure…' And it would be, later, he vowed, struck again by her charming politeness. He was used to women expecting…taking from him. 'I've booked a restaurant on the seafront for dinner…it's not far. We can stroll, if you think you can in those shoes.'

'I'll be fine…' Jane vowed that even if her feet were bleeding she wouldn't say a word; she didn't want a moment of the evening to be spoiled.

He took her glass, and they were almost at the door when she stopped in her tracks by his side in sudden embarrassment.

'I didn't put any make-up on… I can't go out in a dress like this with no—'

Xavier put a finger to her lips, silencing her. He looked at her carefully and came very close, one hand on either side of her face. Then he bent his head and brought his mouth to hers and kissed her.

Taken aback slightly for a second, Jane quickly forgot everything—where they were, where they were going—as the kiss deepened, and she brought her hands up to steady herself on his chest, the beat of his heart starting up a throbbing in her own pulse. With masterful expertise Xavier plumbed the depths of her mouth, and then, achingly slowly, traced her lips with his tongue before delving back in and stoking a fire that had heat travel from the molten centre of her all the way up to where she could feel her breasts aching heavily against their confinement.

He lifted his head, breathing harshly. Jane opened her eyes reluctantly. He saw her cheeks flushed with a burgeoning arousal, her eyes glittering like stars under long black spiky lashes, and her lips… He almost kicked the door closed behind him, painfully aware of his own arousal… Her lips were full and swollen and moist, like two crushed petals.

'There…' he said gruffly. 'You don't need any make-up.'

Taking her hand firmly in his, he pulled her behind him. Jane stumbled to keep up, bringing a hand up to sensitised lips. What did he mean by that?

When she caught her reflection in the elevator mirror a few seconds later she saw exactly what he had meant, and blushed from her toes to the tip of her head.

The restaurant was exclusive. When they arrived the bouncers fell over themselves to be the one to admit Xavier and his guest. The maître d' fawned and fussed as he led them to a table tucked away from the main floor by an open window. Strategically placed plants ensured the kind of privacy that allowed them to see the rest of the room and yet not be observed themselves. A white tablecloth, sparkling silverware, gleaming glasses. Candlelight. Jane sighed and smiled. She couldn't have done better if she had actually written it down on paper.

'What's so amusing?'

She looked at him across the table, so at ease in these surroundings, supremely confident. He would never understand where she was from…where she had to go back to. How special this was for her.

She shrugged lightly. 'Nothing…I'm enjoying the spectacle of all the minions tripping over themselves to impress you.'

'But not you, Jane…you didn't trip over yourself to impress me. You're different.'

Different… Which made reference to all those other women…

A short, sharp dart arrowed its way into her heart. She spoke lightly to disguise it.

'Well…my cunning plan worked, didn't it?'

'Ah…as I thought. You're as mercenary as the rest of them…'
See?

'Yes…' A brittle laugh came out of somewhere. 'You see, I've actually been stalking you for months, and I devised the best, most effective way to get your attention.'

'I thought you looked familiar in the street that day.'

He wagged a triumphant finger at her. Even though they were joking, she felt sad. Though he hadn't let it appear too often, she knew he harboured a well-worn cynicism.

The waiter appeared and took their order. Jane pushed aside all reservations, judgements, fears, and focused entirely on the moment—and Xavier. All too effortlessly she succeeded, and the conversation flowed like a burbling stream. Joyfully, easily, and far, far too seductively to resist.

She barely noticed the courses being delivered. She must have eaten, but for the life of her she couldn't remember what. She found herself watching him talk, committing every part of his hard-boned face to memory. The way his eyes crinkled ever so slightly when he smiled, the glimpse of bright white teeth. The way he inclined his head, encouraging her to go on when she faltered during a story.

All too soon it was time to go. The last drops of wine had been drunk, the espresso cups were taken away. A bare table-cloth sat between them. Xavier stood easily and held out a hand. She allowed him to pull her up, a little unsteady with the effects of the wine. He slipped an arm around her waist and together they walked out. His scent was heavy and potent in her nostrils. She had to stop herself from turning into his chest and breathing deeply.

Instead of going back the way they had come, he led her down by the beach. She hesitated for a second, before taking off her shoes and then reaching up under her dress to pull down her stockings.

'Wait.'

Her hands stilled as Xavier crouched down in front of her.

They were sheltered from the main promenade by a tree, the sound of the sea only feet way.

'Let me.'

Jane stood and closed her eyes as she felt his hands come up under her dress to encircle one thigh, fingers stalling, and slowly snagging the stocking top to bring it down. Exquisite pleasure. Especially when his hands seemed to take far too long to travel their way up her other leg. She was shaking, her hands heavy on his shoulders by the time he reached his destination and pulled the other stocking down, trembling with the unbearable desire for him to keep going up…fingers reaching higher until they found…

He stood up lithely, dangling her shoes and stockings with one hand. On impulse she reached up and tugged at his bow tie until it came loose and free, then undid his top button, tongue between her teeth when it proved stiff and unwieldy.

When she had finished she looked up to find him staring down at her, eyes fixated on her mouth. She innocently moistened her lips with her tongue.

He took her hand with urgency, and led her onto the beach. 'There's a quick way back to the hotel from here…'

Jane barely took in the magical view as they made their silent way across the beach, the moonlight bathing everything with a milky glow, sounds of laughter and muted music coming from the strip on the other side of the bushes.

Soon they were at the steps that led up to the gardens at the back of the hotel. They stood there looking at each other, lost in the moment. Then he handed her the shoes and stockings and disappeared—before she felt an arm coming under her legs and herself being lifted and held against his broad chest.

'Xavier…you can't.'

'There's gravel on the ground up here, and I can't wait for you to put your shoes on… As sexy as you are walking in them, it'll take too long…'

'Too long for what?'

'To get you where I want you...on my bed...under me.'

She buried her head in his shoulder as they approached the hotel, arms around his neck. She felt extraordinarily cherished and protected and desired. They avoided bumping into anyone, and took the service elevator all the way up, coming in to the penthouse from another entrance. He didn't put her down until they reached the bedroom.

Shoes and stockings fell from nerveless fingers as he slowly lowered her down his body. When her feet touched the floor they were standing so close that she could feel his heart beating against her chest.

In what felt like slow motion, her zip was pulled down, buttons popped open, catches undone. There was the whisper of clothes falling to the floor, skin meeting skin, soft and hard and silky, tongues touching and tasting, legs buckling, falling onto the bed in a tangle of limbs. Jane shut her eyes and ears to the voices in her head, concentrating on Xavier's hand as it glided over her breasts and down across her belly, down further...

When Jane woke the next morning she was alone in the bed. Just then the bathroom door opened and Xavier emerged, with an indecently small towel around his waist. She felt a blush coming on when she remembered the previous night... To think of how wanton she'd been...had become in the space of a few days. Where on earth had she ever got the nerve to do those things to him?

He watched the expressions flit over her face. Did she have any idea how beguiling she looked? How much it turned him on to think that he was the only lover she'd ever known? She looked at him, sleepy eyes, flushed cheeks, biting her lip, pulling the sheet up. He strode over to the bed and came down on his arms beside her. Her eyes widened, the pupils dilating. It firmed his resolve for what he was going to ask her. But not yet. Later. He pressed a quick kiss to her lips and straightened.

'Morning, sleepy. I'm sorry about this, but there's an emergency with the hotel in Malaysia and I have a crisis meeting to attend… Stay put, and I'll be right back. We can have breakfast together.'

'OK…'

Jane watched dry-mouthed as he let the towel drop and unselfconsciously pulled on his clothes. What a body.

When she heard the main door close she rolled over, burying her face in the pillow. She had to face it. Couldn't block it out any more. Especially after last night. He had brought her to the height of something so beautiful that she knew without a doubt that she would never experience anything remotely close with another man.

She had fallen in love with him. Hard and deep and fast. Irrevocably. Unbelievably. Needless to say he had made no indication that to him this was anything more than a brief diversion, which was ending today. She wouldn't allow her thoughts to fly ahead a few hours, when she would have to think about leaving. As if ignoring it would make it less of a reality.

Forcing herself to block the dangerous thoughts, telling herself she had to be crazy, she got up and went to have a quick shower, noticing faint marks on her body and colouring when she remembered herself urging Xavier to go harder, how she had assured him that he didn't need to be so gentle. She groaned under the powerful jet of water.

After towelling her hair and donning a voluminous robe, she wandered into the suite and opened the windows, looking out over the pool area and the sea beyond, breathing in the warm morning air.

There was a knock on the door. That was funny—didn't he have a key? Jane went and opened the door, a ready smile on her lips.

'Missing me already?'

CHAPTER SEVEN

HER smile faded fast when she saw who it was at the door.

Sasha.

His assistant looked sparkly and bright. As if she'd been up for hours. Before Jane knew what was happening, Sasha had sidled past her and into the room, looking around with interest.

'If you're looking for Xavier, he's gone for a meeting—'

She turned and fixed Jane with cold eyes. 'I know *exactly* where he is. I *always* know where he is.'

'I'll tell him you called...' Jane stayed by the open door and hoped she would take the hint.

'Actually, I came to see you.'

Sasha sat on the couch, crossing one elegant leg over the other. Where was this going?

'Did you enjoy last night? The pampering....the restaurant?'

How did she know about that? Jane felt a stillness come into her body, as if it were preparing for some kind of attack. Her hand gripped the knob of the door.

'Yes, thank you,' she said faintly, dimly thinking to herself, Well, maybe she booked it for him, so she'd be bound to know...

'Oh, yes! I nearly forgot about the champagne and everything else...'

A dull roaring sensation was beginning somewhere in her head as Sasha continued.

'I hope I organised it all to Xavier's satisfaction. I thought I'd check with you to make sure I did a good job…'

'You…you organised everything?'

She knows about the dress?

Sasha threw back her head and laughed. 'Of course, silly! You don't think someone like Xavier has time to go around booking restaurants and making facial appointments do you?'

Jane's brain was barely taking in her words any more.

And the notes? Surely not those…

Holding onto the door as if it were a lifeline, she fought for composure. 'Sasha, why don't you say what you want to say and get out…I have to pack.'

'I wouldn't be doing my job if I didn't make sure that *all* of Xavi's women were looked after.'

She stood up and sauntered close to Jane, who held her breath, just wanting the other woman gone.

'I have to admit, it gets a bit boring after a while. I keep telling him not to be so predictable, to vary things a bit…' Sasha smiled indulgently. 'But I guess he's just old-fashioned. That's why I'm here, Jane. I can see the type of woman you are. You're not like the others.' She looked at Jane closely before a cruel smile twisted her lips, 'You've fallen for him haven't you?'

Jane said nothing. Couldn't move a muscle.

'You poor thing… It'll be someone else next week, you know…the same thing all over again. Like I said, you seem nice, and I'd hate to see you get hurt. He hates clingy women. *Au revoir.*'

And just like that she sashayed out of the room.

Jane felt as though she'd been punched in the stomach. She actually couldn't suck enough air into her belly for a minute, and had to take calming breaths to prevent working herself into a panic attack. She stumbled over to the mini-bar and pulled out a bottle of water, taking a deep gulp. She felt shivery and nauseous. She sat down on a chair and stared blindly in front of her.

Stupid, stupid Jane. Allowing herself to fall in love with him. If Sasha had picked up on it, then who was to say he hadn't either? Utter humiliation rose up and swamped her. Words that Sasha had said dropped like stones into Jane's numbed brain: *So predictable…someone else next week…all of Xavi's women…*

She stood suddenly. Well, she wouldn't be waiting here for him like a lame duck. She tripped over the robe in her haste to get into the bedroom, and packed quickly and feverishly, throwing on trousers and a shirt, uncaring if they matched or not. The dress lay on the floor, where it had landed last night, a cruel reminder. She didn't bother to call for a bellboy in case they alerted Xavier.

She was outside the hotel and hailing a cab, sitting in it with the driver looking at her expectantly before she could function. She still had hours to go before her plane that night. She directed him to the villa. It was the only other place she could think of. She'd wait there until she had to leave.

Up in the villa, she felt as though she could breathe again. Despite all her brave ideas, notions, how had she ever thought she could walk away unscathed? Sasha hadn't told her anything she hadn't suspected on some level, she had just pointed out the truth…showed her the proof, so to speak. And it hurt like hell. But better that it hurt now. Better than if she'd been waiting in the suite for him to come back. Better than if he'd seen something in her eyes. She could well imagine the panicked look that might have crossed his face, the pity in his eyes as he gently had to tell her that it had been fun…but it was over. No, Sasha had done her a favour.

She heard the low rumble of an engine, which got louder before finally stopping outside the front door. She jumped up. The unmistakable sound of a door being slammed came, and a large shape appeared on the other side of the front door, a harsh knock on the glass.

'Jane! Jane, are you in there? Open this door now. I know you're there…'

Xavier.

She stood behind the wall for a moment, her heart thudding so loudly and heavily that she felt a little faint. The nausea was returning with a vengeance.

She went on shaky limbs to open the door, pasting what she hoped was a bland smile on her face.

He stood there bristling, dark glasses covering his eyes, hands on hips.

'Xavier…'

He pushed his glasses onto his head, and with the sun behind him Jane was blinded for a moment. He took advantage and walked into the open-plan hall. Jane stayed by the door.

'Well? Are you always this rude, or is it just with me?' he asked with deceptive calm.

Every line in her body screamed from being held so tightly. 'What's the big deal, Xavier? I wanted to come back here to collect some things I'd forgotten, and was hoping to get to say goodbye before leaving…'

He came and stood far too close. 'Liar. You were planning on leaving. Sasha told me.'

'What?'

'When I went back to the room and you were gone, I went looking for you. I met Sasha in the lobby and she told me she'd just seen you get in a cab—said you'd told her that you were leaving.'

'But she—' She stopped. What could she say? That Sasha had told her exactly how it was…what his little routine was…how she had organised everything, made it all too easy for his holiday *fling*?

She would not humiliate herself.

'Well?' he asked softly.

Jane wasn't sure what Sasha was playing at. Maybe she

wanted him for herself…maybe she already had him… The thought made Jane feel sick again… Maybe she was tired of accommodating his long line of women. But what did it matter anyway? It didn't change the fact that he would be entertaining someone new next week. Why didn't he just let her go? She looked up into his eyes and felt her equilibrium falter, tried to remember his question. Looked away.

'Nothing, Xavier… Look, I have to leave in a few hours, so what's the point? We're never going to see each other again.'

His hand reached out and caught her under her chin, forcing her face to his. The warmth of his fingers made her want to lean into him. She clenched her jaw.

'I wanted to talk to you about that.'

'What…?' She was having trouble concentrating on what he was saying.

'Never seeing each other again… Forget about this morning. Why don't you stay on for a while? You said yourself you're subbing at the moment, without a permanent teaching position. You're free to do what you want.'

The confusion showed in her eyes as she gazed up into his. She hadn't expected this. Her mind, trying to make sense of what he was saying, seized on the banal.

'But…but I can't just stay here… I've got a mortgage…bills to pay.'

'I could take care of all of that,' he dismissed arrogantly.

The treacherous wings of something that had taken off in her heart were fast crumbling. Jane reached up and brought his hand down. 'So…effectively you would pay for me to stay here?'

He shrugged. 'Yes. I could make it easy for you.'

Jane tried to make sense of it.

'You would keep me here as some sort of…paid woman…a mistress? For an affair?'

'Well, it wouldn't be exactly like that.' His hand sliced the air impatiently. 'You make it sound almost sordid.'

He took her hand and lifted it, not letting her pull away. One thumb rotated in her palm, making slow circles. She could feel herself responding. Her body and head going in completely opposite directions.

'Jane…I haven't had enough of you yet…and I know you feel the same way. Stay…for as long as this lasts.'

For as long as this lasts… That was the problem. It wouldn't last for ever for him, and when it was over he'd move on, desire sated and she knew she'd be feeling about a million times worse than this very moment. *He's used to doing this.*

Jane pulled her hand out of his with a jerky movement. The nausea that had diminished rose again, making her feel light-headed, and dirty, tainted, when she thought of how Sasha had set up last night's date for him, as if Jane were some kind of concubine. It lent a harsh quality to her voice.

'No, Xavier. I don't want to be your mistress. You'll find a replacement soon enough. This week has been more than enough for me.'

She'd had enough? Who was she kidding? She'd never get enough of this man. A lifetime wouldn't be enough…and anything less wouldn't do. And he was not in the market for lifetime commitments. How could she have forgotten that first night by the pool? Sherry had told her about his reputation.

She could see the muscle twitch in his jaw, knew she'd made a hit. She held herself erect. His ego might be wounded, but that would be it. He'd get over it. She, on the other hand…wouldn't.

'I'm not interested,' she said, as if to drive the point home.

He took a step back and Jane felt a rush of air between them and a wave of desolation washed over her. The shuttered look descended. A look she hadn't seen since that first time they'd spoken. It made her want to reach out and touch him. He backed away again and put on his shades.

'If that's what you want.'

She nodded miserably, trying to maintain a look of bland indifference. He turned and went through the door.

And then he was gone. The engine gunned fiercely, and with a spurt of gravel it died away into the distance. Jane couldn't keep it down any longer, and just made it to the toilet—where she threw up violently.

Xavier forced his hands to relax their death grip on the wheel as he sped away. What a fool he'd been, allowing her to get under his skin so easily. How dared she turn him down? His hand slapped the wheel. She thought she was too good for him.

An utter fool. That was what he was. She was nothing but a tourist, looking for a story to bring home. The sooner he put the last week and her out of his mind for good, the better.

CHAPTER EIGHT

Nearly Four Months Later

JANE shouldered her way through the door of her one-bedroom ground-floor flat, shutting out the noise of the traffic and wailing sirens. She was soaked. Autumn was here with a vengeance. She dropped the bags of shopping and kicked off her shoes with relief, taking off her layers and leaving them to drip dry in the bathroom. She ran a quick hot bath and afterwards wrapped herself in her dressing gown, feeling a little better. She would have to be more careful. She sat gratefully on her sofa, placing a hand on her belly. She still couldn't believe she was pregnant. But she was.

She remembered the shock of that day when, after weeks of relentless nausea on her return from France and then no sign of her period, dread had settled in her heart. Finally, one day after work, she had worked up the nerve to buy an over the counter test. A positive result. Confirmed by the doctor.

She hadn't told anyone yet. Not even her mother. Even now she was barely able to contain her heartbreak. It was far, far worse than she had imagined. She had fobbed Lisa off when asked about the holiday, being vague, and Lisa thankfully had responded with her usual exasperated roll of the eyes, before launching into the latest adventure of her own love-life.

Her hand moved abstractedly over her belly. She had never contemplated not keeping the baby. That wasn't an option. She sighed heavily as the object of her every waking and sleeping thought intruded.

Xavier.

She knew she couldn't live a lie, couldn't have the baby and not have the truth known. She had to let him know. But how to tell him? How to get in touch with him? How to be prepared in case he got heavy-handed and demanded…what? Jane remembered him telling her that he was last in his line. No doubt an heir figured somewhere in his future. Just not with someone like her.

But would he demand she hand over the baby? She felt a sliver of fear. She didn't think he would be capable, but then he was so powerful. An heir to his fortune was important, necessary for the survival of the island…

She would have to be strong and not let him bully her. She doubted he'd want to be saddled with a small baby anyway. It would seriously cramp his lifestyle.

She grimaced. She'd gone from a world where Xavier had never existed to one in which, since she'd come home, every paper she opened seemed to have a picture of him. In New York, Paris, Milan… In each place a new fortune being made, a new woman on his arm. Each time like a knife in her heart.

She got up wearily and went through the motions of cooking dinner, eating it and tasting nothing. Afterwards she went into the bathroom and saw the pool of water on the floor under her dripping clothes. She went to get the Sunday papers she was about to throw away, opening them out on the floor to soak up the water.

For a second she didn't even notice that she'd stopped breathing, then shook her head as if to clear it. The photo and the words didn't disappear. It was the business section. His face stared at her starkly from the page under a headline:

FRENCH BILLIONAIRE IN UK TO SAVE AILING
HOTEL CHAIN

Xavier Salgado-Lézille, the French entrepreneur, owner
of Lézille island and the exclusive hotel chain of the
same name, is in London this week in negotiations to
save the once luxurious chain of Lancaster hotels…
In recent times they have deteriorated…
Has his own offices in the City…
Other companies interested in his expertise…
Why do we have to look abroad to be saved…?

The words swam up at her from the page. She sank down
oblivious to the wet floor. Checked the date. Yesterday. That
meant he was here this week. Incredibly.

She read it again. He had offices in the City. She went to
her phone book and checked with nerveless fingers. Sure
enough, there it was, the address and phone number. Why
hadn't she thought of that before? She checked the clock. It
was still business hours. Just.

Before she could think or lose her nerve she dialled the
number from the book. A crisp voice answered. She asked to
be put through to Xavier's personal secretary.

'Hello, Molly Parker here.'

'Hello…are you Mr Salgado-Lézille's personal secretary?'

'Yes, I am. May I ask who is calling please?'

'It's…my name is Jane Vaughan. Could you tell him
please that I'd like to make an appointment to see him?'

Her heart was beating so hard and fast she was surprised the
other woman couldn't hear it. Her hands felt slippery with sweat.

His assistant sounded suspicious. 'Very well—please hold
for a moment.'

After a couple of agonising minutes she came back on the
line. 'Mr Salgado will see you at ten-thirty tomorrow
morning. He's very busy, you know—'

'I'm well aware of that. I won't take up much of his time, thank you.'

Jane put down the phone with a shaking hand. Automatically she placed a hand on her belly and sank into the sofa. The phone rang again, shrill in the room. She jumped violently, picking it up warily, as if it would bite her.

'Oh, Mum it's you… No, I wasn't expecting anyone else—don't be silly.'

In the course of the conversation Jane decided it was time to break the news. Now that she was going to see Xavier and tell him. After all, she was beginning to show.

Her mother was disappointed that Jane was going to have the baby on her own, knowing all too well how hard it had been for her after Jane's father died, and she was worried because she and Arthur were going to be leaving England, but Jane made sure to reassure her on that score. The last thing she wanted was to be responsible for Arthur not being able to take his new bride away to their new life. He had grown up in South Africa, and after the honeymoon he had persuaded her mother to emigrate to the warmer climes of Cape Town.

Jane knew her mother was stubborn and that Arthur would do whatever she wanted. They were due to leave in three weeks, and Jane was determined that they go. She hoped she had done the right thing in telling her.

As if the telephone wires were buzzing, the phone rang again shortly after. It was Lisa. She decided to tell her too, feeling a little more weight lift off her shoulders. She refused to say who the father was, only that she was going to see him the next day and that, no, he wouldn't be a part of her life.

After the initial screech Lisa was for once stunned into silence. Jane managed to see the humour and appreciate this uncustomary role-reversal. It was nice to have the support of a friend, but she declined her offer to come with her. She had to face Xavier alone.

* * *

The following morning in the cab, Jane tried to quell the mammoth butterflies in her stomach. She felt nauseous, and knew it wasn't morning sickness. She hadn't had that in a few weeks now. The thought of seeing Xavier again had her blood running cold through her veins. Then hot. How would he look in this climate? Somehow less? As if! She knew all too well that he would stand out like an exotic hothouse flower.

Luckily, after an intensely busy period with work, the teacher she had been subbing for had returned from sick leave, and Jane as yet hadn't been placed anywhere else. She couldn't contemplate it right now.

The cab drew up under an ominously grey sky outside a huge gleaming building.

Salgado-Lézille Enterprises.

After she got out she fought the urge to turn around, step right back into the cab and tell the driver to go back to her flat. Instead she put one foot in front of the other.

Inside the building there was a hushed reverence more in keeping with a cathedral. No doubt because the boss was in attendance, she thought darkly.

At the reception desk she gave her name and got a security tag. Then she was directed to the top floor. The lift was entirely glass, and she could see the ground floor slip away. The panic rose again.

After agonisingly long seconds it came to a stop and the door swished open with a little ping. She stepped into a luxuriously carpeted hall. A pretty girl behind a desk took her name again, and told her where she could wait on a comfortable couch just outside some huge imposing oak doors. Jane had dressed down, in jeans, sneakers and a sweater. She didn't want him to think she was coming here for anything else. And she was protective of her small telltale bump.

The door opened and her heart jumped into her mouth. It

revealed a matronly woman with a neat grey bob. She emerged, holding out a hand.

'Hello, dear, you must be Jane. I'm Molly, Mr Salgado's UK assistant. Please come through.'

Jane stuttered a few words and followed her into an office where Molly took her coat and stopped outside another set of doors. It was like Fort Knox. She rapped lightly on the door, and opened it before turning to let Jane pass through. She felt a hysterical moment of wanting to bury her head in this woman's chest and have her tell her it would all be OK. But she didn't.

When she walked in she couldn't see Xavier at first, the office was so big. She felt at a serious disadvantage. The door clicked shut behind her.

Then she saw him. Standing with hands in his pockets in an exquisite suit before a huge window that took in the whole of London, or so it seemed. His tall dark shape was silhouetted against the skyline. Master of all he surveyed.

The blood rushed to her head and there was a roaring in her ears. He was saying something, coming towards her. She could feel herself swaying for an interminable moment, but just before she fell strong arms came around her and then she was half-sitting, half-lying on some sort of chaise longue. Xavier was crouching down beside her, holding a glass with some dark liquid.

'Here—take a sip of this. You're whiter than a ghost.'

In such close proximity every cell jumped to zinging life. So much for hoping that any attraction might have diminished. It was still there, like a plug going back into a socket. The energy running between them was palpable.

She moved to sit up. 'I'm sorry, I don't know what happened…'

'When was the last time you ate?'

'What?'

'Food—you know, we use it to stay alive. You look as though you haven't eaten a square meal in weeks.'

Jane stifled a defensive retort. She knew she'd lost weight since she'd got home, but she just hadn't had time...and the doctor had reassured her that it was quite a normal phenomenon to actually lose weight when first becoming pregnant.

'I'm fine...it's isn't any concern of yours what I eat or don't eat.'

He left the untouched glass on a table beside her and stepped away. 'Of course not... To what do I owe the pleasure of your visit?'

Jane stood, not liking the way he was towering over her, and was relieved that the dizziness had dissipated somewhat.

'I've come to tell you something.'

His gaze slanted down at her, no trace of warmth on his face. 'Ah...could it be that you're having second thoughts about my offer? Back in the cold, grey reality of England you're realising what an opportunity you passed up?'

She looked at him blankly for a second before exploding, nerves making her reaction stronger. 'Unbelievable...how arrogant is that? You know, I never thought you had such an inflated sense of self, but obviously I was wrong.'

'Well, then, why are you here?' he sneered. 'Hardly to catch up on old times, eh? As I seem recall you were only too eager to see the back of me that morning...couldn't even wait to say goodbye.'

Her head started to pound. This wasn't going to plan. First almost fainting, and now he thought she wanted to be his mistress after all.

'No...I mean yes. Look, I really do have something to tell you, and it's not easy...' She looked at him beseechingly.

She breathed a sigh of relief when she saw him sit down behind his desk. Space. She sat down on the other side, her hands held tight together in her lap.

'The fact is...I know I said that I thought it was OK, but I was wrong...the truth is...'

'Yes?' he bit out impatiently.

She squared her chin and looked at him unflinchingly. 'I'm pregnant.'

The words dropped into a deafening silence. He didn't react. His face was like a mask, Jane had a moment of clarity when she knew that was why he was so successful at business—a perfect poker face. He got up and went to stand at the window with his back to her.

'Xavier…'

'I heard you,' he said, in a curiously flat voice. Then he turned around abruptly, green eyes pinning her to the spot.

'It's mine?' A slight inflection made it a question.

She stood angrily, her whole frame quivering. 'Well, of course it's yours…how dare you imply that you might not be the father? I haven't had time to do anything since I got home much less find a new lover and try to get pregnant in the gleeful anticipation of tracking you down and trying to pass the baby off as yours.'

He ran an impatient hand through his hair, and for the first time she noticed lines on his face that she didn't remember. He looked tired.

'Look, I'm sorry…it's just a bit much to take in. How much…when are you due?'

'In March.'

'It must have been that first time.'

'Yes.' Jane felt a blush ascending from her chest all the way up to her face. Couldn't stop the torrent of images that were all too frequent, haunting her imagination. She tried to avoid his focus. She started babbling. 'Ah…look, I just wanted to let you know. The last thing I want is for you to feel that you have to be responsible for anything…I don't expect anything from you at all. I'm going to bring the baby up myself. Of course you can come and see him…or her…whenever you want. Why don't I let you get used to the idea?'

She placed a card on the table. 'That's my address and number.'

She was practically at the door before he seemed to break himself out of his stupor. 'Jane, wait…we need to talk about this.'

Just then the door opened, and Molly appeared with some men behind her.

'Not now, Molly, please.'

Even Jane balked at the barely leashed anger in his voice, but Molly seemed to have weathered worse, and stood her ground.

'Mr Salgado, it's the men from Tokyo…remember, they only have one hour in London before they have to fly to New York? You yourself specifically requested this meeting.'

Jane took full advantage of the opportunity and fled before he could stop her, grabbing her coat, mumbling a goodbye to Molly.

Xavier tried to keep his mind on the meeting after Jane left but, the truth was that he was blown away. Everything was distilled down to her and the fact that she was pregnant. He still felt remnants of the pure elation that had surged through him when he had seen her again. Then the concern that had ripped through him when she had gone so white and almost collapsed. The feel of her slender body in his arms…his inappropriate response.

Alone again in his office, he held her card in his hand. The truth was that he had been in possession of her address for a couple of months now. It hadn't been hard to trace her. He wasn't sure if he'd really planned on getting in touch with her. But one thing was for certain: he hadn't been able to get her out of his head. Oh, he had tried. With various women. But when it had come to it, he just couldn't. Her face, the smell of her body…the way she had responded to his touch…would flash into his head and render him more or less impotent.

Him…impotent!

He obviously just hadn't had enough of her—needed to get her out of his system once and for all. When he'd heard she had phoned he had thought it was because she'd realised the same thing. But it wasn't.

Pregnant. The word fell heavily into his head. It brought up images, memories... A dark emotion threatened to rise up. His fists clenched. He wouldn't think about that now. Things were complicated. However, he knew what he wanted with a fierceness that surprised him. He didn't want to look too closely at his reasoning yet, or why it was so strong, he just knew it was the only solution. And he knew exactly how to get to her to comply, whether she wanted to or not. Uncomfortably he was aware that it was more than likely *not*. And he didn't like how that felt.

That evening Jane tried to relax. It was impossible. Her whole body felt as though it had received an injection of some vital life force energy. When she had got back to the flat she'd changed into tracksuit bottoms and an old baggy sweatshirt.

Xavier was in the country, and as long as he was she couldn't rest easy. She hoped that he would just leave her alone. Let her get on with things.

The doorbell rang.

It couldn't be...could it? She went towards the door, her hands balled into fists, opening it warily.

'Dominic.' She breathed a sigh of relief, but also felt a stab of disappointment. Lisa's brother stood on the doorstep. She hadn't seen him since she'd got back, had avoided his persistent calls.

'Come in...what are you doing here?' She ushered him into the sitting room.

He was shy, as usual, not really able to meet her eye. 'Look, I won't beat around the bush...Lisa told me about your...being pregnant.'

A blush stained his freckled cheeks, and Jane's heart went out to him, but she didn't interrupt.

'The thing is, Jane...well, you know how I feel about you.

I came to say that I'm here if you need someone to lean on. That is, if you'd have me, I'd marry you.'

A lump came into her throat. 'Oh, Dominic...that's so sweet. I'm very flattered that you would offer to marry me, but the truth is—'

The doorbell rang again. Jane muttered an apology and went to open it.

Xavier.

Standing on the doorstep, crowding the small doorway.

The breath was driven from her lungs and her body reacted spectacularly, a million miles away from what her head was trying to impose on it. She felt a tremor start in her legs.

She had completely forgotten about Dominic until she heard him behind her. 'Janey, love, are you all right? Do you know this man?'

She came out of her reverie.

'Yes.'

She let Xavier pass her to come into the small hall, feeling a hysterical giggle bubbling up from somewhere deep in her belly.

'Dominic, this is Xavier Salgado-Lézille. Xavier, this is Dominic Miller—an old friend of mine.'

The men looked at each other with deep suspicion. Jane knew she had to put Dominic out of his misery. She threw a quelling look at Xavier and showed him into the sitting room, shutting the door behind him.

Leading Dominic away from the door, she said, 'Xavier is my baby's father...and it wouldn't be fair to take you up on your offer because...' her voice gentled '...I'm not in love with you.'

'Are you in love with him?'

She nodded her head mutely.

'Is he in love with you?'

She shook her head. 'But he will take care of me and the baby if I so wish. I know that. You don't have to worry about me.'

She pressed a kiss to his cheek, making him colour again.

'Are you sure you're OK…? I can stay if you want.'

Jane shook her head, ignoring her rapid pulse. Dominic was no match for Xavier.

She let him out, the difference in the two men comical as they passed in the hallway. At the sitting room door took a deep breath before going in.

Xavier was pacing the small room, dwarfing it with his size and presence.

'Who was that?'

She bristled at the proprietorial tone in his voice, hating the effect he was having on her.

'He's my best friend's brother.'

'What did he want?'

'It's none of your business what he wanted.' She sat down to disguise the trembling in her legs, then contradicted herself, saying disbelievingly, 'As a matter of fact, he asked me to marry him.'

'Did you say yes…*Janey, love*?' Xavier's voice was sharp.

She looked up. His face was shuttered, his eyes giving nothing away. Her heart twisted at the mocking way he repeated Dominic's friendly endearment.

'What's it to you? I can marry whoever I want.'

He hauled her up against his chest so quickly that she didn't have time to protest before his mouth descended and his lips found hers. After a second of shock she was like someone dying of thirst who had found water in the desert. With a small whimper she wrapped her arms around his neck, and their tongues collided in a heated feverish dance.

Time stood still.

She was home.

Then he thrust her away from him.

'*That's* why it's my business. You're carrying my baby— and don't tell me you react like that with everyone.'

Shocked blue eyes clashed with blistering green.

'That's why, if you marry anyone, it'll be me. No one

else. Our baby deserves to be brought up within a marriage. He is going to be my heir, and as such will be afforded the necessary ceremony for his inheritance.'

The shock of what he was suggesting rendered her speechless for a moment.

'I will not marry you just for the sake of an heir. Don't be so ridiculous… It would be a sham…and anyway it could be a girl,' she pointed out somewhat pedantically.

He threw off his overcoat and jacket, loosening his tie. He was like a panther in a confined space. Hands on hips.

'Boy or girl… You would deny our child—possibly the only child I may ever have—its inheritance?'

Jane gasped. 'Are you threatening me? That if I don't marry you then you will effectively deny its existence?'

'It won't be up to me… Before my father died he added a codicil to his will stating that should I have any children outside marriage they wouldn't be entitled to anything. It was his way of ensuring the line would continue in our family's name, ensuring that the island stays in the family.' He shrugged. 'He was very conservative, and there's no way around it.'

She had a sudden memory of the numerous pictures of Xavier with countless women in the press, and words tumbled out, barely coherent to her muddled brain.

'You've had to check that out already? Maybe you have other children dotted around the world—Milan, Paris—?'

He took her by the shoulders. 'No, I don't. I don't make a habit of jumping in and out of bed with countless partners, and I always make sure I'm protected…. Just with you…with you something happened.'

His hands were biting into her shoulders. Something had happened, all right, and she could see how much he hated to admit it. It was in every strained line in his face. He had been taken over by the lust of the moment, whereas she had been taken over by much, much more. She could remember all too well what had happened. She had let good sense out and madness in. She tried to avoid his probing gaze.

'OK…maybe you don't, but what you're suggesting is positively medieval. Surely in this day and age—'

'Did you really think I'd just walk away? I'm offering you everything on a plate…security, respectability, a name for our child.'

Everything but yourself… This heir is everything to him… as important as she had suspected.

She sought for rational words in a brain that was fast becoming fuzzier and fuzzier. 'He or she could still take your name, if it's that important. I can't…please don't make me…'

'There's no need to go green. It doesn't have to be a completely unpleasant experience. We're still attracted to each other—you can't deny feeling it too, the minute you walked into my office today.'

He didn't have to remind her of that mortifying fact. She brought huge wary eyes up to his. 'Yes, but that's all, isn't it?'

His face was expressionless. He shrugged negligently. 'It's more than a lot of people start out with. Jane, I'm thirty-six. It's time I got married and produced an heir.'

She felt a hysterical laugh bubble up again. 'It's almost as if I've fallen in with some cosmic plan to save your family legacy.'

The lines in his face were harsh, and suddenly she didn't feel like laughing. This was all too real.

'Don't mock me, Jane. There aren't many women who would turn down an offer like this.'

Even though his words reeked with arrogance, she didn't doubt for a second that what he said was true. She just happened to hold the ace. His seed inside her belly. Lucky her. She had pipped all the contenders to the post. She tried another tack.

'Yes, but most people start out with love, however misguided…at least it's there to start.'

'And where does it leave them in the end? At least we would be going into this with eyes open—without the illusion of love to cloud things. I believe we have something we can work on, Jane. I wouldn't suggest it otherwise.'

She shifted out from under his hands and sank back down onto the couch, feeling hunted.

Something we can work on...

She knew all too well what he meant. It saturated the air around them.

He hunched down before her, not letting her evade his compelling gaze. 'Jane, the future of Lézille is at stake if I don't provide an heir. This could be my only child.'

She looked at him, helpless.

The doorbell rang again. Xavier went to answer it. She didn't even notice. But she did when she heard the voices. Her mother and Arthur. She closed her eyes. It couldn't get any worse.

Her mother came into the room with one brow arched so high that it almost met her hairline.

'Hello, Mum.' Jane hugged her, feeling the onset of tears in her maternal presence.

She quickly made the introductions, without saying precisely who Xavier was, but she could see that her mother had deduced exactly what his role was.

Unbelievably, Xavier offered to go into the kitchen to make some tea, leaving them alone for a few minutes and making her feel even more confused. How could he come in here and take over so effortlessly? Her mother and Arthur were certainly looking after him with barely disguised awe.

'So that's...?' Arthur nodded in the direction of Xavier's retreating back.

Jane nodded miserably.

'Well, darling, you don't look very happy about it,' her mother whispered.

I'm not!

Her mother and Arthur looked at each other before linking hands. The lump grew in her throat again.

'Dear…we've had a long think, and we came to tell you that if you're still determined to go it alone…we're going to stay here in England.'

Jane started to protest and her mother shushed her, holding up a hand. 'Now, I know what you're going to say, but it's decided… There is no way we can leave you here on your own to bring up that child, and that's final.'

Despite the encouraging smiles on their faces, she could see how hard it had been for them to make this decision. And there was no way she could let them. Her Mum's happiness involved Arthur too. And right now they came first. She could mess up her own life, but not the life of this woman in front of her, who had sacrificed so much already.

She heard Xavier's step approach the sitting room and knew what she had to do. She went with her gut. In that split second she knew she was about to make a choice that was going to change her life. She hoped and prayed that it was the right one. She didn't have time to consider the ramifications.

He came in to the room with a laden tray. Jane waited until he had put it down and the tea was passed out before speaking, and tried to keep a steady voice.

'Mum, Arthur…I really appreciate what you want to do for me, but you see there's no need.'

She glanced at Xavier's ever unreadable face. She wasn't going to get any help there. She took a deep breath.

'You don't have to stay here because…you see…I'm not going to be here.'

Her mother and Arthur looked at each other blankly, then at Xavier and then at her.

'What are you talking about, dear?'

Jane mentally crossed her fingers and took poetic licence with her recent conversation with Xavier. 'Xavier has asked me to marry him…and I am going to say…yes.'

She could hear a splutter of tea come from his corner of the room. Then she was enveloped in hugs and tears and congratulations. Xavier joined in and answered questions vaguely. She was very aware of his sharp, assessing eyes on her all the time.

She knew she had done the right thing, however, when she saw the badly disguised relief on their faces at the prospect that their dream would be fulfilled after all.

Finally, after what seemed an age, they were gone. She went back into the sitting room to find Xavier standing at the window. He turned around and fixed her with hard eyes.

'I gather that little charade was for the benefit of persuading your mother that she and her husband could emigrate after all?'

'Well, it's not going to be a charade unless you won't marry me.'

He approached her softly, coming dangerously close. 'If you were trying to call my bluff then it didn't work. We *will* be getting married. I suppose I should have thanked your mother for helping you to come to your decision…' He gave a short harsh laugh. 'You couldn't have made it clearer that it's the last thing you'd be doing otherwise.'

'You're right. I hate you for this.' Her chest felt tight and restricted, her hands clammy.

A savage intensity flashed over his face so briefly that she might have imagined it before it was gone, and he drawled, 'That hate will just fuel our passion…because it is still there.'

She vowed there and then that there would be no passion. If he so much as touched her, she wasn't sure that she could contain her feelings—and if he guessed for a second…her life would be hell.

He left with a promise to return and discuss things in the morning, and after the door shut behind him Jane sagged against it, the stuffing knocked out of her.

Despite everything that had just transpired, somewhere

within herself she felt curiously at peace. Was she so straight that once she had agreed to doing 'the right thing' she felt good? It couldn't be. What was more likely, she feared, was that she was such a masochist that even though being married to Xavier spelt certain heartbreak, it also meant she got to be with him…and seeing him again had proved how completely he held her heart in his hands.

The baby. How could she deny this little person access to his or her father? To their birth heritage? Especially one so rich—and not just in monetary terms. She knew instinctively that Xavier would be a good father.

Her mind went a more incendiary route. Would he be faithful if she refused to sleep with him? A man as virile and highly sexed as Xavier would not stand for a celibate marriage. How could she hope to live side by side with him and resist him? All she knew was that she had to, for now. Her emotions were too raw…too close to the surface. Maybe in time, when they were more under control, she could… remain detached. As if there ever could be such a time.

She went to bed with a heavy heart and slept fitfully.

The next morning when she opened the door to admit Xavier he took in her pinched face and the dark smudges under her eyes. The pang that struck him when he realised that he was the one who was making her look this unhappy gripped him unawares. He quashed it ruthlessly.

Jane eyed him warily with crossed arms as he effortlessly commanded her small flat again. He was dressed in a suit that hugged his frame, making him seem even more powerful, dynamic. He looked exotic and foreign, his tan standing out against the grimly grey backdrop outside. Stupendously gorgeous.

'I've arranged for us to be married here in London in just over two weeks time at a register office. It's the earliest I could arrange… Also it should be easier for your mother and Arthur to attend before they leave for South Africa. If there's anyone else you want to witness it…'

His efficiency and ability to make the powers that be fall into his plans stunned her—and his unexpected sensitivity to accommodate her mother.

'Well, yes…' She thought of Lisa. 'There's one or two people, maybe…'

'*Bien.* I have to go to New York today, and will be gone until the day of the wedding, so I trust that will give you time to pack up here, tie up any loose ends and inform your work. Molly can arrange to have this place let or sold, whichever you prefer.'

She spoke quickly. 'Let…that is, I don't want to sell it.'

Somehow the thought of severing all ties was too much just now.

He shrugged as if he didn't care.

'Fine. As you wish. I'll let her know she can go ahead with arrangements and find a suitable agent?'

Jane nodded dumbly.

'After the wedding we will stop over in Paris for a short honeymoon. We can replenish your wardrobe there.' He eyed her casual attire critically. 'You'll have a certain role to fulfil as my wife, and will need to be dressed suitably.'

His bossy tone was too much.

'I think I know how to dress myself, thank you very much… You don't have to spend your money on me.'

'Very commendable, darling, but somehow I don't think you could afford even the price tags on the kind of clothes I'm talking about,' he drawled, with infuriating arrogance.

'Fine…' She threw her hands up. 'If you want to spend thousands on making me into something I will never be except on paper, then go ahead and be my guest.'

He came and stood right in front of her. She could feel his breath warm on her face. Her heart lurched as he drifted a finger down one cheek and underneath to her neck, where her pulse was beating crazily against her skin.

'Oh, but you will, Jane…you will. Trust me on that.'

CHAPTER NINE

Two weeks later Jane was trying to contain herself as she felt an increasing sense of panic threaten to overwhelm her. Lisa and her mother fussed around her as she got ready to go to the register office, their chatter skimming over her head:

'...and poor Dominic is heartbroken, but he happened to mention that Xavier is gorgeous...'

'Oh, he is, dear—wait till you see him...'

'And he really owns a whole island?'

'That's nothing...his hotel chain...'

'Still waters, eh, Mrs V? Who would have thought our little Janey had it in her? And to think of all those holidays spent with him under my nose—the time I wasted on those waiters...'

Jane cut in with wry exasperation. 'You know, I *am* here, guys.'

'Yes, dear, don't mind us...now, let's have a look at you.'

She was wearing a fitted cream silk jacket and a matching skirt that was cut on the bias and fell in soft swinging folds to her knees. The material clung to her curves, and the buttons on the jacket closed under her bust, with a lace camisole just visible in a slightly darker shade of off-white. An effective camouflage for her thickening middle.

Her mother hadn't grilled her too much since her revelations and announcement. She assumed she and Xavier had

had some sort of lovers' tiff, and was blithely unaware of the circumstances—which Jane was quite happy with.

She contemplated the rest of the outfit—sheer tights, and high heels covered in the same material as the suit. It wasn't bad for the last minute. Lisa had secured her hair with a flower, and stood back to regard her subject, resplendent herself in a vibrant hot pink dress that clashed magnificently with her red hair.

'Janey, you look like a model… Honestly, what I wouldn't give for your height and figure… When I get pregnant I'm going to be the proverbial whale from day one.'

Right now Jane would have given anything to switch places with Lisa. But of course she couldn't. She had to do this, for the baby and to ensure her mother and Arthur's future. And if she was honest she had to acknowledge the dark part of her that *wanted* to go through with this—wanted to tie herself to Xavier, whatever the cost.

When she saw him standing at the table in front of the registrar she faltered for a moment, her nerve failing her, but in that instant he turned and saw her. They hadn't seen each other since that morning in her flat. It all fell away. Some intensity in his eyes held her. Didn't allow her to break contact. She looked neither left nor right, just went towards him as if he was some kind of homing beacon in a fog. Then she was next to him. It was only the voice of the registrar that brought her back into room and their surroundings.

The words were meaningless. She hoped she made the appropriate response at the right time because she felt disembodied from everything. Before she knew it Xavier was taking a ring from his pocket and placing it on her finger, his hands cool and steady. Then, remarkably, Lisa was handing her a ring—where had that come from?

Jane put it on his finger, it slid on effortlessly. He didn't let go of her hand until the end of the ceremony.

Once it was over they went outside. Xavier told her that

he had arranged for a celebratory breakfast to be held at his London hotel. He led her to a waiting chauffeur-driven Bentley. She could see that there were more people than she had initially noticed, and that there were cars lined up for everyone. He had organised all this?

In the back of the car they were alone once he indicated to the driver to raise the partition. He brought a couple of glasses from a hidden compartment and poured them both some sparkling water. She couldn't help but be aware of his huge frame encased in the dark grey morning suit. The material stretched over hard thighs only inches from hers.

'A poor replacement for champagne, but necessary.'

Jane didn't want him to guess how her insides were churning, the confused anger and frustration she felt at his matter-of-fact tone.

'Let's drink to us.'

'A bit of a lie, don't you, think? There's no one around to fool.'

'Let's drink to a truce, then, because we're sure as hell not going to last one week if you stay in that filthy mood. You've looked like you were going to your own funeral since you arrived.'

Hot tears threatened. She clinked his glass and took a sip, feeling like a fraud.

'I'm sorry…it's just a little overwhelming… Within weeks of seeing you again I'm married and about to emigrate…'

He surprised her by taking her hand in his and lifting it to his mouth. The heat of his lips pressed to her skin made her insides melt. Along with the look in his eyes.

'Don't think about it now…let's just get through the next few days. It's not exactly been easy for me either, you know.'

For a moment they shared an intense communication. There was something in his face…but then it was gone. A bland expression replaced whatever it was, and Jane couldn't help but feel he was talking about being forced into a marriage he didn't want. She reminded herself how single-minded he was. He hadn't even made an attempt for them to talk about things, get to know one another again. He'd taken off as soon as he knew she'd comply with his demands, spent the last two weeks in New York, and come back only at the last minute. Arrogantly sure of her response.

The car drew to a smooth halt outside the hotel, and they were ushered out and into the melee.

Jane was introduced to so many people that they were soon blurring into one, and her cheeks ached from smiling. Her feet ached too, and for the first time since becoming pregnant she felt exhausted. She was ever conscious of Xavier, and where he was. Whenever she caught his eye he held it for long moments, until she began to get flustered and looked away.

She had just seen off her mother, Arthur and Lisa, whose own parents had come too. Jane had been delighted to see Lisa's dad, looking so well after his scare. Her friend had promised to visit soon, and her mother was planning on coming when the baby was born.

Standing alone in the doorway of the function room, she felt awkward with all these unknown people. Some of them were friends of Xavier's and seemed perfectly nice; others were business acquaintances.

Suddenly he materialised at her side, slipping an arm around her waist, and for once she sank gratefully into him, glad of the support.

'Let's get out of here,' he murmured into her ear.

'Yes, please.' She couldn't disguise the relief in her voice.

He brought her up to the penthouse suite. The staff had left out a bottle of champagne and there were rose petals all over the bed.

What a waste...

She turned to face Xavier as he closed and locked the door. He came towards her, pulling off his bow tie and opening his shirt. She could see his eyes darkening and saw the intention in them. It reached out and caressed her across the room, and she could feel every part of herself respond. It was too much. Her feelings were too raw. She backed away.

'Xavier…please. I'm tired…I want to go to sleep.'

He kept coming. 'So do I. With you.'

'No!' She hadn't meant for her voice to come out so strident. 'Just…I need a little space, and I am exhausted.'

She had been exhausted earlier, but now an excess of energy was causing her body to hum, making a lie of her words. Since seeing him again an ache had settled into every cell, an ache that she knew only he could assuage. He stopped in his tracks and she wanted to throw caution to the wind, throw herself at him with an animalistic instinct…rip off his clothes, have him take her right where they were. The strength of her reaction shook her.

'I don't know what you're playing at, but I'll give you the benefit of the doubt for now. I'll go back downstairs for a while. You take the bed…I'll sleep on the couch.'

'Xavier, there's no need—'

'Save it, Jane. If you think we can share that bed tonight without anything happening then you're lying to yourself.'

The door closed ominously quietly behind him.

Jane began to get ready for bed, feeling even more miserable. As if she had somehow cut off her nose to spite her face. Her body still hadn't cooled down since that electrifying look.

She sped through her toilet in record time, and was soon under the sheets, breathing harshly and feeling very silly. After waiting as long as she could, she finally gave in to her exhaustion and slept, not hearing her bedroom door open or Xavier come in and spend long moments looking at her.

The next day on Xavier's private jet, as they flew to Paris, she tried to control her conflicting emotions. She studied him covertly from under her lashes, and twisted the slim white-gold band on her finger as he looked through some paperwork in the seat across the aisle from her. He looked totally at ease, with not a care in the world. Unlike her. She looked out of her window and tried to force herself to relax.

What seemed like only moments later she felt someone shaking her gently. It was Xavier. His face was very close to hers. She could see the darker flecks of green in his eyes. It brought back a vivid image of his pupils dilating as his head descended to hers before he took her mouth with his. She hunched back in the seat to escape the potent memory.

He frowned at her movement. 'What…what is it?' she asked, her voice strained.

'We're here…in Paris.'

She looked out of the window. Sure enough they were on the Tarmac; she could see a waiting limo just at the bottom of the steps. None of the usual Customs or red tape for Xavier and his wife.

Once in the limo, it wasn't long before they were in the thick of traffic in the city. Jane looked out with undisguised awe.

'Have you never been here before?' Xavier asked incredulously.

She shook her head. 'Never had time…or the money. When I left school I worked straight away through college. I wanted to start paying Mum back for all the years that she'd worked her fingers to the bone.'

'If I didn't already know you I'd say that was a line…'

Jane looked at him, shaking her head. 'So cynical…how can you bear it?'

'Not everyone sees the world through rose-tinted glasses.'

'Well, mine are rapidly turning more opaque.'

She could feel his sharp look of enquiry, but didn't elaborate.

She picked out the Eiffel Tower, Notre Dame…and before long she could see that they were going over an ornate bridge on to what looked like an island in the middle of the river.

'Wow…' she breathed.

'This is the Île St-Louis—one of a few islands on the Seine…it's mainly residential.'

I'll say, Jane thought to herself. Chic, immaculately made-up women walked their beautifully coiffed dogs. And she had thought that image of Paris was such a cliché!

They drew to a smooth halt outside one of the buildings and were effusively greeted by the doorman. Jane was fast becoming accustomed again to the bowing and scraping people did in Xavier's vicinity. In the lift she wasn't surprised to see that they went all the way to the top floor. Nothing but the best.

The doors opened straight into a hall with one door, which Xavier opened.

'This is where I come and stay when in Paris on business or for stopovers on long haul journeys—have a look around.'

Jane tore her eyes away from his and did as he asked. It was the quintessential bachelor pad. The age of the building meant that the shell and windows were still of a certain period, but the whole of the inside had been remodelled. The colours were dark, and it was full of sharp corners, with abstract art on the walls, state-of-the-art sound and TV systems. The kitchen was worse, all gleaming steel and not a hint of homeliness in sight. She hated it.

He stood back, arms folded, and watched her face with amusement. She couldn't hide a thing. He felt a sharp, uncustomary burst of pleasure, remembering her refreshing honesty, and became aware of just how much he had missed it…

'You hate it, don't you?'

'I'm sorry…' She blushed. 'It's just so cold and characterless.'

And he became aware of how he'd missed her blushes.

'I suppose I'd be offended if I'd actually had a hand in the decoration, but thankfully for my ego I didn't. I allowed a friend who was trying to build up his interior design portfolio the run of the place. I'm here so infrequently that it doesn't really bother me.'

He thought of the women that he had brought here. He couldn't remember one who hadn't oohed and ahed delightedly over every room. Either they had all loved it or, more realistically, said what they thought he wanted to hear. Now he could see it through Jane's eyes he hated it too, and vowed to rip it all out and do it up again.

Her heart hammered when he suddenly took her hand. He led her to a bedroom, where he faced her again.

'What…what are you doing?' she asked desperately, hating the effect just holding his hand was having on her, but determined not to pull away and reveal the extent of her discomfiture.

He indicated with his head round the room, starkly decorated in creams and browns. 'This is your room.'

The relief on her face was comic. 'Thank…thank you.'

He rested heavy hands on her shoulders. 'Your hands-off signals are loud and clear. Rest assured, Jane, I've never forced myself on a woman and I'm not about to now…but you know you're fighting a losing battle, don't you? This scared virginal act is wasted on me. We both know you're no virgin.'

He brought his face down to hers, his mouth close to her ear, and she closed her eyes weakly. His breath tickled the sensitive part of her neck just below her ear. The fine hairs standing up.

'But if you think for a second that you can hold out for ever…then you're very, very mistaken. It's only going to be a matter of time. It's there, vibrating between us like an electric current, and it's not going to go away. Do you know what happens when you suppress something? It just gets stronger and stronger.'

He straightened up, his eyes taking in her flushed face, the bead of sweat on her brow, the pulse hammering against the base of her neck, and he had to use every ounce of his will-power not to pull her into him, mould her body to his and make her acquiesce—which he knew he could do.

He would wait until she was shaking with longing, weak with desire. Until she could barely look at him because of it. He wanted her. Badly. But that was all it was. Sheer, unadulterated lust. Nothing else. This was why he'd been unable to get her out of his head the past few months.

'Settle in, and I'll get lunch ready.'

He walked out of the room. Jane pressed her hands up against flaming cheeks. That was her reaction after mere words! What would she do if he kissed her? Or if she lost control and grabbed him? Which seemed more likely right at that moment. She'd go up like tumbleweed to a lit match on a dry day.

All the more reason to be strong.

And what then…?

One day at a time. That was the only way she was going to handle this.

CHAPTER TEN

THE next morning Xavier insisted on a day of sightseeing.

In the early evening they emerged from the Louvre. Jane was bone weary, even though the ever-present limo had whisked them from place to place.

Bone weary because at every opportunity during the day he had touched her—usually just the slightest glance of physical contact, a brush of a hand here, a light touch on her waist or shoulder...pressing close against her in the crowds. But it had been enough to set her nerve-ends jangling, almost as though he knew exactly what he was doing. His face each time she'd sneaked a look had shown pure innocence.

By the time he took her hand outside the great museum she was worn down from trying to escape him, and just left it in his without a word. That contact, chaste as it was, was torture in itself.

'I let Pascal go home... There's a restaurant near here I thought might be nice for dinner. We can get a cab later.'

'I'm not dressed properly...' She indicated her jeans and sneakers.

'Don't worry, it's a low-key place.'

She shrugged and allowed him to lead her through the streets. They came to a charming little bistro, tucked into a small side street, with only a few tables that were already full.

Xavier was greeted like a long-lost son by the proprietor,

and when he introduced Jane as his wife there were shouts and a woman came running out. Jane was enveloped in hugs and warm kisses, and couldn't help but be charmed. The older woman at one point looked at Jane's ring finger and unleashed a stream of French at Xavier that Jane couldn't follow. He looked shamefaced after it.

Once they were seated at a free table that had appeared as if by magic, Jane had to ask, 'What on earth did she say to you?'

'Madame Feron pointed out that you don't have an engagement ring.'

Jane lifted her hand stupidly. 'Oh…I hadn't even thought about it myself.' She looked back to him. 'I don't need one, you know…it'd be silly just for the sake of it. Plenty of people nowadays just wear a wedding band.'

'Nevertheless, she's right. We will do this properly. I'll buy you one tomorrow.'

His tone brooked no argument. His businesslike attitude reinforced her will to resist him at all costs. This was nothing more than a mutual agreement, each having their own reasons: him to secure his heir and its future, her for the baby's sake and to secure her mother's future in South Africa.

But maybe down the road when the baby was born they could negotiate a separation? Surely by then any inheritance would be safe? Jane knew in her heart of hearts that sooner or later her will would break, or Xavier would succumb to another woman, and either scenario would be untenable for long. She knew that now, as she looked at him across the table.

Her appetite still wasn't back to normal, but she forced the food down, not wanting to insult the couple who couldn't stop beaming at them.

That night when they got back to the apartment Jane fled into her room as soon as she could. She rested against the door, breathing heavily with eyes closed. She heard Xavier's step pausing outside her door and her mouth went dry, her pulse tripping.

'Goodnight…' he called softly through the door.

But he may as well have said *coward*. It was what he meant.

She got under the covers a short while later and pulled them over her head, as if that would block out the images, the vivid memories that played like a home movie every night in her dreams. Her body felt as though it had a fever. What was wrong with her? She was pregnant…how could she be feeling so…so…*sexually aware* of herself and him?

She slept fitfully. Again.

The following morning Xavier informed her that they would spend the day shopping and return to the island that evening. When he saw the less than enthusiastic expression on her face he frowned.

'What is it? Are you feeling ill?'

'No…it's nothing…just that I've always hated shopping. The crowds…trying things on. It bores me to tears. But as you say, I have to keep up appearances now.'

He shook his head, once again struck dumb. Reminded of how different she was from the women he was used to.

An hour or so later, when they approached the door of a designer shop, Jane caught his hand and dragged him back. The memory of years of scrimping and saving rushed back in lurid humiliating detail, her mother's face lined with worry and strain as she struggled to let down another hem, trying to get another year out of a school skirt.

'We can't go in there…those clothes cost a fortune. Look, why don't you just let me go off for a few hours? I'll find some high street stores and kit myself out. Honestly, you can trust me…'

'Woman!' he exploded, stunning her into silence. 'I'm normally dragged on these expeditions, reduced to nothing more than a walking credit card, but you—' He shook his head. 'You have to have morals. Jane, without insulting your intelligence too much, will you please trust me when I say that if I let you go off and *kit yourself out*, as you put it, within weeks we will be at some function where it will be horrendously obvious to everyone that I can't afford to dress my own wife. This isn't just for you. As much as I agree with your sensibilities, unfortunately society hasn't caught up with us, and I have a certain standard to maintain.'

Her mouth opened and closed ineffectually, a red-hot poker of pain striking her at his reference to what must have been many other trips like this...with other women he had indulged. She walked into the shop without another word, hoping to distract him from her hurt.

By that afternoon she'd lost count of the shops... Dresses, casual clothes, shoes, underwear—which thankfully he had absented himself for—and last but not least maternity wear. She had worked very hard at putting images of other women out of her head, and berated herself for not expecting as much in the first place.

Xavier had arranged for everything to be sent straight to the plane and loaded up. Once they were on it themselves, later that day, Jane felt a pang of guilt mixed with fear. Xavier saw the look on her face.

'What is it?'

She shook her head rapidly. 'Nothing...nothing at all.'

Everything!

She averted her head and looked out of the window. When she thought about the afternoon she had to admit that she had enjoyed it on some level. Who wouldn't have? Assistants fawning all over her. Well, over Xavier's credit card, to be accurate. And what on the surface must have looked like a doting husband indulging his new bride. The covetous looks of the other women hadn't gone unnoticed. At one point she had even felt the old warmth creep up, when one of the women had been particularly sycophantic. Jane had looked to Xavier and caught his identical look, and a bubble of delighted communication had almost transformed her face, made her forget why she was there. But that would be far too dangerous. What they had shared in the summer was not who he really was. She had to remember that.

Once the small plane was cruising, and the seat belt signs were off, she saw Xavier turn towards her from the corner of her eye.

'Jane, I have something for you.'

She turned to look.

'More? What could you possibly—?'

She went silent when she saw him reach into the inside pocket of his jacket and pull out a small box, which he offered her across the aisle. She looked at him and her hands shook slightly as took it. When she opened it she gasped. Nestled in a bed of cream velvet was the most stunning sapphire ring in an antique square setting of tiny diamonds and white-gold. It was beautiful. How could he have picked exactly what she would have gone for herself?

'How did you know…?'

'I remembered something you told me once about sapphires being your favourite stone…'

She couldn't help but be touched that he had remembered.

'We can change it if you don't like it,' he said stiffly.

She looked up quickly. 'I lo—' She stopped herself and amended her words. 'It's beautiful.'

She put it on her finger with a tremor in her hand. A perfect fit.

He went back to his papers; she went back to looking out of the window, with the sting of tears in her eyes at the sterility of the exchange.

They landed at the private air strip on Lézille in the early evening.

Xavier's four-wheel drive was parked nearby, and he expertly negotiated his way out of the tiny airstrip and towards the castle, silhouetted on the horizon against a darkening sky.

This time it wasn't empty. A retinue of people were lined up to welcome them home. Most of the names and faces were a blur as Jane struggled to hang onto them. A gardener, cook, maid…and at the head of the queue Xavier introduced her with obvious affection to Jean-Paul and Yvette who, he told her, had run the castle since he was a baby. They had the same dark distinctively Spanish features of the rest of the islanders.

Before she knew what was happening, Xavier had lifted her up to carry her over the threshold. When he put her down again she stood back, trembling and breathing hard…disconcerted. Another tear threatened….for about the third time that day. She told herself it must be her hormones, emotions too close to the surface. She couldn't read his face, searching desperately for some indication that his motivation wasn't ironic. Or an act purely for the staff, who were looking on delightedly. She had to admit that was more likely. But his face was shuttered, expressionless. She controlled her wayward reactions.

Yvette shyly led Jane upstairs to the master bedroom. It all looked familiar, and exactly how she remembered it. Little had she known that she'd ever be back…married and pregnant. She sank onto the side of the bed and looked around, feeling a little removed from everything. Her life had changed so completely within just a few months, a total one-hundred-and-eighty-degree turn. Goosebumps prickled across her skin and she wrapped her arms around herself, feeling a sudden chill.

She went to look out of the window. The scenery was as vividly breathtaking as she remembered, just slightly less lush than it had been in the summer.

A movement out of the corner of her eye made her look round. Xavier had appeared in the door, holding one of her bags.

With sudden panic and clarity she realised something. 'Xavier…this is your room.'

'Yes. And now it's your room too.'

He walked in, closing the door behind him, coming uncomfortably close. Jane wrapped her arms tighter around herself, forcing herself to remain calm. But it was difficult. The bed in the corner of her eye loomed large and threatening; the memories were rushing back.

'We are not sleeping together.'

'Yes, we are.' He enunciated each word with chilling softness.

'No.'

He ran an angry hand through his hair and Jane could feel the energy crackle around them. 'Jane, we are going to share this room if I have to lock us both in here every night. If the staff see us sleeping separately, word of a fractured marriage will spread before morning. And I will not have that. We may as well not have bothered getting married.'

Jane threw her hands in the air and moved away jerkily, pacing back and forth. 'Don't be ridiculous. If I sleep in the other room I can make sure the sheets are pristine every morning…I'll—'

'Now you're being ridiculous. Tell me, Jane…why the great resistance? Don't you remember how it was between us?'

Didn't she remember?

Her stomach dropped with sudden panic under his narrowed gaze. Resisting him…and this overwhelming desire…was the only way she knew how to protect herself. He *couldn't* ever know…and if he started to look at her motives…

She wouldn't even contemplate that scenario. She placed a protective hand on her belly. It might as well have been over her heart. She mustered up a look that would have frozen boiling water, her blue eyes chips of ice,

'This baby is the only thing I care about. I'm pregnant, Xavier, I don't feel those…*urges*.'

She hated using the baby like this, but she needed all the armour she could get. Anything that would keep him at a distance. She knew that he would not step over the line…

unless she gave the word. Which she was determined not to—until she knew she could stay detached, if such a time existed.

A savage intensity flashed over his face. The hell she didn't feel those *urges*. Every part of her quivered lightly before him; she was taut as a bow, just waiting for his touch. His eyes dropped to the hand over her belly, before they took in the rise and fall of her chest. He wanted to walk over and shake her, and call her a liar to her face. He caught her darting a glance to the bed, the slight flush under her skin. He moved closer.

She backed away.

He gestured to the bed, taking in her reluctance to follow his gaze with something akin to triumph. 'It's a king-size bed. Plenty of room for two people on opposite sides to never come close to touching.'

'I don't trust you. No way.' She eyed him warily from under her lashes, arms back around her body.

'Oh, Jane, be honest…it's not me you don't trust, it's yourself.'

Of all the conceited…!

Jane's blood boiled; her arms dropped. 'Fine. If you can keep your hands to yourself, then I certainly won't have a problem keeping my hands off *you*.'

'Good.' He smiled smugly. 'I'm going to catch up on some calls. Yvette will bring the rest of your things up shortly, so you can get settled in.'

When he left the room Jane could have kicked herself for allowing him to goad her. But she couldn't back down. Somehow she knew it would be more dangerous if he suspected for a second what she suspected herself. That he was absolutely right about her not trusting herself to share his bed. He was playing a game with her, she knew. She would not be the one to crack.

But in a deep, dark corner she was very much afraid that she would indeed be the one to crack…

CHAPTER ELEVEN

'I PRESUME you won't mind me leaving you to make some calls, as you've barely said two words over dinner…?'

Jane looked up sharply. In contrast to her tense form, spine as straight as a dancer's, he lounged at the opposite side of the table, long legs stretched out, a brow quirked mockingly.

'Not at all…' she replied sweetly.

The heavy potent atmosphere was giving her a headache. She was more than uncomfortably aware of him. His scent, his large body mere inches away across the table. During dinner she'd been transfixed by his hands, until she'd realised she was staring. Still in a state of shock to be back here…with him…again.

In a way, she reflected when he'd taken his leave and her pulse had finally returned to normal, it would be easier to have people around. It would have been too much to have the slumberous heat outside and the entire place to themselves. Things were more formal with the staff here. There was none of the seductive easy intimacy of the summer…making dinner in the kitchen, eating outside. The outer changes just reflected their own inner reality. Everything was different.

She went up to the bedroom and changed into the most unrevealing nightwear she had—a pair of silk pyjamas—buttoning them up as far as possible, and automatically went to the side of the bed that she'd used before, aghast at how natural it felt.

Scooting down under the covers, she felt her body rigid with tension, and she lay like that for at least an hour, until she heard his footfall and the door open. She stopped breathing, her eyes shut tight as he came into the room.

Forcing herself to take long shallow breaths, it was torture as she heard his movements and tried not to imagine what he was doing. The whisper of a shirt sliding off, a belt buckle opened, a button being popped. When she heard his trousers hit the floor, and the barely discernible sound of his underwear being tugged down, a corresponding heat flooded her lower belly. She had to bite her lip to keep back a moan.

She heard his footsteps pad to the bathroom and water running, being turned off, and then the footsteps come back to the bed. She felt the dip as he pulled the covers back and got in. She was curled in a ball, as far away from him as she could get, the covers tucked around her like a wall.

She only fell asleep once he'd stopped moving and she heard his deep breaths even out.

When Jane woke the next morning she was in the same position she'd fallen asleep in, and she could feel how the tension had cramped her muscles. With a wary look over her shoulder, she breathed out when she saw that Xavier was already up, the sheet pulled neatly back. She took advantage of the solitude and got up, taking a quick shower and dressing before going downstairs, meeting Yvette on the way.

'Oh, *madame*! You should have stayed in bed. You must be tired…I was going to bring you breakfast.'

Jane smiled warmly at her. 'There's no need. I'm sure you have enough to be doing…I'll come and get something in the kitchen myself.'

She looked up over Yvette's head and saw Xavier at the bottom of the stairs, watching her intently. She could see a muscle work in his jaw from where she was. Had he slept well last night? She searched his face for signs, but he looked remarkably well. Vibrant. She proceeded down the stairs, fighting to look cool.

'Morning.'

'Morning.'

'Did you—?'

'I hope you—'

They both spoke at the same time, and Jane took the lead, saying airily, 'Oh, like a log. I didn't even hear you come in. Was it late?'

He took her arm and led her across the hall before leaning down close and breathing into her ear, 'Liar.'

Before she could react, and quell the butterflies he'd set off in her stomach, he straightened and said in a normal voice, 'We have visitors to see you, darling…' He looked back to Yvette. 'The Vercors are here. Bring some tea and a selection of things please…' He dropped his voice again as he walked her to the door of the sitting room. 'I remember what a large appetite you have, even if you don't want to.'

Her mouth was open and her face pink when he man-oeuvred her into the bright room. He smiled benignly down into her face.

'Darling, do you remember Sophie Vercors? And this is her husband Paul.'

Jane forced herself to tear her eyes away from his mesmer-ising pull and looked at the couple. She immediately recalled the glamorous woman from that day when they'd bumped into her on the road, on the way down to the beach. The sudden memory of it had her cheeks flame red.

She stood to greet Jane warmly. Xavier's hand on her back propelled her forward.

'Jane! It's good to see you again…I had a funny feeling I might.'

Sophie's eyes twinkled with mischief, and Jane found herself responding to her warmth gratefully.

'And this is my darling husband, Paul.'

She pulled the man forward. He was quite a bit older than Sophie, balding and with a definite paunch, but he had the kindest eyes and a look of mischief to match his wife's. It was clear, despite their mismatched appearances, that they loved each other deeply.

'Shame on you, Xavier, for getting married in London… and the baby! What great news…'

Xavier slanted a privately mocking glance down at Jane. 'What can I say? It took four months before I could win her back.'

Sophie clapped her hands. 'Jane…you *are* the one for him. I knew it. No other woman would have run rings around him like that!'

Jane smiled weakly, wanting nothing more than to swing for Xavier, who was still clamping her to his side. They settled down to chat, Sophie clearly delighted to have another woman of similar standing on the island.

'It can get so boring sometimes…especially in the winter.' She winked at her husband cheekily. 'But now you're here we can do all sorts of things. Though you'll probably spend a lot of time on the mainland, with Xavier when he's working…'

Jane was quite happy to let her prattle on, horribly aware of Xavier's thigh pressed hard against her own on the small couch. What would they say if they knew that their marriage was a sham?

Before long they were in the hall, saying their goodbyes. Sophie embraced Jane. 'So don't forget the Winter Ball will be coming up next month. That calls for at least a few shopping trips… You lucky thing—at least it's in Xavier's hotel, your home from home.'

When they were gone, Jane turned to Xavier. 'How can you deceive your friends like that? Let them think that you're happily married?'

'What makes you think I'm not?'

Jane frowned at his obtuseness. 'But of course you're… we're not. How can you say that?'

His eyes narrowed on her face, a shuttered look descending, making a chill run down her spine.

'Jane, I am very happily married, believe me. I've got the most important thing I always wanted and expected to get out of a marriage. An heir.'

She staved off the ice that settled around her heart at his words. 'How can you be so cold?'

He smiled, but it didn't reach his eyes. 'You call me cold? You're in this for your reasons too, or have you conveniently forgotten them?'

A stillness came into the air around them. Nothing moved; not a sound came from anywhere. She found her voice and it sounded remarkably calm. 'No, I haven't. I'm doing this for the baby. And I want my mother to be happy. They are the only reasons I said yes. Certainly not for anything else.'

Liar…

She felt her throat close over and wanted to get as far away as possible right at that moment, but she forced herself to stand strong.

He brought a large warm hand to her neck, caressing, and the pulse thumped crazily against her skin and his. Every muscle tensed as she fought against reacting, against closing her eyes. When, oh, when would she be free of this debilitating desire for him?

'You'll never be free of me, Jane. You'll come to me. Sooner or later. I'll wait. And until you do we will share our bed. We both know you curled up in that tight ball beside me to stop yourself reaching out and experiencing the passion you know is still there.'

Her eyes widened as his words echoed her thoughts, as if he had read her mind. Belatedly she remembered his uncanny ability to do just that. But his arrogant assumption helped to dampen her clamouring body. She tore his hand away from her neck.

'It's good to clarify things and know that at least we agree on our motivations for the marriage. It'll be a cold day in hell, Xavier, before we make love. I'm going for a walk.'

And she stormed out of the house, feeling as though the hounds of the Baskervilles were at her heels.

Xavier watched her go and felt rage surge upwards. He stormed into his study and poured himself a shot of whisky, gulping it back. His hand was a white-knuckle grip around the glass. How was she able to enrage him so? He'd never allowed any woman to affect him like this… How could she stand there so coolly and say those words?

A bleak expression crossed his face and he rubbed a weary hand over his eyes. It was nothing less than he'd said to her.

Why should it bother him that she felt exactly the same way? That she wasn't what he had imagined all those months ago? He had allowed himself to imagine for the first time ever something elusive, ethereal. A glimpse of fulfillment—what he saw Sophie and Paul share…he'd stupidly hoped that perhaps he too could have that sense of coming home…

He crushed the empty feeling. A foolish daydream, that was all it had been. He'd been wrong…it existed for others but not him. Never him.

A newly familiar surge of guilt rushed through him, and he swallowed back another shot to drown it out… Guilt was an emotion he had little time for. He conducted every aspect of his life with ruthless precision…so why should he feel guilt that maybe he…what? That he'd bullied her into marrying him? As she had just told him, she had her own very concrete reasons for entering the marriage. He shook his head. No way would she have given in unless she'd wanted to.

But she needed to…not wanted to. She told you she hated you for doing this to her, for not offering her another way…

He cursed the voice that mocked him.

It was just physical frustration. That was all. He'd never been denied a woman he desired before now. Her and her damned insistence that she didn't feel those *urges*. She hated the attraction. This was just her way of claiming control over the situation… The guilt rose again like a spectre. He swallowed another shot.

It had taken all the strength and will-power he possessed not to reach across the bed and pull her into his arms last night. Her achingly familiar sweet scent had tantalised his senses as he lay there, his body aroused to the point of pain, testing him beyond endurance. But he wouldn't do it…he couldn't. She was his *pregnant* wife, dammit. She would have to come to him.

When that day came…when she did come to him…maybe then that voice would disappear.

Another shot didn't help.

A few days later, a wan-faced Jane came into the dining room where Xavier was finishing breakfast. She eyed him warily. She'd had the most vivid dream last night. That he had pulled her close and tucked himself around her so completely that she'd felt unspeakably comforted, safe and cherished. She'd even felt love from it. And then she'd felt his hardness against her back, and it had started up a throbbing need that had woken her with its intensity. When she'd woken with a start, the bed had been empty. Xavier hadn't yet joined her, and the loneliness that had lodged in her chest had been so heavy that she still felt it this morning.

He looked at her over the rim of his coffee cup, and Jane hid her churning emotions behind a mask of bland happiness.

'Morning. Did you sleep well? Are you going to the mainland today? Isn't it lovely outside? I might go for a drive later, explore a bit.'

He frowned at her inane chatter, clearly not taken in.

'We're having some people over tonight—business colleagues, friends. A small dinner party. About ten people. Sophie and Paul, and Sasha will be there too. So you'll know a few.'

At the mention of Sasha's name, Jane nearly fell into her chair, her face paling. She'd managed to put the other woman out of her head, but now that awful morning came back vividly. Her own humiliation.

'Oh…that sounds nice.'

What else could she say? Don't you dare invite that woman?

'You'll act as hostess, of course.'

She just nodded her head. Still thinking about Sasha, distracted.

'I have to go to the hotel…I'll be back around seven p.m. The guests are due to arrive at eight.'

He drained the last of his coffee and got up to go. Just as he did Jane felt a flutter of something in her belly, and gasped audibly. Xavier came around to her side quickly.

'What is it? Is something wrong?'

Jane shook her head, her hand on her belly. 'I think I just felt the first kick.'

She turned to face him, smiling, her eyes gleaming with excitement. He crouched down beside her chair and she had the irresistible urge to reach out and take his hand, place it on her belly. The air around them grew heavy. She couldn't take her eyes from his. She saw his hand come out towards her, and suddenly checked herself. The feeling that he had read her mind was too strong, that he might have seen something on her face.

She flinched back. A tiny movement, but he saw it. His hand stopped. She saw his eyes harden. His face was inscrutable. A muscle twitched in his jaw.

'So you're all right.'

Jane gathered herself together. God, she was so transparent…she had to control these impulses.

She forced her voice to be light. 'Yes. It's nothing. It's probably not even the baby at all.'

She felt the acute disappointment that she couldn't share the moment with him. But she was far too vulnerable and weak in his presence; she had to maintain her guard at all times. Looking at him with welcoming eyes, wanting him to feel the baby move—that would have led her down a very dangerous path…

After helping Yvette and Jean-Paul prepare for the dinner, despite their remonstrations, Jane took a drive all the way up to the memorial at the other end of the island. It was bitter-sweet to be back there again and remember that day in the summer. She placed some flowers in the vases and lit a candle that was sheltered by the wind.

As she looked out to the sea, churning in a grey froth, she asked herself yet again what she was doing. Did she really have the strength to go through with this?

And then she felt the flutter again, barely perceptible, low in her abdomen. She turned and contemplated the view to the north. The view she had contemplated that day she'd come up here with Xavier, so full of optimism and joy, delighted expectation. And that night…that night was when this baby had been conceived. She unconsciously rubbed the bump beneath her jumper. That was why she was here. Loving Xavier was unfortunate, incidental, and not giving in to his potent seductiveness was her main priority. She had to remember that.

She was dressed and ready that evening when Xavier returned. His sharp, assessing eyes took her in. A long indolent look up and down that left her breathing faster. She cursed his ability to weaken her.

'Very nice.'

'Thank you,' she answered tightly.

She had tied her hair back in a loose knot, and was wearing a midnight-blue silk button-down dress. Demure and classic.

He reached into his pocket and pulled out a small box, handing it to her. She looked from him to it, a small frown creasing her forehead as she took it. When she opened it she had to hold back a gasp. Sapphire drop earrings glistened against the velvet background. They were stunning. Priceless. Her eyes flew up to his.

'But…what's this for? I can't take these; they're far too expensive.'

His voice was almost harsh, his face closed. 'Just take them, Jane. I got them to match your ring… You'll be getting plenty more jewels in time, and I'll expect you to wear them.'

Of course he would. She had a certain standard to maintain, didn't she? As his wife, she would be expected to wear jewels, compete with the other women in their society. The rush of pleasure she had felt initially at receiving such a gift was quashed.

As he'd said, they were to match her ring. He hadn't put any more thought into it apart from that.

She could be just as closed. She took them out of the box and put them in her ears, feeling as though they were piercing her heart, not the lobes of her ears. They felt heavy. She handed him back the box.

'Thank you for the gift. Excuse me. I have to help Yvette get the dining room ready.'

And with a straight back she walked away, barely hearing him take the stairs two at a time.

Jane threw herself into helping get the dining room ready to take her mind off their exchange, and it was just before the guests were due to arrive that Xavier appeared again downstairs. She was putting the finishing touches to a vase of flowers she'd picked herself on her excursion earlier, and looked up, her hands stilling of their own accord as she took him in.

He wasn't formally dressed, but had changed into a dark grey suit and a snowy white shirt with the top button open, giving a tantalising glimpse of dark skin and hair just underneath. Jane could almost feel the heat emanating from his chest as he paused on the bottom step. He took her breath away. Literally. Cleanshaven, hair swept back, sardonic eyes taking her in.

She burned up with colour at how she'd been caught staring to intently. Had she lost her mind? She was meant to be keeping him at arm's length, not drooling over him—and certainly not so obviously.

'Still blushing, Jane…? How remarkably sweet.'

Before she could answer, the doorbell pealed and Xavier took her arm.

'Time to act the loving wife.'

She smiled her way through the introductions as everyone seemed to arrive at once—Sasha being the last. She came in and threw her arms around Xavier's neck, pressing an eager kiss to his cheek. Jane couldn't take her eyes off the display, the way Sasha looked so sexy draped in his arms, blonde contrasting with dark. Xavier caught her eye and pulled himself out of Sasha's arms.

'Sasha, you remember Jane…my wife?'

Was there a subtle possessive inflection there? Jane wondered. Or was it just wishful thinking on her part?

'Sasha, how nice to see you again,' she said, lying through her teeth. 'Please come through. What would you like to drink?'

Sasha avoided Jane's eye, clinging on to Xavier's arm as they went into the main drawing room, where the rest of the guests were enjoying their aperitifs.

By the time they were on coffee and desserts, Jane's cheeks ached from smiling. Thankfully Sasha was at the other end of the table, beside Sophie, who had thrown Jane a few pained looks during dinner. At least now she didn't feel as though her dislike of Sasha was just in her own head.

Back in the drawing room afterwards, she rested on the arm of a chair, talking to the very friendly wife of one of

Xavier's older colleagues. She felt a prickle of awareness, and looked up to catch him staring at her from across the room.

The weight and intensity of his gaze caught her by surprise and, not having the time to react and school her features, she felt her body responding to his look, crying out for fulfilment. Her breasts grew heavy, and she felt her nipples harden into tight points, and that treacherous all-revealing flush stain her cheeks. She was unable to tear her gaze away from his, as if he'd put some kind of spell on her.

Sophie finally broke it, when she rolled her eyes and said to the room at large, 'Newlyweds! What is it the Americans say? Oh, yes! Get a room! We didn't come here to see you two devour each other with looks.'

Everyone laughed, and Jane blushed even harder. How had she ever thought she could handle this enforced celibacy?

And it was about to get worse.

Xavier, taking full advantage of the situation, strolled over and caught Jane up to him with one graceful move. He bent his head, taking her mouth with such a sweet kiss that a wave of longing made her shudder in his arms. His action was so swift that he took her off guard, much as he had with his look.

When he pulled away, her mouth clung to his, reluctant to let him go, and with a dazed look she realised that they were still in the room, and it hadn't been some dream. She couldn't let go of the feeling that had surged through her body, every point sensitive to his touch, his presence…the sheer sexiness of it, her breasts crushed against him.

She looked into his eyes and saw them flicker around the room. Reality crashed around her. An act…that was all it was. An act to unnerve her and for the guests.

She spoke quickly to hide her vulnerability, afraid he might read something into her easy acquiescence. 'I hope that was convincing enough for you?'

When she tried to pull out of his arms, they tightened. His

eyes flashed down at her. 'If I'd known you were going to be so happy to comply and act along then I'd have taken advantage a lot sooner…but rest assured I'll remember next time.'

And with a casual kiss on her wrist, he calmly strolled back to the other side of the room.

Xavier watched Jane from under hooded lids. She was studiously avoiding looking anywhere near him. He was only half taking in Paul's conversation, glad that there was a third person so he could watch her without appearing rude.

The kiss had unsettled him. How quickly he'd become aroused, like a flash fire. Rapidly devouring any sense of reality except what he felt when he touched her. He had felt how ripe and lush she was, more curved, rounded. The feel of her belly, pressing low against his groin… The intense possessiveness he'd felt had nearly floored him…she was *his* woman…carrying *his* baby. The thought of other men looking at her blooming beauty, the burgeoning curves, made his hands curl into fists.

Only registering the presence of their guests had held him back from hauling her up into his arms and out of the room…much like the caveman impulse he'd felt when he'd first brought her into this house. Amazingly, after all this time, he still felt the same out-of-control desire—if anything it had grown even stronger, and with it he felt…weak. Like Samson and Delilah, he thought with a small hard smile to himself. As if she was sucking his strength. Taking his power.

He could see how her chest rose and fell with uneven breaths, the V of her dress giving tantalising glimpses of her breasts, which pushed against the silk. He'd felt them through the fabric of their clothes. He wondered if they looked different now she was pregnant. Were they already fuller, harder?

His erection grew again, and he shifted uncomfortably. Then he remembered that morning, in the breakfast room.

When she'd turned that innocent gaze on him, so full of delight at the joy of their baby. Her hand on her belly, feeling something that he could only imagine. He'd ached with the sudden need to reach out and share what she was feeling, share the experience, and he had been sure the invitation had been in her eyes, her face. But then…just when he'd reached out…she'd flinched back, and the icy cool look had come down. Something inside him had shrivelled up. He had done that to her. She could barely bring herself to look at him.

That the baby could bring such effortless joy to her face but not him… He resolutely turned away from her and back to the conversation, a heavy feeling in his heart. A place he'd never given much thought to…until now.

Finally the last guests left, and Jane closed the door wearily. She'd told Yvette and Jean-Paul to go to bed long ago. Thank God that was over. She rubbed a hand over her tired eyes and pulled her hair free at the back of her head, massaging her scalp.

Xavier stood in the doorway of the drawing room. 'Care for a nightcap? Non-alcoholic, of course,' he added dryly.

She had a sudden overwhelming urge to walk over, run her hands under his jacket, lean into his tall body and say, *Take me to bed. Make love to me until we can't move any more.*

As if that scenario existed in some parallel world. A world where he loved her as much as she loved him.

But it didn't. She quashed the seductive daydream and instead moved towards the stairs, every cell in her body screaming to go in the other direction.

'No, thanks. I'm tired.'

'Of course. Wouldn't want you to miss out on any sleep. It mightn't be good for the baby.'

She looked at him warily as she got to the bottom step, saw him tip his glass back and drain the contents with something savage in his movements.

'Goodnight.' And she fled.

CHAPTER TWELVE

A MONTH later Jane was getting ready for the Winter Ball, which was that evening. Her hands shook as she put earrings in her ears, smoothed back her hair and flicked some lint off her dress.

Her nerves were wound so tightly now that she jumped at the slightest sound or movement. The last few weeks had been an exercise in torture. Self-inflicted torture. On the outside she was the picture of a glowing pregnancy. The sleepless nights, waking with muscles cramping from tension, hadn't yet told on her face, apart from faint dark circles. Xavier hadn't touched her again since that devastating kiss in front of their guests, but she could hardly look at him for fear of him seeing the naked desire on her face. She avoided him whenever she could. Slept late or got up early. Whatever was required.

He spent some nights on the mainland, and those were the only ones she slept. On a rational level she welcomed this, but on every other *honest* level she missed his presence with a physical pain that was almost unbearable. One day he'd brushed past her, barely touched her, and it had caused such an intense spiking of desire to rush through her that she'd had to restrain herself from grabbing him.

That was just what he wanted. Her to give in, beg him for release.

And…in weak moments…she had begun to entertain treacherous thoughts of doing just that. But each time she did, she'd remember why she couldn't... What if she couldn't keep her feelings hidden?

She sighed loudly in the empty room, and turned side-on to check her reflection. She smoothed the black empire line dress over her bump. It was growing every day, still neat, but now very evident.

A sound made her jump. Xavier stood against the doorjamb nonchalantly, devastating in a tuxedo. A memory of the first time she had seen him like that, by the pool in the hotel, came rushing back with such sudden force that she felt faint, and grabbed on to the table beside her to stay steady.

In two quick strides he was by her side, a hand curling around her arm.

'What is it?'

She shook her head, warding him off. 'No...nothing. Just a dizzy moment. I'm fine.'

He dropped his grip as though burnt, and ran an angry hand through his immaculate hair, leaving it tousled. 'For pity's sake, Jane, would you expect me to leave you lying there if you'd collapsed? I haven't laid a hand on you in weeks. Your startled jumps and fearful glances aren't exactly arousing me to passionate heights.'

He was furious, his pulse beating erratically against the skin of his neck. And all she wanted to do was reach out and press her lips against it. Feel the flutter under her mouth, taste his skin, see if it still had that musky tang...

She closed her eyes. 'I'm sorry. Of course I don't expect you to jump on me.'

The way she was feeling, she was more likely to jump on him.

She was a mess. A mass of churning frustrated emotions and desires...he was the cool one.

'The helicopter is ready; the Jeep is waiting. I'll be downstairs.'

He left the room.

Jane turned back to the mirror. Noticed her cheeks burning up, the fever-bright glitter of her eyes. Her breasts pushing against the fabric of the dress felt heavy and full. It was herself she needed protection from, not him. She closed her eyes at her reflection in despair.

By the time they got to the hotel she was calm again. Relatively. It was her first time back there since returning to France, and the memories rushing up were kept down with difficulty. She'd had plenty of opportunity to go to the mainland before now—Sophie rang nearly every other day to check in and ask her out—but Jane kept begging off. Somehow she knew she wouldn't be able to cope with Sophie's easy friendliness. She was just holding it together for herself. The island had become something of a sanctuary.

She followed Xavier to the main ballroom. He stopped her just before entering, the muted sounds of an orchestra coming from behind the doors.

'Ready for the performance of your life?' he drawled.

She nodded jerkily, avoiding his eye. She suddenly felt exhausted, as though she was conducting an impossible immense uphill battle.

'I am if you are.'

'Oh, I've been ready for some time.'

She ignored the implication in his tone. He took her hand in his and led her into the huge main ballroom, the crowd and sounds stunning Jane for a second after the peace of the island.

She nodded and smiled her way through the crush. With the help of Yvette she'd been picking up more and more French, and was now able to converse haltingly at Xavier's side.

A couple of hours later, after speeches and auctions in aid of charity, Jane was trapped by a very boring colleague of Xavier's. Some sixth sense made her realise that they'd become separated. She looked around and found him on the other side of the room. It wasn't hard. He stood head and shoulders above everyone else. His dark head was inclined towards someone. Jane couldn't see who, but then the crowd cleared and she had an unimpeded view. It was Sasha, in a stunning cream backless gown that showed off a smooth, tanned expanse of bare back. She was holding Xavier's arm, her head thrown back, throat exposed, laughing at something he'd just said.

Jane felt a red-hot poker right through her heart, and shook with the desire to march over there and rip every tousled blonde lock out one by one.

'She's a piece of work, isn't she?'

She looked around suddenly, aware that her heart was racing and shocked at the intensity of her feelings. To her relief she saw that the man had gone and Sophie was beside her.

They kissed each other's cheeks in greeting. Jane tried to make sense of her comment.

'What do you mean…piece of work?'

Sophie nodded her head towards Xavier and Sasha.

Jane feigned uninterest. 'Oh, that…'

Sophie flicked her hand in a very gallic gesture. 'Sasha…she's nothing. No, my dear. The women you need to watch out for are the ones giving you dagger looks.'

'What?' Jane followed Sophie's gaze and saw all the beautiful women dotted around the room, and she did indeed catch some looks that were none too friendly.

'Who…who are they?'

'They're the ones who thought they had a chance, who want to be where you are—married to Xavier and expecting his child.'

Sophie caught her husband gesturing at her from across the room and winked at Jane, 'My man wants me… I know what you might think, chérie, but you're quite welcome to your Alpha man…I'll take my pot-bellied version any day!'

Jane had to laugh at Sophie's outrageous sense of humour as she disappeared into the crowd.

Her smile faded, though, as she took in the women who had just been pointed out. More than a few speculative looks *were* coming her way, and she suddenly imagined them all shooting come-hither looks to Xavier.

She felt a huge surge of possessiveness and jealousy. So strong that she shook with it. Her first time out in public with her husband and she wanted to rip the head off every woman in a ten-mile radius. This didn't bode well.

She looked across the room again. Sasha had now been joined by two other beauties. They surrounded Xavier. Vying for his attention. A cold rage filled her body. Acting purely on some primeval instinct she was barely aware of, she started to walk over to him, not even thinking about what she would do when she got there.

She kept getting bumped and jostled by the crowd. Suddenly a tall man appeared in front of her, didn't move. She looked up…for a second her brain stopped working and then cleared.

'I don't believe it…Pete?'

'Jane!'

She kissed him on his cheek. 'You're still here! It's so lovely to see you…'

It all rushed back—her blind date with Pete, the night she'd met Xavier properly for the first time. She remembered his easy, unthreatening presence, and it was like a soothing balm to her soul. She smiled up at him widely.

'I was due to return home in September, but I met someone just before I did…and decided to stay on.' He blushed endearingly. 'We're getting married in the spring.'

'Oh, Pete, I'm so happy for you. That's wonderful news.'

Impulsively she reached up to kiss him again, a silly jealous dart rising unbidden at his exuberant happiness. When she stepped back, he had a funny look on his face.

Jane frowned. 'What…what's wrong?'

But she knew. She felt the familiar prickle of awareness.

An arm snaked around her waist, holding her firm. Xavier held out a hand to Pete. Jane could feel the tension radiating off him in waves.

'I'm Jane's husband…and you are?'

Pete visibly swallowed. 'Pete Sullivan.'

Jane couldn't believe Xavier was being so rude. Pete mumbled something and made a quick escape—Jane barely had a chance to say goodbye properly. She rounded on Xavier, pulling herself out of his embrace, but he had other ideas. He clamped a hand around hers and pulled her into an alcove where they were hidden from the room.

'Who the hell was *that*?' he snarled.

'Well, if you'd been acting like a human being I could have introduced you properly.'

'You were all over him.'

'Hardly, Xavier.'

'Well?'

She crossed her arms in front of her chest. 'I'm not going to dignify your behaviour with an explanation.'

'Oh, yes, you are…' A funny look came into his eyes. She recognised that darkening, that intent as he bent towards her, and instinctively pulled back, her hands coming up.

'Xavier…no.'

Hard hands took her arms. 'Yes, Jane. If you can kiss perfect strangers in front of the whole room, then you can kiss your damn husband.'

'He's not a stranger!' she cried desperately.

It was the worst thing she could have said. All she had was a glimpse of flashing green before the light was blocked and Xavier's mouth slanted over hers.

Her drew her in close to his body and kissed her with raw, unchecked passion. She tried not to respond, but her hands weren't obeying the order to push away…they rested between them, ineffectual.

The fire that had been simmering for weeks turned into an inferno…and on a deep sigh, she gave in. It was too strong for her to fight. And she was so tired of fighting it.

When he realised she wasn't resisting him, his arms relaxed and one hand moved to cup her bottom through the silk of her dress. The other threaded through soft hair, tilting her head, allowing his tongue to delve deeper.

Her hands uncurled and with sweet hesitancy climbed up his chest, until they were around his neck, holding him tight. She traced his lips with her tongue, her breath coming in short, sharp gasps, fingers tangling in the silky strands of hair that curled over his collar. He didn't allow her any quarter. His hand moved up, skimming, touching her more rounded curves, over her belly and up, until she felt him cup the heavy weight of her breast.

She'd never felt as womanly, as desirable. She tore her mouth away with a moan as his thumb found a jutting nipple and flicked it through her dress. With her increased sensitivity everywhere, it nearly pushed her over the edge.

His head dipped and he took her mouth again, remorseless, until Jane was weak and clinging to him with a powerful desire pulsing through her entire trembling body.

He finally tore his mouth away, both of them breathing hard. She pulled back, and this time he let her go. Through the haze of desire that pounded in her blood, Jane couldn't believe she'd let him kiss her like that. Or that she'd kissed him back. All of her precious barriers, so carefully in place to guard her weak heart. Torn down with a kiss. And it was blatantly obvious that her so-called *urges* were very much there.

She shook her head dumbly, suddenly remembering seeing him surrounded by that bevy of beauties. He was just staking his claim. On his property. In case she was getting any ideas.

Xavier looked at her, colour high on his cheeks, his lips curled derisively. 'Don't look at me like that, Jane…you wanted it as much as I did.'

She turned quickly and half-ran, half-walked back through the room, praying that he wasn't following. She muttered apologies as she crashed into people, unseeing. All she wanted was to get out of there. Suddenly she felt more claustrophobic than she'd ever been in her life.

Finally she stumbled out into the lobby on unsteady legs, breathing hard. Xavier was right behind her. She backed away.

'Xavier, please leave me alone.'

'Jane, you were with me back there every step of the way…you were very responsive.'

So responsive, in fact, that his body tightened again just at the thought.

Her eyes flashed and the possessive rage coursed through her again. 'Only half as responsive, I'm sure, as Sasha…or any of the other willing ladies in there.'

Someone walked out of the room and Xavier grabbed Jane's elbow, leading her to a quiet corner.

'What are you talking about?'

'I'd like to know exactly what is going on with you and Sasha.' Fire spat from her eyes.

He frowned for a second. 'What on earth do you mean?'

'I saw you with her…it didn't exactly look innocent. Every time she sees you she jumps all over you, and hisses at me like a cat.'

And what about the other women?

He took her shoulders and she tried to break free, but he wouldn't let her. 'I've known Sasha since she was a baby. She's had a crush on me for years…a stupid crush.'

He paused and looked at her assessingly, dangerously.

'Jealous, Jane? You won't let me touch you, but can't stand the thought of other women?'

She snorted, hiding the panic. *What was she thinking?*

'Hardly…don't flatter yourself.'

But the words sounded weak to her ears. She tried to evade

his gaze, but it was impossible. She realised that what he said was true. She didn't want those other women near him with a passion that scared her.

His hands tightened. 'Who was he?'

She looked up, feeling sudden relief that his attention had been taken from her disastrous admission of jealousy, from her raw emotions.

'Pete?'

Jane could feel him barely reining his temper in. His heavy-lidded gaze bored into her.

'Yes…who is he?'

She contemplated not answering him, but knew it was futile. And she certainly didn't want him focusing on her reaction to Sasha again.

'I met him the night I came here for dinner after the day trip. He was my blind date… He's living here, working in town. He was just telling me about the girl he's getting married to.'

She looked into his eyes, something twisting in her heart. 'What a coincidence, both of us finding our true loves here…'

Her sarcastic comment bounced off him. She could see his rapier-sharp mind make the connection, recognition drop. He straightened up to his full intimidating height and let her go. She swayed precariously. It was all too much…the crowds, the other women, Sasha, the kiss…and underneath it all this all-consuming, still raging desire for this man who just wanted her for the baby in her belly.

She felt herself being lifted against his chest and closed her eyes, a blessed numbness taking over. Felt herself being carried through a door and then carefully put down. She realised she was sitting on the edge of the bed in the penthouse suite.

Xavier was at her feet, taking off her shoes. 'What are you doing?'

He shot her a quelling look. 'Relax, Jane. You're obviously exhausted; you need to rest. Lie down for a while and I'll come back to check on you.'

He pushed her down onto the bed and drew a cover over her in the darkened room.

But then, instead of moving, he rested on his hands over her for a timeless moment. Jane looked up, transfixed by his eyes. It was as if time stood still. She saw something in the green depths, some expression of desire and blatant need that connected with the deepest part of her so strongly that she felt energy course through her system, exhaustion forgotten.

Xavier closed his eyes for a split second. She could see the pulse throb in his temple. Then he stood and straightened, looking down from his great height. Distant and remote, he stepped away from her.

He opened the door, about to walk out, and stopped. Jane's breath stopped too. He shut the door again and rested his hands on it, his head bent. Then he turned around with a sudden savage movement and strode back towards the bed, taking off his jacket as he did so. Jane's eyes widened, the breath coming jerkily in and out of her mouth as he came back and leant over her on his arms.

'Xavier…what are you…?' Her hands came up automatically between them when she saw the feral glitter in his eyes. He kept coming down, closer and closer. Her hands tried to push but he was immovable. She could feel her blood throbbing through her body, that energy pulsing through every cell.

'I want to sleep with my wife…I've waited long enough, and after that kiss…' His mouth tightened. 'God, Jane, how can you deny us this?'

He came closer, his torso practically touching her chest. She could feel her breasts swell against her dress, the nipples peaking into hard points. Her hands still pushed ineffectually at the hard wall of muscle.

Closer and closer.

She shut her eyes as she felt his mouth near her ear, his lips a breath away from touching. She was trembling all over.

'If you push very, very hard, push me away, I'll go back downstairs and leave you alone. But know this. I need you, Jane. I want you so much it hurts.'

His words resounded and echoed in her, through her. She hurt too. All over. The heat from his chest enveloped her, his scent arousing her beyond anything she'd ever felt. But she couldn't do this…had to resist. She pushed. Nothing. He didn't budge. Pushed again, harder.

Xavier expelled a harsh breath and started to pull away. Suddenly Jane had a vision of him walking out through the door, back downstairs to all those predatory women. Saw an aching lonely void when he left the room. It was the same as the kiss…she was suddenly tired, so tired of fighting herself, him…*this*.

Her hands stopped pushing. He stopped. She looked into his eyes and knew with fatal clarity that she could not let him walk out. She needed him with an aching, craving desire that obliterated all coherent thought and washed through her with such force that she shook.

Her hands moved up and around his neck. She pulled his head back to her.

On a mutual sigh of relief his arms came around her tightly and his tongue entered her mouth with one igniting stroke that mimicked another form of penetration so vividly that Jane moaned deep in her throat, her tongue meeting his, melding and mating and dancing.

She couldn't think beyond the here and now. She was too far gone. She'd worry about it later. Their kiss quickly got out of control as her hands roved over his chest, back, wherever she could reach. It was heaven to be able to finally touch him…and she wanted him to touch her…all over.

He drew back, breathing harshly, and pulled her up to a sitting position. His hands ran over her shoulders, glanced down over breasts that ached against the confines of her clothes.

'Take it off. I need to see you…'

She pulled the dress over her head awkwardly, feeling suddenly shy. She hadn't been naked before him since the summer. Xavier gazed at her wonderingly, a hand reaching out to cup her breast. They strained against the lace cups of her bra, bigger, the veins visible under the translucent skin, and then his hand moved down to her belly, the proud hard swell. He bent his head and pressed a kiss to the skin, his hand visibly shaking as he traced the smooth contour. She felt immeasurably moved.

He flicked open the front clasp of her bra, letting her breasts tumble free. The clamouring of her pulse got louder and she sucked in a hard breath, her head thrown back as his hot mouth bent and suckled there. A throbbing heat pulsed between her legs.

'You...I need to see you too,' she muttered thickly, coming up on her knees to pull off his bow tie, and open his shirt, her hands trembling. A button popped, and then she was smoothing it off his shoulders, baring him to her hungry gaze. How had she survived till now without this?

He sat back for a moment, watched as she bent forward, pressed her mouth against his skin, found a hard flat nipple, nipped gently. His hand threaded through her hair, holding her head, and she heard the whistle of his sucked-in breath.

Hands on her shoulders, gently he put her away from him, and she watched with a dry mouth as he stood and kicked off the rest of his clothes.

His body was even more beautiful than she remembered. The long lean lines, every muscle and sinew taut, the warm olive gleam of his skin rippling as he stepped back to the bed. Her gaze travelled down and her pulse ratcheted up a few notches when she saw his erection. It was bigger and harder than she remembered, and she felt a liquid burst of desire in response.

He caught her look and said wryly, 'It's been a while.'

He must mean since getting married, Jane thought dimly.

And then couldn't think as he took her shoulders and pressed her back down onto the bed. He rested over her on strong arms, the muscles bunching. She reached up, revelling in the feel of him, the satin warm skin, the musky scent. The strength of his body poised over hers made her quake with the need to take him into her, know him again.

His mouth was hot on her neck, on her pulse, beating out of control. He rested on his elbows over her, careful to keep her shielded from his full weight. She could feel the entire length of his body against her, his hardness against her belly. She writhed in response, a small moan escaping when his hair roughened chest stimulated her breasts unbearably.

He pulled back slightly, brought a hand up to skim over her shoulders, down over her breasts, before his mouth dropped and paid homage to each hard thrusting peak in turn. She was not herself any more. She sucked in jerky breaths, arching against him. His breath tickled as his mouth finally moved down, over her belly and lower, where she felt his fingers hook around her panties and pull them down, stockings following.

When she was naked, he pulled her into his body, torso to torso, legs entwined around hers, every part of their bodies touching. Jane could feel the tremors run through her. It was too much, too heady after so long…her breathing was laboured. She needed him, wanted him so badly.

He spoke her thoughts out loud. 'I don't think I can wait…or go slowly…'

'Me neither…' She arched as his hand caressed between her legs, fingers finding the moist centre of her desire. Stroking back and forth.

'You're so ready.'

She was half crazed with the need to feel him inside her, and instinctively lifted her leg over his hip, bringing her into intimate contact with his erection. It jumped and pulsed against her body. Xavier moved down slightly, keeping her leg lifted, and with one smooth thrust entered her. Jane cried out with the sensation, her walls tight around him after all this time.

'Have I hurt you?'

He went to withdraw and Jane grabbed him. 'No…don't stop.'

He started to thrust upwards, one arm around her back holding her steady, the other on her leg, holding it over his hip. And all the time came that delicious building, tightening, as they climbed and climbed, his strokes going deeper, harder, filling her exquisitely. She blindly sought his mouth and kissed him, unable to contain her instinctive drives any more. She arched towards him and felt every part of herself clench as with one last thrust Xavier sent her into a huge explosion of stars that left her quivering around his body just as he joined her in his own climax. She felt his power spill into her, deep in her body.

It was unbearably, exquisitely intimate, lying like this, still joined, face to face, their breath mingling, every inch of skin in contact, legs entwined.

When they were finally breathing normally Xavier shifted himself free of Jane's embrace, causing her to gasp again, her body still painfully sensitive.

He turned her gently, so her back was tucked into his chest, pulled a sheet over their bodies and pressed a kiss to the back of her head. A heavy, possessive arm lay around the swell of her belly, a hand stretched out to cover it.

She felt a kick in her belly under Xavier's hand and stilled.

'Did you feel that?'

It came again, stronger, and she turned a shining happy face up to him, holding his hand firm against her belly. 'Oh, Xavier, did you feel that?'

As he looked down into her face and felt the baby kick, he felt something inside him close off. Shut down.

He had to get away. Now… He couldn't trust himself here with her. He felt raw, exposed. They had just shared the strongest climax he could ever remember experiencing, and he'd been pretty sure it was the same for her, and yet…it was the baby that was giving her that glow of happiness, that smile as she looked up into his face.

Images and sensations rushed through him…the red mist of anger that had settled over his vision when he'd seen her talking to Pete…the feel of the baby kicking under her smooth skin…her happiness for that but not him—and the fear. The fear that he was falling into some place that he'd never find his way out of again…

She was just giving in to carnal desires—desires she had been resisting. She'd almost pushed him away; he'd almost left the room. It was laughable. Instead of the mocking voice in his head stopping, now it was all he could hear. He had to get out.

Jane felt the tension in Xavier's body, tried to gauge the look on his face.

He pulled his hand away from under hers and pulled himself out of the bed. She drew the sheet up over her chest, feeling a sudden chill. Xavier was stepping back into his clothes, a million miles away from the man who had just tucked her into his body. A cold look of detachment on his face, the angles harsh in the dim light.

'I should go back downstairs in case we're missed.'

He picked up his jacket and cast her a quick glance as he left the room.

'I'm glad you've decided it's time to be my wife. *Properly.*'

CHAPTER THIRTEEN

JANE lay in the bed, tucked into a curled-up position, for some time. Until the air began to chill her skin and she had to pull another blanket onto the bed to stop her teeth chattering.

This was exactly what she had feared. Sleeping with him had opened her up, taken the scab off the wound…and now she was afraid there would be no way to stem the flow of blood. This intimacy had cracked her heart open completely. And there was no going back. No closing it off again. After this…she couldn't.

What had she done…?

The next morning when she woke she was in the bed alone, and knew that Xavier hadn't joined her at all. Her body ached with a betrayingly pleasurable ache as she got up and belted a robe firmly around her waist. When she went out into the suite she paled visibly when she saw him standing at the window, pristine in a dark suit. He ran a cool look over her as she emerged, feeling sleepy and tousled in comparison. Her heart hardened when she saw the lack of anything on his face.

'Morning.'

'Morning.'

'I have to go to Paris for a couple of days…something's come up.'

She exuded what she hoped was an air of extreme unin-terest, fighting the reaction of her body to the musky scent that reached her nostrils, the smell of which was bringing last night back to vivid life. Her voice sounded strained to her ears.

'Fine...I'll go back to the island later on. Sophie said something about meeting for lunch, so I might do that.'

Xavier was very still as Jane helped herself to coffee and a croissant. She moved over towards a chair at the other end of the table and had to walk past him. He blocked her way, and she nearly jumped out of her skin. He took the cup and plate out of her hand and put his hands on her arms. She care-fully schooled her features before looking up, but started trembling when she took in the green eyes, smoky like last night, took in his mouth and quickly returned to his eyes. His mouth was far too potent.

'Jane...no more of the startled rabbit. We can't go back after last night.'

He took his hands away and ran one through his hair im-patiently. 'Hell, Jane, you stopped pushing me away. I almost left...'

Every self-protective mechanism kicked in. She shrugged negligently. 'It's no big deal, Xavier. I'm quite aware of what I did. We both got what we wanted.'

A hand came to her jaw, forcing her face up to his. She flinched inwardly at the hardness in his face. The lack of emotion.

The voice in his head would stop. He'd make it...and this was how.

'Good. Because when I get back we are going to be man and wife...properly...from now on.'

Jane refused to give in to the desire to run as fast as she could, stood her ground. She had got herself into this and there was no way that he would ever know how much it was going to kill her to be intimate, how much she feared her heart was going to break with every encounter, every time he left her so dispassionately afterwards.

Why, oh, why had she been so weak? She'd hit the self-destruct button. Spectacularly. And she couldn't even blame him! As he had pointed out, she had pulled him back to her, had made the choice.

Xavier held her jaw in a light but firm grip and bent his head, his breath tickling her face for a moment before he touched his mouth to hers. Even now, despite her pain, the pull was too strong, the desire overwhelming to just sink against his body, pull him close, allow him full access.

'I'll see you in two days…'

Two days later, back in the castle, Jane was like a cat on a hot tin roof. Listening out for the helicopter or the Jeep. Trying to read and giving up. Watching the TV and giving up. She knew she was irritating Yvette by getting under her feet, and took herself out for a walk to burn off the excess energy.

As much as she dreaded seeing Xavier again, she hungered for him now in a way she never had before. She had convinced herself in the past two days that she could do this…maintain a physical relationship and keep her feelings back. She couldn't fight him again. If she did, that razor-sharp mind would focus on her motivations and not let go until he'd found the beating heart of her.

And that weak heart, so brimming over with love for him, was what she had to guard against. She had nearly revealed it that night, when she'd felt the baby kick. And that was what had driven him from the bed. She was sure of it. She had seen the dawning horror on his face, the cool detachment as he had firmly extricated himself from her embrace.

She wouldn't make that mistake again.

When she returned to the castle there was still no sign of him. She tried not to worry, and picked up the phone countless times only to put it down again. He'd love that, wouldn't he? No doubt he'd laugh at her attempt to be a concerned wife. But the truth was she *was* concerned. She paced back and forth in the sitting room, looking out of the window at the skies that looked ominously grey.

Yvette appeared at the door, an indulgent smile on her face. '*Madame*, don't worry…he will be here. You should go to bed.'

Jane smiled weakly and nodded. 'Maybe you're right.'

It was a relief not to have to hold back her feelings with the other woman. Yvette assumed, of course, that Jane was madly in love.

She climbed the stairs and once in bed eventually fell asleep, despite the niggling worry.

Xavier walked into the bedroom, every bone and muscle in his body screaming with fatigue. Two days of intense negotiations and then he had flown himself back to the island on the plane. Ordinarily he would have stayed overnight in Paris. He had never had the overwhelming desire to come home before…

But now he did. And the reason was curled up under the covers. Her hair was fanned out on the pillow, lashes long against her cheek, and he could imagine the hidden curves. Her arms were bare and his body hardened in an instant at the thought of her naked.

He stripped and got into the bed, pulling her body close into his, breathing in her sweet scent. He felt the flimsy silk of her slip. She'd never worn this before…was it because she'd been waiting for him? The thought made him harder. His hand was firm on her belly, just under the weight of her breasts, and he cupped one full heavy mound, delighting in the way her nipple sprang to hard life in his palm.

He couldn't shut out the thought: She might want this for now…but you know she would resist if she could…she's going to hate you for this…sooner or later…

He blocked it out with every ounce of will-power, pushed it into some dark recess. It was too heady…too seductive… being here, having her in his arms like this…

Jane was half asleep and moaned softly in her drowsy state. She couldn't believe it. She was having that dream again. When would it stop?

She wiggled to try and force herself to wake up, but instead of the feelings subsiding as she became more awake, they got stronger. The pulse beating between her legs was all too real, as was the hand on her breast, the nudging of a very aroused man low at her back.

She came to full tense alertness. Her head falling back. 'Xavier…'

His mouth was busy trailing a hot blaze of fire down the back of her neck. Relief coursed through her. She tried to stay coherent for a moment, not in this all too dangerous dream-like state where anything could happen, anything might be said…

'Xavier…where were you?'

He lifted his head and she could just make out the glittering green in the darkness. His voice was sardonic, but didn't quench her desire, which was fast spiralling out of control.

'You missed me…?'

She blustered, 'No, of course not.'

He was pulling up her silk slip, up over her thighs. She hesitated for a split second and then lifted them to help, and felt his moan of approval against her back as he slipped her free of the flimsy garment entirely with one swift move.

Had she somehow subconsciously picked it because, if she was honest, she'd imagined this very scenario…?

She turned her head so that her lips were close to his. His mouth hovered over them for an infinitesimal moment and then he took them with a drugging, heated kiss, his tongue invading, exploring, plundering her weak, non-existent defence.

His hands on her breasts roused them to hard, engorged

points, and she gasped when he took his mouth away from hers. Keeping her back to him, he brought an arm under one leg, lifting it slightly, opening her up for him to explore with long fingers, feel the telling wetness, arousing her to even further heights.

She bit her lip to stop from crying out as she felt him guide his hard length into her tight passage, his chest pressed close against her, his hand holding her in place as he smoothly thrust in and out.

She was fast being borne away in an ever tightening need, the eroticism of the position, the hunger with which they both sought to reach the pinnacle, something almost animalistic in their movements helping them to reach a simultaneous climax of such strength that Jane felt everything go black for a split second…and then came back down on the shuddering waves of her orgasm, her body clenching and pulsating around Xavier for long moments.

How was it that they could reach this intoxicating peak every time without love? Words trembled on her lips. She turned her head and blindly sought his mouth…every buried wish and desire naked for him to see…if only he could.

Then she tensed abruptly. This was what she had to fight. This uncontrollable awful need to blurt out her feelings.

Xavier felt her distancing herself and pulled free from her body. He needed no further indication. They had scratched their itch.

He lay on his back by her side, and didn't pull her into his arms as she curled away from him. Jane lay for a long time staring into the dark. Long after Xavier had turned away on the opposite side and his breathing had slowed and deepened.

Two weeks later…two long weeks of similar nights…nights of blinding, all-consuming passion followed by each of them turning away from the other…Jane walked into the dining room, the toll now obvious on her face. Dark circles were evident under her eyes, and no amount of make-up could disguise the puffiness. She knew she couldn't keep going on like this. Despite her grand justifications to herself. She had hit the wall of as much emotional pain she could take.

Xavier took in her appearance with a sharp look.

'You don't look well.'

She bristled at his tone. He didn't have to point out to her what she knew herself. The bloom had gone. In the past few days she had even begun feeling nauseous again.

'It's called being pregnant, Xavier. I'm sorry, but not everyone feels amazing all the time. And I certainly don't at the moment.'

'You didn't seem to be feeling unwell last night…'

'Well, you wouldn't have exactly noticed, would you?' she snapped.

'Are you saying you didn't want me? Correct me if I'm wrong, but from what I recall you were a very willing partner—couldn't even wait for me to get out of the shower.'

She flushed a dull red, her body reacting to the image his words evoked, a tide of humiliation burning her up inside. A muscle twitched in his jaw. His face was hard.

'Xavier, it's just desire, purely physical, and, yes…I feel it too. Believe me, if I could switch it off I would.' The ringing bitterness in her tone surprised even her, and she stopped, avoiding his eyes.

He got up with a sudden violent movement, his chair scraping back, loud in the silence of the room. Jane flinched.

'I have business to attend to in the hotel. I'll be back this evening.'

A huge lump grew in her throat and tears blurred her vision as she sat there, miserable after he'd stalked out, unable to take even a sip of coffee. They were no better than bickering children…and it would only get worse. She knew the barbs would get sharper, cut deeper.

She blinked back the tears and hid her face when Yvette

bustled in and clucked like a mother hen. She went up to the bedroom and tried to take a nap, but it was impossible to sleep. She went down and helped make lunch, and prepared for dinner later as it was Yvette and Jean-Paul's night off, but her mind still churned, her stomach feeling acidy. In the afternoon, feeling as though she was going to go out of her mind, she made her escape and fled. She took the car on a drive, not knowing where she was headed.

She found herself arriving at the small cove where they'd spent their last day together in the summer. Grey skies and pounding waves reflected her mood effortlessly. She remembered the sweet happiness she'd felt that day...feelings that had long been submerged by now.

Her thoughts went inward. All along, since they'd met again, Xavier had professed to being motivated by nothing other than wanting this heir. The warmth they had shared in the summer had been the smooth, urbane playboy part of him. The seductive man beneath the cynical, ruthless businessman. She only had to remind herself of how, once he had taken the decision to marry her, he'd gone to New York for two weeks, not to see her again until their wedding day. Supremely confident that she'd acquiesce.

She had thought she was doing the best thing for the baby, for her mother...but all along she had to admit that she had harboured a deep fantasy that maybe things would change, that he would look at her with the same tenderness she remembered from the summer.

She knew it was that that had prompted her to give in to her overwhelming desire...an effort to recapture some elusive dream, maybe change the status quo... But she'd made things worse, not better. And she knew, sadly, even if she could go back to the penthouse suite and that night, she still wouldn't have the strength to watch him walk out through the door. That had been inevitable, a force of nature.

But, because of it, all that stretched ahead for now were

long, lonely days. Nights filled with passion, maybe. But afterwards he would pull away from her, exactly as he had each night up till now, and she would stifle the words that begged for release… She knew it was only a matter of time before she revealed herself, and to do it in a moment of weak passion would annihilate her.

She knew then what she had to do. With a clean, clear certainty in her heart, she felt relieved for the first time in weeks. She would go to him and tell him. She would tell him she loved him, calmly, with dignity, not in a moment of passion.

If there was any way he thought he could feel anything at all beyond a purely physical attraction, then she would stay and try to make the marriage work. But if he couldn't…and that thought made her feel weak…she would leave. As much as it would kill her to do that, it was the only way she could hope to survive.

She could go to the mainland, stay in Lisa's villa, figure out what to do. After all, they were married now, surely the inheritance had to be merely a formality? She wouldn't even insist on a divorce for now, if he didn't want it. But she was sure he would one day…he would meet someone else. How could he not?

Jane got back into the car, a nervous knot in her belly, wanting nothing more than to finally be honest with him…and herself.

By the time she got back to the castle it was much later than she had realized—early evening, the light darkening in the sky. Xavier's Jeep was back already, and Jane felt her stomach plummet. Her hands felt clammy as she gripped the wheel after she'd come to a stop. Could she really go through with this?

Then she saw him at the door, his tall body tense. He strode towards the car, pulling the door open.

'Where the hell have you been?'

Her churning emotions, what she had to do, made Jane

match him in anger. 'I went for a drive. Is that permissible? Don't worry, Xavier, your precious cargo is still safe.'

He frowned down at her as she got out, barely allowing her enough room to move. She clenched her jaw as she brushed against him.

'Cargo...what on earth are you talking about?'

Blue eyes blazing in her face, she looked up after slamming the door shut. 'The baby...the reason we're here.'

His mouth compressed. 'Of course. How could I have forgotten.'

He took her by the elbow and pulled her inside.

'Xavier, let me go. I'm perfectly capable of walking by myself.'

He dropped her arm and rubbed a hand over his eyes. Jane suddenly noticed that he looked terrible, and there was a slight smell of alcohol on his breath.

'Have you been drinking?'

Hard green eyes regarded her as his head came back, nostrils flaring slightly. 'Yes, dear wife. You're driving me to drink...happy now?'

Jane walked towards the kitchen. 'You need a cup of coffee.'

He grabbed her arm and swung her around, bringing her into intimate contact with his whole length. He looked and felt dark and dangerous, dressed all in black. She closed her eyes at the dismayingly predictable way her body responded to his heady proximity. With an effort she held herself stiff as a board in his arms and slowly opened her eyes.

She shook her head at him. 'Xavier, let me go...we can't do this...'

This just firmed her resolve for what she was going to do. Their passion, if unchecked, would soon make them bitter with their need for each other. It was already happening. She pushed herself out of his arms with effort, more from her own self than Xavier holding onto her.

'You're right.' A bleak look crossed his face and he stepped away. 'I'll go and make some coffee. I came home early to talk to you…and then when you weren't here…'

'I…I wanted to talk to you about something too…'

'I'll get us both coffee and bring it into the sitting room.'

He went towards the kitchen and Jane took off her coat, hanging it up and going into the sitting room. She felt ridiculously nervous, pacing up and down, biting her lips, wrapping her arms around her body, sitting down and then standing up.

He appeared at the door silently, with two mugs in his hands. She took the one he handed her. She wrapped her hands around it as if to pull some of the heat into her chilled body. Take some comfort where she could.

She sat on the couch while Xavier stood pensively by the fire.

'Jane, I—'

'Look, Xavier…'

They spoke at the same time. Jane put down her mug and stood up, feeling at a disadvantage sitting down. She locked her hands together to stop the betraying tremor. She needed to calm herself before launching into the hardest confession of her life. She needed time.

She gestured to him. 'You go first…'

He stood for a minute, looking into the fire, before turning towards her. She'd never seen him look so serious, and so distant that it scared her a little. She felt an awful foreboding trickle down her spine.

'Tell me, Jane, does the sight of me really disgust you so much that you can't look at me without your body being rigid with tension?'

'Of course not…how can you say such a thing…?' Her eyes widened in reproach, confusion in their depths, her body going even more rigid despite his words.

'Because ever since we got married you've been like a deer

caught in the headlights…flinching whenever I come near you…rigid like you are now, with that cool icy look in your eyes. Oh, I know how to make you relax—' he laughed harshly '—it's very apparent to both of us how we can make the tension disappear. But then afterwards you can barely wait until I've pulled free of your body before you shut down again.'

Jane blanched at his crude words, remembering all too vividly the night in the penthouse when *he* had been the one to pull away, get out of there as fast as he could. And her humiliation and self-derision rose again like bile.

'It seems to me to be mutual.' She couldn't disguise the bitterness lacing her voice.

He noted it with a look, and emitted an audible sigh. 'I've been thinking all day today about…us. And not just today, if I'm honest. It's something I've tried to avoid thinking about.' He looked into the fire for a moment before looking back at her. 'There's something I should explain, though.'

'Go on.'

She marveled that she sounded so calm.

He thrust his hands into his pockets. 'My parents weren't happily married. By the time my mother died when I was five I was being used as a pawn in their relentless bitter feuds with one another. That's why my father never remarried; he was bitter his whole life, and he took it out on me.' His lips thinned. 'Everyone assumed he never remarried because he loved my mother so much, but it was the opposite. And…I'm afraid that I can see the same thing happening with us. Jane, this morning we were sniping at each other like…exactly how they used to.'

He looked at her, his eyes fixing her with their green luminescence. She took in his words, dimly remembered every time she'd brought up his father, only to have him change the subject, the look that would cross his face. It made sense now. She had to focus when he spoke again.

'I won't bring a child into that again…so that's why I'm

prepared to give you a separation if you want. At least if we're apart, we might be able to maintain respect for each other.'

She stopped breathing. 'What…what do you mean…?' she asked faintly.

'I think we both know this marriage isn't working. You went into this with the clearest of motivations, intentions… and I took advantage of that. The inheritance is assured by our marriage. I shouldn't have brought you back here…'

She couldn't understand how everything wasn't crumbling around her, disintegrating. She sank down onto the couch behind her, her eyes unseeing, unfocused on the ground in front of her.

Xavier's voice continued, like a relentless battering ram against her heart,

'Believe me, I'm tempted to do the cowardly thing, indulge our physical attraction, keep going as if nothing is wrong—and I know you might too, up to a point. I thought it would work…that it would be possible with just…just what we had. But it's not. We're becoming bitter, and that will poison any chance of a civil relationship.'

He was talking about their attraction being the only thing he thought they could have worked on…and even that wasn't enough now.

He paused and took a deep breath. She knew he hated the admission with every bone in his body. It would be hard for him to admit to any frailty, weakness, and their marriage not working would fall under that.

She found herself nodding her head. It was the worst-case scenario. Even knowing that this had happened, *was* happening, she could feel the tiny part of her that had clung to treacherous hope…die.

Just don't make me speak… I can't speak, can't breathe.

'I can set you up wherever you want. If you want to stay

here, I'll go to the mainland. You'll be taken care of… I would just ask that you consider staying in France, so I can have more access to…our child.'

He sounded so cold, so clinical.

She forced herself to stand again, not wanting him to see the devastation on her face, in her body. Well, now she knew. He'd done her the unwitting favour of allowing her to keep her dignity intact. He'd never know how much she loved him.

She looked up, focusing on a point just beyond his shoulder, the lines in her face rigid. He came towards her, she backed away.

'Jane? You can't tell me you're happy…you're not the same person I knew in the summer.'

Neither was he…

'No…I'm not happy.'

That much at least was true.

They faced each other like strangers. A gaping chasm between them.

'You wanted to tell me something?'

She looked at him then, and she had to keep back the slightly hysterical laugh that threatened to bubble out of her mouth. 'Would you believe it was to ask for a separation, too…?'

He sighed heavily. 'Yes, I would. At least it seems we're agreed on this.'

She turned blindly and walked out of the room, just managing to stop herself from running out through the door.

'Jane—wait. We should talk about this now…what we're going to do.'

She turned with huge effort at the door, her face white, her eyes huge blue pools. 'I'm very tired. I'd like to lie down for a while.'

'I'll take the spare room tonight.'

That was all she heard as she walked across the hall, her

singular desire right then to get away to some private space where she could be alone with her pain.

Just as she approached the stairs she had the strangest sensation of not feeling her legs—before a blinding cramp seized her middle and she doubled over in pain. It was so intense that she couldn't breathe. She was vaguely aware of someone calling her name, arms supporting her...and then she collapsed.

She came to for a second, was only half aware of Xavier picking her up into his arms, and then she thought of the baby. Completely forgetting the recent conversation, the uppermost thing in her head with crystal-clear clarity was this baby—and what the future would hold if anything should happen to it

Nothing.

He would send her away, let her go. She clutched his jumper in a white-knuckle grip.

'Xavier...the baby. Nothing can happen to the baby... I need it so much... I love...' And she passed out again.

CHAPTER FOURTEEN

JANE opened her eyes slowly and realised that she was lying on their bed, dim light casting shadows into the room. Then she saw Xavier standing at the base of the bed, talking to some man in a suit. That was weird. Why was she on the bed? And what was that man doing in their room?

She tried to speak and a croak came out. The men turned to face her. The older man hurried to her side. He lifted her hand and took her pulse.

'Hello, my dear, you gave us quite a fright…'

His words meant little to Jane as she struggled to take things in.

'What…what happened?'

She looked from Xavier to the man with a frown on her face.

He sat on the bed and kept her hand in his. 'Jane, I'm Dr Villeneuve. Xavier called me when you collapsed a short time ago. Luckily I was here on the island, doing my rounds, and was close by…otherwise you would have been taken to the hospital on the mainland.'

Suddenly it all came back—every single second of what had happened. Her hand went straight to her belly, her face white.

'The baby…?' But even as she felt her bump, she knew it was all right. The relief she felt made her feel giddy with light-headedness. She caught Xavier's eye, but his face was immobile, shuttered.

Dr Villeneuve patted her hand and looked at Xavier. 'If you'll excuse us for a moment, Xavier? Now that she's awake I'll need to do a thorough exam, just to make sure she's safe to rest here for the night. But she will need to go to the hospital first thing tomorrow.'

'Of course.' Xavier's voice was terse and he left the room.

The doctor helped Jane to undress, and examined her for any signs of anything more serious than a cramp. When she had changed into nightclothes, he came back and sat beside her on the bed.

'Jane…I'm happy enough that nothing is wrong. It's clear that this is stress-related, and it can be common enough, although very frightening. I know it's your first pregnancy, and it can take a lot out of you. You need to take care of yourself…is there anything bothering you?'

She looked into his kind, jovial face and felt like crying.

Only that Xavier doesn't love me and wants to separate…

She shook her head. 'No…don't worry, Doctor. I'll take care of myself and the baby.'

He gestured to the door with a smile. 'And that man out there, wearing a hole in the floor! I've never seen him so frantic. He pulled me out of my car before it had stopped moving. I shudder to think what he would have done if I hadn't been passing. He's asked me to stay for the night, and I'll come to the hospital with you in the morning…he's a very persuasive man.'

She smiled weakly. Xavier's concern for the baby was admirable, but not exactly a soothing balm to her spirit. The doctor left her, and when he was gone she heard his and Xavier's steps echo down the hall.

She sank back into the pillows. The last thing she remembered was Xavier wanting to talk things through, and then that awful pain. She focused on her breathing and staying calm. She wouldn't think about what they had said now…knowing very well that her cramp had been brought on by the sheer shock of Xavier informing her he wanted a separation.

Thank God she hadn't spoken first. To have to separate and have Xavier know how she felt would have made him look at her with such pity...at least this way she could leave, dignity relatively intact.

The door opened and he stood framed in the doorway. Jane's breath stopped, and then quickened as her heart leapt.

'Xavier, the doctor doesn't have to stay. The poor man probably wants to go home to his family.'

'I'm not taking any chances. He's staying, and that's that.'

His tone brooked no argument. He closed the door behind him and came further in, shedding clothes as he did. Jane's mouth went dry as she watched him.

'What are you doing? I thought you said you were going to sleep in the spare room.'

'The doctor is using the spare room.'

'There are at least five more,' she pointed out, an edge of panic strangling her voice.

'And they're all the other end of the house...I won't have the doctor that far away, and you are not sleeping on your own. Anything could happen.'

She averted her face, closing her eyes to his naked body climbing in beside her, her hands clenched under the covers. The doctor had said to stay away from stress—surely this qualified as stress? She could feel her pulse skyrocket.

She lay on her back, eyes closed, and heard the light click off, felt the darkness surround them. Their breathing was unbearably loud to her ears in the quiet room. She could feel a heavy cloud of need and desire hover over them, felt her body coming alive against her will.

Suddenly a gravelly cough from across the hall broke the spell. The doctor. Imperceptibly Jane breathed out a sigh of relief, and turned on her side, willing her body to calm down.

She sank into a deep, dreamless sleep, half waking during

the night to feel herself tucked into Xavier's chest, his head resting on hers, arms tight around her belly and chest, spooning her lower body. In blissful half-consciousness, able to ignore reality, dangerous thoughts, she snuggled in tighter and drifted off again. She told herself this contact was inevitable if they were in the same bed. She knew well enough that morning was just around the corner. And perhaps it was the last time she would ever share a bed with him.

When she woke, sunlight was streaming into the room. Jane took a moment to remember the previous night's events. When she did, a hard weight lodged in her heart. No more hope…no more maybe….no more possibility that perhaps he could come to feel something…

She pulled herself out of the bed, feeling a hundred years old. A small reassuring kick deep in her belly focused her thoughts and reminded her of how close she'd come to nearly losing everything. At least with the baby she'd always have a piece of him.

A movement caught her attention, and she looked up to see Xavier come into the room. He was carrying a tray, and looked smart and cleanshaven, but there were lines around his mouth and circles under his eyes. She willed down the concern that rose up.

'Here's some breakfast. Dr Villeneuve is downstairs, ready to go when you're dressed.'

'I feel much better today. I'm sure I'll be fine. There's no need—'

'Jane. We're going to the hospital.'

He left the tray and walked out. He'd hardly even looked at her.

She forced herself to eat something small, but it tasted like chalk in her mouth. She washed and dressed in jeans and a simple smock top before making her way downstairs.

In no time they were in the chopper, landed, shown to a

waiting car, and then Jane was being settled into a private room at the hospital. The whole thing happened so fast it made her head spin. The nurse left, and then it was just the two of them.

A heavy silence settled over the room. Xavier crossed his arms and rested back against the sill of the window.

'Tell me, I'm interested to know why you were going to ask for a separation…you never did say.'

Her hand stilled on the sheet. The conversational tone he'd used, as if it was as innocuous a comment as asking about the weather, made her see red. The pain and anger she'd been holding in since yesterday evening, the pain that had caused her to cramp, rose like acid bile on her tongue, and she wanted to lash out. Lash out at his cool façade, his reserve, his perfectly articulated reasons why he thought they should separate. As if he was in supreme control, capable of these rational judgements. She wanted to smash through that control…say something to make him squirm…run out through the door and perhaps finally leave her in peace.

She hitched up her chin, looked him in the eye, and with an unwavering voice she was proud of said, 'Would you believe that I was going to ask for a separation because…?' She faltered. Faced with those devastating eyes, her brave façade crumbled, her heart skipped a beat.

'Well…?' he taunted softly, quirking a black brow over cool, sardonic eyes.

It was all the impetus she needed. White hands clenched the bedspread. The full weight of her heartache settled over her like a dark cloud. She felt her voice quaver but didn't care. The words came stumbling, rushing out, tripping over each other…

'Because…Xavier…I love you. I love you so much I can't breathe with it. Every time I look at you I want to make love to you. I hurt all over, but especially in my heart, because you don't love me, and if we don't separate then I'm afraid that by the time this baby is born there won't be anything left of me. Because I just can't bear to be in the same room as you and want you so much, and know that it's only physical attraction you feel, and that you only want me for this baby…' She paused for a second, drawing in a gulping, shuddering breath, too distraught to see how he had straightened and paled. 'And that you don't, can't, *won't* ever love me…that's why…and it's just as good a reason, if not better, than yours.'

Tears blurred her vision and she fought to stop the wobble in her lip, feeling more raw and exposed than she'd ever felt. In shock at what she had just said.

She turned her head away, closing her eyes, the tears trickling down her cheeks as she waited to hear the click of the door. Waited to give in to the huge sobs she could barely hold back, her chest heaving silently.

Instead of the door opening and closing, she felt the bed dip beside her, and a warm hand under her chin, turning her head around. She kept her eyes shut tight, bringing a hand over her face in a pathetic attempt to hide her anguish.

Xavier brought her hand down. The sobs were threatening to break free. She choked them back, opening pain-filled streaming eyes. 'Just go, Xavier…please, leave me alone.'

He was intense, his eyes roving over her face. 'Jane, it's the baby you love, not me.'

How could he do this to her? Humiliate her? Wasn't it enough that she had laid her heart bare for him, and now he had to trample it into the ground? Why wasn't he walking away?

'Xavier, if you can't handle the truth, then leave. This is why I want to separate.'

'But, Jane, all along you've said…' He stopped, started again. 'When you collapsed it was the only thing you mentioned before passing out…'

She pulled his hand down from her chin, saying with a choked voice, 'Of *course* I love the baby…but, like it or not, I love you too. I was scared because this baby is my only link to you. There—are you satisfied? Now, just go and leave me be...*please.*'

He still didn't move. He dropped his head, his hands fists on the bedspread either side of her body. She wiped at the tears on her cheeks and waited for him to stand up and leave, a little hiccup escaping her mouth.

He brought his head up and fixed her with a look of something indefinable that she'd never seen before. Her breath caught in her throat. She couldn't escape his eyes, pinning her to the spot, their brilliant green reminding her of their first meeting.

'Jane...I did think it might be best to separate because of what I told you about my parents. But the stronger reason was that I couldn't live with myself any more for making you so unhappy. Because every time we slept together you were hating me a little more...every time I saw joy in your face for the baby I felt jealous...'

A numbness was taking her over. She recognised it as a form of self-protection. What was he saying?

He went to reach for her hand, but she drew back. He could see the trepidation in her eyes.

'Jane...let me explain. Ever since that night in the penthouse—'

She cut him off, her body taut with tension. 'You were the one who left. And the next morning...you were so cold...'

'I left because...sleeping with you again blew everything out of the water. My feelings didn't go away, they got stronger. And I was jealous...insanely...of your joy in the baby when...when we had just shared...' He stopped himself, a rare vulnerability in his eyes. '*You* were so cool, so blasé about it. As if you'd decided sleeping together was nothing more than giving in to our overwhelming physical urges. I told myself I didn't need feelings to be involved...' He gave a short sharp laugh. 'You were handing me exactly what I thought I wanted, and suddenly it wasn't enough.'

'All *you* want is this baby...'

'I told myself that at the start. I used the baby to justify how much I had to have you, no matter how it happened. When you came to me in London, so self-contained and full of independence, I followed the strongest instinct I've ever felt and did all I could to make you marry me, sure that you'd fall into my bed and we'd pick where we left off and I wouldn't have to examine my feelings.'

'But you—Feelings? You weren't even *thinking* about me...'

'Wasn't I?' He lifted a brow, a rueful look on his face.

Jane still clung onto the protective shield.

'I had your address for two months before I saw you. I had you traced a month after you left... I'll admit I wasn't sure if I was going to get in touch, but I know that I wanted to...and believe me, I didn't like feeling like that.'

She frowned, shaking her head. 'But how...? What about all those women? I saw the papers, all the models...'

He hung his head and groaned before coming back up, his gaze on her mouth, her eyes. 'I took them all out...wined them, dined them...even kissed a few—and as soon as I did the memory of you would break through and any desire I felt disappeared. It happened with infuriating regularity, and no woman...*ever*...has had that effect on me.'

She resisted the pull...dampened the spark that wanted to erupt in her chest.

'But when you asked me to marry you...you left me alone...didn't come back until the wedding.'

'I couldn't be near you. It was too intense. I was terrified of losing you again, and so in denial about how I was feeling that I went as far away as I could...'

He looked away for a moment, then back, a sad light in his eyes. 'After witnessing my parents' fighting, my father's bitterness, I never dared believe I could feel the real thing...I didn't know what it was. This summer you reached a part of me I didn't know existed...then, when you left...'

He looked shamefaced. 'I think on some level I wanted to

tie you to me, sate my desire, which I told myself was the root of all my feelings, and punish you for making me feel so vulnerable. I was so sure you felt nothing for me. But then…it was slowly killing me inside to know how unhappy I was making you. It was the hardest thing I ever did, telling you that you could leave.'

'What…what exactly are you saying?'

She had to be strong. His words still didn't necessarily mean what she thought, hoped. It could just be pity…guilt… and that would kill her all over again.

His eyes stunned her with their intensity. 'Jane, I have not stopped thinking about you since that day you…*we* bumped into each other. It was a *coup de foudre*—love at first sight. I know that now, but it's taken me the longest time to just give in and admit it to myself…'

He grew blurry again through her tears. The spark grew; her heart cracked open.

He tenderly wiped her cheeks with his thumbs, his hands warm around her jaw. She put her hands over his.

'I've been in love with you for so long. I couldn't believe I'd fallen for you that week…' She hiccuped again. 'So stupid.'

'Shh, you don't have to say anything…'

'But I do. I didn't stay in June because I couldn't bear to be just your mistress, especially after Sasha—' She stopped, the pain of that morning still vivid.

Xavier frowned. 'After Sasha, what?'

'She came to the suite that morning and told me that she had organised everything for our date… She told me that it was your usual routine—the pampering, the champagne, dinner…that she did this for all your…women.'

His whole body tensed, his hands dropped. 'No wonder you left… She must have seen that you were different. You have to believe me, Jane. She must have heard me on the phone… I'll bloody kill her.'

He looked so fierce that Jane took his hand. 'I do…I do believe you. I know now that she's no threat.'

She looked down at her hand on his, still not really sure if she could believe. She wanted to tell him…everything.

'When we got married, I didn't sleep with you because I thought you'd guess straight away how I felt. I was so raw and emotional with the pregnancy, and seeing you again…but of course you were right.' She smiled a watery smile, 'What I suppressed only got stronger—the *urges*—God, how I hated using that word—were always there. But using the pregnancy was the only way I knew to try and keep you at a distance. At the ball I wanted to rip the head off every woman there…'

He shook his head ruefully. 'Not sleeping with me was the smartest thing you did…it forced me to face myself. And as for the ball, when I saw you with Pete…he's lucky he got to walk away.'

He looked at her, his face suddenly serious. 'Jane, do you really mean what you said? Are you sure it's not just the baby…?'

'My darling, I loved you long before I found out about the baby…'

He brought his hands up to frame her face again. Jane could feel them tremble. 'When you collapsed in my arms…' He closed his eyes, his skin suddenly ashen. 'If anything had happened to you, I don't think I could have lived. I love you so much that it terrifies me…'

'I'm not going anywhere… I love you, Xavier, with all my heart and soul.'

'And you and this baby—' he bent and pressed a kiss to her belly '—are my heart and soul, *mon coeur*. Without you, my life would be over.'

Then he took her lips in a sweet, healing kiss, a kiss of benediction, and with such reverence that fresh tears streamed down her cheeks—just as the door opened and the doctor walked in.

'What's this? I said no stress.'

They couldn't take their eyes off each other. Jane smiled. 'Everything is just fine.'

Six months later, at the annual summer fête, the island was celebrating. Xavier tucked Jane into his side and held Amelie against his shoulder while she cradled Max against her chest.

Jane's mother and Arthur bustled over. 'You young people need to have fun and relax. We'll take care of the little ones.'

Giving in to a greater force, Jane chuckled as she handed over her son, and watched as Xavier handed over his daughter with comical reluctance and care.

'Will they be OK?' he asked, looking anxiously after the doting elders holding their precious bundles.

Jane slipped her arm around his waist, pushing a hand into one jeans pocket and cheekily squeezing his firm behind. 'Yes, darling, they're taking them for the day—which means I have you all to myself.'

He managed to drag his worried eyes away and brought Jane around to face him, drawing her in tight against his body. She blissfully laced her fingers around the back of his head and moved sinuously against his pelvis, exulting in his low, appreciative groan.

'As I'm not flying in "one of those death traps", as you so succinctly put it—this year or ever again if it reduces you to the terror that you told me it did—then why don't we go somewhere a little more private?'

'Yes, please.'

They walked towards the castle, which wasn't far in the distance, arms wrapped tight around each other.

'Do you think we can find out well in advance if there's any likelihood of twins again? I don't know if I could handle the shock.'

Jane had to laugh out loud as she remembered the moment

that day in the hospital when, during a check-up scan, they had discovered for the first time that she was carrying twins. The doctor had informed them that it was rare, but nevertheless quite possible, for one twin to mask the other until relatively late in the pregnancy.

She pretended to think for a second. 'You know, I must ask Mum. I'm nearly certain there are triplets somewhere on her side…'

He lifted her up into his arms. 'You witch…you just want to see me go into Neanderthal protection mode again…'

'But you did it so well…' She batted her eyelashes up at him.

He claimed her mouth in a hot and desperate kiss. All joking fled from her mind as her pulse speeded up and a familiar throb of desire pulsed through her veins. By the time they got to the front door they were both breathing heavily, with flushed cheeks.

He looked down into her face with such naked love and desire that her heart sang.

'Do you have any idea how happy you've made me?' he asked huskily.

She brought a tender hand up to caress his face. 'If it's half as happy as you make me every day, then we have enough happiness to last a few lifetimes.

THE SPANIARD'S
MARRIAGE BARGAIN

This is for Dr. Larry Bacon, Dr. Louise Campbell and Dr. Jim Holden, with much thanks.

This is also especially for The Inspiring Ladies of the fledgling Women's Writers Circle in Scariff in County Clare, and even more especially for Ruth McMahon—who is soul sister, friend, guru and wisewoman.

CHAPTER ONE

ROWAN CARMICHAEL faltered slightly as she stepped into the minimalist lobby of the small boutique hotel. She hadn't realised it was so exclusive. Even though she was well dressed, well enough to look as if she belonged here, she felt as though everyone must surely be able to see under her skin to the very heart of her, that beat so unsteadily. It had been so long since she'd been in a place like this. Another lifetime, another woman. She should have picked a more down-at-heel hotel. This kind of hushed luxuriousness reminded her of too much and made the skin on the back of her neck prickle.

She was completely oblivious to the several appreciative looks she drew, with her dark red hair and flawless creamy skin, which contrasted with her ever so slightly awkward grace as she moved.

Her expressive full mouth tightened as she looked for a seat, willing herself not to let the rising panic overwhelm her. She couldn't think of the past now. It was gone, and with it— Her step faltered again as a slicing pain ripped through her, stunning her with its intensity, with its rawness, its newness… even though it was old. And she felt old—a lot older than her twenty-seven years.

She found an empty seat and sank into gratefully. Within

moments a waiter had come to take her order for Earl Grey tea. She sat back and crossed her legs, taking a deep breath. She had to get it together. Had to be in control and above all *calm*.

She would have to discuss with a solicitor in less than ten minutes how she could best contact the husband she'd walked away from two years ago…and her baby. That slicing pain gripped her again, and she was made aware of how tenuous her control was. She needed time to gather herself. Perhaps she'd been silly, scheduling the appointment so soon; she was literally just off the train. This was the first time she'd been out in public again in two years. In the busy, heaving metropolis of London. Somewhere she'd truly never expected to be ever again.

No. She couldn't think like that. She'd be fine. After all, hadn't she been through so much worse?

This was the first day of the rest of her life. A new page, a new chapter.

A new beginning. And perhaps… A tiny alien bird of hope fluttered in her chest. Perhaps another chance at happiness? Even though in truth she'd had precious little happiness in her life so far…

Just then her attention was taken by a little boy, who was running and fell headlong at her feet on the marble floor. With instinctive and unquestioning swiftness Rowan was out of her seat and bending to lift the boy gently, her hands under his arms, a reassuring smile on her face.

'It's okay, sweetheart. I don't think you've really hurt yourself, have you? You look like a very brave boy.'

He stood unsteadily on chubby legs, his face veering between crying and not crying, a lip wobbling. He was adorable. Dark blond hair, olive skin and huge eyes…they were the colour of violets. Unusual and distinctive.

Too unusual and distinctive.

Shock slammed into Rowan like a punch in the gut. They were, in fact, the exact unique shade of violet that looked back at her in her own mirror every day. With that thought came a surge of something so instinctive, so primal, *so inexplicable* Rowan felt the world flip over and right itself again at an angle.

She held onto the boy. He'd obviously decided against crying, and looked at her guilelessly, his mouth cracking into a huge grin, showing tiny baby teeth. He rubbed his forehead and babbled something unintelligible, but she didn't hear him. The shock was so intense that she couldn't breathe.

This couldn't be him…*couldn't* be.

Had she dreamt of this moment for so long that she was hallucinating?

That was it. And perhaps arriving back like this was too much. Perhaps… But as she looked into his face, those eyes, she knew rationally it couldn't be possible. Yet her heart told another story, every instinct clamouring loudly.

She started to feel slightly desperate. Was this going to happen every time she saw a boy his age? Surely someone had to see her, had to *know*? Had to take him away from her— because she didn't think she would be able to move ever again. Or let him go.

Black-shod feet had appeared behind the boy. A man. There was a blur of movement and she had a sense of his size, his magnetism, even just in that quick moment as he bent down to pick the little boy up. His scent washed over her. *It was familiar.* Her heart had already stopped beating. Blood froze in her veins. Her hands dropped.

A coolly cultivated deep voice came from far above her head. The man spoke with a slight accent that was barely noticeable '…need eyes in the back of your head, they move so fast…'

She couldn't believe what she was hearing, or seeing. He

was tall, so tall that even when Rowan stood fully—she didn't know *how*—he towered over her own not inconsiderable height. He was so sinfully handsome that her brain seized—exactly the way it had when she had seen him for the first time.

Nearly three years ago.

This couldn't be happening. This was too, too cruel. Life *couldn't* be this harsh. And yet she knew well that it could.

He was still talking. And then abruptly he stopped, and the warm smile faded. Dark blond brows drew together over piercingly light blue eyes. The colour of blue ice. They pierced all the way through to Rowan's heart and soul, ripping her open, laying her bare to the myriad expressions crossing his face: the shock of recognition, disbelief…and then something much more potent. Disgust, anger…hatred. *Rejection.*

Rowan felt her mouth move as if to speak. But nothing came out. Everything seemed to hurtle around them in fast forward, but they were cocooned in an invisible bubble. Suspended in time. She looked at the little boy held high in his arms, and that was her downfall. She felt as if her heart would explode. It was all too much. She had one coherent thought before she slid into a dead faint at her husband's feet: *my baby.*

Isandro Vicario Salazar stood at the window of the bedroom in the suite that he'd carried Rowan upstairs to just a short time before. He looked at the distinctive telecom tower in the near distance, the bumper-to-bumper traffic in the streets down below, and saw none of it. His eyes were narrowed.

Rowan Carmichael. Rowan Salazar. His wife.

His mouth twisted into an even thinner line. His *errant* wife. The wife·who had walked out on him and abandoned her own baby just hours after the birth because *she hadn't been ready to deal with it.* A drumbeat of rage, barely contained, beat under the surface of his skin. In his blood.

Stunning him with its force. That day he'd left her to rest after the birth, and returned some hours later—only to find her gone. He'd not laid eyes on her from that moment to this. He still reeled with the shock of seeing her. He reeled with the torrent of emotions that seeing her had evoked within him— emotions he'd suppressed long ago, *that day*, when she'd revealed her true nature and had shown him how unbelievably duped he had allowed himself to become. But not a hint of his inner emotions showed on his face even now.

A faint sound from the bed made him tense, and slowly he turned around.

Rowan waited a moment before opening her eyes. It was something she'd got used to in the past couple of years. A moment before reality rushed in, a moment to take stock, do a body-check, feel the sensations, feel if there was pain present…feel if she was *well*. But this time, as the muted sounds of car horns and traffic came from just outside, albeit a long way down, she tensed. The previous moments rushed back. The last thing she cared about right now was physical pain or if she felt well.

Her eyes flew open and there he was. It hadn't been a mirage. Her husband stood with his back to the window, hands deep in pockets of what she knew would be superbly crafted bespoke Italian cloth. Like his shirt and his jacket. The clothes moulded to his form, hugging every hard contour, emphasising every part of his tall, broad-shouldered and powerful body. Exactly how she remembered…but even more devastating in the flesh.

She knew on some level that it was the cushion of shock that allowed her to be so coolly objective. He was, if anything, even more handsome. Although in fairness handsome was too trite a word, too *pretty*. He was altogether too male for a word like handsome. And he was right here in front of her, living, breathing…not a figment of her imagination. The exquisite pain of seeing him again when she knew well what he must think of her was mercifully not allowed to penetrate too deeply.

'So…' he drawled with a sardonic edge, 'you were obviously shocked to run into me. Surprising, really, considering this is my hotel.'

Rowan felt the numbness fade, the protective shock starting to shatter. *His hotel?* Since when had he owned a hotel in London? Even though he'd had to do a lot of business here, he'd never hidden his antipathy for the place. And how had she unwittingly chosen this hotel…out of a million others?

She'd quite literally come back and walked directly into the lion's den—like an industrious ant following the scent of a familiar pheromone.

How had she got up here to this room?

And then she remembered. It was too joyful and painful to bear, slicing through the shock and opening a raw wound. Her baby, her son…she'd seen him, held him. It *had* been him. She hadn't conjured him up. That knowledge was still too much for her to cope with fully; she knew that. Her brain would be close to going into meltdown if she focused on what had just happened too intensely.

'Did I…did I frighten him?' Her voice felt scratchy.

The cold flash of sheer disgust that crossed her husband's face was like a slap. If she'd had any doubts about his reaction they were laughably quashed now.

'No. If you had I wouldn't be here right now.'

The protective tone in his voice was unmistakable. Rowan pushed herself up to sit on the side of the bed. Her head still felt light, as if stuffed with cotton wool. Warily she looked up at Isandro. It almost physically hurt to see him like this after all this time. She'd dreamed of this moment for so long…but of course she had to concede that never in her imaginings had she fooled herself into believing that Isandro would be pleased to see her. That had been confined to her fantasies.

'Did you call him Zacarías?' she asked with a husky catch. Her eye was drawn to a muscle clenching in his jaw. But his curt, tight voice brought her eyes back to his.

'Zac. Yes.'

'After your grandfather…'

A look of disdain flashed across his face. 'Please let's not pretend that you actually care.'

Rowan winced, her face paling. She'd known exactly what she might expect when she confronted Isandro, but she just hadn't expected it so soon. She'd wanted to be in control, to have the chance to explain, be ready… Who was she kidding? In that moment she felt like she'd never be ready to explain.

'Your lover was sent on his way.'

Rowan had been in the act of standing, and promptly sat back down again. Isandro watched her coolly, but he felt anything but cool inside. It was taking all his self-control not to walk over, haul her up and demand…*what*? He shook inwardly with the force of the emotions running through him. The strongest of which felt suspiciously and awfully like jealousy. But he told himself it was only his pride that he cared about, that this vortex threatening to consume him couldn't possibly be linked into *feelings*. He'd learnt that lesson two years ago.

'My what?' She looked at Isandro incredulously. Now she really felt removed from reality.

'Your lover,' he spat out. 'The man you had come to meet. No doubt you have a room booked here somewhere? Is this how you've spent the last couple of years? In a debauched world tour of hotel rooms with insignificant men? Is this what you meant when you said you weren't *ready* to deal with marriage and motherhood?'

Insignificant men?

Rowan's head throbbed, and she put a hand to her temple, struggling to make sense of what he said. And then it hit her as a benign, friendly face swam into her mind's eye. She looked up at him again, her eyes wide. 'You must be talking about David Fairclough. He's my solicitor. I was due to meet him downstairs, just when…just when…'

Isandro snorted contemptuously. 'A likely story. You really wanted to rub my nose in it, didn't you?'

Rowan barely heard what he was saying. She finally found the strength to stand, her hands balled into fists at her sides. 'It is true. I was meeting him…' She faltered. She really hadn't planned on it happening this way, but there was nothing she could do now. She hitched up her chin. 'I was meeting him to discuss how best to contact you and talk about seeing my son.'

Isandro crossed his arms across his chest, making him look even more powerful, formidable. He blocked the light coming in from the window behind him and it made a shiver run down Rowan's spine.

'I can tell you right now that that is *not* going to happen.' His whole stance screamed rejection of her claim.

Panic coursed through Rowan. She stepped forward jerkily. 'But I have a right to see my child, no matter what's happened. You can't stop me.' To her utter chagrin her throat tightened with tears. She fought to control herself. She couldn't fall apart—not here, like this. She needed to be strong.

'I can and I will.' Isandro was icy and controlled. She shook her head and opened her mouth to speak, but he cut in ruthlessly. 'I wouldn't be surprised if you'd forgotten till today that it was a boy you had, you left so fast.'

Rowan's mouth closed, and the pain that lanced through her was raw and overwhelming. Her voice sounded thready to her ears. 'I... Of course I knew he was a boy. I've thought of nothing else but him every day since—'

Isandro took two quick strides and gripped Rowan's arm painfully. 'Enough!'

She took a sharp breath to disguise the pain. This was far worse than she had anticipated. She couldn't afford to forget that this man wielded a power that was on a par with the world's most prominent politicians. Would telling him what had really happened make him see...make him understand? She'd hoped it would, with the cushion of distance between them. The lingering rawness made her feel as though a layer of skin had been stripped from her body. The truth would lay her bare completely, but right now, having met her son when she'd truly believed she'd never see him again, shock was making her reckless.

'Isandro. Please, I can tell you what happened. Maybe then you'll understand—'

He cut her off harshly. 'Understand? *Understand?*'

His face was so close that she could see the fine lines spreading from the corners of his eyes, could see his skin, golden and taut over those high cheekbones. She held herself rigid, would not give in to her body's demand to allow herself to really acknowledge what his proximity was doing to her. How could she when he was looking at her with such unbridled hatred, making her feel confused and inarticulate?

Scorn dripped from every syllable of his every word. 'I know what happened. You left a note...remember? There is not one thing, not one word, not one lame story you could dream up to excuse what you did that day. You took away an innocent baby's most important source of nourishment and love. Security. There is no one and nothing on the planet that could absolve you of that crime. You gave up your right to be a mother to him when you walked away, just hours after he was born.'

And you gave up the right to be my wife...

The words, unspoken, hung heavy in the air.

Rowan's inarticulate explanation died on her lips. His stark, cruel words resounded in her head. For a short, blissfully deceptive moment she felt no reaction to them, was numbed, and then like poison-tipped arrows they joined with the ever-present debilitating guilt and sank deep, deep into her heart, robbing her of words, of any explanation she might give.

He was right. She couldn't say a word. Not right now anyway. How could she expect him to understand that which she had barely come to terms with herself? That which she'd only just very painfully started to forgive herself for? She *had* walked away from her own newborn baby. Had she really thought that telling him her reasons might absolve her? She didn't deserve that.

Her control was close to breaking, but she knew she couldn't afford to crumble now. She had to face the consequences of her actions, not seek absolution. She dredged up some much needed strength and pulled away from his iron grip jerkily.

Isandro watched her dispassionately. She backed away farther, her hand going to rub her arm where he had gripped it. His anger was cooling to a contained icy rage. She turned away for a moment, offering him her back, and his eyes flicked down. In her smart suit and high-necked blouse he could see for the first time that she was slimmer than she had been. The short jacket and straight skirt didn't hide much. Desire burned low and insistent in his belly, even though everything in him rebelled at his unwanted response. She'd always been slim, but there was an unmistakable fragility to the lines of her body now that hadn't been there before.

He hated to think it, and quashed it almost immediately, but was there also a *vulnerability*? Her Titian hair had been long before, down her back, but now it was much shorter, exposing the line of her elegant neck. She still had that quintessential upper class deportment that couldn't be faked. She'd been his access into a world notoriously hard to break into for outsiders: the upper echelons of the English banking system, an ancient and tightly guarded group of the super-wealthy elite.

With what had been an extremely uncharacteristic failing to read another person, she had been the first person *ever* he'd so badly misjudged. Monumentally. Catastrophically.

She turned around to face him again and her eyes were flashing, taking him by surprise. But then his resolve hardened. *This* was the real woman he had married. But unaccountably, even as he thought that, his eye was involuntarily drawn to the crest of her breasts, pushing against the fine silk of the blouse. He felt his body tighten even more in response to their fullness, felt sensual tension flooding his veins. His reaction was so unwarranted that it momentarily stunned him. And then she spoke, cutting through the haze in his brain. He told himself it had to be shock.

'Whether you like it or not, I have rights. Any court in the world will recognise that. Whatever I did, I will be allowed to see my son. Eventually.' Her voice was clipped, her breeding coming through with every well-enunciated syllable, taking Isandro's mind off the unpalatable reactions in his body.

Rowan watched his reaction warily. He mustn't know what it was costing her to stand here and speak to him like this. She felt as if she was back in elocution class. But it was the only way she was clinging onto that flimsy control.

Isandro's face was a stony mask of non-reaction as he took her by surprise, starting to walk away. 'You will remain in this room for now. If you attempt to leave there is a bodyguard outside this door who will bring you back inside.' All he knew was that he had to put some distance between them, take stock of what had just happened.

Rowan watched incredulously as his long powerful strides took him towards the door. Belatedly she went after him, stumbling a little. 'Wait—where are you going? We haven't finished discussing this.'

He turned at the door and the cold force of his gaze stopped her in her tracks. 'Oh, yes—we have. For now. Just remember this: you deserted your son and left him with me. I can make this easy or very, very hard. It's up to you.'

When he opened the door, Rowan saw the great big hulking shape of a bodyguard just outside and heard a small voice chatter excitedly. 'Papa—Papa!'

The door closed and she felt the bed at the back of her legs behind her. Hearing that small voice was too much. Her legs crumpled and she slid to the ground. For a long time she sat like that, with her legs tucked under her, stunned by everything. It was only after a few minutes that she realised her cheeks were wet with tears, and she held a fist to her chest as if she could soothe the pain in her heart.

Eventually Rowan got up and went into the bathroom, where she splashed some water on her face. Towelling herself dry, she studied her reflection. Her face was white, her eyes huge. She looked and felt like a deer caught in the headlights. She needed to look in control, not half shocked out of her wits and terrified. Out of the corner of her eye she noticed her bag on the bed. Isandro must have picked it up from where it had fallen when she'd fainted. She wished she had some make-up, but she didn't have a thing—make-up had been the last thing on her mind for a long time.

She went back into the bedroom and tried pinching her cheeks to restore some colour. Standing at the window, looking out on the view that Isandro had seen only a short time before, she held her body tense. She still couldn't believe how the fates had brought them together. It was laughable. She'd chosen this hotel primarily because it was close to St Pancras, where she'd gotten off the train from Paris, and because her solicitor's office was uncomfortably close to Isandro's London offices. It had been under A on the internet, for Alhambra Hotel. But in the end she would have been safer meeting David Fairclough at his office.

She felt a fleeting moment of ironic humour. She'd counted on being able to gather all her information, had banked on the fact that Isandro would most likely be in Spain. They would contact him by letter to let him know of her wishes, her intentions to get to know her son... But instead here they were. The chance to explain in depth her reasons for leaving that day by the luxury of a letter was gone. Faced with Isandro's virulent anger, she knew he was in no mood to listen—possibly for some time. And now he believed that he'd caught her in the midst of an afternoon tryst. The worst possible start to any kind of meeting.

And then there was her son. Her baby. *Zac*. He was so beautiful. Rowan put a hand to the curtain, gripping it tight as she felt weakness flood her, her legs turning to jelly.

Meeting Isandro again was something she'd been somewhat prepared for. But how did you prepare to meet the child you thought you'd never see ever again? Every step of that walk away from him was etched into her memory like a searing brand. She'd woken from nightmares reliving that walk almost every night for the past two years. Her bruised and battered heart beat unsteadily against her chest. That indescribable pain and the lingering joy of seeing him all swirled together, making her feel like crying and laughing at the same time.

Rowan heard the door open behind her. Her hand tightened on the curtain before she released it from her grip. She took a deep breath and turned around. Isandro. His face was so harsh and austere that Rowan sucked in a breath. He *hated* her. She could feel it tangibly as he came and stood in front of her, head back, looking down at her with heavy-lidded disgust. His blue eyes were like shards of ice.

'I have some business to attend to here in the hotel. You are by all means free to go if you wish.'

Her mind and heart seized in a painful spasm at his *volte face*. The thought of being so close to her son and being sent away now was wrenching and unbearable.

'No.' She shook her head. 'I'm not going anywhere. I came back to London to get in touch with you. Believe what you want, but I had no idea you owned this hotel. I'm not leaving now until you agree for me to see Zac.'

His mouth tightened with unmistakable displeasure. He obviously hadn't expected that. But there was also something she couldn't put her finger on. A hint of resignation? Did he realise that he couldn't just dismiss her?

'Very well. In that case you will remain in this room tonight, and tomorrow morning we may discuss things.'

Rowan looked at him sceptically. She'd expected more of a fight. Why wasn't he flinging her out on the steps? He was playing with her, a master tactician.

'No need to look so suspicious, Rowan. You are, after all, my wife—are you not? Naturally I am overjoyed to see you again.'

With a mocking look on his face he backed away before

turning and leaving the room. When an outer door shut too, Rowan knew that she was finally quite alone. Hesitantly she opened the door into the outer part of the suite and looked around. Her suitcase had also been transported upstairs. Breathing a little easier for the first time in hours, Rowan went to a couch and sat down. Half distracted, she felt something underneath her and plucked it out. It was a furry toy animal.

Zac. With a shaking hand she brought it close to her face and breathed deep. The well of emotion was rising to consume her again and she couldn't keep it back. Clutching the small teddy, Rowan curled up on the couch and gave in to the storm.

Much later that night Isandro found himself at the door of the suite just down the hall from his own private rooms. What was he doing here? He opened the door and stepped in. The light was dim, the curtains still open, and it was only as he walked towards the bedroom that he saw the shape on the sofa.

His heart fell. Why couldn't she have just disappeared?

He knew damn well why.

She was back to get everything her greedy little hands could carry. No doubt including his son. Look at her. He almost laughed out loud when he saw Zac's toy clenched in one hand, close to her face. She'd come back from whatever rock she'd been hiding under, like an actress poised in the wings of the stage, ready to make her entrance.

Yet, much to his dismay, faced with her benign sleeping form, Isandro was helpless against a rush of memories. The first time he'd seen her across a packed function room where he'd come to meet Alistair Carmichael. Rowan's father had been a man in dire straits, about to become publicly bankrupt unless Isandro agreed to a mutually beneficial deal. Carmichael had known that Isandro wanted in, and Isandro had known Carmichael needed saving from public humiliation and ruination. In the middle of it all had been Rowan. Part of the deal.

He'd seen her across that crowded room and, like an old cliché, their eyes had met. He'd felt a little poleaxed by their intense shade of dark violet-blue, their seriousness, when so many women looked at him with another expression entirely.

She'd been unbelievably gauche-looking—too gauche, in fact, and he now knew for a fact that it had all been an act. Then he'd spotted her father by her side and he'd put two and two together. *This* was the daughter the old man wanted to marry off. Carmichael had baited him with the fact that if she married she'd come into her mother's sizeable inheritance.

He had let Carmichael believe that he might want a bride who came with a dowry, suspecting that the banker had designs on much of his daughter's inheritance himself. Isandro had had no need for the dowry, of course. But what he had needed, much more importantly, was another level of acceptance. Social acceptance. Without a *bona fide* English society wife, his taking control of Carmichael's chair at the bank would be for ever frowned upon. He'd be as socially ostracised as a beggar on the streets. However, if it was a merger of two great families—one Spanish, with links to the formidable banking industry there, the other English—then that was a different story. Acceptance would be immediate, and would consolidate his control over banking in Europe.

Which was exactly what had happened.

His mouth tightened in rejection of the way his thoughts seemed to be defying him, leading him back to a place he never wanted to visit again. What he hadn't counted on was the place that his meekly unassuming new wife would take in his life. And what it had done to him when he had discovered the true depth of her avaricious and shallow nature. What it had done to him to come back into that hospital room to find her gone. Leaving nothing but a note and her wedding rings. It had made him the biggest fool—because all along, right up until that moment, he'd believed her to be different.

He stepped noiselessly back out of the room and vowed with everything in his body that she would pay for her actions a million times over.

CHAPTER TWO

THE next morning Rowan sat tensely in a chair and watched the door of the suite. She'd woken early, to find herself stiff and uncomfortable on the couch, still holding Zac's toy. With the arrival of the morning things were clearer in her head. She could not let Isandro intimidate her. She had to make him see that she had rights. She cursed her own lack of foresight. Today was Saturday, and she didn't have her solicitor's home or mobile number. She should have rung him yesterday, after Isandro had left…but she'd been feeling so shocked. She knew that it was a mistake that could cost her dearly.

The truth was, she'd only contacted her solicitor in anticipation of the worst-case scenario—that Isandro, on being contacted, would prove intractable and unforgiving. She was still too much of a coward to admit to herself that she had harboured the wish that somehow, despite everything, once he knew, they could be a happy family. A hundred jeering voices mocked her naïve fantasy.

But they had been happy. They had had *something*. But, she had to concede painfully, that had been *before*, in the earlier months of their time together. Isandro had been the first man to draw Rowan out of herself, the first man she'd slept with…the first man she'd fallen for. He'd made her feel beautiful, desirable. And, to her shame, she found she was remembering that, and not her discovery of what he'd really felt for her: which was *nothing*.

That brought her mind back to reality. No doubt Isandro would already have consulted with an army of legal advisors on how best to deal with the reappearance of his wife. His ability to adapt and react to situations had always awed her. This would be no different. She could well imagine that David Fairclough would have been intimidated out of his skin yesterday, faced with Isandro's wrath.

Suddenly the door opened, taking her by surprise, and Rowan jerked up to stand, all of her clear-sightedness deserting her with the arrival of her husband. Her body was rigid with tension as she took in his dark blond good-looks, his hair slightly tousled, as if he'd been running a hand through it.

Isandro closed the door softly behind him, watching her. Her face was still as pale as alabaster, her eyes like two huge bruises of colour. His own eyes ran up and down her form. She trembled as lightly as a leaf, barely perceptible.

'I trust you slept well?' he asked innocuously, with no evidence of the will he was imposing onto his body's response to seeing her. Anger at this renewal of response surged through him.

'Very well. The bed was most comfortable.' Rowan was not going to pretend for a second that she hadn't had a night of perfect restful sleep.

A fleeting expression that she couldn't decipher crossed his face as he pushed away from the door and came close. Rowan fought against backing away.

This morning his jacket and tie were gone, shirtsleeves rolled up. She noticed what looked suspiciously like dried food on his shirt. Had he been feeding Zac? An overwhelming urge to see her son again nearly floored her. She needed to see that he was *real*, that she hadn't imagined him. That he was as beautiful and healthy as he'd looked…

Isandro folded his arms. Everything about him was forbidding. Rowan forced her swirling emotions down.

'Your timing is impeccable…but then I guess you've proved that already.'

Rowan's eyes met his cold ones. She ignored his barb. Waited to hear what he would no doubt explain. He brushed past her to the window, as if in deliberate provocation, and Rowan sucked in a betraying breath at the way he took her off guard by coming so close. At the way her skin prickled uncomfortably. His cool and musky scent wrapped around her, and another scent…that baby scent. Her heart lurched in reaction.

He stayed with his back to her for a moment. For some reason he couldn't trust himself to face her, and he hated that. He spoke in a monotone. 'Two months from now it will be two years exactly since you walked out of that hospital. You've returned now because we can both file for divorce and you can get your hands on the money agreed in the prenup. I see you've been careful not to go beyond the two-year desertion mark, which would have biased things against you. It must be killing you to come back and disrupt your *plans*, but once the divorce is through you'll be off again.' He turned around and fixed her with those laser eyes. 'Yes?'

Rowan struggled through waves of shock at his cool mention of divorce to understand what he'd said. She had no concept of time or legalities. She'd come here now because she was able. *Because she was finally well enough…*

His arms were folded, every line in his face regal, hard, uncompromising. Her betrayal and his own shaming lack of judgment seared him again now he was faced with her wide-eyed act of shock. He laughed briefly, harshly. 'Come now—even you, with all your guile, hardly expected us to play happy reunited families?'

Rowan shook her head. His words, which committed to dust that childish and secret fantasy, had rendered her momentarily speechless.

His voice assumed a bored tone which did even more damage to her heart. 'You've done me a favour. If you hadn't turned up now I wouldn't have been able to seek a divorce without your consent, so you've saved me the tedious job of having to track you down.' His expression changed in an instant, and he moved closer, looking at her assessingly. 'Let me guess. You've run out of your inheritance?'

Rowan blanched, going even paler. The sizeable inheritance from her mother *was* almost gone, but not for the reasons he'd so obviously guessed. But it was too late. He'd seen her reaction. A hard, triumphant glitter made his eyes icy.

'As I thought.' He shook his head. 'You know, it disappoints me how predictable you women are. But then I don't know why I'm surprised. I should have known this was on the cards.' He continued. 'So now you're back, seeking to cash in on a prenup which will give you a nice nest egg…although at the rate you got through your mother's money, I can't see that mine will last much longer.'

Rowan's anger built with a white-hot flash. She felt colour bloom in her cheeks and welcomed it. 'I have no desire for your money, Isandro. The only thing I desire is to see my son.'

He looked bored. 'I can see how he will be a good pawn for you, but please do not insult my intelligence. Turning up now shows just how deeply your mercenary streak runs. Being the mother of my son is an added insurance, to make sure you get as much as possible. No doubt this was all part of the grand plan.'

The grand plan? If only he knew…

'Tell me,' he said thoughtfully, 'have you already planned your public defence? Are you going to go with postnatal depression, which is what the papers hinted at as being the likely cause of your curious absence from my side?'

Her mouth fell open. 'Postnatal depression…you mean people don't know?' Rowan had feared that the press would have heard how she had deserted her child after she'd gone. She'd been prepared to deal with it, and it was more than surprising to her that Isandro hadn't leaked the news for maximum benefit… Yet how could she forget that towering Spanish pride?

Isandro's eyes narrowed on hers. 'Why are you doing this? Why are you pretending you don't know?'

'But… I don't…' Rowan felt woolly in the head. For the first six months after her departure she hadn't seen one newspaper. Or the news. And by the time she'd been exposed to it again she'd never seen any mention of Isandro. She'd fought the urge to go looking, because every time she felt it, the guilt would rise up and overwhelm her. Her husband was the type of man rarely mentioned in tabloids or the common press. His power and astronomical wealth were such that he was effectively removed from such banal speculation or scrutiny. Protected.

However, the papers must have read *something* into the fact that Isandro Vicario Salazar's wife had seemed to suddenly disappear from the face of the earth.

He answered her unspoken thoughts. 'Nobody is aware of the fact that you deserted this marriage. They lost interest when I returned to Spain with Zac, believing that you had simply taken refuge from prying eyes at our…*my* Seville home.'

Rowan struggled to take it all in. 'And your family…?' She

remembered his mother's austere and pain-lined face. The coolness with which she had endured the wedding in London, patently hating every minute of it. Rowan also remembered the equally cold and suspicious face of Isandro's older sister, Ana. Neither had offered any form of welcome.

'Oh, they know exactly what happened. Somehow they weren't surprised.'

Rowan knew she had to sit or else she'd fall. She walked unsteadily to a chair in the corner and sat down. She felt incredibly weary all of a sudden, and the magnitude of the fight she faced was sinking in. She couldn't let the stark reality that he fully expected them to divorce overwhelm her. He didn't have to know how little she'd prepared for this, and now she welcomed the prompt which had led her to seek a meeting with her solicitor.

'All I want is to be able to see my son. That's why I was meeting Mr Fairclough yesterday. Even I know that as Zac's mother I *will* be allowed see him.'

Isandro fought down the anger that rose when she mentioned Zac's name. He decided to go with his own plan and see how far he got. But he didn't doubt that Zac was the golden ticket in Rowan's plan.

'I can have divorce papers drawn up today.'

Rowan's heart sank. She was going to be faced with Isandro's full ammunition.

'If you agree to divorce proceedings, and agree to the terms I'll outline for granting you access to Zac, I'll triple the amount stipulated in the prenuptial agreement and it will be transferred into your account immediately.'

Rowan blanched. That sum of money would keep a small country running for some years. But she had no interest in money.

She stood up from her seat and raised her chin. She had to

be strong. She could crumble later. She had to focus on Zac, because to think of anything else right now was too much to bear. 'No.'

'No?' Isandro's face darkened with anger. He was caught in a bind and he had no doubt that she knew it.

'I'll agree to…to…' To her utter chagrin her mouth and tongue stumbled on the words. She felt herself flushing. 'To the divorce, by all means. It's not as if this marriage was ever a love-match. I'm well aware of that. But I will not put my name to anything that signs away my rights to Zac. Those are bullying tactics, Isandro, and I won't be bullied.' She folded her arms to conceal their shaking.

Isandro had to admit to feeling slightly flummoxed. He'd never been accused of being a bully before, and it didn't sit well with him. Bullies acted without intelligence, on frightened instinct, and he had to concede now that he *was* frightened. Frightened of what she could do to his son. Frightened of a lot more than he cared to name at the moment.

'He's my son. I carried him for almost nine months. I gave birth to him. You can't take that away from me. You can't—'

Isandro crushed the surprise he felt as she stood up to him so calmly. 'And yet despite all that you were able to walk away without even a backward glance.'

Rowan's throat closed over again. *She'd put her son first. If she had looked back then she'd never have left, and that would have meant…*

She stopped her painful thoughts with effort and controlled herself. 'I don't care about your money. I just want to know my son.'

Who was she kidding? He had to stop himself from laughing out loud. This was a woman who had married him to get her hands on her inheritance and had got pregnant in a calculated bid to extract as much money as she could from him. And here was the evidence. Right in front of him. She was wily and canny. He'd give her that. She knew exactly what she was doing by returning just before two years was up. It meant that any claim he made of desertion would be called into question, might be investigated. And even though he had the note she'd left as evidence, he knew that if she were conniving enough she could turn it around to work for her.

The sheer evidence of her premeditation stunned him anew. This wasn't the meek, shy wallflower he thought he'd married. She'd been a virgin on their wedding night! The ultimate in innocence and purity. She'd even maintained the façade right through her pregnancy— He halted his thoughts with effort and dug his hands deep in the pockets of his trousers, tightening the material across his groin. His shirt, open at the neck, hinted at the dark olive skin underneath, with crisp whorls of hair just visible.

For a second Isandro's physical presence hit Rowan hard between the eyes, and out of nowhere came a vivid memory of herself underneath him, his naked body pushing down over hers, chest to chest. She remembered taking him into her on a single breath, he'd thrust so deeply that she'd truly believed in that moment that he'd touched her heart.

She shook her head faintly, feeling acutely warm and breathless. The room—it must be the room. It was too hot, she told herself.

Isandro was speaking again. 'You leave me no option, then.'

'No option...?' she repeated stupidly fighting an urge to open her own shirt at the neck and let some air get to her skin. She was feeling constricted.

It utterly galled Isandro that even though she'd behaved reprehensibly as Zac's mother she *could* swan back onto the scene like this and have rights. Any court in the world would see the importance of a child being allowed to bond with its mother. His own lawyer had advocated that he should not be seen to stand in the way of reasonable access; it would only damage him down the line. As much as he wanted to turn around, walk away, forget she existed, he couldn't.

He didn't know why she wasn't taking the small fortune he was offering, but thought it could only be because she believed she'd get even more with this charade of belated concern. He had to be seen to give her a chance. But if he was going to do it then it would be on *his* terms, on *his* turf. He couldn't trust that if he left her behind now she wouldn't try and do something dramatic, using Zac in order to wage a public campaign for custody—and ultimately for the millions she no doubt craved.

'If you mean what you say about being here purely to see and get to know Zac, then you will return to Seville with us within the hour.'

His words cut through her body's inexplicable response. She focused on the clear blue of his eyes and felt as if they were impaling her. 'Go on.'

'You will come and live in my house for a sufficient amount of time to prove your…good intentions towards Zac. You will be allowed a certain amount of supervised access—'

'But—'

'But nothing. These are my terms, Rowan, and you're not in a position to argue.'

Rowan swallowed as she acknowledged her weak position. 'I told you—my only concern is being with Zac as much as I possibly can.'

'Well, then, you can't *possibly* have a problem with this.'

Living with him in his house…in such close proximity… her every move watched and monitored…

Rowan looked up at him. 'I…don't—I just…couldn't I stay somewhere nearby?'

Isandro waved an impatient hand. 'That is not practical. If you are serious about getting to know Zac it's best to see him in his own environment. I won't have you coming along, disrupting his routine, taking him out of his home. No way.'

Rowan wrung her hands. 'Of course I wouldn't do that. I didn't mean that, I just…'

'This is it, Rowan. Take it or leave it. You're hardly in a position to negotiate.'

He watched the turmoil in her eyes. No wonder she was balking at his suggestion. It proved how false her intentions really were. To go from two years of hedonistic freedom to being holed up in his home in a small town outside Seville— she'd be climbing the walls within weeks, if not days. Not to mention spending time with a small toddler who had the smile of an angel but who would test the patience of a saint.

'I'll give you five minutes to think about it.'

Rowan watched, still slightly dumbstruck, as he turned and left the room. The door shut softly behind him, the sound incongruous in a room heavy-laden with atmosphere and tension.

Rowan paced up and down. She had to think fast. Isandro was not used to having to wait for anything or anyone. She knew what she should do was stay in London, meet her solicitor and see what her options were. But that would be next week now. In the meantime this tenuous connection would be broken. Isandro would be back in Spain with Zac. And with his obvious determination to divorce, who knew how hard he'd prove to be to contact once the matter was in his legal team's hands? It could be months, even longer before she got to see Zac again. She had no doubt that Isandro would do whatever it took to make her look as bad as possible, and she had to concede that wouldn't be hard at all… How would it look if it emerged that she'd turned down an offer to go and live with her son?

Perhaps that was what he was hoping? That she would shoot herself in the foot...

She had to put aside her feelings for Isandro. Her one priority was Zac. When she'd seen him, touched him yesterday, she'd *known* him—incredibly. That primal recognition and joy struck her again.

This was the moment she had to let go of the fantasy. The wish that somehow something of *before* could be salvaged. She'd irretrievably damaged everything. Fate and circumstance had led her down a difficult path. And she had to remind herself that no matter what she'd led herself to believe, to hope for in their marriage, she'd been living in a fantasy all along anyway.

She firmed her mouth. Now was not the time to indulge in old memories. Once she'd unwittingly overheard that conversation with his sister well into her pregnancy she'd known exactly where she stood, how he felt. Their marriage obviously hadn't become for him what it had become for her, no matter what she'd thought at the time. *Or hoped...* She'd berated herself for her fanciful notions—what had she known, after all? She'd been a virgin when they'd first slept together. And he... She flushed hotly. Well, he certainly hadn't. She pressed cool hands against her cheeks to try and stem the heat.

Zac was here. She'd seen him. There was no way she could walk away again. She didn't have it in her. She didn't want to be miles away, not knowing, missing even more of his life. She would prove herself to her husband if it was the last thing she did. And then he would *have* to acknowledge her role in their son's life.

'Well?' Isandro stood at the door, dressed impeccably in jacket and tie again, every inch of him the banking giant whose influence induced fear and awe among adversaries and colleagues alike. Her eye caught that muscle twitching in his hard jaw. The fact that he wasn't as controlled as he looked was no comfort.

Rowan looked at him steadily and said, very clearly, 'I'm coming with you.'

After that things happened with scary swiftness. Isandro plucked a phone from his pocket and made a call, unleashing a stream of Spanish that Rowan only understood bits of. Her once fluent command of the language was rusty from lack of use.

He finished the conversation and pocketed the phone. He had an implacable expression on his face, but she could sense the underlying anger and impatience. He did not want her coming with him. She was quite sure that he had most likely been advised by someone that to offer to bring her back to Spain was a good idea. And he had expected her to say no. To be so unwelcome made her feel a little queasy.

'Where do we need to go to get your things?'

Rowan shook her head. 'Nowhere. I have everything with me.'

Isandro's body stilled. He flicked a derisive glance to the tiny case by her side. 'Everything?'

She nodded. 'It's all in there. And I have my passport in my handbag.'

'You haven't been living here?'

She shook her head, unbelievably stung by the evidence of his uninterest. He really had taken her note to heart. He hadn't tried to find her. And while that had been her objective in leaving the provocative note…it still *hurt*.

He took a step closer as he straightened his cuffs. 'Care to tell me where you *have* been living? Or do you expect me to believe you've been living out of a suitcase that size for two years?'

Rowan blinked and swallowed painfully. She had, actually.

If he looked hard enough he might recognise that it was the case she'd had with her in the hospital, when she'd given birth to Zac…might even recognise that this, her one and only decent suit, was also two years old. But of course he wouldn't. His questions were cutting far too close to the bone. Literally.

'It doesn't matter where I've been, Isandro. What matters is that I'm here now.'

His eyes were intensely blue on hers for a long moment. And then he shrugged. 'Come. It's time to leave.'

Rowan hitched her bag on her shoulder, and had caught the handle on her suitcase when he surprised her by coming back and leaning close, to take it out of her hand with a brusque movement. Their hands touched. She was so shocked at this contact that she snatched hers back, as if burnt. She could feel her eyes widening, her breath quicken, her heart race, and knew she looked shocked, but couldn't hide her response.

He stood to his full height and, helpless, Rowan could only gaze up into his eyes. That small physical contact was unleashing a maelstrom of sensations, images, memories, and, as if Isandro knew exactly what was going on inside her, he looked her up and down with studied insolence. His look, when it came to rest on her face again, was remote, utterly cold, and Rowan was in no doubt that he had just read her perfectly and did not welcome her reaction. Rejection flowed from every line of his tautly held body, and she had never felt so humiliated in her life.

By some small miracle he said nothing, merely turned on his heel, carrying the case and walked out of the room, not even checking to see if she was following. She caught up with him at the lift. He was staring resolutely ahead. She still burned.

'Where…?' She hated the tentative sound of her voice. 'Where is Zac?'

The bell pinged and she followed Isandro into the lift. He

waited till they were descending and said coolly, 'Zac has gone on ahead to the plane with his nanny. By the time we get there he should be down for his nap, so will have the minimum of disruption to his schedule.'

'Oh.' She was struck, heartened to see how closely attuned to his son's life he obviously was.

The lift doors pinged again and opened onto the lobby. Isandro strode out. Rowan struggled to keep up. A very attractive woman in a suit hurried over to speak to him, and when he stopped Rowan could see that she wore a manager's badge. She had huge blue eyes that looked up at Isandro with undisguised appreciation. He smiled down at her easily, and for a second Rowan couldn't breathe, such was the force of his smile. She'd forgotten just how potent his charm was. Not that he'd ever had to lavish much on *her*; she'd been a conquest he hadn't had to woo, after all.

The manager was speaking in an efficient yet slightly breathy tone that grated on Rowan's nerves. 'When we get that analysis report you requested I'll have it sent over to Spain immediately.'

'Thanks, Carrie.' Isandro started walking again, with the other woman beside him, effectively shutting Rowan out as if she didn't exist.

Then they were outside, where a sleek limousine was waiting with doors open. Isandro gestured for her to get in, careful not to touch her, Rowan noticed. When she sat in the car she was slightly out of breath. She watched as they pulled away from the hotel and eased into the morning traffic.

'I thought you hated London.' She could remember his irritation when business had kept him tied here after their perfunctory wedding, and then her advancing pregnancy which had precluded moving back to Spain until after the birth.

He flicked her a hard glance. 'I do.'

'So why this hotel?'

This time he did turn more fully, and settled back into the seat. Rowan instinctively inched back as far as she could.

'Why the interest, Rowan? Already adding it as a possible to the portfolio you're hoping to receive if the money's not enough? You should have taken me up on my first offer. It won't come around again.'

She decided to ignore that. 'I was just wondering, that was all.'

She faced the front. Isandro studied her profile, the straight nose, determined chin. Long sweep of black lashes. Surprisingly full lips…soft and inviting. He despised his unwarranted lack of control, over a woman so completely without morals, despised the fact his desire could not be governed by his intellect. Back in the suite just now, when she'd looked at him with such naked desire, for a second he'd actually forgotten just who she was and had felt his body quicken to a hot response. Exactly as she'd no doubt intended.

He forced his mind away from that. He needed words. To speak. Cut through the images…the memories.

'I bought the hotel after Zac was born. I can't ignore the fact that he's half-English. This is part of his heritage. It'll serve as an investment for him for the future, should he ever decide he wants to come here.'

Rowan didn't answer. She was too shocked by the tender feelings his words evoked, the memories of other times when she'd seen that tenderness come through. It had made her fall irrevocably in love with him, the contrast between hard-nosed ruthless businessman and his much more secret side. A side she thought only *she* had been privy to. A side that she had come to believe in—which she should *never* have believed in. She welcomed the hardness that settled around her heart. She had to protect herself. To remember.

She cast a quick glance at him. The aquiline line of his nose and full lips gave him a profile that spoke of sensual knowledge and promise. He gave no indication of knowing he was under scrutiny. Then his head turned and those eyes snagged hers. Dead on. Heat flared upwards from the pit of her belly and Rowan turned away. She could almost feel the mocking, knowing smile that curved his lips.

CHAPTER THREE

THAT sensuous profile was mocking her, coming closer and closer. Rowan felt panic rise and struggled to get away from the cruel smile, the icy eyes. She felt someone tugging, pulling her back, and suddenly found herself being jerked back to reality by a very definite and persistent pulling at her skirt.

Rowan opened her eyes. They felt gritty and tired. She was on the plane. She must have fallen asleep. The tugging registered again. She looked down, straight into the huge violet-coloured eyes of her son. Her heart stopped. And started again painfully. He was trailing an old and faded blanket. His cheeks were still sleep-flushed, his hair standing up. And her heart clenched so tight for a second that she felt in serious danger of fainting again. She willed it down.

Hungrily her eyes roved over him, as if checking a newborn for all his fingers and toes. She longed to pull him up and hold him close but didn't. She knew it might scare him. Just this moment alone was worth everything—put things into perspective. Isandro and his threats faded into the background.

Her voice was husky with emotion. 'Hi, Zac.'

One chubby hand clung to her leg for support. With his other hand he proudly mimicked her, pointing to himself. 'Zac!'

Then he put a hand to his head and made a face, obviously making the connection between Rowan and the previous day, when he'd fallen.

'That's right—you fell. Did you hurt your head?'

Zac nodded and rubbed his head. Rowan bent down and pretended to feel for a bump, exclaiming and making a fuss as if she'd found one. Her hands shook with the intensity of her emotions. Zac started to giggle.

Just then an older woman in a dark dress came up behind Zac. She looked Spanish. She bent down and took Zac's hand to lead him away, looking curiously at Rowan.

'I'm María—Zac's nanny…'

Rowan held out her hand. 'I'm Rowan…' She balked then. What did she say? *I'm Zac's mother? I'm Mrs Salazar?*

But the nanny didn't wait for elaboration. She smiled, shaking Rowan's hand perfunctorily. 'Excuse me—he needs to have something to eat.'

Rowan nodded jerkily and waved goodbye to Zac, who was already speeding off, his interest taken by something else. She turned back and looked sightlessly out of the window at the blanket of whiteness. She was too numb for tears and her heart ached. Yet she couldn't help but feel deep-seated relief at seeing Zac so well and healthy. That had always been her only priority…to see him flourishing so beautifully…it justified her decisions. Not that she'd ever needed justification. She'd acted from day one on a primal instinct that had been so strong she'd had no choice but to follow it. Above all she hadn't wanted him to suffer a moment's pain, which a selfishly prolonged departure would undoubtedly have brought. Even for a baby.

The one thing she hadn't counted on was *this*. Being in this situation. She wondered if she was being selfish coming back, seeking Zac out…wanting to get to know him. She knew rationally that she wasn't, but somehow she still didn't feel deserving of this. This luxury of seeing her son, this happiness. Perhaps she should have stayed away, said nothing. Let them get on with their lives. But with shameful weakness she knew she hadn't had the strength to do that. As soon as she had known that things were different, that she had a chance…

'You were hungry?'

Rowan's head whipped around. She'd been so caught up in her thoughts she hadn't heard Isandro come and sit down in the seat across the aisle. He was tieless and jacketless again, as if being in a suit even for a short time constrained his vibrant male energy. His shirt was open at the throat, revealing the strong brown column…. What was wrong with her? Although she'd been undeniably attracted to Isandro from the moment she'd first seen him, she couldn't remember experiencing this carnal level of attraction before.

'Yes. Starving.' She glanced at her plate, which was wiped clean of the delicious paella and salad she'd been served.

Isandro frowned as he recalled her curled up figure on the couch last night. There was something defenceless about the image that tugged at him. He ignored it. 'You didn't eat at the hotel?'

Rowan flushed and shook her head as his eyes ran up and down her form disparagingly.

'You've lost weight.'

He sounded accusing, and Rowan bristled. 'I know.'

He didn't have to spell out with that look just how unappealing she was to him. In that moment a blur of blond launched itself at Isandro, and deftly he plucked Zac up into his arms before he could do some damage or bump into something.

He glanced over to Rowan, showing the first tiny chink of something approximating warmth. 'As you've seen already, he's at the stage where he hasn't quite got the ability to stop once he's started.'

Rowan felt a lump come into her throat as she saw Zac wrap his arms around Isandro's neck, hugging him close only to just as abruptly squirm his way down Isandro's body, toddling off again under Isandro's watchful gaze until his nanny reclaimed him. The easy intimacy between them was a reminder of something she'd once foolishly allowed herself to believe in, and she could see now how potent it was when it was truly lavished on someone else. All she'd experienced however had been the surface emotion. Not the depth.

She couldn't quite meet his look. 'You've done an amazing job. He's beautiful.'

'Surprised?' came the dry response.

Rowan looked up, her eyes snared by his. She shook her head. 'No. I had no doubt that you would be a good father—' She stopped herself abruptly because she'd been about to say *My only concern was that you would not make enough time for him...* But that would have been revealing too much, and she could lay that fear to rest now. Clearly Isandro thought nothing of taking Zac with him on business trips.

Something in her tone made Isandro's eyes narrow on her for a second. Her eyes seemed to swirl with something indefinable, and for the first time since seeing her again he saw shadows, depths that hadn't been there before. *Pain?*

She looked away for a moment, and when she looked back her eyes were clear. They were so like Zac's that it took his breath away momentarily. But the ambiguity in their depths had gone. A trick of the light. That's all it had been.

At that point the hostess came to tell them the plane was preparing to land. When she had moved away, Isandro surprised Rowan by moving swiftly out of his seat to crouch in front of hers, a hand on either arm of her seat, effectively trapping her.

She could feel the heat from his body. Instinctively she pulled back into the seat, feeling claustrophobic. He was looking up at her with such intensity that she had to force herself to speak— 'What? What is it…?'—just to try and veer her mind off the dangerous track of previous experiences…moments when he'd looked at her before with that same intensity.

His eyes held her with all the easy hypnotism of a magician. His voice was deceptively light. His words were anything but.

'Just this, Rowan. If you come close to doing *one thing* to endanger, hurt or harm a hair on Zac's head then, believe me, not a court in this world will grant you custody when we divorce. I won't hesitate to use the full force of my power, and you'll be lucky if you even get to read about him in the papers as he grows up.'

He smiled, and it was so cold that Rowan could only stare. Transfixed by this absolute stranger. Then he stood and moved to a seat at the back of the plane with the effortless grace of a panther. Rowan stared at the place where he'd been. She felt cold inside. What would Isandro say if he knew she'd already laid down her life in order to protect Zac? Not much, she guessed bleakly. As he'd said himself, nothing would ever absolve her of that crime in his eyes. Rowan sighed and looked out of the window, just as the plane landed with a bump on Spanish soil.

Their journey to the east of Seville did not take long. Rowan looked out on the rolling plains of La Campina, barely able to take in the surroundings, still struggling to absorb everything that was happening. Isandro drove the Jeep. She was in the front, and María was in the back with Zac in his car seat. The bodyguard, who had been introduced to Rowan as Hernán, followed behind in another vehicle.

She was momentarily diverted when they entered the exquisitely picturesque town of Osuna, Isandro's birthplace and home.

'It's beautiful.'

'Yes.' Isandro glanced at her briefly but she didn't notice, too enthralled with the tiny, winding, climbing streets. He'd been watching her surreptitiously as they'd driven out of Seville, waiting for her reaction of dismay at leaving civilisation behind, but she hadn't given anything away. If anything she'd seemed uncomfortable with the bustling crowds—jumpy...almost slightly overwhelmed. But then he hadn't expected her to be so obvious so early.

They were at the top of the town now, overlooking the impressive baroque-style municipal buildings. Isandro took a quiet road which Rowan soon realised was a cul-de-sac. They came to a set of wrought-iron gates, with high walls on either side, overhung with trees. Isandro entered a code into a security pad from the window of the Jeep, the gates swung open and a security guard came out of a hut to greet Isandro, who waved back.

Rowan was not prepared for what appeared around the bend. She'd vaguely expected some kind of *hacienda*. Instead she saw a huge baroque mansion, emerging like something from a medieval fantasy. Cream-coloured, it seemed to shimmer in the sunlight, windows glinting, a profusion of flowers tumbling from pots along the steps and front of the house. Her jaw dropped. Isandro had parked and was already out of the Jeep, walking around the front to get Zac out of his seat in the back. Zac was bouncing up and down with excitement, having been cooped up for too long and clearly recognising home.

Rowan got out slowly, and the huge front door opened as if by magic, to reveal waiting staff. With trepidation in her breast she followed her husband and son into the house.

After a quick succession of introductions that had left Rowan's head spinning slightly, Isandro issued a stream of instructions and Rowan found herself being ushered upstairs, the housekeeper following with her bag. Rowan tried to take it from her, but she was having none of it. The chattering of Zac faded behind her as she was shown into her room.

It was a haven of dusky cream and rose. For some reason that she couldn't quite put her finger on at that moment the colours soothed her. And then it hit her. It wasn't the dreaded white of her nightmares. Of her recent past.

The housekeeper was showing her where everything was, and she welcomed the distraction from her inner demons. After she'd left, Rowan took a deep, steadying breath and explored for herself. A huge antique four-poster double bed had white muslin drapes caught back with ornate ties. The room had typically floral baroque features which were toned down by the simple colours. She went to the open French doors and took in the sight laid out before her with wide eyes, walking out as if in a trance.

A small stone balcony with ancient steps led down to a private inner courtyard, complete with a small pool inlaid with dark green tiles and glittering mosaics. She moved down the steps slowly, in awe of the stillness and beauty. The pool was surrounded by flowering bushes and olive trees. Scent hung heavy on the air. It was like something out of a dream she'd always had but never realised until now. Turning around in a circle, taking it in, she started when she saw Isandro standing with hands in his pockets outside another set of double doors, just feet from her own, with an identical balcony and steps leading down into the courtyard. His room? Her heart seized at that thought.

He came towards her, every step resonating with barely leashed menace. Rowan couldn't step back or she'd end up in the pool.

'You like what you see?' he asked tightly.

Rowan nodded, barely aware of what he was asking, her mouth suddenly dry at seeing him against this backdrop. He looked *golden*. Vibrant.

'You really messed up, you know.' He took one hand out of his pocket and gestured around them abruptly. 'You could have had all this the last two years, and now it will never be yours.'

Rowan's heart twisted in her chest. He thought she wanted this—the material evidence of his wealth. She started to shake her head, but couldn't get a word out. The sneer on his face stopped her.

'Just don't forget, dearest wife, that you are here purely at my behest and on the advice of my lawyers. They think it will serve me well to show how magnanimous I'm being in allowing you to get to know Zac, despite what you did. So don't get greedy and imagine for a second that you are entitled to a square inch of this place. You will not make a move that isn't watched and controlled. You will see Zac when and only when I allow it.'

Rowan forced her mouth to work, wanting to stop his words. 'That's all I want. I'm not here to take anything from you, Isandro. I don't have any interest in anything you own. My interest lies purely in Zac.'

He made a small rude sound. 'And in what you can make from the spoils of a divorce. Give me a break, Rowan. If I'd been less blinkered, less taken in by your innocent act of naivety, I would have realised long ago—'

'You'd have realised what?' she interjected bitterly, her emotions bubbling up, 'That the woman you married purely to raise your own standing in English society was just that— nothing but a trophy wife?' She'd known her actions when leaving would paint her in the worst possible light, and she knew she was being irrational, but the fact that he so easily believed her to be that kind of person lacerated her insides.

Isandro was momentarily taken aback. Her words brought back all his own humiliation—and he hated to admit it— his *disappointment*. And yet as she stood here now in front of him, a faint line of perspiration along her upper lip, her arms crossed defensively, pushing her breasts up, all he could think of was the desire pooling low in his abdomen. As much as he wanted to reject her in every way possible, he knew that with each moment spent together desire was growing stronger…

The disturbing arrow of lust he felt firmed his resolve. If he had but known it, he would have realised that the hot passion lying in wait beneath her cool exterior was a sign of things to come. She might have been a virgin on their wedding night, but he'd awoken her, and as soon as she'd been free of her baby she'd run. He'd never planned on their marriage being consummated, but when it had it had felt so right. And then when she'd become pregnant— He cut off his runaway thoughts and let hard ruthlessness rise. This woman in front of him represented his one fatal weakness.

'Our marriage was never meant to be anything but a business arrangement. You knew that. I knew that.'

'Of course it wasn't. I did know that…' Rowan gulped miserably, unable to continue for a moment, furious with herself for allowing him to goad her. The last thing she wanted was to draw his attention to her vulnerability to him. Or to the memory of how wanton she'd been during their short-lived marriage. Or to hear him say it had been a mistake. 'I never expected anything more.'

She felt hot in the afternoon sun as it beat down on her head. Hot and tired. She didn't have the energy for this. She didn't have to remind herself how clinical their conversations had been before the wedding. Didn't have to remind herself of how their marriage had never been meant to turn physical. *And yet it had.* She'd thrown herself at him. Shame clawed her insides.

In a series of meetings and dinners before they'd married Isandro had made everything crystal-clear. His words were still etched into her brain.

'I am marrying you so that I can save your father from bankruptcy, and by doing so I will take his position as CEO of Carmichael's Bank. You are marrying me in order to fulfil the terms of your mother's will and receive your maternal inheritance. As this won't be a real marriage, if I take a lover I will do so with the utmost discretion, and I would ask the same of you. In a year we can review things, talk about a divorce. A year with you by my side should be enough to establish my place. By then we will have both got what we wanted and my control of the bank will be assured.'

At the time Rowan had blinked at him slowly, finding it hard to move her gaze from his mouth to his eyes. Eyes which had been cool—cool enough to dampen her silly, girlish ardour. She'd been sitting there daydreaming, imagining him saying…*what*? That he'd fallen in love with her the minute he'd seen her and known she was the one for him? That he was as overwhelmed with lust for her as she was for him?

She returned to the present and swayed betrayingly as the heat seemed suddenly to intensify. Little had she known just how inconsequential she had been to him—that at no point had he *ever* entertained the possibility of feelings, no matter what she might have fooled herself into believing…

With an almost rough movement, Isandro took Rowan's arm and ushered her back up the crumbling steps and into her room. 'You need to get out of the sun. You're not used to the heat.'

She stood away from him, feeling better now that she was back inside, and looked at him warily.

He put distance between them, rocking back on his heels, tall and dominant. He laughed harshly. 'Silly me—how would I know what you're used to? After all, you could have been anywhere for the last two years.'

Rowan blanched. She knew she would have to tell him sooner or later exactly where she had been. But right now, feeling so rawly vulnerable, coming to terms with everything, was not the time. If she could just stay out of his way for the moment, focus on Zac... When she was feeling more in control of herself and her see-sawing emotions she would tell him then. Because when she did, it was going to invite all sorts of questions. Questions she certainly wasn't equipped emotionally to answer yet.

He backed away from her to a door she hadn't noticed in the wall as it was painted the same colour, almost camouflaged. It must be the adjoining door to his room. Her heart stopped and started again painfully. He saw her wide-eyed look. A smile mocked her.

'No one here expects us to pretend we're a happily married couple, enjoying the conjugal bed, so rest assured, Rowan. I won't be knocking on your door at night.'

No, she thought with an alarmingly sharp pain in the region of her heart. No doubt Isandro would have had a string of lovers to keep him company and must have a current one. She didn't have to remind herself of the disparaging remarks he had made about her to his sister. *That* conversation was a lane too far to travel down in her memory right now.

She breathed a sigh of relief when the door closed behind him, shutting away his disturbing presence. She sat on the bed, feeling exhausted, her mind a whirling minefield of memories. She pressed a hand to her chest, as if to slow down her thumping heart. To no avail. He had come to her room on their wedding night when she had least expected it. Had looked at her as if seeing her for the first time. She could still remember the aching longing she'd felt as his blue eyes had looked her up and down. She'd willed him to find her attractive, and she'd watched with bated breath as he'd come closer and closer. She'd known he'd come just to say goodnight, to be polite. But it had been as if her yearning body and heart had spoken out loud. And when, unbelievably, as if hearing her unspoken plea, he'd taken her in his arms…kissed her…he'd aroused a passion within her that still shocked and scared her to this day.

Rowan shook her head, as if she could somehow dislodge the painful images. She'd been so wanton, so full of ardour. With a groan Rowan stood jerkily and started to unpack, busying herself with the mundane task. It worked. Her feverish mind cooled. She gave in to the lure of a long hot shower, and afterwards belted a clean robe about herself and sank into the soft depths of the bed, letting the wave of blackness engulf her. She was with her son again. That was all that mattered. It had to be, because she couldn't hope for anything more.

She was back in that room. The white room. Two sets of double doors. She knew she had to get out, that if she didn't get out she'd never leave, never see her baby again. Panic gripped her, making her movements clumsy. She couldn't seem to get off the bed. She could hear footsteps approach, and knew they were coming to lock her in. Two sets of doors. She tried to scream, but no sound emerged. Her voice was gone. The covers on the bed were hampering her, trapping her. With the scream strangled in her throat Rowan felt salty hot tears fall down her face, and then she was being shaken. Terror froze her limbs…

Rowan became conscious of two things at once. It was the dream. The same dream, although a slightly different version.

It was just the dream. And she *was* being shaken. Her eyes flew open and clashed immediately with glacial blue ones. Isandro looked down at her, impatience stamped all over his face. She was in Spain, not in that awful room.

'What the hell is wrong with you? You were almost screaming the house down. Zac is asleep just across the hall.'

Zac.

The terror of the dream was still so real that she shuddered. She felt completely disorientated. It was dark—the curtains leading outside fluttered gently in the warm breeze. Isandro's big hands were still on her shoulders, his body half sitting on the bed, uncomfortably close enough for her to smell his scent, feel his heat. She jerked back.

'What time is it?'

He let her go when she moved, and glanced at the platinum watch encircling one wrist.

'Half past eleven.'

Rowan shook her head. 'At *night*?'

He nodded and stood up. 'Julia, the housekeeper, looked in on you at dinnertime, but you were sound asleep so I told her to leave you alone.' He studied her, and then asked harshly, 'What is it? Are you jetlagged?'

Rowan shook her head. 'No. Just…tired. It was just a bad dream. I…I had no idea I was crying out.' She put a hand to her temple. It was throbbing slightly. She became aware she was dressed in nothing but the robe and it was gaping open. She pulled it closed and awkwardly got up off the bed. 'I must have been more tired than I realised, that's all.'

Isandro put on the small bedside light and it threw long shadows across the room and his autocratic face. Rowan could see that he was still in his clothes.

'I was on my way to bed when I heard you.'

'Oh…' She felt as if he'd read her mind, and a blush came up to stain her cheeks. 'I'm sorry.'

'If it's likely to happen again I'll have to move you to the other side of the house, away from Zac. If he gets woken at night he's impossible to put back down.'

'It won't.' Rowan sent up a silent prayer. The dreams were a regular occurrence. Mainly they were tinged with sadness, and she woke crying, but this one had been more intense. It must be just because of the recent events. 'Really,' she assured Isandro, wanting his disturbing presence to be gone. 'It won't happen again.'

Isandro looked at her. Her skin was pink, her hair sexily tousled. Had this been some sort of ruse? To lead him in here, to try and seduce him? Was she aware of her effect on him? Had she become practised in the art of seduction these last two years? That thought made something knot deep in his gut. He couldn't put out of his mind the way she had felt under his hands just now, the frailty of her bones. Her clean, slightly musky scent. And yet the terror in her voice had been real enough, and the sound of her screams.

'See that it doesn't.' His voice sounded constricted to his own ears, and he was aware of the irrationality of his state-ment. If she had been in the grip of a genuine nightmare, of course she wouldn't be able to control her responses. He turned and left the room, shutting the door behind him. Damn the woman for coming back.

Isandro went across the hall and pushed open Zac's door, looking in to see his son sleeping peacefully, half on the bed, half off. He went over and placed him back safely in the middle, his heart swelling with love for this little boy. He hated the fact that he had to dance to Rowan's tune—hated the fact that as Zac's mother she could be allowed access to a child she had so callously walked away from. His hands clenched into fists. He had no choice but to allow her this access, but God help her if she thought he was going to allow her to take him away.

The following morning Rowan felt groggy, her head heavy. She had woken to a knock on the door, and now looked as a young maid came into the room. She pulled back the drapes farther, letting sunlight stream into the room, and opened the French doors wider. A bird called outside. Warmth came in on the light breeze and Rowan felt herself respond to it instinctively, letting it into her bones. It felt *good*.

'*Buenos Días.*'

'*Buenos Días.*' Rowan echoed, sitting up in the bed. She smiled at the girl hesitantly, and was rewarded with a shy smile. She was informed that breakfast would be served downstairs in fifteen minutes.

After a quick shower, and dressing in a plain skirt and T-shirt—one of about three outfits she owned—Rowan went downstairs. She felt self-conscious, well aware that she must look shabby. She just hadn't had to worry about clothes in so long, and she certainly hadn't expected to be *here*. Her mind flew from those concerns as she approached what must be the dining room door. She could hear the shouts of Zac.

With her heart thumping painfully she took a deep breath and went in. Two sets of eyes turned towards her. One she did her best to block out and one a mirror image of her own. She focused on Zac as she came in, unable to help a smile from spreading across her face. He was a mess, with food everywhere—all over him and his face. He grinned up at her from his high chair as she approached the table.

For one very normal and wry moment she didn't doubt for a second that his winning grin could change in an instant to tears and tantrums. But even that thought made her heart twist, and the longing to just sit and study every single aspect of him was overwhelming with its force.

Reluctantly she looked away and greeted María, who sat on the other side of the table, also eating breakfast. The woman sent her a hesitant smile, and Rowan reciprocated, feeling grateful. She sat down, and the housekeeper bustled in with a plate heaped high with food. She indicated to where there was fruit, croissants, and poured Rowan some steaming and fragrant coffee.

'I trust you slept well?'

Rowan glanced briefly at Isandro, whose tone was as arctic as his eyes. 'Yes, thank you. The room is more than comfortable.'

María broke the uncomfortable ensuing silence. 'It is a stunning house. I've often thought it must have been a magical place to grow up. Zac is very fortunate.'

Isandro slid a mocking glance at Rowan, and then a more benign one to María. 'Yes, isn't he?'

Rowan felt the weight of a myriad insults in that comment, but either María was oblivious to the tension or else she was a very good actress, and she chattered on about the house, asking questions. In truth Rowan was relieved that the other woman was there, to divert Isandro's attention from her.

Isandro was deftly feeding Zac, making all sorts of emotions run through Rowan. In answer to something María said which Rowan hadn't heard, he said, 'This isn't my original family home. My sister lives there, on the other side of Osuna, with her family and my mother.'

Rowan's insides clenched in instinctive self-protection at the mention of his mother and sister. At least they didn't live *here*. Relief flooded her. She needed to be thankful for small mercies. As it was she was sure she'd have to face them sooner or later, and she didn't believe that time and circumstance would have made either of them any more amenable to her.

Just then María stood up, excusing herself. Isandro stood too, and took Zac out of his high chair, handing him over. 'I think he's had all he's going to eat for now.'

'I'll take him up to get dressed…' The older woman deftly lifted him and took him out.

When Isandro sat down again Rowan's breath caught in her throat. She'd only just noticed that he was dressed down, in jeans and a T-shirt, the material doing little to disguise the breadth and power of his chest. He looked at her over the rim of his coffee cup.

'No more dreams last night?'

She shook her head. 'No.'

She looked away and down, and Isandro noticed the faint purple shadows under her eyes. Something kicked him in the chest as he recalled his impatience the previous night, and he did not welcome it.

'I'm sure,' he drawled conversationally, 'that it's just your guilty conscience.'

Rowan's head jerked up. His words had cut right through her with the precision of a knife.

For a second Isandro couldn't believe what he was seeing—abject pain in the depths of those deep violet eyes. He couldn't believe it because it wasn't there, he told himself. Wasn't he already witnessing her shy, hesitant smiles with Zac? The way she was charming María…?

'Isandro…' Rowan's voice felt unused and too husky. 'All I ask is for a chance. That's all. I'm here on your terms. I won't do anything you don't want me to do. I just want a chance. That's all.'

He sat back in his chair and saw her ramrod-straight back, her tightly held body. It was too thin. The shortness of her hair highlighted her long neck, and the bones in her wrist seemed so fragile—as if he might break them just by taking hold…

'You're getting the best chance you'll ever get or deserve. You're here, aren't you?' he gritted out. He hated being so aware of her.

She nodded and looked down, her hair falling forward across one cheek to shield her eyes from him. He had to stop himself from putting out a hand to pull it back, tuck it behind her ear.

'Thank you.'

He had to get out of there, away from her sham act of vulnerability. Abruptly Isandro stood from the table, dropping his napkin. He looked at Rowan sternly. 'You're here, as I said, primarily because I have no choice—and also because I know you won't last a week.' His eyes flicked disparagingly over her worn clothes. 'All this effort and play-acting...you really don't need to bother, you know.'

He turned, about to walk out of the door, and Rowan gathered her strength from somewhere, storing her hurt at his words deep down. She stood up, the sound of the chair harsh on the floor.

'Wait.'

He stopped and turned, impatience and intransigence stamped on every line of his body.

'When...when can I spend time with Zac, please?'

She held her breath. If he was going to refuse her—

'You can see him for a couple of hours before he goes down for his afternoon nap.'

He walked back in then, and came to stand close. Rowan gripped the table with one hand, slightly off balance after the way she had stood up.

'I'm off work for one week, Rowan. I'll be around, watching your every move, so don't get any ideas.'

Rowan watched as he walked away again, and out of the room. *Off work for one week?* Since when had he taken more than a day off work? She sat down again, trembling all over.

Had having Zac been what it took to make him change? Because undoubtedly he had. It was that softness she'd noticed. Not directed at her, by a long shot, but a softness nevertheless, and certainly a different attitude to work if this behaviour was anything to go by.

But she had seen it before, and it was this side of him, so rarely on display, which had given her the confidence to leave Zac—because she'd known above all else that he wanted and would love his son. The first time she'd really seen that side of him had been with his sister's children, who must be aged three and five now. He'd had an innate patience and an ability to communicate with them that had surprised Rowan when she'd seen them together at the wedding. It had bowled her over. And after she'd conceived, on their wedding night, she'd known instinctively that he'd be a good father.

Despite the fact that he'd been so ambitious that he had coldly married her in order to take control of one of the biggest banks in England, he'd welcomed the news of impending fatherhood. Clearly, though it had never been expected from her, he'd been happy to be having an heir.

She'd been halfway in love with him before they'd even married, and that had coloured her own decision to allow herself to be persuaded into the cold business deal of a marriage. Not that she'd had much choice... But when it had turned physical, and she'd fallen pregnant, then she'd foolishly and naively hoped for so much more.

She angrily took a sip of her tepid coffee, not wanting to remember but unable to forget. Her ailing father had pointed him out to her at that function in London's Savoy Hotel. But in truth she'd seen him the minute he'd come into the room. Anyone there with a pulse had. He'd appeared like a golden lion in the midst of lesser beings, mortals. There had been a moment's hush before the energy and conversation had zinged up a few notches. All the women had gone into preen mode; all the men had paled into insignificance. And he had just stood there, eyes constantly roving, assessing, blatantly uninterested in the conversation around him. Faintly sneering.

Rowan had been unable to take her eyes off him. Like every other woman there, she didn't have to remind herself. And yet she'd caught his eye—*or so she had stupidly thought*—and he had walked over towards her with singular intent. Rowan had been shaking, trembling, her eyes huge when he'd stopped in front of her and she'd finally realised that he wasn't looking at her, he'd been looking at her father. With the briefest of acknowledgements for Rowan—and she could remember the way those cool eyes had flicked over her—he and her father had shaken hands and retired to a private room, where they had hashed out the deal. The deal that had included her and changed her life.

She could still remember her misery when she'd over-heard some women talking in the powder room shortly after-wards. 'Did you see Rowan Carmichael's face when he walked over? The girl practically had her tongue hanging out. I mean, really, who would have her? She's twenty-five and still a virgin, I bet! And that dress—*honestly*. I wouldn't be surprised if it had been her mother's…'

They had gone on and on for what seemed like ages. When Rowan had emerged she'd gone straight outside and taken a cab home, her confidence in ribbons.

Rowan realised that she was gripping the small coffee cup so tight that she was in danger of breaking it. She relaxed her hold and put it down, took in a deep breath. So much had happened since then. *So much.* She couldn't allow being here to bring back those memories. She had to focus on the present and *Zac*. That was how she would get through this.

CHAPTER FOUR

'FORGIVE me, Mrs Salazar, it's just that…this situation is a little unusual.'

Rowan grimaced inwardly at the way María had immediately called her Mrs Salazar in her broken English. She tried out her rusty Spanish. 'Please, María—call me Rowan.' She looked at the other woman with sympathy. 'I know it must be strange for you to suddenly have me arrive like this, but my only concern is Zac and getting to know him.'

The other woman was obviously taken aback to hear Rowan speak Spanish, but still looked tense, worried. Not sure how to handle this situation.

'Look,' said Rowan, 'all I want to do is spend time with you and Zac for the moment. After all, he doesn't know me, so he's going to have to get used to me.'

A look of relief crossed María's face, and she wondered if Isandro had told her not to let Zac out of her sight while Rowan was there? She wouldn't put it past him.

María started to tell her what their routine was as Zac happily played on the lawn with an array of toys, mainly cars. Rowan could feel the back of her neck prickle, but didn't turn around. She was very aware that Isandro would be watching from one of the windows that looked out onto the main lawn.

She firmly pushed all thoughts of her husband out of her head. She had two hours with Zac today, and she was going to make the most of it. She also pushed down the well of emotion that threatened to erupt on a continuous basis every time she looked at her beautiful sturdy son. His personality was already ingrained, strongly apparent. More than a hint of his father. He toddled over to her and she shot a reassuring smile to María as she let him take her by the hand so he could pull her down onto the ground to help him play with his cars.

Isandro looked out of the window, arms folded tightly across his chest. He watched as Zac appeared to be happily welcoming Rowan into his life—as if she hadn't walked away from him, as if she hadn't already *rejected* him in his most vulnerable moment.

Rage burned upwards on behalf of his son, and he had to restrain himself from going out there and pulling Zac away from her grasping hands. And yet…he looked happy. And she wasn't looking bored or irritated. He hated to admit it, but Zac was naturally cautious with strangers and yet with Rowan, from that first moment in the hotel, he'd shown none of that caution—almost as if he'd recognised her. Isandro shook his head. That couldn't be possible…

Rowan was down on the ground, patiently nodding as Zac babbled incoherently with all the seriousness of a child on a mission who believed himself to be absolutely understood. She was still dressed in that tatty skirt and T-shirt, and the skirt was riding upwards to show a long length of leg, pale and smooth. His insides contracted, and resolve hardened inside him. He turned abruptly from the window and strode to his desk to pick up the phone.

The following day Rowan went back into the house. Zac had just been taken away for his nap. She hurried through the hall, thinking that maybe one day she would be able to spend time with Zac and not feel as though her heart were being ripped from her chest every time she looked at him.

Her foot was on the bottom step of the main stairs when she heard her name being called autocratically. There was to be no respite, then. It was as if Isandro was some sort of magician, catching her at her most vulnerable moments. She turned reluctantly and hoped her eyes didn't look too bright. Isandro stood framed in what she guessed to be his study door—she could see a big desk in the background.

'Could you come in here, please?' His tone made a mockery of the *please*.

She nodded briefly, tersely, and walked towards him, avoiding his eyes. He stood back to let her pass and she held her breath, not wanting to breathe in his scent. His essence. For a second she was so wrapped up in trying to avoid being aware of him that she didn't even see the man who had stood and was now holding out a hand. Isandro was introducing him.

'This is my lawyer, Ricardo Sanchez.'

Rowan stepped forward to shake his hand, still a little stunned that she hadn't even noticed him. 'Señor Sanchez.'

Her heart stopped and started again. The divorce papers. It had to be. She felt a self-protecting numbness spread through her. Even though she'd been expecting this from the moment they'd come to Spain, still it shocked her that he was giving her no time to prove herself…that he was carrying out his threat.

'Please sit down, Rowan.'

Rowan sat heavily into the seat that had been brusquely indicated by Isandro, and watched as he walked around the desk and sat down. Even in jeans and a T-shirt he looked formidable, frighteningly powerful. The sun slanted in at that moment and gilded his hair with a dark golden aura. She blinked and looked away to his lawyer, who was seated to her right. He was relatively young—she guessed him in his mid-forties—and handsome, albeit in a very buttoned-up way. He looked at her then, and smiled. Rowan was momentarily taken aback at this common courtesy after the past forty-eight hours of tension, and she smiled back, her mouth feeling strange in the movement.

'Ricardo.'

The name was called in a staccato of impatience. Rowan flushed and looked away, feeling guilty and not knowing why.

Isandro glared at her, and then at his lawyer. 'If you wouldn't mind showing my wife the papers, please?'

'Of course.' Isandro's lawyer bent and smoothly pulled out a sheaf of papers. He handed one set to Isandro, another to Rowan, and kept one himself.

They were in Spanish, but Rowan could make out the unmistakable. They were indeed the divorce papers. Something hard and unyielding settled into her chest, making her feel slightly breathless.

'I think you will find that everything is in order. Very standard.' Bitterness tinged Isandro's voice. 'Your entitlement under the prenup is unchanged. After careful consideration I fear that it will only cause more trouble than it's worth to fight your right to it—which undoubtedly I could do after your…disappearing act.'

Rowan looked up, her hands clenching around the papers. 'Isandro, I've already told you that—'

He flicked a lean hand, cutting her off with the violence of his gesture. 'Spare us. Señor Sanchez is well aware of the circumstances. Your acting isn't necessary here.'

She glanced to the other man, who now avoided her eye

and looked uncomfortable. Very well. Isandro wasn't going to listen to her. If he insisted on giving her the money then she would simply lodge it straight into a trust account for Zac, and perhaps give some to—

'So, if you could just sign the back page here…'

Rowan looked at Isandro incredulously, to see that he had flipped back the numerous pages filled with technical legalese to point to a dotted line. Indignation coursed through her. 'You have got to be kidding me.'

Isandro slammed down the papers, brows drawn together. 'If you're thinking of turning on an act to try and make me believe that you don't want this—'

Rowan stood up jerkily, every cell screaming at her not to let him see how this was affecting her. How hard it was for her to be faced with the stark reality of their marriage ending for ever. 'Of course I'm not. But do you really think I am so stupid that I would meekly allow you to shove this under my nose and expect me to sign it without so much as a by-your-leave?' She threw the papers down on the table as if they'd stung her, terrified that he'd see them shaking in her hands. 'It's entirely in Spanish, which isn't my first language—'

'You're fluent—'

'Yes, I am—but not in legal terms. How do I know you haven't added in a clever clause about custody, signing away my rights to Zac?'

He stood now too, and bristled at her from across the desk. Clearly she'd piqued his honour.

'Of course I haven't. These are divorce papers, pure and simple.'

'Well, I'm not signing a single thing until I've spoken to my own solicitor and he's looked them over. When he says they're okay, then I'll sign.'

Isandro felt impotent. Caught. And yet he knew that what

she said made sense. In another circumstance, if she were a different person, he would have advised her to take exactly the course of action she'd just outlined.

In Spanish, Rowan heard the lawyer say nervously, 'She's right. We need to send a copy to her own people.'

Rowan looked down at Isandro's lawyer. 'And you can send them in English. I won't take on the added expense of my solicitor having to bring in a translator.' Her bravado was masking intense pain.

'Of course,' the other man assured her, with something approaching respect in his dark eyes.

She looked back to Isandro. 'I'd also like to ring Mr Fairclough now, to advise him of this.'

She'd hitched up her chin, and with her arms crossed defensively Isandro felt inexplicably as if he should apologise. He quashed it down. This woman had committed a crime that not many would forgive. What right had she to be coming over all moral with him? He clenched his jaw and picked up the phone, handing her the receiver. She just looked at it. And then back to him.

'In private.' Her tone could have peeled paint from the walls.

Isandro looked at her for a long moment. The tension tautened and crackled. Rowan felt a little sorry for Señor Sanchez.

It didn't sit well with Isandro at all that he'd acted so out of character. But he couldn't deny the visceral way she made him feel. It had led him to convene this meeting, to get papers drawn up in record time. He spoke with exaggerated courtesy. 'I'll have one of the maids bring a cordless phone to your room. You will have all the privacy you need there.'

'Thank you.'

And with her head held high Rowan stalked out of the room. She sagged once outside, though, and then hurried up the stairs, almost as if Isandro might call her back, or bring her back bodily and force her to sign. She knew that no matter what had happened he wouldn't have done something so underhand as to add in a clause regarding custody. It wasn't his style. And yet she knew she was right to assert herself. She'd be a fool if she let him think he could walk all over her.

Once in her room, she went and stood by the open doors and looked out onto the courtyard. Its beauty and hushed stillness soothed her. And made her aware of the pain in her heart. The pain that had lodged there when it had become so blatantly obvious that Isandro would have divorced her there and then if he'd had the choice. Got rid of her as if she was nothing more than a piece of gum under his shoe. She shouldn't even be feeling like this. If she was, then it meant that—

A brief knock came at the door, startling her, and she opened it to reveal the maid who had woken her the other morning. She took the cordless phone with a strained smile, dug out David Fairclough's number and made the call. She explained briefly what had happened, and warned him to expect to receive divorce papers.

That done, she took a deep, shuddering breath. This was it. The beginning of the end. The beginning of the end of their marriage of convenience. Of a marriage that had never been meant to be consummated, that should never have resulted in a baby. But it had. And she didn't regret that for a second. Not even when it had caused her more pain and grief than she'd believed herself capable of enduring. And she would keep enduring it until she had proved herself to Isandro and come to some arrangement whereby she could live her own life *and* see Zac—be a part of his life too.

For the rest of that week Rowan avoided Isandro as much as possible. She saw him at breakfast, and in the evenings, when they would conduct stilted conversations at dinner. But for the rest of the time he would either be shut up in his office, out riding, or with Zac.

She relished her short time with Zac every day, when she got to see him before his nap. And relished even more how María was obviously feeling more relaxed with her presence, more inclined to use the time that Rowan had with Zac as a little break for herself. She'd bring a book and read as Zac and Rowan played.

Today, though, as María was taking Zac away for his nap, he let out a cry of distress, clearly wanting to keep playing with Rowan. Her heart broke. María smiled sympathetically. 'He's taken to you in a big way. But I'm afraid Señor Salazar's instructions were explicit.'

'María, don't feel you have to explain. I'm here on your territory—and Zac's.'

The woman blushed uncomfortably as Zac still wailed in her arms. 'I know, but you seem…' She blushed again. 'Nice. And you are his—'

'What's going on here?'

Their heads turned in unison, to see Isandro striding across the lawn. He took Zac from María and inspected his tear-stained face. The quivering lip.

María rushed to speak. 'He's just tired, Señor Salazar. It's time for his nap, but he was having too much fun playing with Row—' She stopped. 'Mrs Salazar.'

Isandro looked from her to Rowan, as if he suspected something had happened. He looked so grimly protective that Rowan's heart lurched.

'I'll…I'll go inside. I don't want to upset him. María's right. He's just over-tired.'

Before he could say another word Rowan hurried inside. Feeling agitated and restless, she balked at going up to her room, where she always retreated every day. Instead she went into the main drawing room. She whirled around a moment later when she heard heavy footsteps and saw Isandro darkening the door, coming in to shut it behind him.

He advanced with lethal slowness, and Rowan backed away instinctively.

'What is it?' she asked flatly, because she had no doubt that Isandro was about to fill her in on her latest crime.

'What are you doing to my son?'

Rowan shook her head and it felt fuzzy. 'Nothing. Just playing with him.'

'He was upset. *You* must have upset him.'

Rowan's eyes grew round. She couldn't believe the unfairness of his attack. 'He was tired, that was all, Isandro. Children his age get over-excited easily. He's had someone new to play with this week. By next week the novelty will have worn off.'

Isandro scowled. Her reference to *next week* made all sorts of hackles rise. 'Since when did *you* know so much about kids?' His voice was scathing.

Rowan steeled herself to withstand it. 'I'm a woman. I've *au paired*. And apart from anything else he's my son. I—'

She stopped. She'd been about to say *I love him*, but knew that would bring down a whole torrent of abuse on her head.

'He's my son, Isandro,' she said simply instead. 'And you're going to have to get used to it. I'm not going anywhere. I'm going to be around for the rest of his life.'

Isandro raked his blistering blue gaze up and down. 'Until you've got your hands on what you came back for, you mean. Then he'll be dropped like a hot potato again, and this time it'll be worse because he'll have got to know you.' He swung away from her with a violent movement. 'I can't believe I'm allowing this—' He stopped, his voice full of self-recrimination, and came back close again, eyes blazing.

Rowan couldn't back away any more as a chair was behind her. He'd come so close that she could see the flecks of lighter blue in his eyes. Smell him. *Dear God.* If he knew for a second—

'I know what you're doing. But know this. With me as his protector you can be damn sure that if you so much as cause one tear of distress to fall from his eyes *you're gone.*'

Rowan's throat closed over as she felt a well of sadness rise up. She could feel Isandro's pain. His uncertainty. She could feel it because she'd been through it, a million times over. It was one of the reasons she'd walked away. She wanted to reach out and reassure him, and her hand even stretched out impulsively.

Immediately he jerked back. He looked at her hand suspended in the air as if it were toxic. Couldn't believe that he'd almost, for one second, responded to her gesture. 'Don't come near me. You disgust me.'

With a chilling look he turned and walked from the room.

Rowan couldn't move. She was locked in stasis. Paralysed by the venom in his expression just now. The very real evidence of his absolute hatred and unforgiveness. Hot tears filled her eyes, splashing down her cheeks. She pulled her hand in and cradled it against her chest as if he had struck it. Because, worse than anything else that had just happened, there was another emotion that she had to acknowledge. And it shamed her beyond belief. It had been jealousy. Jealousy of her own son. Because Isandro loved him so completely, so utterly, that she knew he had the capacity to do what she had done. Lay down his life for his child. And the fact that she represented that level of a threat to him hurt her more than she could bear.

For the last couple of days of Isandro's week off he had watched Rowan even more closely. Instead of leaving her alone with Zac and María in the afternoons, as he had done before, he joined them. His reluctance to leave Rowan unsupervised with Zac was palpable. It had made something harden inside her. She would not let him scare her. She was stronger than that. He didn't know how strong she'd had to become. So she endured his company, his looks, his obvious distrust.

Even so, her nerves were stretched to breaking point by the time Sunday night came. They were in the dining room drinking coffee, having finished dinner. Rowan took another sip and closed her eyes to savour the aroma and taste as much as to block Isandro out.

When Julia came in to bid them goodnight, Rowan got up quickly, wanting to leave, to avoid being subjected to more of Isandro's scathing looks, ascerbic comments. But a hand snaked out of nowhere and caught her wrist, enveloping it in shocking heat. The physical contact threw her so much that she stumbled backwards. If not for Isandro standing to catch her shoulders she would have fallen.

She looked up with startled eyes. His hands were like a brand, burning through the threadbare material of her thin sweater. He seemed to be caught too. His eyes flared. Rowan stopped breathing as the air around them seemed suddenly charged with electricity. It couldn't be. He despised her. And yet…*this* was what she'd felt that night. The night of their wedding. And countless nights over the months of her pregnancy. Nights of passion…white-hot consummation. The memories of which had become her fantasies.

In an instant he'd moved even closer, and one hand came off her shoulder to tip her chin upwards. To better see her face. Her neck seemed to be made of elastic as her head fell back.

'I wonder…'

'You wonder what…' Rowan croaked out.

'What tricks you've learnt in the past two years. For no doubt you've been busy becoming more *experienced*.'

CHAPTER FIVE

ISANDRO'S words didn't make sense at first, and it was only when his mouth was dropping towards hers, his eyes closing, that she realised what he was doing. She felt her body sway towards him, helpless. The sensation of wanting this, wanting him to kiss her, was so overwhelming, so intense that she couldn't help it.

And when his mouth touched hers softly, and then harder, his lips firming over hers, she gave a little moan of acceptance. Her own mouth opened under his, seeking for closer intimacy. Seeking for his tongue to find hers, seeking for his arms to pull her close and let her feel the strength of his body against hers. She'd craved this for so long. For ever. And had thought she'd never experience it again. She'd stored up her memories of this like a miser with her gold, taking it out every now and then, allowing herself to revel in it…guiltily.

Despite the clarity he'd felt when he'd started this, the reluctant yet insistent desire to prove something to himself, now Isandro's arms itched to pull her pliant and yielding body even closer. To feel her breasts crushed against his chest. He could feel her soft mouth opening, hesitantly, as if she was unsure…and like a douche of cold water he pulled back, so suddenly and harshly that Rowan stumbled backwards. This time, however, he made no move to steady her. He'd told her just the other day that she disgusted him, and yet he'd just proved otherwise. He hated that she'd made him lose control. Hated to be faced with the evidence that he still wanted her. Badly. In spite of her actions.

Cruelly he wiped a hand across his mouth, as if to wipe the imprint of her lips away. 'You've perfected the art of the virginal act, I see. It might almost lead me to believe that perhaps you were more experienced than I remember. It's not unknown for a woman to become so practised in the art that she can make every man feel like it's the first time.'

Rowan gasped, and struggled to contain her wildly see-sawing emotions. She was hurt beyond belief at the way he'd wiped away her kiss. Yet her body still hummed, felt raw with desire. How could she have just let him do that to her when his motives couldn't be anything but transparently hurtful to her? Hadn't the way he'd looked at her the other day in the drawing room had *any* effect? The words he'd said?

'How dare you—?'

She made to get past him, but he caught her arm, swinging her back. His face was harsh, the shadows in the room making his hair look dark. His lips thinning. The evidence of his own monumental lack of judgment where she'd been concerned struck him anew.

'You married me for no better reason than to secure your inheritance. But you tricked me, Rowan. You went one step too far. In a bid to secure your future for ever you got pregnant as an added insurance. With no intention of ever being there for your child.'

Rowan's voice shook, and she could barely mask her hurt and pain. 'You have it so wrong it's not even funny, Isandro.' She wanted to say something—anything to cut him down, minimise the hurt—but she had no defence. Because she knew well that even once she'd been pregnant nothing had diminished her passion. If her only aim had been to get pregnant, then why would she have thrown herself at him so ardently night after night?

So she used the only arsenal she could think of to distract him from that glaring anomaly. 'You're forgetting the little choice I had in the matter. It was part of the deal, remember? To ensure your social acceptance and save my father's face I *had* to marry you.'

He looked her up and down, took in the rapid rise and fall of her breasts. Her words made something jar uncomfortably inside him. Made something inexplicably painful surge upwards.

Rowan finally ripped her arm free. Right at that moment she hated him with an intensity that shook her to the core— but if she was honest she knew it just masked a much scarier emotion. This was exactly what she was protecting herself from. The fear that he would guess for even a second how much he did affect her. And had affected her.

'Go to hell, Isandro.'

He recovered himself. 'Not without taking you with me.'

I've already been there... The words trembled on her lips but she bit them back.

'I'm not going anywhere, Isandro. So get used to it.' And with those parting words she walked on jelly legs out of the room and upstairs.

That night she had the dream again. She was trapped in the white room. Couldn't get out. But when she woke with wet cheeks and her heart thumping she was alone, and thankful that she hadn't caused a disturbance as the house was silent.

The next day, as Isandro sat in his office in Seville, he felt an almost overpowering urge to leave, get into his car and go home. She was there, in his house. Alone and unsupervised apart from María and his staff. He could see that María had been confused as to how to treat her. He saw how Rowan had been twisting the other woman around her finger. Was he mad to leave her there? He stood up and ran a hand through his hair.

A call came through. He picked up the phone and barked into it.

'Good morning to you too.'

'What is it, Ricardo? I'm busy.'

His lawyer wasn't stupid. He took the hint. 'I thought you'd like to know that your wife's solicitor has instructed us that the papers are good for her to sign. He's just rung her at the house to inform her of this.'

Isandro sat down into his chair. An immediate heaviness had entered his chest. Which was ridiculous. He should be elated.

'Fine. They're still in my study at home. If you can meet me there tonight we'll sign them.'

'Of course.'

Isandro let the phone drop.

On the other end his lawyer smiled wryly. He wondered what would have been the reaction if he'd said no, that actually he had a date tonight? He shook his head. Men as powerful as Isandro were never given excuses. So he picked up his phone again and called off the date with his girlfriend.

With Isandro's disturbing presence out of the house, Rowan felt herself relaxing somewhat for the first time in days. She knew María had been given strict instructions not to allow Rowan any more time with Zac than had been discussed, but the woman bent the rules a little. Rowan was so pathetically grateful, it was ridiculous. Without Isandro looking over her shoulder she could really get to know Zac. She knew well, though, that it was galling for him to know she was there.

Every evening when he came back he looked in on Zac, and at her suspiciously, as if she might have done something to him.

Rowan had signed the preliminary divorce papers a couple of evenings ago, and since then a heaviness had weighed her down inside. But she told herself it was only natural to feel pain at the thought that she and Isandro wouldn't be able to provide Zac with a stable family...

Dinner on Friday evening passed off without incident, and Rowan managed to escape without being detained. Up in her own room, she was too restless to sleep and took confidence in the fact that Isandro would no doubt be in his study, working. She went out into the patioed garden and tipped her head back to see the stars, drinking in the night.

Suddenly weary and feeling very vulnerable, she sank for a moment onto the bottom step and let her head fall back. The warm Andalucian air caressed her. She closed her eyes and breathed in deeply. Until a sound made her head jerk up. She stood hurriedly when she saw a dark shape peel itself from the wall. She knew well who it was. A stranger would have caused less panic.

'Isandro.' Thank goodness her voice was steady.

'Did you think it might be a burglar?' he asked lightly.

Rowan held onto the wall beside her as he walked down his steps with leonine grace.

She shook her head and smiled tightly, thinking of all the bodyguards. 'With the security system here?'

He came and stood in front of her. She was still on the bottom step, so she stood slightly taller than him, and in the dark star-filled night she had a sudden urge to put her hands around his face, lower her mouth to his to kiss him and feel him put his arms around her waist.

She shook inwardly with the effort it took to clear her mind of the image.

'Isandro, what do you want?'

She couldn't read his face. But his eyes were hard. He opened his mouth to speak and she braced herself for censure but just then a noise sounded from inside Isandro's room. Someone calling his name. And the panic in that voice was unmistakable. Immediately Rowan recognised it, and hairs rose on the back of her neck. Everything else was forgotten.

'María…' she breathed. Instinctively she followed Isandro's swift return to his room, where María stood wringing her hands, her face as white as snow. Rowan could see that she was in shock and panic, almost about to faint.

Isandro went and took her shoulders, but the woman was incoherent. Rowan tried to get her to calm down.

'María what is it? Just try to breathe and tell us.'

Rowan could sense Isandro's swift sideways look of annoyance that she had followed him.

The other woman finally managed to say, 'Zac—it's Zac. He's having some kind of fit—I don't think he's breathing.'

Shock slammed into Rowan even as she registered Isandro reacting like lightning and thrusting María aside. No… No! her mind screamed. Not now. Not after everything.

On numb legs she followed Isandro into Zac's room. She could see that Isandro was dangerously close to panic as well. With an instinct she wasn't even aware she possessed, she pushed him aside to have a look. María had followed them, clearly verging on full-blown hysteria. Rowan somehow forced herself to remain calm and look at Zac properly.

As she did, she felt an intense burst of relief. He had stopped convulsing and was now rigid on the bed, his skin turning blue. He was unconscious, but breathing. She stepped in front of Isandro and knelt down by the bed, quickly turning Zac towards her and onto his side. Then she loosened his pyjama top. Felt his forehead. He was burning up.

She looked at María and issued a rapid instruction. María just stood there, in shock. Rowan snapped out her name, and it woke María from her trance. She ran into the bathroom. That seemed to wake Isandro too. Rowan felt his hands on her shoulders, as if to pull her back. His voice was hoarse with fear.

'What are you doing? You're going to hurt him.'

Rowan shook him off. 'He's going to be fine. He's having a febrile convulsion. Go and call an ambulance or a doctor.'

She looked up at Isandro, who hadn't moved. He looked so pale that she felt scared. '*Go*—call an ambulance. We have to get him to hospital. He'll be awake by the time you come back, I promise.'

Her urgency finally penetrated, and he left the room. Rowan had instructed María to get a glass of cool water and a baby paracetamol. By the time Isandro came back Zac was indeed coming round.

Rowan felt shaky with relief. She made sure to keep him in the recovery position and spoke to him softly. He was groggy and disorientated, a little grumpy, which she knew could be expected after a convulsion. When she deemed him to be sufficiently recovered enough to swallow, she gave him the paracetamol María had brought, and made him drink some water.

'What's that?' Isandro stepped forward, his hands clenched by his sides. Rowan read his mood in an instant. He hated being impotent—hated seeing the power that she had just displayed.

'It's baby paracetamol. To bring down his temperature.'

Just then they heard banging on the door downstairs, and Rowan breathed a sigh of relief. María ran out. Rowan focused on Zac, making sure she was keeping him cool and comfortable.

When the paramedics arrived she explained what had happened. Isandro had lifted the still sleepy Zac into his arms to bring him downstairs, and they met the doctor, who had also arrived. He quickly checked Zac over and confirmed him safe enough to move.

Rowan stood at the door and watched as they got into the ambulance. She felt weak and limp in the aftermath. At the last minute the doctor looked at her. 'Aren't you the child's mother?'

Rowan stood up straight. 'Well…yes—yes, I am. But—'

'Well, you must come with us. The child will want you too, and he's going to be disorientated enough.'

'But—'

The doctor was impatient. 'You must come to tell them what happened so they can determine if it is serious enough to keep him in.'

Rowan's eyes met Isandro's, where he sat in the ambulance cradling Zac. His features were tight and drawn. 'He's right, Rowan. Get in.'

So she did. They travelled to the small local hospital some ten minutes away, and Rowan didn't take her eyes off her son. He was recovering rapidly. Rapidly enough so that by the time they had arrived at the hospital he was looking around him with big eyes, although still groggy.

After Zac had been thoroughly examined the doctor deemed that he should stay in overnight, just to be safe. Isandro immediately declared that he was staying with Zac. Rowan said nothing, just walked with María out to the front of the hospital. She'd followed them, with Hernán. The woman was inconsolable.

'I'm so sorry. I just froze. I got such a shock when I saw him convulsing…I *knew* what it was, but I've never seen it before…'

Rowan put her arm around María's shoulder. 'María, don't worry. You did the best thing by coming to get Isandro.'

María looked at her with something like awe in her eyes. 'But *you* knew what to do. *You're* his mother.'

'María, you should go home. And take Rowan with you.'

Rowan looked at Isandro. He had followed them out and he looked exhausted. She wouldn't fight with him now, but she had no intention of going home. Isandro went back inside, and she saw María out to the Jeep and sent her off. Then she went back inside too. She didn't go into Zac's room, where she guessed Isandro was, she just sat on a chair in the corridor. A different bodyguard hovered discreetly nearby. All she wanted was to be close, in case anything happened.

That was when she started to tremble. Uncontrollably. Shock was setting in at what had just happened and where she now sat. A hospital. Just like the clinic. With white walls.

Isandro came out of Zac's room for a moment, to make a quick call to Hernán and instruct him as to what time to come and pick them up in the morning, and that was when he saw her. He reeled. Rowan was staring straight ahead, her hands shaking in her lap, and she was so pale that he was surprised she was still sitting up. He quashed his immediate reflex to demand to know why she hadn't left.

'Rowan…'

No response.

'Rowan?'

No response. He moved closer and sat down. Eventually took her hands in his.

Rowan felt warmth coming from somewhere. But she was locked in a living nightmare. She knew she wasn't asleep. She was surrounded by white walls. Eventually something pierced her consciousness.

'Rowan.'

Someone was pulling her head around. Forcing her eyes to meet…blue ones. The only ones she'd ever dreamt of. The warmth of his hands was seeping through to her chilled bones and body. Like a life-giving force. And with that sanity and reality returned.

'Rowan?'

Isandro was looking at her, and it wasn't his usual impatient look. It was something different. Assessing. Speculative.

'I couldn't leave. I'll just sit out here and wait, if that's okay?'

Isandro willed down the concern rippling through him. She was in shock. Of that there was no doubt. But it was a shock so deep and raw that he'd never seen anything like it.

'Will you be okay if I leave you for a second?'

Rowan nodded, and watched as he put her hands back in her lap and walked away. She felt like calling out after him. But just as swiftly he returned and put a steaming hot cup of tea into her hands, encouraging her to drink. The tea burnt its way down her throat into her stomach and warmed her.

As he watched the colour slowly come back into her cheeks, Isandro remembered coming out onto his balcony and seeing her with her head tipped back, eyes closed...there had been something intangibly vulnerable about the lines of her body. Then he remembered the way he'd felt when he'd come to stand in front of her. All that had been on his mind was that he'd wanted to kiss her. How could he think of that at a time like this?

'How did you know what was wrong with him?'

Rowan looked at Isandro warily. 'I read about febrile convulsions in one of my baby books while I was pregnant.'

His eyes speared her, intensely blue against the white background. 'You *read* about it in a book?'

She nodded. 'They're not uncommon in children his age.'

Isandro stood up and stuck his hands in his pockets. 'And yet not I nor María knew what to do—and I am his father and she is his nanny. Dammit, that woman was meant to be the best of the best—trained to deal with anything.'

Rowan rushed automatically to María's defence. 'It's all

very well to know something in theory, but when you're faced with a child in a convulsion, turning blue... She knew what it was, Isandro, she just got a shock.'

'And yet with no training you knew exactly what to do.'

Silence hung heavy and awkward. What could she say? Sorry? She looked down at the ground and saw Isandro's feet come into her line of vision. She suddenly felt tired.

'I never said thank you.'

She looked up and shook her head, hiding her shock at his apology. 'You don't have to. I'm just glad I could help.'

And I couldn't. The words reverberated in Isandro's head. He'd never felt so impotent in all his life, never so much at a loss. He'd had to let someone else take control, and it had almost killed him.

Rowan could feel him looking at her. What was he thinking?

He stretched out a hand. 'Come on.'

She looked up. His face was inscrutable. She stood up and let him take her by the elbow. He steered her into Zac's room, where he lay sleeping, and made her sit down in the comfy chair in the corner. He took the upright chair beside Zac. She started to protest but he shushed her.

And in the half-light of the hospital room, with her son's chest rising and falling easily, Rowan let herself relax... She fought it for a long time, her eyes going from father to son, but finally she slept...

Back at the house the next day, María appeared, still looking shaken and shamefaced as she greeted them and took Zac for his morning nap.

Isandro looked at Rowan. 'You should get some rest. You can't have slept well on that chair.'

And what about you? she wanted to ask. But he'd already gone to follow María and check on Zac.

He didn't go into the office those first couple of days after the weekend, clearly still shaken by the experience. Rowan was aware of a subtle softening in his treatment of her, but knew it was far too dangerous to allow any feeling of complacency to creep in.

It was the evening of the first day that Isandro had returned to work. He'd just taken a shower and now strode towards the dining room doors for dinner, knowing that Rowan would be sitting beyond them. Inarticulate rage twinned with something much more disturbing beat in his chest. All day he'd felt a black mood engulfing him, distracting him from his work.

In the last couple of days he'd been feeling so many things, and that fear…the awful bone-numbing terror he'd felt when he'd seen Zac so defenceless…was still potent. And Rowan—the woman who had deserted them—was the one who'd been there, fulfilling her role as mother for all the world as if she'd never left, making Isandro feel blurred and ambiguous.

He came close to the door. She was dangerous. He had to remember that, despite her heroics. She had the power to do so much more harm this time. To Zac. *To him.* Isandro's eyes narrowed and his mouth thinned. She didn't have any power over *him*, it was Zac he thought of. Not himself. But still the black cloud enveloped him a little more suffocatingly as he opened the door, only to come face to face with his wife on her way out. Her eyes widened, looking up into his, scrambling her thoughts and making the rage burn more fiercely.

Rowan stared up at her husband, the breath still knocked out of her after the suddenness of his arrival. He was looking effortlessly gorgeous in a white shirt, black trousers, his hair still wet from the shower. His scent enveloped her…she fought for breath.

'Sorry… I was just… I didn't know if you were…' She

cursed herself and started again, drawing herself up straight. Immediately she knew all was not well as he glowered down at her, and couldn't begin to wonder what had precipitated it. 'I was just going to tell Julia I'd eat in the kitchen as I thought it would only be me for dinner…' She wished she had something to cling onto—and then her eyes slid treacherously to his broad chest, just inches away, and she felt heat flood her cheeks.

Finally he broke the spell and moved past her, gracefully, stealthily. And he drawled, 'There's no-one else here, Rowan… Who are you trying to impress?'

Rowan ignored him, and the silly pain in her chest at this evidence of his filthy humour. Like this he was very dangerous. She turned to follow him back into the room. 'Well, as you're here, I'll stay.'

He swept an arm out as he sat down. 'Oh please—don't stay on my account. By all means go and eat in the kitchen if you want.'

But just when she would have taken him at his word and left, she heard the door, and Julia arrived with the soup. Rowan knew it would be futile to get into a big long explanation of why she wanted to eat in the kitchen, and she didn't want to embarrass the other woman, so she sat down and busied herself with her napkin.

For the past couple of days Isandro had been somewhat civil, but that civility had obviously run its course. She avoided his eye and they ate their soup in oppressive silence. Rowan was quite tempted to just pick up her bowl and leave the room, but she was also determined not to show how he affected her.

Julia returned with the main dish, and a bottle of red wine to go along with the beef. Rowan accepted a glass and speared a morsel of the succulent meat. It almost melted on her

tongue, and it had been so long since she had had anything
so exquisite that she closed her eyes for a second, unconsciously savouring the taste.

When she opened them again she caught Isandro staring
at her with a hard look.

'The beef is delicious.' She knew she sounded defensive.
'It's just beef.'

Rowan took a swift sip of wine. That too begged to be
savoured but she stopped herself. They continued to eat in
silence, and Rowan did her best not to be aware of his lean
brown hands, big but graceful, as he handled his silverware.
She saw him take his fork into his left hand to eat and remembered that he was left-handed. She wondered absently if Zac
might have inherited that trait.

When they were finished, Isandro put his napkin down by
his plate and leaned forward, cradling his wine glass in one
big hand. Rowan instinctively sat back into her chair. She
couldn't help but look at him. She knew her eyes were
growing big and round, but couldn't help it. He filled her
vision like nothing else she'd ever experienced. She felt as if
he could see right through her. As if they'd gone back in time
and it was one of the first times she'd seen him all over again.

Isandro watched her intently, and in that moment he felt
inexplicably like pushing her, goading her into revealing...*something*. Anything. *Something that would make
things easier for him to understand?* He quashed the annoying
voice, and asked, 'Why did your father want to marry you off
so badly that he made you a part of the deal?'

Rowan's mind seized. This was the last thing she'd expected
to hear. 'Why on earth do you want to talk about that now?'

Isandro shrugged negligently, dangerously. 'Call it making
conversation.'

Rowan stifled a reply. If she made a fuss, he'd know that

this was a sensitive subject for her. He was playing with her like a cat toying with a mouse, that was all. In keeping with this weird mood he was in.

She affected a shrug, much like his, and willed Julia to return. Anything to break this up and change the subject. 'I thought you knew why.'

Isandro waved a hand. 'Well, for your inheritance, I believed. But as he never made any play to get it after we got married I could never figure out why.'

Rowan was genuinely surprised. 'You thought my father wanted my inheritance?'

Isandro's gaze narrowed. 'Didn't he? He was going bankrupt. I thought he saw you as his ticket out of lifelong debt. That he was offering you up for marriage for that reason.'

Rowan's head swirled, and she put a hand to it. He had deduced *that*?

As if reading her thoughts, he added, 'It was obvious there was little affection lost between you, Rowan. Anyone could have seen that.'

She glared at him. This was getting far too close for comfort. Her own secret humiliation open for scrutiny. The fact that she'd been unwanted. Unloved. Tolerated. By her only family.

Rowan lifted her glass of wine, her hand trembling slightly, and took another sip. He was being too invasive, and yet she couldn't escape that intense regard. He would settle for nothing less than blood. This was the price she was expected to pay for wanting to be here. For leaving in the first place.

'There's something you obviously weren't aware of.'

He inclined his head, taking a slow sip of wine. 'Go on.'

Tension spiralled through Rowan. 'The truth is that my father was sick. No one knew how bad it was apart from me and his cardiologist. He had a degenerative and inoperable heart condition. It's why he lost control of his business and work. Why he looked for someone to bail him out. He wanted to save face before he died.' She shrugged minutely. 'As for me—he just wanted to see me married to a suitable husband. He had no interest in the money.'

Isandro was frowning. 'I had no idea he was ill. But why was it so important to see you married?'

Rowan could feel anger rising. Was he intent on humiliating her completely? She deliberately kept her voice as light as possible to hide the long-buried pain.

'Because he'd made a promise to my mother on her deathbed that he'd see me married to someone worthy so I'd safely inherit her fortune.' Rowan's lips thinned in self-deprecation. She'd gone inwards. 'I don't think he'd counted on it taking so long. He knew he was dying, and he needed to ensure Carmichael's safety, my inheritance. You came along and effectively killed two birds with one stone for him.'

Isandro's eyes narrowed sharply on her tense face, at her staccato words.

She smiled tightly, looking up at him briefly before looking down again, white fingers playing with her napkin. 'No doubt you were well aware that I was groomed from birth to be the perfect wife. I went to finishing school. I speak five languages. I can converse on topics as diverse as the possible extinction of the mountain gorilla in Rwanda and the theory of the butterfly effect.' She gave a little laugh then, as if revealing herself cost her nothing. 'When I was eighteen my father threw away the bi-focals I'd worn since I was nine and made me get laser eye surgery. All the better to make me a more appealing wife.'

For a long moment Isandro said nothing, and Rowan realised that her breath was coming jerkily, as if she'd just been running. And then he said softly, 'Perhaps he could see how beautiful they are.'

Rowan's heart flipped in her chest and she sent him a quick shocked look, for a second catching his eye. He coloured slightly, as if he too was shocked at his words, but then that scarily cool mask was back in place and he diverted his attention to filling his wine glass again. He was making her feel thoroughly confused. Acting so mercurial. Moody.

'So why didn't you get married before?'

Had what he'd just said about her eyes been her imagination? She shook her head faintly. 'I don't know…'

But she knew well. She thought of the men she'd been introduced to over the years. Insipid. Boring. The minute she'd seen Isandro she'd *known* him. She'd felt something deep within her spring to life, as if she'd been asleep until that moment. She hadn't believed it when her father had said he was interested in being introduced to her. But then she hadn't realised the extent of his interest in her as a trophy wife. More fool her.

That first time they'd had dinner she'd got to the restaurant before him and had sat facing away from the door. She'd cursed herself, but had been too self-conscious to get up and move. She'd waited like that, with her back so straight and tense it might have cracked, and then she had *felt* him. She could remember closing her eyes for that split second just before he'd come into her line of vision, and then he'd surprised her by asking, 'Excuse me, is this seat taken?'

She'd looked up, and he'd been smiling down at her. A half mocking smile that had been so confident, so seductive, so sure of himself. She'd blushed from that moment right through the whole meal, but amazingly the ice had been broken with his self-deprecating introduction. She'd always felt slightly guilty after he'd proposed, as if they were so completely mismatched that she'd surely taken him away from a far worthier, more soignée woman. And she'd never had to nerve to ask him why *he* hadn't married before…

She certainly didn't have the nerve to ask him that now, but she wanted his focus off her as to why she might have agreed to marry him. Her inheritance had never been important to her, and if he guessed that…

'You married me to get your foot in the English banking door. Tell me, has it worked?' She hated being reminded of a time in her life when all she'd been was a commodity to be passed off, because her father was doing no more than ticking the boxes before he died.

Isandro was calm and implacable, infuriating her with his coolness. 'Yes. You could say that,' he answered equably. 'I now control a majority share in the biggest bank in England.'

She darted him a look. 'You must be happy, then. You got what you wanted.'

He shrugged and drained his wine glass. 'Happy? I wouldn't say happy, exactly, Rowan. Satisfied, perhaps. Can you say that your frittering away of your own inheritance in these last two years has made *you* happy?'

And just like that she was brought back to the present with a mighty bump. She shook her head, not really seeing him any more. 'No. I can't say it has.'

There was a bleakness in her tone that was unmistakable. But she missed Isandro's quick glance.

Julia came in then, with coffee and dessert. Rowan thanked her for the beautiful dinner and waited till she had left. Then she put down her napkin shakily and stood up.

'I'm feeling quite tired now. I think I'll go to bed.' She felt raw and open inside. Flayed.

Isandro grabbed her wrist as she went to leave. She took a deep breath and willed the emotion out of her eyes as she turned to look down. She even managed to raise a nonchalant brow in question, even though her pulse beat crazily against his hand. She prayed he wouldn't notice.

'Tell me. Is that why you left, Rowan? Because you wanted to escape the box your father had put you in?'

No... The word ached to come out but she couldn't let it. Not yet. It was still too much to share. Especially when he was in such a dangerous mood.

So she tossed her head slightly and saw a flare of something—anger?—in Isandro's eyes. 'Yes. That's why I left.'

He gripped her hand a little harder. His mouth thinned. 'You expect me to believe that you were just a poor little rich girl, Rowan? A poor little sheltered rich girl, who ran away at the first opportunity…?'

'Yes,' she said wildly—anything just to get away from him.

'Well, I hope it was worth it, Rowan…'

It was…

She tore her eyes from his with a will she hadn't known she possessed, and snatched her hand back. She ran from the room, all pretence of insouciance gone. Once outside she walked blindly through the house and out to the garden, where she gulped in the night air. He was so right and yet so wrong. She had been exactly that. A poor, gauche little rich girl. Unbelievably naïve. Her father had done all he could to make her a biddable wife; he just hadn't counted on her chronic shyness and innate lack of grace and style thwarting his efforts.

And she hadn't run away at the first opportunity. She'd fallen stupidly in love at the first opportunity. With a man who had made her dreams of love look like a silly garish cartoon, complete with love hearts and flowers.

CHAPTER SIX

ISANDRO poured himself another glass of wine and his hand wasn't completely steady. What on earth had compelled him to rake up old ground? He'd never cared before why Rowan had married him. She just had—she'd been willing, part of a package. She'd *appeared* to be refreshingly unlike the other women of that society, which was why he'd decided to marry her as opposed to any other.

He'd clearly stated the terms of their marriage, and had thought he would be doing her a favour by making sure her father didn't get his hands on her inheritance. But he'd died soon after the wedding, and if what she'd just said was true he'd never planned on doing her out of it anyway. That bugged him now. He wasn't used to reading people wrong. His mouth thinned. And yet what had his wife turned out to be? He slugged back a gulp of wine. *A monumental thorn in his side...*

The truth was, she'd touched a protective instinct in him. From the first moment he'd seen her, and that unbelievably naïve quality about her. He'd read her outward shell of unconcern to be just that—a shell. And yet she'd played him for a fool from that first moment.

His feeling of vulnerability these last few days came back

to him and rocked him to his core. From the first moment he'd seen her again he'd viewed her as a dangerous threat. But she'd become the complete opposite... And when he'd walked into the dining room earlier all he'd seen were those huge eyes, staring at him, full of *something*. Looking at him as she'd looked at him before. When he had stupidly believed that perhaps his wife felt more for him than she had shown.

She'd asked him if he was happy. It had touched a nerve. Zac had made him happier than anything else he'd ever known, and for someone who'd meticulously planned out a life built around gaining power it had been...a revelation. A revelation that *she* was responsible for. Anger coursed through him again. He welcomed it.

More than a week had come and gone. Why wasn't she bored? Why hadn't she made an attempt to go into Seville, to the city? Why was she insisting on wearing those three tatty outfits day after day?

Was that why he'd felt compelled to goad her, to prod her? To ask her about things that had never concerned him before? To drive her to reiterate why she'd left? So that he could remember and not forget? Was he in danger of forgetting? He downed the last of the wine. He *would not* forget. And as soon as their divorce was through he would move her out of his home and they would establish her access to Zac. That was all their relationship comprised now.

When Rowan came down the stairs the following morning it was bedlam. Zac was in Isandro's arms, and he and Julia the housekeeper were trying to talk above Zac's screaming, crying. His face was puce, and Rowan guessed it was because he was being ignored. Her arms itched to take him and calm him down. It couldn't be good for him to be getting worked up so soon after the convulsion.

'What's wrong?'

Her voice seemed to cut through the mayhem and they turned to her. Even Zac halted with a hiccup. Isandro glared at her. But what had she expected after last night? They'd taken two steps forward and about three hundred back.

'María has left.'

Rowan's churning thoughts stopped dead. Much like Zac's screaming. 'María's left? But why?'

Isandro held out a note. 'Here—you seem to have a lot in common.'

Rowan ignored his barb and read the note. In effect María was saying that she felt she hadn't handled Zac's convulsion well, and now that his mother was here she didn't see that she had a role.

Rowan looked up at Isandro, speechless. He glared at her briefly, before trying to calm Zac down. He was rapidly working himself up again.

'Here—give him to me. Let me give him some breakfast. He must be hungry.'

Rowan watched as Isandro handed Zac over to Julia. She had a nervous fluttering in her belly. It was patently obvious who Isandro blamed for this. She crossed her arms.

'Isandro, I'm sorry to hear María has left—'

'Of course you are. No doubt you're loving this. Tell me, did you pay her to leave?'

Rowan's mouth dropped open inelegantly and she sputtered indignantly. 'How dare you? Of *course* I had nothing to do with her leaving. If you hired someone unprofessional enough to leave at the first sign of a crisis then you cannot blame me.'

He moved close and said silkily, 'And yet everything was running smoothly before you came back.'

His conscience pricked at that. In truth he'd begun to have his doubts about María within the last month, but he was too incensed faced with Rowan right now, her face flushed prettily with anger, to be rational or fair.

Rowan glared at him belligerently, her hands now down at her sides and curled into fists. 'Well, I did—and I'm here to stay. Are you going to accuse me of bringing on Zac's convulsion too?'

For a long second they glared at each other. His anger was tangible and awe-inspiring. Then Isandro broke the spell. He stepped back slightly and ran a hand through his hair.

'No. Of course not.' That conscience struck him again when he recalled his paralysing fear that night, and how Rowan had been the only one to retain any calm sanity. He'd just gone a step too far.

'I have to go to Kuala Lumpur today, for a three-day emergency meeting. It's something I just can't get out of. Believe me if I could I would.'

The bitterness in his tone told Rowan exactly how trapped he was feeling.

'Well, at the risk of having you jump down my throat with threats and insults, I would love the chance to take care of Zac while you're gone. You're hardly going to get a replacement nanny in such a short space of time.'

He battled to keep his face impassive, to hide his frustration. 'I know. And believe me, the only reason I'm even *considering* this is because my mother and sister are on holiday for a week. Otherwise he would stay with them…'

He ran an impatient hand through his hair again, his gesture saying it all.

'Needless to say, Rowan, I leave him here in your care with the utmost reluctance. It is only because I know your every move will be monitored and reported back to me that I do this. Hernán will remain here with you. Julia can help.'

She hitched her chin. So she was to be a virtual prisoner.

Still…it meant time alone with Zac. When she spoke her voice had lost its belligerence. 'I have no intention of going a step outside these grounds or these four walls. All I want is time with my son. I swear.'

Her eyes had turned a soft darker velvet colour, and a wealth of emotion lay in their depths even though Isandro knew instinctively that she was trying to hide it. He didn't want to know *how* he knew that. His eyes moved up and down her body, taking in the swell of her breasts under the thin material of her shirt, her worn jeans. One of those three outfits she'd been circulating since she'd arrived. Her eyes, her body, her scent threatened to scramble his thought processes…he had to push her back.

'I'll be checking in regularly.'

'I wouldn't expect anything less,' she said softly.

He looked for triumph, for any sense that she'd won a victory over him, but saw nothing of the sort. Her response, far from confirming what he'd expected, made confusion rush through him. And something else. Something very nebulous and disturbing.

Rowan watched her son sleeping. It had taken a while to put him down that night, he was too excited with the change in routine and having Rowan there every moment, as opposed to María. She was exhausted. And yet happier than she could ever remember being in her life. She bent down and lovingly tucked a lock of fallen hair back, and in doing so she was reminded of a moment once snatched, when she'd watched Isandro sleeping after they'd made love. Her heart beat so painfully that it hurt. After a long minute of just looking at Zac, she went and curled up in a chair in the corner of the room, eventually falling asleep. She didn't want to leave him for a second.

* * *

A week later Isandro stood in his study and looked out onto the lawn through the window. His return had been delayed due to a sudden crisis on the Asian stock market that had necessitated his continued presence. He'd never have gone if he'd known that might happen. He could see that Zac was working himself up into one of his increasingly frequent tantrums—a side-effect of his fast-approaching second birthday. As Rowan tried to placate him, he hit her. Isandro's insides immediately clenched in fear that she would retaliate, and he made to move—only to find himself obeying some instinct and stopping again.

As he watched he realised that Rowan wasn't reacting to the slap. Zac hit her again and Isandro winced, this time for Rowan. Again she didn't respond. She completely ignored Zac, and got up to tidy his toys away. Eventually Zac started to calm down, perplexed by this non-reaction. It made Isandro suddenly nervous of how María might have reacted in a similar situation. That niggle of conscience rose again.

After a while Zac toddled over and got Rowan's attention, and she bent down to his level. She appeared to be talking to him, and showed him where he had hit her. Isandro could see even from here that her skin was red. She seemed to be trying to explain to him that it was wrong, and then Zac threw his arms around her and kissed her. Rowan hugged him back, and Isandro felt the most curious tightening and falling feeling in his chest.

He turned away abruptly to leave the room and go outside. The feeling that seeing them had precipitated in his chest just now was terrifying with its force. Rowan Carmichael was a very real threat. He just wasn't sure which direction the threat was coming from any more.

* * *

Rowan knew he was there—that awareness gripped her. She didn't look round, though, and waited for Zac to react when he saw him. He screamed and ran towards him, and she let him go before turning around herself—only to have her heart flip over in her chest. He was so gorgeous. He was dressed in a steel-grey suit, dark tie and an impeccable shirt, and his slicked-back hair was now fast becoming tousled by small hands.

Rowan felt shy and awkward. He strolled towards her, putting Zac down as he squirmed out of his arms. She wasn't aware of how her eyes roved over him hungrily. Or of the surprised flare of response in his eyes as they were hidden by shades.

'How did it go?'

Rowan smiled wryly as she automatically checked what Zac was doing before looking up. 'Well, as it's barely two hours since you last called, there's nothing much to report.'

Isandro had to stop his reflex to return her smile. Instead he gestured to her arms, and the fading red marks from Zac's slaps. 'Zac?'

He saw her flush and quickly shake her head before stopping and smiling a little self deprecatingly. 'He's not aware of what he's doing. It's no big deal. He's just testing his boundaries. I'm trying to make him see that he can't…' She crossed her arms and put her hands around the offending marks, suddenly scared. Would he think she'd hit him back?

Her immediate reflex to protect Zac surprised him. It was almost as if she hadn't wanted him to know. 'You handled him well. I saw you.'

Her mouth opened. Something cold settled into her chest. Of course he hadn't trusted her for a second. 'You mean you spied on me?'

He shook his head and removed his shades, his eyes so blue

that they took her breath away. 'No, I just saw you out of the window before I came out.'

'Oh…' Rowan bit her lip. 'Then I'm sorry.' She looked down at Zac again. 'It's time for his nap now.'

'Why don't you put him down and then meet me in my study? I have a couple of things I'd like to discuss with you.'

Like custody…or is the divorce through already? Rowan knew rationally that it couldn't be, but it didn't stop her heart from clenching. She just nodded and scooped Zac up into her arms to bring him inside. At the last second Isandro stopped her to bend down and kiss Zac's head. His own head came close to her breasts, and Rowan could feel them respond. She closed her eyes weakly and willed him to step away. When he did, she set off on shaky legs.

A short time later Rowan knocked on Isandro's door and opened it. He was on the phone, but gestured for her to come in. She felt too antsy to sit down, so she wandered around, looking at the books on the shelves, feeling all over the place. After a week of not seeing him? How pathetic was that? Especially when he so obviously despised her.

'Sit down.'

She whirled around guiltily. She hadn't heard him terminate his conversation. She sat down warily, with her hands in her lap, and forced herself to look at him steadily.

He leant back in his big leather chair for a second before standing up. All the air seemed to have contracted in the room as Rowan watched him approach. He was jacketless and tieless again. He sat on the edge of his desk and the action pulled the material of his trousers taut over one powerful thigh. She swallowed past a dry throat and hoped she had enough self-control not to let her eyes drop.

'I've arranged for some nannies to come tomorrow for interviews.'

Rowan immediately sat up straight. 'But—'

He silenced her with a hand. 'It's not a reflection on how you have cared for Zac this last week. I'm sorry I was away for longer than intended.'

Rowan shrugged and avoided his penetrating eyes. 'It was no hardship—no work, Isandro. He's my son. I'd take care of him every day if I could.'

He quelled a quick surge of irritation. 'Well, we both know that's not how things are going to work out.'

'Yes. I know.'

He stood up then, as if restless, and paced the floor behind her. She had to turn awkwardly to look at him. He stopped and faced her, thrusting his hands into his pockets. He hadn't planned on discussing this with her now, but somehow it felt right.

'I would like it if you would sit in on the interviews. I don't want a repeat of what happened with María, and perhaps you'll be adept at seeing how qualified they are.'

Rowan stood too, to face him. She knew that it must have killed him to say that, and only his concern for Zac would have prompted it. However, this was the first time he'd accorded her anything approaching respect for being Zac's mother. It made her voice husky. 'I'd appreciate that. Thank you. But…if you feel that you're not ready to hire another nanny I'm more than happy to keep looking after Zac.'

He shook his head, negating her words. 'No. As I told you before, I won't have him become so attached to you that it will cause him undue pain when you're not around on a permanent basis. And I'm going to need another nanny more or less immediately, because you're not going to be on hand all the time.'

Rowan sat down heavily. He was sending her away. She quickly did some mental arithmetic. Perhaps she could rent a small apartment in Osuna, stay close by.

'Rowan?'

Her head jerked up. 'I'm sorry—what?' She hadn't heard a word of what he'd just said.

'I said that we're going to have to go into Seville to get you some clothes and do something with your hair.'

She stood again, feeling totally confused. 'What are you talking about?'

He frowned at her. 'What I just said. The Feria de Abril annual ball is next week, and I need you to come with me.'

Rowan shook her head again and translated out loud. 'The Festival of April ball?'

'Yes. It's one of the biggest dates in the Seville calendar.' He started pacing again. 'Last year you weren't here—that's when people started to speculate. As one of the patrons of the festival, I have to make a speech every year, and naturally there is a lot of media attention.' A flash of cynicism crossed his face. 'As we have the good fortune of your presence this year, you will accompany me and help to put wagging tongues to rest.'

Rowan automatically started to protest for many reasons—not least of which that it would be a total sham. But he silenced her, taking a hand out of his pocket and coming to stand close. Too close.

'Don't you think it's the least you could do?'

She was feeling dizzy, looking up at him. 'Well, I...of course... But won't people think it weird? And what about when it becomes apparent that we're divorcing? Won't it be obvious that something was up?'

He dismissed her words with a hand. 'I'm not concerned about that. I'm only concerned with the here and now. I'm involved in an important deal with a bank in Madrid, and their CEO has been invited. It will look good for me to show that my marriage exists.'

A week later, as Rowan got ready for the ball, she reflected on Isandro's words and shivered again. That coolness, that level of ambition, was something that had been all too familiar. Somehow, seeing him be such a good father to Zac, she'd been seduced into believing in a side of him she'd thought existed when she'd first got to know him, when she'd fallen in love with him. But that was dangerous. He'd just reminded her with his actions that he was in fact a cold-hearted businessman with no room for love or emotion in his life. Unless it was directed towards his son. She had to remember that, or she'd be the biggest fool.

The past week had flown. Isandro had taken her into Seville three days ago, on a whirlwind tour of the shops. He'd bought her a veritable wardrobe full of clothes. She'd protested, but to no avail. And when they'd come home he'd personally overseen her own tatty clothes being thrown away. She'd bristled at his high-handed behaviour but he'd ignored her again. In truth, being back in a bustling, vibrant city had been almost too much for her. She'd found the sounds, the traffic, everything a little overwhelming. She knew she'd get used to it again in time, but hadn't missed the funny looks Isandro had given her. She would have to be more careful.

She twisted in the mirror now, trying to reach the zip of the silk dress she'd chosen to wear, when she heard a voice.

'Do you need me to do that up?'

She jumped around, her heart thumping crazily, and held the gaping front of her dress in her hands. *'Excuse me!'* She hid her surprise and panic behind affront.

He strolled easily towards her and she couldn't breathe. In a black tuxedo, white shirt, white bow tie dangling undone, he was a virile picture of masculine perfection. And even though she'd seen him like this…it had been *before*. She'd been pregnant then, and later she'd had other concerns. But now every sense seemed indecently heightened. On full alert.

He took her shoulders and turned her stricken body around. She felt his hands come to the zip, pulling it up slowly, his fingers grazing her back. The hairdresser Isandro had taken her to had cut her hair into a more defined bob, and now it fell in soft waves to just below her jaw. The back of her neck was exposed, and there was something about that that made her feel intensely vulnerable...

She hadn't been able to wear a bra with the dress, and as the zip ascended now she could feel the dress being pulled up, tightening around her breasts, chafing against nipples that felt sensitive. She felt so tense that she feared she might snap in two. His hands stopped somewhere around the middle of her shoulderblades, and was it her imagination or did his fingers linger there for a second?

He turned her around again and looked her up and down, not a hint of warmth in his eyes. It helped to cool her pulse a little. That, and her mortification that her nipples must be like two hard pebbles under the material.

'And now if you could return the favour...'

Rowan looked up at him, dazed. And then she realised that he was talking about his bow tie. Her heart lurched. He'd never been able to do one up, and had always had to ask her. Those moments had been stolen guilty pleasures... She had a sudden intense memory of doing it once, her pregnant belly pressing into his body, feeling his burgeoning arousal. And then they had arrived late to the function. She really didn't think she could do what he was asking now and stay in one piece.

'Don't you have a ready-made one?' she asked with not a little desperation.

Isandro's brows snapped together. 'It's too much for you to do?'

He felt absurdly angry. He cursed himself for giving in to the impulse to come in here. He went to turn away but she caught his arm. She was looking up at him, something indefinable in those violet depths thrown into stark relief by the creaminess of her flawless skin and darker cream of her dress. For a second he felt as if he couldn't breathe.

'Wait. Let me try. It's just been a while, that's all.'

She stood in front of him and reached up to his tie. He lifted his head back automatically to help—and to avert his eyes from her gaze. Her clean, unmanufactured fragrance drifted upwards. She moved closer and Isandro could feel the soft swish of her dress against him, the fleeting glance of her body against his, but she pulled back so sharply when that happened that he looked down swiftly. She apologised.

And then he couldn't look away. Her face was flushed, her tongue protruding slightly through small even teeth as she concentrated on his tie. Her lashes were unbelievably thick and dark, so long that they cast half-moon shadows on her cheeks. He could see the dip of cleavage in the dress, the way it had pushed her breasts up slightly. They looked full and voluptuous. Once more she swayed against his body, and he had to clench his jaw so tight that he felt his teeth would snap. His erection was hard and heavy against his underwear, and he hadn't felt this hot for a woman since—

'There.' There was more than a little breathless relief in Rowan's voice as she stepped back. Tying that bow tie and remaining standing had been like her own personal Everest quest. She couldn't look up. She babbled. 'I just have to put on my shoes and get my wrap and bag and then I'm ready to—'

'Here—you're going to need these.'

Rowan glanced up quickly, and then down to where Isandro was holding her wedding ring and engagement ring in his palm.

'You still have them…' she breathed. She'd loved those rings. Her wedding band was simple platinum and her engagement ring was an antique. She'd picked it herself, a square green diamond surrounded by tiny clear diamonds in an Art Deco setting. She watched as he took her hand and held it out, efficiently slipping the rings onto her ring finger. She'd lost weight and they were looser.

'I'll have to get them re-sized.'

'What's the point?'

Rowan looked up and willed the sharp pain down. She couldn't *believe* she'd just said that. 'Of course. I wasn't thinking.'

'I'm going to look in on Zac. See you downstairs.'

When he left, Rowan took a deep, shuddering breath. That whole experience had taken more out of her than she cared to admit. She looked at the rings glinting on her finger and felt like an impostor. She cursed her big mouth again.

Checking herself quickly in the mirror, she stopped, and her hand went to touch her hair. What would Isandro's reaction have been if he'd seen her this time last year? With that thought came the uncomfortable truth. Sooner or later he would know…and what would that do?

'I like Ana-Lucía. I think we've made the right choice.'

Rowan looked at Isandro in surprise across the back of the car as they drove to the function. His helicopter had brought them to a small private airfield just outside the city. His use of 'we' had made her heart stop.

'I like her too…'

When they'd interviewed nannies the other day, for the first time they'd both agreed on something. Neither of them had liked a single one of them. They'd either been too interested in making eyes at Isandro, in the house, or in how much money they would be paid. Rowan could remember the jealous bile that had risen within her when yet another simpering blonde had cooed coquettishly at Isandro.

Then Julia had told them of a friend of hers who was looking for work. They'd met her and known immediately that she was the one. Rowan much preferred to hire someone local, and Isandro had seemed to agree.

The car was drawing to a smooth halt outside a huge, impressive Moorish building. Rowan tried to hide her awe, feeling gauche. Isandro followed her look.

'This is the Palacio de Don Pedro. It rivals the Alhambra in Granada in its preservation of drawings and carvings.'

He stepped out of the car and Rowan saw his hand stretch in to take hers. She had a moment of remembering other occasions like this, how attentive he'd been to her, making her feel secure, at ease. Emotion rose and she struggled to quell it. She took a deep breath and tried to emerge gracefully, taking his hand.

Once standing with him at the start of a red carpet, she registered the flashing bulbs of the paparazzi, numerous milling crowds, stunningly beautiful women bedecked in the finest fashions and jewels. Handsome men. But none as handsome as the man by her side. She felt momentarily stunned, in awe and fear of the obvious exclusiveness of the event.

The ball was taking place in the spectacular Salón de Embajadores. Rowan was mesmerised by the ceiling, which was a wooden dome with thousands of star patterns. She was so entranced that she gaped. When she looked down again she caught a couple of women looking at her and laughing slightly behind their hands. Her face burned crimson as the memory came back of overhearing those poisonous women in the bathroom in London. But, she reassured herself, she was different now, stronger.

'Who are they? Do you know them?'

Rowan heard Isandro's voice close to her ear and fought the urge to move her stricken eyes. She shook her head. 'No. I was taken aback by the ceiling, and I'm afraid I must have shown a little too much awe than is appropriate for such a gathering.'

He slanted a probing look down at her. Rowan looked away and took a sip of her champagne. It slid down her throat like a fizzy starburst. There were so many sensations that kept taking her unawares.

Isandro took a closer look at the women Rowan had been looking at and his heart sank. One of them was Mercedes Lopez. He hadn't been entirely honest with Rowan in his reasons for wanting to bring her along. Although it was serving him to have her here, to reaffirm his respectability after she'd made a mockery of their marriage, it was also to deter the advances of the other woman—and he could see Mercedes bearing down on them now.

They'd been lovers some years before he'd married Rowan, and with the recent notable absence of his wife she'd been agitating to resume the affair. Isandro had hoped that having Rowan by his side might send her a message. He couldn't say what it was about her that turned him off so completely now, when before she'd appealed to him, but something just did.

Unconsciously he pulled Rowan closer, and could feel her stiffen in response. It made him angry and he looked down at her, but she was looking at the other woman with wide eyes. Unaccountably, he felt protective.

Mercedes spoke in rapid and intimate Spanish as soon as she reached them, putting her arms around Isandro's neck and taking total liberties with the traditional warmth of a normal Spanish greeting. Her kisses on both cheeks lingered for far too long. And far too close to his mouth. She was beautiful, thought Rowan. And undeniably she must be his lover, for there was a wealth of intimacy that couldn't be manufactured in the woman's every sinuous movement.

She was very seductive. Tall, dark and slim. Flashing brown heavily kohled eyes, her perfect breasts moving and swaying with her dress as she gestured. Lush hips and a tiny waist.

Rowan's rising and very fledgling euphoria at being in such a beautiful place with Isandro was about to burst like a cheap balloon. She was transported back in time. The gauche outcast again. But she wouldn't feel sorry for herself. This was all a game, and she would play it as if her life depended on it. When they were divorced Isandro could do as he pleased, but right now they were married. And, God help her poor battered heart, the jealousy rising within her was about to explode.

She inserted herself expertly between Isandro and the other woman. She could feel his initial shock and held her breath momentarily. And then let it out as she felt him take her lead, moving behind her and bringing both arms around her waist so that she lay against him.

Rowan held out a hand and spoke in clipped upper-class English. 'How do you do? I'm Rowan—Isandro's wife. I don't believe we've met before?'

The other woman had to take a step backwards. A fleeting glower transformed her perfect features before it was gone. Rowan almost felt sorry for her.

'*Querida*, this is Mercedes Lopez—an old friend of mine and head of the biggest PR company in Southern Spain.'

A knife twisted in Rowan's heart. *Yeah, right.* She was glad she couldn't see Isandro's face to read what his expression might be. What little secret look he might be giving the other woman. To her intense relief, Mercedes made her excuses and left, clearly taking the hint—or else some indication from Isandro that he would see her again soon.

'Come—there are some people I'd like to introduce to you.'

And before she could dwell on the other woman, Isandro took Rowan's hand and led her through the crowd. No doubt this was the object of her role here, to be the dutiful wife, her presence proving that all was well, all was respectable.

Isandro's body still pulsed. When she'd made that cute little move to block Mercedes she'd taken him completely by surprise. And turned him on. She'd never shown any proprietary urges before.

That's because now she's back for your money and she'll do whatever it takes...

But another voice reminded him that she'd been pregnant before, and unwell for a lot of the time, not able to attend functions, so how would he know how she'd act?

Rowan found that the people Isandro had taken her to meet were genuinely nice. Other couples, also colleagues from the banking world. And none of the women were looking at Isandro as if they wanted to devour him. She was happy to speak and get used to her Spanish here, and she'd caught a warm glance from Isandro that had made her feel absurdly happy.

She was tuning in and out of the conversation a little later when one of the women took her arm, and Rowan just got her last few words. '...market crash.'

Rowan frowned apologetically. 'I'm sorry—what?'

'The European market crash of eighteen months ago...don't you remember? The absolute carnage that resulted in the economy practically sparked a global recession.'

Rowan racked her brain feverishly to try and remember if she'd heard anything. 'I'm sorry... I just don't recall...'

Isandro was frowning, giving her an intense look.

Conversation had halted around them. She knew well why she hadn't heard anything. She affected a look of delayed surprise and self-deprecation. She laughed nervously.

'Oh, *that* crash—of course I do. I'm sorry, I wasn't sure what you meant.'

The woman laughed. 'How could you be married to the man who controls finance in Europe and not remember that? You'd have to have been buried under a rock!'

Or near enough…

Rowan smiled weakly and wished the ground would swallow her up. She felt Isandro's arm tighten on her waist and looked up warily. She met that clear blue gaze tinged with ice again. He clearly hadn't been fooled by her bad acting.

And the night wasn't about to get any easier. Rowan's heart sank to her shoes when she saw who was approaching them now. Ana. Isandro's sister. Too late to escape. The crowd melted away and it was just them—and Ana and her husband.

CHAPTER SEVEN

ANA greeted Isandro and then stood back. She shared the same colouring as her brother. The same tall, lean physique. But she had her mother's eyes. Dark and hard.

'So.' She looked Rowan up and down. 'The prodigal wife returns.'

'Ana,' she heard Isandro say warningly.

His sister sent him a blistering look. 'What? You mean to tell me that after what she did to you and *to my nephew* you're just letting her waltz back in to clean you out?'

Rowan felt shaky. She could remember another conversation. One between him and his sister. That very day when she'd come home and known her life was going to change. Ana had travelled all the way from Spain to see him. Rowan had returned to hear them arguing in the sitting room. Their voices had been so raised that she hadn't been able to help herself stopping. And it was all coming back in lurid detail.

His sister's voice had been a strident shriek of indignation. 'After all the years of pain and humiliation our father put our mother through, put *us* through with that English whore of his, *you* take an English wife and now she's having your baby? *You* would do that to us?'

Isandro's own tone had sent shivers down Rowan's spine.

'Ana, nothing has changed. This is a business arrangement. The fact that she is now bearing my child is an unexpected bonus. It will save me the bother of marrying again in order to secure an heir.'

His sister's voice had lowered dangerously, reeking of suspicion. 'Are you in love with her?'

Isandro had laughed quickly, harshly. 'Of course not.'

'Then why did you sleep with her?'

Isandro's voice had turned icy. 'That is none of your business.'

'I can't imagine it was fun.' Ana's voice had been so scathing and so dripping with disdain that Rowan had felt weak. 'She's like the original ice queen.'

Their voices had got lower but no less heated for a minute, and Rowan had been too frozen with horror to move. Too shocked. Too hurt. And then Isandro's voice had risen again.

'She means nothing more to me than a means to an end. She never did; she never will. I don't *care* what our father did. That has no bearing on how I am going to live my life. I will not be dictated to by his misdeameanours, and I will certainly not be dictated to by you. She has more than fulfilled her function as my wife and you *will* accept that.'

'She's truly trapped you now, brother dear…' Ana had finished tauntingly.

Slowly Rowan became aware of her surroundings again. Ana was still standing there, hissing at Isandro. Her husband looked sheepishly apologetic beside her. Rowan felt clammy and cold.

And then Isandro was saying to Ana, *'Bastante!'*

His sister halted in mid-tirade. With a strangled sound she grabbed her husband and stalked off. Rowan felt as though she'd been punched.

Isandro turned to face her. He was shocked at how pale she looked. Her eyes were wounded. He cursed, and took her over to a quiet corner. When he almost acted on instinct and pulled her into his chest she stepped back jerkily. It made a rush of self-mockery run through him. He was getting that soft?

Rowan felt very close to the edge. Isandro had reached for her, but she knew that if he touched her she'd dissolve. And the fact that he'd almost offered to comfort her was doing even worse things to her head.

But then, as if she'd imagined it, Isandro spoke, and his tone was frigid. 'She had no right to subject you to an attack like that here.'

It helped Rowan to claw back some equilibrium. She shook her head vaguely, as if to negate what he said. He couldn't see how badly his sister had affected her. But she'd let her get to her *again*. She'd thought she'd blocked out that awful conversation, but it was still there like a brand burnt into her memory. It had been timely, though—she had to remember that. Because if she hadn't heard it when she had she'd have told him…everything. And that would have lost her the only sliver of pride and dignity she'd managed to retain.

When he asked abruptly, 'Are you ready to go back inside?' Rowan just nodded, hoping that none of the turmoil in her belly was evident on her face or in her eyes.

'Yes, of course. I just…needed a moment…the heat…'

For the rest of the evening Isandro was attentive but distant. Unbelievably cool. Perhaps seeing his sister had put things back into perspective for him? Reconfirmed his suspicions that Rowan had indeed set out to trap him? Perhaps he regretted bringing Rowan with him? Perhaps he was wishing he was with his lover?

All the way home he barely said two words to her. Thunder rumbled ominously as they got out of the car, and Rowan looked up to see rolling clouds racing across the sky, the full moon appearing and disappearing. The air was warm, but there was a storm on the horizon. A little shiver of something went down Rowan's spine. Of foreboding or something—she wasn't sure what.

Once inside the house, Isandro yanked his tie free. 'I'm having a nightcap—care to join me?'

Rowan shook her head. Not that he was even looking at her. 'No. Thank you. Goodnight.'

Something stopped her at the bottom stair and she found herself asking, just before he stepped into the drawing room, 'Is that woman your mistress?'

His broad back stopped. He turned slowly, and Rowan could have bitten her tongue. She had no right to know. She couldn't read the expression on his face.

'Why?'

She shrugged awkwardly. 'I was just wondering. You seemed...close.'

'We were lovers a long time ago. But, no, she's not my mistress.'

'Oh...well, goodnight, then.' Rowan fled before her mouth could get her into any more trouble. Even so a curious fizzing sensation filled her veins. Upstairs, she took off her shoes and checked in on Zac. He was sleeping peacefully. She straightened the covers over him, pressed a kiss to his forehead and went to her own room.

When Isandro walked into Zac's room a while later he could smell Rowan's scent lingering on the air—barely there, but *he* could smell it. He could see that she'd already tucked Zac in properly. He sat down heavily in a chair in the corner of the room and looked moodily into space for a long time.

An hour after trying to get to sleep Rowan still lay tossing and turning. Images, memories, emotions—all were swirling through her head. And most vivid of them all an image of Isandro. Tantalising and torturing her. The air in the room seemed oppressive, and she noticed that her French doors were closed. She heard another roll of thunder. She craved air, a breeze—*something*. So she got up and went to open them.

The air outside was dense, warm and unbearably heavy, redolent with the imminent storm which still hadn't hit. Rowan stepped out and looked up. Almost unbelievably drops of rain started to fall, as if they had been waiting for her cue. She stretched out a hand as they fell, heavier and heavier. Within seconds it was a torrential downpour, and jagged lightning lit up the sky.

Rowan stepped out farther, the rain drenching her in seconds. She didn't care. The moment was magical, the kind of thing she'd dreamed of over her long and hard recent months. She went down the steps and stood in her nightdress, her face tipped up to the menacing black clouds as the rain teemed down over her, plastering her hair to her head. She felt as if she were being cleansed. An intense joy filled her.

She had survived an unspeakable nightmare and she was with her son. Despite the pain of knowing Isandro wanted a divorce, she could ask for no greater happiness than that. Lifting her arms, she welcomed the rain like a benediction…

'What the hell do you think you're doing?'

Rowan dropped her arms feeling instantly silly and whirled around, her heart thumping heavily. She could barely see Isandro through the driving rain, although she could sense his tension, his irritation. He stepped closer. She could see that he was dressed in nothing but brief boxers. Rain was running in rivulets down his chest. He was already as soaked as she was.

'I…I'm standing in the rain,' she answered lamely.

'I can see that.'

He could also see that her short nightdress clung to her body like a second skin and had become translucent. His eyes dropped. He couldn't help himself. The outline of her body was clearly shaped, from her waist to her hips, down long, long legs. The dark shadow of promise between them was a tantalising invitation. The drenched material moulded to her breasts, still high and firm, their tips hard. Desire beat through his blood, hot and insistent.

'Sandro…'

He looked up. 'What did you call me?'

There was a look on her face, a yearning look that slammed into him. He'd seen that look before. His eyes were drawn to where her chest was rising and falling rapidly. He couldn't hear the rain any more. All he could hear was the beating of his heart. The beating of his pulse.

'I said Sandro.'

Isandro shook his head. He had to break out of this spell. 'No one calls me that.'

'I did,' she said simply.

A pain gripped him inside, and he was reminded of his instinctive move to comfort her earlier. 'Rowan…go back to bed.'

She moved a step closer, but not to move past him.

Feeling a surge of intense irritation, Isandro closed the distance and took her by the shoulders. 'Dammit, woman, what's wrong with you?'

Rowan was being guided by a stronger force than she could resist. It went beyond mere desire, although that was there too, burning her up so that she couldn't even feel the rain. She put her hands on his waist and felt him stiffen. She prayed it wasn't in rejection.

'Sandro…please…'

'Sandro, please *what*?' He knew he shouldn't even be engaging in dialogue, should just walk away. But there was something about her, something…different. Earnest. He felt he'd never met this woman before—or he had…but in the past, when he had believed—

'I want you.'

The three simple words exploded into his head. He tried to move but he couldn't. Her hands were on him and he wanted them on him, all over him, around him, touching him, caressing him. Her hair was plastered to her head, huge drips falling onto her shoulders. And yet some self protective instinct kept him from acting on the strongest desire he'd ever felt in his life.

'Rowan…' His voice was hoarse.

Rowan moved closer. Close enough for their bodies to touch lightly. It was as if they were both filled with attracting ions—she could feel the force of how strongly they were being pulled together. It *had* to be real. It couldn't be her imagination. The electricity in the air wasn't just coming from the sky.

'Please.'

He shook his head. But *please* sank in and reverberated through his aching body. He could see her eyes. The rain was stopping, water drops glistened on her skin, clung to her long lashes, and he wasn't strong enough to try and pull back, analyse what was going on.

With an urgent movement and a guttural moan dredged up from somewhere deep inside, Isandro put two hands around Rowan's head, cupping it, and jammed their bodies together. Then he lifted her face and met her mouth with his.

His kiss was passionate, and everything Rowan had ever dreamt of. She sank into his body, her arms wrapped around his lean waist, her breasts crushed to his torso. She couldn't believe this was really happening, but the rain and the storm had added a magical, other-worldly element to everything.

Isandro was still cradling her head, his hands around her

face, not letting her move an inch as he plundered her mouth. His tongue sought hers, tangled and danced. Rowan could feel the heat rise from a pool low in her belly. She was oblivious to the wet clothes clinging to her body, could feel only the hard evidence of Isandro's arousal against her. A fierce exulting force moved through her.

When Isandro drew back she opened eyes that felt heavy-lidded. His were dark blue, stained with desire. Without a word he bent and caught her up against him, an arm under her legs. He turned and walked swiftly to his own room, and Rowan had a quick impression of dark colours and a huge bed before he put her down in front of him. Her legs felt weak.

She looked up at him, acutely conscious now of her clinging wet nightdress, and suddenly awful reality wanted to intrude.

As if Isandro read her doubt he swiftly put out a hand and tipped her face to his, shaking his head. A hard smile touched his mouth. 'There's no going back from here.'

And before she knew what he was doing, he'd brought his hands to the top of her flimsy cotton nightdress and ripped it from neck to hem. Rowan gasped. He slipped the garment from her shoulders so that it fell behind her, and had pulled off his own briefs in a second.

They stood naked, facing each other. Before, Rowan would have been cringing from her toes upwards—but now…she was gone beyond that. For any number of reasons. Not least of which was that her desire and the memory of how he could make her feel was burning through her, making a mockery of any show of embarrassment.

She could feel raindrops from the ends of her hair falling onto her skin and shivered slightly, breaking into goose-bumps. Her breasts felt tight, aching. Her breath stalled in her throat as she watched Isandro's eyes drop, his hand come and cup one breast. Rowan's breath returned jerkily.

Isandro lazily took the weight of her breast in his hand. All of Rowan's nerve-endings were stretched and pulled, the centre of her breast screaming for his touch. He bent his head, his breath feathered, and Rowan's eyelids fluttered closed. But then, instead of taking that straining peak into his hot mouth, she felt his tongue come out and lick where a drop of rain had fallen on the upper slope.

She put her hands on his wide shoulders to steady herself. Past and present were meshed. All that remained constant were the sensations and the way he was making her feel. Rowan gave herself up to it, and deep down thanked whatever God had given her a second chance.

She opened her eyes and speared his wet hair with her hands, lifting his head and stepped right up against him. His erection was heavy, trapped between their bodies, and then she stretched up to kiss him.

Passion gripped them, overtook them. They kissed furiously. Isandro's hands roamed over Rowan's back down to her buttocks, which he cupped in his two big hands. He pulled her up and into him, so that the aching jut of his arousal was right *there*. Rowan responded, her own hands searching, seeking to touch him all over, and then she inserted a hand between them and let her fingers close enticingly along his length.

Isandro broke away, breathing harshly, eyes glittering. 'Enough.'

Rowan felt a moment of pure fear that he meant to bring her to this point only to reject her, but then he was carrying her over to the bed and laying her down. Relief swamped her. She watched as he reached for something in a drawer nearby and sheathed himself with protection. As she watched him, something inside her fell. It didn't feel right to have that barrier between them, but she couldn't speak up—not with the weight of history heavy around them. She said nothing.

Isandro, totally oblivious to the turmoil in her head, lay beside her and ran the palm of his hand down over her breasts, their tight peaks, her belly, and down farther. She opened her legs instinctively and saw something dark cross Isandro's face for an instant. Then it was gone again.

He bent and licked around the aureole of her breast for a second, his hand delving in between her legs to find that moist heat. In the same instant that he finally took one turgid nipple fully into his mouth two fingers thrust into her slickness, his thumb instantly finding the sensitive swollen bud of her desire. Rowan nearly jumped off the bed. She'd never been so aroused, so sensitive.

She moved against his hand, her eyes shut tight, the muscles in her neck corded, as Isandro suckled at her other breast. Her hips lifted in mute appeal. It wasn't enough. She wanted him inside her, where she'd dreamt of him on her long lonely nights.

'Sandro… *Sandro!*'

Isandro almost didn't hear her with the haze of desire that was clouding his brain. She was soft and silky, fragrant, and she felt like paradise on earth. And she was as responsive as he remembered—more unbelievably responsive than any other woman he'd known. That hadn't changed.

She clutched at his shoulders, twisting her hips away. Her eyes were so dark they looked black. He could see her nipples, wet from his ministrations, and he became even harder in response.

'No,' she said breathily. 'I want you inside me.'

For a moment suspended in time they just looked at each other. And then, breaking the spell, Rowan shifted herself so that she was under him. He lay between her legs. There was no hesitation. Isandro cupped one buttock, felt its peachy firmness. Her legs opened farther and, positioning himself carefully, he entered her. He watched her head go back, the way she sucked in a deep breath as she drew him in, and his head went fuzzy. It was exactly the way she'd taken him before. And he remembered every other time as if it was yesterday, as if it was now. And it *was* now.

Coming over her properly, taking his weight onto his arms, he started to thrust in and out. Rowan had released her breath and looked up as he'd withdrawn. Now she drew her legs around his waist, and Isandro couldn't stop his moan of intense pleasure when he felt himself go even deeper. He was buried so far now…

For a long time they rode the wave, eking out the pleasure until the very last moment. Rowan knew she couldn't prolong it any more. She could feel tremors building, that delicious tightness taking over, building and building. Isandro's tempo increased, sweat glistening on his skin. The raindrops were long gone—evaporated in the heat of passion—and in one second Rowan's world erupted around her into a million stars.

She'd hung suspended for a long moment, and now, as she fell, she was hardly aware of Isandro's own completion. His body jerked and pulsed in the aftermath, still thrusting sporadically, still wringing out the final pleasure, until finally he lay over her, and she held him tightly within her, within her arms.

After a long moment Isandro found the strength to move and release Rowan from him, from his weight. Pulling free of her body caused a yearning, aching feeling to surge up, and to disguise it he got up off the bed and walked into his bathroom to deal with the protection. After he'd done that, he looked at himself in the mirror of the bathroom, with the door shut firmly on the woman who lay in the bed just feet away.

The words *What the hell just happened?* reverberated in

his head, but it seemed almost too banal to try and articulate how he felt about what had just happened. All he knew was that one moment he'd been standing in front of her in the pouring rain, asking her what she was doing, and the next…the next she'd been under him, and he'd been sinking into her like a man in a desert starved of water who'd just found an oasis.

He knew what had happened. She had bewitched him. She'd heard him going into his room, *she must have*, and had gone out there in nothing but a flimsy nightdress in the rain. And she had waited, knowing that he would have heard her door open. Knowing that he would investigate. She'd sensed his vulnerability earlier, and now she had him right where she wanted him. And he…he was completely exposed in his desire for her.

Desire. That was all it was.

He straightened up. He didn't have to feel exposed, or vulnerable. Since when was desire linked to emotion for him? *Since that first night, and now tonight…* Isandro brought his fist down onto the side of the sink heavily. No, it wasn't. He could remember her breathy little *please*…as if she'd really meant it, as if she'd never even left, walked away. Well, she had.

This was nothing more than what she owed him. At some point during their marriage she'd seemed to change overnight, had turned on the ice queen act. He wasn't about to let it happen again—at least not until he'd been thoroughly satisfied. And if she thought these cute little moves were going to get her something extra from the divorce, then it would be a fine moment of revenge when she discovered it had all been in vain.

Rowan lay on the bed. She couldn't move. Aftershocks and little tremors were still pulsing through her body minutes later. Her muscles still clenched minutely. Isandro came out of the bathroom and she turned her head. She couldn't read the expression on his face, but a little shiver went down her spine. She sensed something ominous in the air.

The passion of moments before seemed to cool in seconds, and she was reminded of how wanton she'd just acted—*again*.

He came and stood beside the bed, and she didn't like what was in his eyes. She could see that he was already becoming aroused again and, despite her trepidation, she could feel herself responding. She drew her legs together, even though they wanted to open for him, and brought her arms up over her breasts, even though she felt as if she wanted to arch her back and offer them up to him again.

Confusion and fear warred with potent, aching desire. Perhaps he expected her to go? She made a move to get off the bed, but a large warm hand caught her back and pushed her down.

'Sandro…' She was breathless already. 'I thought… Do you want me to go?'

In the dim light Rowan could see a muscle flex in his jaw. 'I've no doubt that's what you had in mind, but we're not done yet.'

'I—'

But he silenced her with his mouth, bringing his whole body down beside her, trapping her with his arms, drawing a hard-muscled thigh over her legs. And she could feel his insistent erection growing, firming against her body, and knew she didn't want to go, couldn't go anywhere.

Much later the weather had calmed outside. Without looking, Rowan knew the sky would be clear. She lay encircled in Isandro's arms, her back against his chest. She felt sated, complete, and at peace for the first time in almost two years. She'd cried when they'd made love just a short while before, but she'd buried her head in Isandro's shoulder and used her moans to disguise her sobs of helpless emotion. She didn't think he'd heard them. She prayed that he hadn't.

As if sensing her wakefulness, Isandro shifted behind her. Rowan held her breath as she felt him pull his arms from around her and get out of the bed. She closed her eyes tight, and then she felt him come around and scoop her up into his arms. She couldn't pretend to be asleep. The tension in her body gave her away.

'What are you—?' Her words stopped when she saw where he was going. He was striding back towards the adjoining door, and bent to expertly open it before shouldering his way through and depositing her on her own bed, over the covers and naked. Her bedside lamp was still on from earlier, and Rowan felt ridiculously exposed in the soft light.

His eyes, cooled now after their spent passion, flickered down her body and back up, stopping suddenly at her breasts. They narrowed. Rowan felt a snake of something bad. He wasn't looking at her with desire, it was curiosity. Isandro bent down slightly, coming closer, and Rowan cowered back. But he came down on the bed and grabbed her arms, stopping her from hiding herself. With a leaden sinking feeling she knew exactly what he was looking at—what he'd missed earlier, in the dimmer light of his own room. She closed her eyes.

A scar, about two centimetres wide, in the middle of her chest, under her breasts.

'What is that?'

Rowan opened her eyes to see his finger come out to touch. She jerked her arm free, slapping his hand away. 'It's nothing. Just a scar from…' her mind worked feverishly '…a brooch pin that stabbed me.'

He looked back up to her eyes, his other hand still holding

her fast. For a moment it seemed as if he was going to question her, but then he shrugged. And that was like a slap in the face. He didn't care.

He stood lithely from the bed and looked down at her, totally at ease in his nakedness.

Rowan frowned and looked up, feeling very much at a disadvantage. His absolute distance precluded any notion she might have had of telling him exactly what that scar was, what it meant.

'Sandro...about what just—'

'Firstly, don't call me Sandro. I don't like it.'

'But I thought you liked it when we were—'

He laughed harshly. 'Before you deserted this marriage? Before you walked away from Zac? Well, that was then—this is now.'

Familiar pain lashed her inwardly. 'But what about...what about what just happened...?' She hated the uncertainty in her voice, and scrabbled to find covers to pull around her in protection.

Isandro started to walk away, his tall, lean and powerful body a vision of perfection. Gleaming golden skin stretched over hard muscles. He turned at the door.

'That's the second thing. We just slept together, that's all. It means nothing. And Rowan?' He didn't wait for an answer. 'This time I'll expect you to be willing when I want you, for however long I want you. Perhaps you'll be a better mistress than you were a wife.'

CHAPTER EIGHT

ISANDRO stood under the punishingly hot spray of the shower. His whole body was tense, his belly knotted with extreme self-reproach, self-recrimination, *self-disgust*. He had just given in to the weakest of urges—although it hadn't felt weak at the time. It had felt like a force field sweeping him in one direction only: to possess Rowan.

Savage hands spiked through his wet hair as he stood under the intense needles of spray.

Sandro. She'd called him Sandro. The only one who had ever shortened his name. She'd let it slip one day early in their marriage. He could still remember the colour that had turned her cheeks rosy at his expression. And then he had drawled laconically, 'It's fine. I like it.' And the thing was, he *had* liked it. Had thought it had meant something.

But to hear it again now was a shock. It had felt so right. A lot like how it had felt to kiss her and take her to bed. And he was sure she knew. Had *expected* to use it as some kind of trigger.

And how could he have slept with her? Not once, he had to remind himself, but twice. In quick succession. She was the worst of the worst. She had walked out on her baby. On him. Had spent the latter months of her pregnancy freezing him out. Isandro turned the shower to cold for a second, and welcomed the icy clarity the brief pain brought.

She owed him. He'd had no intention of prolonging her stay—he'd already planned on suggesting that she move either into Osuna or Seville—but *now*… Now he might keep her a while. Let this irritating passion for her burn its course. Then he'd let her go and say good riddance. Once the divorce was through, custody agreed in his favour, he would make sure he had as little to do with her as possible. Intermediaries could deal with the moments when she would take Zac, or he would be taken to her.

But with that thought came an image of Zac being shuttled from one place to the next. Isandro dismissed its poignancy immediately. It was no less than what millions of children across the globe had to deal with, and they survived. *But his child shouldn't have to just survive…*

Isandro stepped out of the shower. He told himself that his thoughts were clear. As icy as the water that had just hit his skin. But his belly was still tight, still full of *something*. It was indefinable and uncomfortable. He looked through his bathroom door at the rumpled sheets on his bed. As if to mock him, the tantalising smell of their sex, their bodies, seemed to curl around his senses, and to his dismay the recent cold punishment was forgotten and his body started to react again.

Holding onto the clarity of thought, crushing down the hard feeling in his chest and belly, Isandro strode to the adjoining door and stepped back into Rowan's room. This was all the clarity he needed—the physical kind. After all, she was just his mistress now…

'*Gracias*, Ana-Lucía.'

Rowan took Zac from his new nanny to bring him outside.

She snuggled close and buried her face in his neck, making loud kissing noises, listening to his giggles and feeling pure joy at the sound. When they got outside he started squirming, struggling to be down and running. She welcomed the distraction. Any distraction was welcome from what had happened the other night—and every night since then. Her body was tender all over, aching in secret places.

Her mind still couldn't fully cope with what was happening, what had happened. At the way she'd been so forward, so wanton that night. She'd literally begged Isandro to make love to her, when evidently he'd wanted her to leave.

And yet now he wanted her as his mistress.

And why didn't that thought fill her with the indignant horror it should? Why did it fill her with molten heat? Each night since then, when they went to bed, Isandro would either carry her from her bed to his, or come to her bed. But either way he would leave her alone afterwards. After taking her to paradise and back. Over and over again. It enflamed her, and yet made her very scared of what the fallout might be.

She put Zac down and watched him toddle off at great speed. He'd discovered the art of gardening. The art of pulling up great handfuls of earth and replanting them somewhere else—usually his clothes. She smiled and followed dutifully, but for once her son couldn't make her block everything out. Much as she tried to let him. Erotic images, wanton images, flashed through her mind with disconcerting ease and frequency.

Absently she accepted the wriggling worm that Zac proudly held out. Clearly Isandro meant to take her as he would a mistress as a form of punishment, for whatever time was left of their marriage…

She grimaced. Isandro's frequent absences during their marriage had left enough time for her to be alone and doubt everything she thought…and felt. Yet when they had spent time together those doubts had fled easily, and she'd found herself falling more and more into an abyss of vulnerable feelings. It had been so seductive. To come from the emotional wasteland her parents had offered her to being with a man as dynamic as Isandro, who'd seemed to truly *care* for her. Desire her. Especially as her pregnancy had progressed. But she'd been wrong. Perhaps not about the passion, evidently that was still there, but about everything else…

She looked at Zac helplessly. On that fateful day when she was seven months pregnant she'd found out so much…

'Papá!'

Rowan froze. How had she not sensed him arrive? And yet wasn't he in her brain all the time? With her at every moment?

She looked around to see Zac throw himself at Isandro's legs. Isandro was looking down, smiling, oblivious to the two huge mucky handprints that now adorned his pristine suit. Rowan's heart beat rapidly. He cast her a quick cool look.

'I thought I'd come home early to take Zac riding…'

Rowan stood up awkwardly and brushed off her own filthy jeans. She felt mussed and inadequate. 'Oh…okay.' Once Ana-Lucía had taken over from María, Rowan had assumed Isandro would expect her to follow the original routine. Today her time with Zac wasn't up yet, and she felt a dart of pain that Isandro could so easily wield this control.

He started to move away, with Zac, chattering nonsensically, held high in his arms. Ridiculously tears pricked her eyes, as if her heart was being wrenched from her chest just at watching them walk away.

Before they reached the house Isandro turned around, a mild look of impatience crossing his unbearably handsome features. 'Well? Aren't you coming too?'

For a stunned moment Rowan just stood there, and then

stammered out, 'Well…I thought…I mean, yes…yes, I will— if that's okay?'

He gave a curt nod, and Rowan followed them jerkily as they disappeared into the house. The sensation of being on a string was vivid and unsettling. She had to learn to control herself. Her emotions. But just for now she felt joy zinging through her at Isandro's easy invitation.

That night, as the tremors in Rowan's body started to recede and her heart resumed a normal rhythm, she prayed silently that Isandro wouldn't leave her bed just yet. Pain made her insides clench. Was this how his mistresses felt? Or was he different with them? More tender? As tender as he'd once been with her…before she'd heard his poisonous words. It was too painful to go there. She couldn't allow herself to think about that. He was here now, with her. This time was finite.

He'd pulled away to lie on his side and, craving to touch him, to stay connected, Rowan pressed her front against his back, bringing her legs up to cup his bottom, her arm around his chest. She felt him tense for a second and her mind balked. He was going to get up and go—*again*.

But after a long moment she felt him relax, and rejoiced inwardly. She heard his breaths deepen and lengthen. She felt a huge surge of emotion and pressed her lips to his broad back, as if to stifle words that threatened to spill out. She had no idea what she wanted to say, no idea what the feeling was. And then, as sleep started to claim her body and mind, she knew. She was sorry. Sorry for leaving, sorry for walking away, for not having the courage yet to explain.

Without even realising what she was doing, she pressed another kiss to his cooling skin, higher, closer to his neck, and whispered, 'Sorry, I'm so sorry…' again and again, as she kissed him softly.

Then the world was up-ended, and Isandro was out of the bed, looking down at her with scorn written all over his face before she knew which way was up.

He'd been awake...

Rowan came up on one arm and pulled the sheet around her, her heart thumping painfully as she watched Isandro reach for his trousers and pull them on.

'Sorry?' He laughed harshly. 'Sorry for what, Rowan?'

Rowan felt jittery, shaky and in shock. She had to tell him. Now. She reached for the lamp beside her bed and switched it on. Shadows danced, and the sculpted plains of Isandro's body and face were thrown into sharp relief.

But before she could get a word out Isandro was already walking away, back towards his own bedroom.

She put out a hand. 'Wait!'

He didn't stop. He ignored her and kept walking.

Rowan refused to be dissuaded and got off the bed, pulling the sheet around her and following him into his room.

He heard her and turned around, saying coldly, 'I've had enough for tonight. Please leave.'

Rowan did her best to ignore the shaft of pure ice and pain. 'Please, I need to tell you...to explain—'

He advanced, and she backed away despite her intentions. He was just too big, too intimidating and too *male*. Her body throbbed as if on cue.

'Explanations are not something I'm interested in, Rowan. Explanations are for people who are interested in hearing what the other has to say. My interest where you're concerned is confined to the bedroom and to how I'm going to make sure you don't get a minute's access to Zac that isn't approved by me.'

He took her in: flushed, tousled, sexy. His face tightened. He made a split-second knee-jerk reaction decision. He knew he was doing it, and his weakness made his voice unbearably harsh. 'In fact, I've been thinking. The divorce is underway, and I think you've spent enough time here. I've been more than generous where Zac is concerned, but the time has come for you to leave.'

Rowan's head reeled. They seemed to have gone from zero to a thousand in emotional voltage in a nanosecond.

'Isandro—'

'I see *Sandro* has gone out of the window.' He mimicked her voice in a cruel parody of passion. '"Sandro, I want you so much. Sandro I need you—"'

'Stop it!' Rowan cried out, with such vehemence that he did. He was flaying her heart with a whip, shredding it to pieces, and it was in that moment that she knew for certain that she'd fallen for him all over again—had never really stopped loving him. Otherwise he wouldn't have the power to hurt her so deeply.

'All I want is to tell you where I've been since that day, Isandro. It's not easy for me to tell you—' *Especially when you're like this…*

'And I know why.' His arms were crossed, a sneer on his face.

'Why?' she asked, as if she couldn't already guess the answer.

'Because you've had to try and figure out how to make yourself look as sympathetic as possible.'

He started to walk around her then, making her dizzy, but he wouldn't stop, so she gritted her teeth and stood still.

'Do you need me to show you the note again, Rowan? I still have it downstairs.'

She hid a shudder. She could still remember writing it, the bile that had been in her throat as she did, the unbelievable pain in her heart.

She shook her head, feeling sick. 'No…I don't need to see it.'

'Because you were very clear. "I'm not ready to be a wife

and mother. I have things I want to do, things I want to see…"
Is that about right? Forgive me, I might have forgotten the
actual wording.'

She turned to try and face him, but he eluded her efforts.

'Isandro, I know how the note looked. But believe me—I
only wrote it because I never expected to see you or Zac again.'

He stopped and turned to face her, and she took a step back.
He was livid. She heard her words reverberate and winced.
They had come out all wrong. Well, right *and* wrong.

'No—wait. It's not like that—'

'No, I'm sure it's not. But your inheritance running out and
you not finding another willing sucker drove you back here
to a cushy prenup, using Zac, the convenient ace up your
sleeve, along the way to curry favour.'

Rowan opened her mouth but nothing came out, and in any
case Isandro wasn't finished.

He came and stood right in front of her. Worse than
anything, he just looked emotionless now. 'You've been dead
to me since you left, Rowan, dead to Zac. And in many ways
I think it might have been preferable if you had died, or at least
stayed away.'

He couldn't know what he was saying. He couldn't
possibly have any clue as to how cruelly close to home those
words were. Rowan comforted herself with that as she stood
there and felt ice trickle into her blood and her heart freezing.
There was so much meaning, so much hate in those words that
she had to get away from him. Before he could reduce her
completely. She had thought she'd been to hell and back
already, but this was coming a close second.

She looked somewhere in his vague direction. 'I agree
with you about moving out. I had already thought of perhaps
renting somewhere in Osuna. I'll get on to it tomorrow.'

And then she turned and went back into her room, shutting

the door softly behind her. In a moment of black parody her sheet caught in the door and she couldn't move forward. Loath to open the door again, to face Isandro's wrath and very evident self-disgust, she dropped the sheet and went straight to her bathroom. She pulled on a robe and locked the door, then sank to the floor in the dark and dropped her head to her knees, wanting to curl up into as small a ball as possible. No matter how much she tried she couldn't stop Isandro's words going round and round. And with them was another word: *fool...fool...*

CHAPTER NINE

ISANDRO looked at the piece of sheet caught under the door and waited impatiently for Rowan to open the door again and take it out. But she didn't. What was she doing? Just standing there? His irritation and anger levels had been finally cooling somewhat, but threatened to spike again now. He went and opened the door, only to find the crumpled sheet on the floor and the room bathed in soft light which jarred with his nerves.

The bed was empty. Where had she gone? He trod softly to the bathroom door and was about to knock, not even sure why he had felt compelled to come into the room at all, when he heard a soft noise. A keening sound like he'd never heard in his life. It made the hairs on the back of his neck stand up, his blood run cold.

His hand was still raised to knock on the door. His mouth opened but he couldn't articulate her name. A louder sound came now, and it was so primal, so *private*, that Isandro backed away, his hand dropping slowly. An image came into his head of her face when he had told her that she should have stayed away…and the other thing he'd said, about her dying.

He'd heard the words come out of his mouth and had wanted to swallow them back. But it had been too late, and before he'd been able to assess the consequences of them, of how he might have revealed himself, he'd been diverted by her reaction. She'd gone stony silent, pale as the sheet around her, her eyes dimming. She'd retreated back into the cool shell he remembered so well. It was as if what he'd said had really *hurt* her. And yet if she was nothing but a scheming, gold-digging heiress, looking to cash in on her marriage, wouldn't she have just tried to cajole him back into bed? She could have done it easily.

He couldn't disguise his shaming attraction. It burned like nothing he'd ever experienced, and surpassed even what had left him a little shell shocked after the explosive revelation of their wedding night.

But she wasn't cajoling him back into bed. She was in her dark bathroom, making the kind of sound that Isandro knew he'd never forget. But he couldn't go in there. He knew instinctively that she believed she was without witnesses, and to intrude would be unthinkable. So he left, his mind racing as to what she was up to now, what this might mean. Everything was up-ended all over again—that clarity as laughably elusive as ever.

For a couple of days Rowan studiously avoided Isandro, still raw and hurting after their row. He made no attempt to take her to bed again, or to come to her bed. He hadn't mentioned her moving out again but Rowan had made contact with an agent in Osuna and it hung in the air around them ominously. But that evening at dinner, after a painfully stilted conversation, she was surprised when he said that she and Zac should go to Seville the following day for a visit. For the first time in two days Rowan felt a spark within her erupt. She said yes, not knowing if his offer was as benign as it sounded. When he asked Rowan to come into his study after dinner she followed warily, keeping her eyes averted from the sheer force of his physique in worn jeans and a light sweater.

She stood resolutely behind a chair. Her body was feeling weak. A hunger was starting to rage through her blood at his proximity, but evidently Isandro's passion had burnt itself out. And no way would she be revealing her own vulnerability to him.

She watched as he opened his drawer and plucked something small and shiny out. He came around the desk and handed it to her.

'Here—it's a mobile phone.'

She looked at it, confused. 'But I have my own phone. I don't need yours.'

'You do need it if you're going out on your own and taking my son with you.'

Her eyes met his. 'He's my son too.'

His jaw clenched. 'This phone has all my numbers stored in case something should happen.'

'What on earth could happen?'

'You just need to be careful. We were featured extensively in the papers after that night in Seville. People know you're back on the scene. Change like that makes me and Zac and you vulnerable.'

Rowan felt a shiver of fear. She wasn't stupid. Of course a man as wealthy as Isandro could be a target for all sorts. She still ignored the phone.

'We don't have to go into Seville—'

Irritation shot through Isandro. Couldn't she see he was doing this for *her*? The fact was, ever since he'd heard her crying the other night and witnessed her withdrawing into herself, he'd been…frightened. He wanted a reaction—wanted to make her do something. *Wanted to see her during the day now as well as the night.* His body throbbed uncomfortably and he tried not to let his eyes roam over her hungrily as she stood in front of him.

He was so distracted that he barely noticed when she

finally accepted the phone. 'I still don't see how it's different to my own.'

Isandro shook his head. 'If anything happens just speed-dial me on number one. But I'll send Hernán with you too, so I'm sure you'll be safe.'

Rowan turned the phone over and back. She looked up for a second before she left. There was an intensity in his eyes that she couldn't fathom and which made her legs weak. She had to get out of there. She turned to walk out, but at the door he called her.

She turned back.

'I'll see you at the office. The girls will be looking forward to seeing Zac.'

A moment of pure exhilaration gripped her at his banal words, for all the world as if this was normal, as if they were a happily married couple discussing plans for the next day. And then just as swiftly Rowan felt that everything was crystal-clear. How could she have been so stupid? Anger rose, swift and bright. She walked back into the room, clutching the phone.

She held it out. 'This isn't about security at all, is it?'

Isandro had the gall to look nonplussed.

'You're afraid I'll try to run with Zac if you give me the slightest chance, aren't you? You're testing me.'

Two spots of colour were high on her cheeks and she was shaking. Isandro was genuinely taken aback. He hadn't thought of that for a second, and now he felt stupid for *not* doing so. Because clearly it was uppermost in *her* mind. He advanced around the desk.

'Is it cramping your style for me to know where you are at every moment of your journey?'

Rowan wanted to throw the phone back in his face. She could feel its imprint in her palm. She longed to tell him she didn't want to go to Seville, but she knew this was an important step in the process of making him trust her with Zac. Still words slipped out, helplessly. 'When will you just trust that I have only the best intentions where Zac in concerned?'

His eyes glittered down at her, a stormy blue. 'Oh, maybe on the twelfth of never.'

Rowan backed away to leave again. 'Send an army with us if you wish, Isandro. I don't care.'

But she did, she knew, as she left and went upstairs.

Isandro went and sat down behind his desk, driving a hand through his hair. Even as she had been standing there, mocking him for his own lack of suspicion, he'd been aware of her. Aware of her body, of the rise and fall of those soft breasts under her shirt. He wanted her. Mistress or wife. In his bed. And he hated to admit that he'd been ridiculously comforted to see a spark return to her eyes after two days in which her only animation had been inspired by Zac.

He'd vowed after the other night not to touch her again, but he knew that might be taking his will a step too far. The woman was running rings around him and she didn't even know it. But if she did, or if she suspected for a second...

His phone rang and he answered curtly. He heard his assistant's voice. 'What...? Nothing?' His hand spiked through his hair again. 'Yes, I want you to keep looking. Leave no stone unturned. She can't have just disappeared off the face of the earth.'

He slammed down the phone. He also hated this impulse to find out for himself exactly where she had been all this time. Forewarned was forearmed, he told himself. It was clear she'd been trying to tell him, but he would not listen to her lies before he had the truth in his own hands.

* * *

The next day Rowan looked at the phone for a long time. It seemed to shine up at her malevolently. But at the last second she threw it into Zac's bag of necessities. She knew it would be childish to leave it behind, and she had no doubt that Isandro would be most likely checking up on her.

She couldn't help a frisson of excitement as she settled Zac into the baby seat of the Jeep. The thought of Seville didn't scare her any more; she was feeling so much stronger these days. They loaded up—she in the back with Zac and Hernán driving. They waved goodbye to Ana-Lucía, who was on the steps.

Then Rowan was distracted, because Zac was grouchy and demanding attention. She tended to him for a few minutes, digging out water and a biscuit, so she didn't see Hernán slowing down or coming to a stop until he had, about a mile outside the small town.

She looked around his seat and asked in Spanish, 'Everything okay?'

'No problem. A car has broken down and I recognise it as my cousin's. I'll just check to see if he's okay…'

She looked back through the rear window. The broken down car was some distance behind them. Hernán had obviously passed it before he'd seen it. She made funny faces and played with Zac, and then cast another half-interested look back to the other car.

What she saw made her blood run cold and her heart stop. As she watched Hernán approach the car, a man stepped out from under the hood with a wrench and hit him on the head. It was so unbelievable and so fantastic that Rowan literally did not believe her eyes—not even when she saw another man emerge from the back of the car. Hernán fell to the ground, and the man with the wrench approached her in the Jeep.

She was stuck, couldn't move, but finally, when he was mere seconds away and she saw the flesh-coloured balaclava, she jerked into action and fumbled for the locks on the doors. There was only one thought in her head: *Zac*.

She was too late. The door on Rowan's side was pulled open, and the man grabbed her and pulled her out so fast and with such violence that her head spun. He was shouting at her in Spanish, but she couldn't make any sense of it. Then the other man arrived. He grabbed her too, and said roughly, '*Habla español?*'

She shook her head again, to try and clear it. He took that as a no.

'*Stupido*—Hernán said she's English. She doesn't speak Spanish. Get the kid.'

Rowan forced her mind to clear. Sheer primal protectiveness came to the fore and gave her courage. She made for the other side of the Jeep and Zac, babbling in English. She knew she'd have an advantage if they thought she didn't understand them.

She got to the door before they did. She ranted in English. It worked. The two men looked at her, and then she heard them say, 'Let *her* take the kid. What does it matter? I don't want to hold a screaming brat, do you?'

The other one grunted and gestured for Rowan to open the door. She did. Her hands were shaking so much that it took an age to undo Zac's straps and lift him out. She grabbed his bag too, in a moment of blinding clarity. Zac sensed the tension immediately and started to whimper.

The men shoved her roughly and moved her towards the other car. Everything happened in terrifying slow motion, and yet conversely so fast that before Rowan knew it one of the men had frisked her and she was sitting in the back of the car, arms firmly wrapped around Zac. Rowan's flesh still crawled from where the man had felt her bottom.

One of them put a secure blindfold over her eyes. They then got into the front and started the engine, pulling away with a screech of tyres. She couldn't let herself be scared. Think, think, *think*. She repeated the words like a mantra. The phone. She had to find it and call Isandro somehow. If she didn't it would be hours before the alarm might be raised. She just prayed that it wouldn't ring. She shushed and settled Zac securely into her chest, and then with a free hand started to feel for the bag. She found it—and felt a big hand over hers, stopping her. Her heart thudded painfully.

'Water!' she said urgently. 'Water for my baby.'

'It's okay—she just wants water. Let her get it.'

The hand left hers and Rowan searched. She found the water instantly, and then searched for the phone. About to give up hope, and fearful that the man would take the bag and get the water himself, finally she found it. She could have wept with relief. It was so small she could tuck it into her palm behind the bottle.

When she could feel that Zac had taken the bottle in his hands himself, she surreptitiously moved her hand behind him, to hide what she was doing. The men were talking now, arguing. Rowan used their preoccupation. She felt for where she thought the first digit would be. Then she pressed it, and racked her brain for where the call button had been.

With no idea if she was doing anything right, she pressed a button just as she felt the car slowing, then turning onto what she guessed was a motorway as their speed duly increased. She used the moment to throw the phone back into the baby bag. Was it her imagination or had she heard someone's voice, distant but there? Rowan knew that if she had got through to Isandro this might be her only chance, so she leant forward and said loudly in Spanish, 'Why are you kidnapping us? Where are you taking us? Why did you knock Hernán out? He could be badly hurt—you should call an ambulance…'

There was silence for a second, and then mayhem. She sensed the blow before it came, but it still snapped her head sideways. 'She speaks Spanish!'

Zac started to cry again, and Rowan calmed him down, knowing that their patience was less than thin.

One of them shouted back, 'We're taking you away for a while, to give your rich husband time to think about how much you're worth. And once we have you…' He mentioned in lurid detail what they would do to her, and Rowan blanked her mind. It was the only way. Thankfully Zac seemed to have quietened; she could feel him heavy against her chest. Tears pricked her eyes. She couldn't believe this. If anything happened to Zac… She vowed that it wouldn't. They would have to step over her dead body first.

After what seemed like hours over potholed roads they stopped. Rowan knew they'd been climbing in altitude because her ears had popped. One of the men pulled her from the car and ripped off her blindfold. She blinked painfully. Zac was a dead weight, mercifully asleep.

'No harm you seeing where we are now, because, *querida*, it's too remote to worry about.'

He shoved her in front of him towards a small stone shack. It was up on the top of a mountain, and there was literally nothing else in sight but craggy peaks.

Despair rose. The shack was windowless and cold and damp. She was pushed into a room and the baby bag hurled after her. Alone at last, Rowan put Zac down on a mattress and rummaged through the bag. She found the phone and the screen was smashed. It must have happened when the bag had hit the ground.

She busied herself getting a blanket for Zac to lie on. He was waking up again, groggy and cranky. She only had milk and baby snacks. She gave him another biscuit, which kept him occupied for a while, and then a bottle. She changed his nappy, trying to make things as normal as possible.

But after that his energy was boundless, and she couldn't blame him after being in the car and asleep for most of the day. She tried to encourage him to play quietly, but of course he had no understanding of the situation they were in.

He marched to the door and tried to reach up to open it, crying out when he couldn't. Rowan had been searching in vain for any means of escape, and darted forward just as the door opened, knocking Zac backwards. He started to cry, and the man bent down, his huge hand heading straight for Zac's head.

'No!' Rowan screamed, and pulled Zac back out of danger. She straightened up, breathing harshly, and had no warning of the hand that now came her way, cracking across her face. She felt her lip split and staggered back. The man went for Zac again, but like a tigress Rowan made a leap and caught Zac up into her chest.

Her head was ringing and she could taste blood. 'Don't *touch* him.'

The man stepped forward, but Rowan stood her ground.

He stopped then for a second, as if slightly confused. 'If I hear him so much as breathe I'll throw him down the mountain.'

He left the room and, shaking, Rowan went to the mattress and sat down, taking Zac with her. He was mercifully quiet, his eyes huge as he looked at her and her cut mouth. He put out a finger and pointed. Rowan tried to smile, but pain lanced her head. She spoke softly to try and reassure him, and got a tissue to try to stem the blood coming from her lip.

Losing all sense of time and place in the dim light, Rowan found her eyes closing. Zac had fallen asleep against her chest, and she wrapped his blanket around him to keep him warm. Her head kept nodding, and when she jerked upright some time later and found they were in the same position she had no idea of how much time had passed. She was so stiff that her legs had gone numb, her arms had pins and needles.

She came fully awake in an instant, though, when she sensed something outside. A movement, *something*… Zac woke too, and whimpered. Immediately Rowan was on her guard and stood up on wobbly legs, holding Zac tight within his blanket against her.

This was it. She knew it. They were going to try to take Zac from her and then— Her mind went blank with the horror of what was about to come.

The door opened, light streaming in from a flashlight and Rowan blinked. 'You will have to kill me to get to my son. My husband is on his way, and he knows exactly what—'

'*Rowan? Mi Dios*, what have they done to you?'

Rowan thought she was hearing things. She had to be making it up. It couldn't possibly be—

'Sandro…?'

'*Sí*. Yes. It's me.' His voice didn't sound like him. She couldn't trust it. It couldn't be possible. He came into the room, and more lights blazed behind him. Rowan felt disembodied, wasn't sure if she was standing or sitting or lying down. All she was aware of was Zac in her arms.

And then he stood in front of her. Tall and dark in the light, and so handsome and vital and *real*. If it was a hallucination then she could die happy right now.

CHAPTER TEN

THE adrenalin was still pumping through Isandro's body, and the metallic taste of fear was still in his mouth. When he'd opened that door all he'd seen had been two huge pairs of violet eyes. And such determination and fearlessness in Rowan's. For a second the emotion coursing through him made him stop. He couldn't actually touch them yet because he was shaking so much.

Rowan finally allowed the relief in, the reality, and then all the other emotions she'd been suppressing surged up. 'Sandro, I'm so sorry. I shouldn't have said I'd go to Seville. If we hadn't been going then this wouldn't have happened. Zac should have been at home. I could have gone on my own. You were right. I never should have come back in the first place. It's my fault—'

Isandro's heart clenched painfully. It had been *his* suggestion, his fault. And yet she was blaming herself. 'Shh, Rowan, it's okay. Give Zac to me.'

She stopped, feeling her mouth trembling, her limbs starting to shake. She knew she had to let go of Zac but she just *couldn't*. She tried, but it was as if her arms were welded across him, holding him so tight. A sob broke free. 'I can't—I can't let him go.'

'You can. Here…'

She felt Isandro put his hands over hers and warmth seemed to seep through her chilled skin. She felt Zac move instinctively towards his father, and somehow, finally, she was able to relax her arms from their death grip.

He took Zac and held him close for a long moment, and then she watched incredulously as he handed him to someone behind him. Then he turned to her and took her hands in his again. 'Do you think you can walk?'

She nodded, feeling slightly removed from everything. Why wasn't he just leaving now that Zac was okay?

'Of course—I'm fine—' She took a step and her legs promptly gave way, but as if he'd been expecting it Isandro caught her and scooped her up into his arms.

Rowan's mouth felt funny, and as they came out into the other room her eyes blinked in the intense light. Isandro was looking at her. At her mouth.

'What happened?'

An ugly voice came from beside the door. 'I hit her when your brat wouldn't shut up.'

Rowan tensed immediately in reaction to the horribly familiar voice and knew the two men were there, albeit probably tied up. She felt Isandro tense too. But without a word he walked outside and gently placed her in the back of a warmed Jeep, beside Zac, who was in a baby seat being tended to by a female police officer who smiled kindly at Rowan.

Rowan vaguely took in all the police, the flashing lights. She heard a scuffle and then Isandro was walking back out and cradling his hand. He sat into the front passenger side of the Jeep and the driver expertly swung them around to drive away.

Rowan knew he'd gone back in there and hit the man, and she felt glad. Because she would have hit him herself if she'd had the strength.

Sleep was rising to claim her. She couldn't fight it, but she had to ask, 'Hernán? How is Hernán?'

Isandro turned around, but he was a blur in her vision. 'He's in the hospital. He's going to be fine, thanks to you and the phone…'

His voice got further and further away…

Rowan woke as she was being carried into the house. It took a minute for things to seep into her consciousness, and when they did she tensed rigid. 'Zac—where's Zac? Who has him? Where—?'

'He's fine. He's with Ana-Lucía. She's feeding him and bathing him.'

Rowan struggled to be free from Isandro's arms. 'I don't believe you. I need to see him.'

His arms tightened around her. 'Rowan, relax. He's fine. I need to clean that cut on your lip, and then you need to eat too.'

Rowan forced herself to relax and let him carry her. It felt so good to be held like this, against his broad chest. She felt protected and cherished and safe. It was dangerous.

He let her drop outside his door, let her legs touch the ground. Rowan took a step. They felt shaky, but okay. He held her hand and she followed him into his room and to the bathroom. He made her sit down on the toilet. Then he rummaged for a first aid kit and pulled it down. Coming onto his haunches in front of her, he took out cotton wool and anti-septic. He dabbed at her lip and she sucked in a breath at the sharp pain. She noticed then that she was filthy. Dust and grime everywhere. Blood smeared on her T-shirt.

Isandro cast her a glance. 'You must have been freezing. It was almost zero degrees up there, you were so high.'

Rowan shook her head. She genuinely hadn't felt the cold. 'I don't…I didn't feel it. Had to keep the blanket on Zac in case he got cold…' Her teeth started chattering then, as if his words had unlocked something she'd been clinging onto, some control. She valiantly tried to hide it.

A look crossed Isandro's face, and then he said, 'I'll be back in a second.'

He got up and left the room, and she heard him go out into the corridor. She stood up shakily and looked at herself in the mirror. She was white, with two bright red spots in her cheeks. Her eyes were overbright too. A lurid cut snaked out from the side of her lip and throbbed painfully. Efficiently she started to pack away the first aid kit.

'Leave it—I'll do that. Sit down.'

'Oh.' Rowan hadn't heard him come back. She sat down and watched as he held out a tumbler. The smell of brandy hit her nostrils as he held it up to the side of her mouth that wasn't split, making her drink some. She didn't argue; the shivering was still there. The liquid burnt its way down her throat and she coughed slightly, but she could feel it going to work, warming her insides, calming the uncontrollable shivering.

'I'm sorry—this would never have happened if… I can't believe I put Zac in such danger…'

Isandro crouched down in front of her again and said sternly, 'Stop that. It could have happened just as easily with me.'

Rowan blanched. The thought of Isandro and Zac being kidnapped was more horrific to her than the thought of what those men might have done to her.

She shook her head to clear the fear, the awful image. 'Still, they went for me because they knew—'

He put a finger to her lips. 'Hush. They went for you because one of them was Hernán's cousin. He took advantage of knowing Hernán's movements and thought he'd try and be smart, make a quick buck. They were nothing but stupid thugs. You were so brave, *mi querida*.'

She shook her head, confused by the warmth in his eyes, the endearment. 'No, I was scared.'

'But you protected Zac; you were strong. I never knew you were that strong…'

He came up between her legs and placed his mouth gently over hers, his lips feathering across hers in a benediction, a healing kiss. Rowan wanted to sink into him, into the kiss, wanted to take what he was offering, to take the very essence of him, make it her own. She knew that they had just been through something extraordinary and had survived. He was just grateful, that was all. She knew all about moments like this, surviving. The euphoria would soon fade. His resentment would still be there somewhere, under the surface.

She pulled away gently, even though it felt like the hardest thing she'd ever done. She smiled awkwardly and her lip throbbed. She felt dirty. 'I think I'd like to have a shower…'

After a moment he stepped up and back, a blank expression replacing the warmth.

'Of course. Do you need a hand?'

'No, thanks,' Rowan said hurriedly, too hurriedly. The thought of him being around her when she felt so vulnerable was emotional suicide.

She made her way back to her own room and into the bathroom. She stood under the hot spray and scrubbed at her skin, scrubbing at any part those animals had touched. When she finally felt clean she got out. Throwing on a robe and rubbing her hair dry, she stepped back into her room.

Almost immediately, as if he'd been listening for movement, their adjoining door opened and Isandro walked in. 'Dinner. You must eat.'

Rowan knew better than to argue, and she followed him out of the room and down to the kitchen, where a steaming plate of stew waited for her with some crusty bread. Her stomach rumbled, and Isandro rested back against the sink as she sat and ate under his supervision.

'Do you want some wine?'

Rowan shook her head. The effects of the brandy were already going to her head. 'Just some water, please.'

A full glass materialised in seconds. Rowan glanced at Isandro, seriously nonplussed to see this side of him. He turned from the sink and caught her looking. She blushed and covered it up.

'How long were we…? I mean, when did you know…?'

'You don't know?'

She shook her head. 'I was blindfolded, and we drove for a long time. I don't wear a watch and one of the men threw down Zac's bag and the phone smashed.' She had to repress a shudder.

Isandro came and sat down, as if sensing her need to be near someone. 'My phone rang this morning, when you dialled it, and we found you at six p.m. They'd taken you out to a remote part of the national park. It lies to the east of here. They had you for about eight hours. If you hadn't called and raised the alarm it would have been much later, possibly even tomorrow. We lost your navigation signal when you entered the park…'

Rowan shivered again as it all came back to her. She stood abruptly, her chair sounding harsh on the tiled floor. The panic was returning. 'I need to see Zac. I have to know that he's—'

Isandro came around the table. 'He's fine, Rowan.'

'I don't care—I need to see him.'

She started out of the room and Isandro was right behind her. She had the most irrational fear that was galvanising her movements, making them jerky. She walked to Zac's room and pushed open the door, her heart thumping. Ana-Lucía turned around from where she was tucking him in. He was fast asleep. Rowan sagged against the door. Tears of proper relief stung her eyes.

She saw Ana-Lucía send a concerned look over her head to Isandro, and felt him turn her around and propel her to her room.

'See? He's fine. Now you need to sleep too.'

Isandro knew his voice sounded husky with suppressed emotion. Rowan looked up at him and her eyes were bright. Seeing her here, with Zac, when he'd thought…he'd feared the worst. He couldn't think of that fear, couldn't let it rise again. It had almost undone him earlier. He could still feel his fist smashing into that man's face, the police pulling him back, and knew he might have gone a lot further. He would have put Zac in danger because he wouldn't have been able to control himself, but Rowan had exhibited calm and control and had put Zac first every step of the way.

When his phone had rung in the middle of a meeting he'd almost let it go to message, but he'd somehow known it was her. He'd picked it up, and then he'd realised what he was listening to. He could still feel the acrid fear and panic that had seized his innards.

His churning thoughts halted as Rowan stepped away from him to go into her room. 'Will you be okay?'

Rowan looked at him. She knew she should say yes, that she'd be fine, thanks, and goodnight, but her mouth wouldn't work. *Just for tonight. Please just let me have tonight, and tomorrow I'll get on with the rest of my life.*

She faced him and lifted her chin slightly. 'Would you…? I mean I know that you don't—that we aren't—'

She stopped. She couldn't even string two words together. She turned in mortification and shame but felt Isandro tug her back.

'Do you want to sleep with me?'

Colour scorched her cheeks. She couldn't look up. 'Not like that…but, yes, please. I don't want to be on my own.'

Without a word Isandro took her by the hand and led her along the hall to his door and into his room. In the dim light he undid the belt on her robe. She started to protest that she had nothing on underneath, but he just shushed her. He slipped the robe from her shoulders and then stepped out of his own clothes until they were both naked.

He brought her over to the bed and waited till she was in, then he got in the other side. Rowan thought he was just going to let her lie alone, but immediately she felt the heat and hardness of his body as he pulled her in close to his chest, his legs cupping her bottom. She could feel his body stirring against hers and she shifted slightly.

He pulled her closer, a possessive arm around her belly, and whispered in her ear. 'It's okay. It's something I can't help with you so close. Go to sleep, Rowan.'

Heat and pleasure and warmth and safety fizzed through Rowan's veins. She finally allowed herself to relax back against Isandro's chest. Let his warmth and the strength of his body seep into her bones and skin. She'd said she hadn't felt cold earlier, and she hadn't. But now she realised that she had. She'd just blocked it out. It was a coldness the like of which she hoped she'd never experience again. It was the coldness of hopelessness, and even throughout everything she'd been through before she'd not felt it until today.

She knew she must have slept for a while, because when she woke a little later she could feel Isandro's arm heavier around her. More of a dead weight. She felt in that moment as if she could quite happily lie like that for ever.

Emboldened by knowing that Isandro was asleep, she ran her hand lightly up and down his arm, leaving her hand to rest over his. It felt strong and big, the fingers long and capable. Vibrant and alive. She turned her head to try and see his sleeping face and he moved. She tensed. She was going to break the spell. He'd wake, forget everything that had happened, wonder what on earth she was doing in his bed...

Rowan froze. Isandro moved again and she could feel him against her bottom. He wasn't as hard as before, but he was coming back to life. Her cheeks grew warm in the dark as his hand started to move lazily on her belly, upwards, to the curve of her breast. He cupped it lightly.

Rowan's breath stopped. She sucked her belly in as his hand moved up and over her breast fully, trapping her hardening nipple between two fingers, squeezing gently. There was no point trying to play dumb. Her whole body was humming, singing, and she could feel him move restlessly against her, now rock-hard and *big*.

About to say *Sandro*, she stopped, remembering his mocking words from the other night. 'Isandro...?'

'Shh.'

He pressed kisses all down the back of her neck onto her shoulder. Fire was raging between her legs and Rowan could feel herself parting them in a tacit plea. Isandro took his hand from her breast and smoothed it down in a sensual journey, over the indent of her waist and out to her hip, down her thigh and back up, before going between her legs and opening her up to him. She felt him guide himself between her thighs, seeking the hot, moist juncture.

She gasped when he found it, and his hand came back around her belly to pull her into him even more, fingers long and searching, seeking and finding that spot. He surged upwards in one move and he was there, where she ached for him, thrusting deep. Rowan twisted back further and he came up on one arm, bending down and meeting her mouth with is. His kiss was gentle. The whole experience was so gentle it was breaking her heart. He was careful to stay away from the sore side of her mouth.

His head moved down. He was setting up a rhythm that was fast hurtling her towards nirvana, and when his mouth found one hard peak, thrusting forward flagrantly, and suckled fiercely, nirvana broke all around her, within her. She clutched his arm, his own tempo quickened, and with one last surge she felt him come deep inside her.

They lay like that for a long moment, Isandro pulling Rowan tight in against him, almost as if he wanted to fuse their bodies together. Eventually he pulled free and Rowan lay flat on her back. Isandro propped himself up beside her. She looked at him, still breathless. He just watched her. A fine sheen of sweat made her skin glow. She lifted a hand and traced his jaw. He took it and sucked a finger deep into his mouth.

A pulse throbbed between her legs. How could he have the power to arouse her so easily, so quickly? She knew her eyes had widened.

He frowned lightly. As he watched her expression something crept over him. Could it be possible?

'You...*this* frightens you, doesn't it? The way you are with me here, in bed...'

She just looked up at him, fear and confusion evident in her eyes. He didn't know how he hadn't seen it before. Too blinded by lust. By events.

She nodded slowly, and then said shakily, 'Terrified... I feel like I become someone else...someone I don't know...' She whispered the last words. 'And yet I need it, crave it, and that makes me feel...'

His mouth quirked slightly. 'Wanton? Lusty? Sexy? Sensual?'

Rowan grimaced. 'Well...some of those things.'

He moved over her then and let her feel the evidence of his own resurgence of arousal. He found her hand and brought it down, making her encircle his shaft, moving her hand up and down with his.

His voice sounded rough, hoarse. 'Sex is messy, guttural, wonderful and base…and all I know is I've never experienced it with anyone else the way I do with you. You are all those things, Rowan, and more…'

He took his hand away and rested over her on both forearms, his weight deliciously heavy against her. She kept her hand on him, moving up and down, and watched fascinated as passion glazed his eyes and tautened the skin across his cheekbones. Desire flooded her, but she only cared about giving him pleasure.

When his head went back and the muscles in his neck corded she knew he was close. He reached down and stopped her hand, coming close and pressing his mouth to hers, and then he filled her again. She gasped and arched upwards, wanting all of him, every inch. He started to move and, together again, they reached the blazing heights.

The following morning Rowan awoke to find Julia bustling into the room with breakfast on a tray. Her automatic impulse was to sit up, but then she realised she was naked. She pulled up the sheet quickly. Julia appeared not to notice anything unusual in finding Rowan in Isandro's bed.

She settled the tray beside Rowan and clucked around her like a mother hen, fluffing up the pillows. As she was leaving, Rowan asked her about Zac. Julia told her that Ana-Lucía had already fed him, and that he was downstairs with Isandro.

Rowan sank back. The breakfast looked appetizing, but her stomach lurched. A million things hit her brain at once. She'd spent the night in Isandro's bed. He hadn't left her. They'd made love. Or that was how it had felt. Her heart clenched. She was in so deep now that the thought of leaving again, this time through no choice of her own, was filling her with dread.

She heard a noise and the door opened. Isandro. Her mouth went dry and her cheeks flushed at the thought of last night.

His eyes went from her to the breakfast. 'Not hungry?'

Her mouth tightened as she watched him come in. 'Not really…' She couldn't read his expression. He seemed remote, different from the man who had taken her to heaven and back last night. Who had been so tender.

He stood at the window for a moment before turning around. 'Look, Rowan, about last night…I'm sorry…I never meant for…that to happen. When I offered to sleep with you I meant just that. Sleep.'

Rowan sat up straight, holding the sheet against her. White-hot pain blanked out the previous night and the urge to self-protect rose up swiftly. She rushed to halt any more words. 'Oh, no—please don't worry. I hadn't expected that either. It was just an effect of the day. The extreme circumstances.'

Her cheeks were crimson, and she looked with despair to where her robe was flung on a chair in the corner. He saw her look, and with a rigid jaw strolled over to get it.

All she wanted to do was get out of there and away from the pity he must feel. He'd been offering comfort; she'd taken complete liberties with that. Hadn't he made it tacitly clear after the other night that any desire for her had burnt itself out? Her role as his mistress had been laughably short in the end. But last night, she could almost have believed…

He handed her the robe. She glanced up quickly and saw his face was like granite. She sensed anger and felt bewildered. A knife skewered her heart. He regretted it that much? She'd have to make moves to leave the house soon if she couldn't even be trusted to control herself around him.

She grabbed the robe and pulled it on without managing to show a sliver of flesh. She stood up from the bed. 'I'll eat this downstairs…I'd like to see Zac anyway.'

He stopped her just before she went to lift the tray. 'Let me.'

Rowan felt even more exposed. He must have seen her hands shaking. He took it and walked out, and she followed miserably.

At the bottom of the stairs he turned to her, his eyes guarded. 'The police are due here in about an hour to take a statement from you. Are you up to it?'

Rowan's heart contracted. For all the world he sounded genuinely concerned. She nodded. 'Yes. I'll be fine.'

When she followed Isandro into the dining room after that she was immeasurably relieved to see Zac playing happily with Ana-Lucía, seemingly suffering no ill effects of the day before.

Isandro disappeared into his office after the police had been and gone. He'd sat by her side throughout the interview, and Rowan had felt his tension growing as she'd related the events. Undoubtedly he must blame her to some extent. How could he not?

After playing with Zac until his nap, Rowan retreated to the walled garden of the private patio outside her room. Under the shade of a huge tree she was trying to read, but gave up when she realised how futile it was. Her cheeks burned again, and her insides twisted in embarrassment when she thought of last night. What was going to happen now?

She would have to call that estate agent and see if he had found anything yet. One thing was clear: she needed to leave as soon as possible. No doubt Isandro would allow her a little grace, considering what had happened, but she couldn't take advantage of that. She was too volatile around him, barely able to control herself.

The divorce would most likely be through quickly—Isandro would want to be free to get on with his own life, possibly even remarry. The sooner she made the break, got some distance, the sooner she could start to claw back some control…get on with things. Rowan's fists clenched unconsciously in rejection of her thoughts.

She heard the shrill ring of her mobile phone from inside her room and hurried in to get it. Her heart thumped a little erratically as she realised exactly who it must be. Her past reached out ghostly tentacles to claim her, and she brushed off a feeling of foreboding.

As she'd expected, it was a call to remind her of her appointment. She hung up, and hugged her arms around herself, suddenly feeling cold. At that moment she wished she had someone to turn to, someone who would share her concerns, her worries. For a fleeting moment she wondered wistfully what it might be like to be loved, completely and deeply, by someone like Isandro…to be supported.

Just then a knock sounded at her door. She opened it, and the object of her thoughts and fantasies was standing there, looking grim. She clutched the door. No doubt this was it. He wanted to talk about the arrangements.

'Can you come down to my study? There's something I'd like to talk to you about.'

'Of course,' she said faintly, feeling sick.

In the study, Isandro told Rowan to sit down on the leather couch by the wall-to-ceiling shelves, but she shook her head minutely. 'If it's okay, I'd prefer to stand.'

He went and picked up a file from his desk and came to stand in front of her. A long moment stretched as he just looked at her, as if he was trying to figure her out, and Rowan's nerves screamed.

'How is your mouth?' he asked then, innocuously.

Rowan blinked and had to forcibly ignore an image of his

head coming towards her, and a kiss so light she almost hadn't felt it. She touched it gingerly. 'Fine…much better.'

Her hand dropped. 'What…what did you want to talk about?'

He glanced at the file in his hand and looked up, a harsh glitter in his eyes. He held it up. 'This is the result of the investigation I've had done into your whereabouts for the past two years.'

He knew? The thought set panic racing through her. This wasn't what she'd expected. She shook her head, as if to clear it. Had she heard right? 'I don't know what you're talking about… You investigated me?'

He nodded grimly. 'A little after the fact, I'll admit, but I didn't do it at the time because of extenuating circumstances: namely becoming a single parent, and shortly afterwards a stock market crash that threatened the livelihood of millions in Europe.'

The market crash that woman had mentioned at the party…

As if he had read her thoughts, he said, 'The crash that you appear to know nothing about.'

Rowan wanted to sink onto the couch behind her, but wouldn't. She wasn't sure she was ready for where this was inevitably headed, especially in light of her recent phone call. Feeling cowardly she played for time.

'I'm not sure I know where you're going with this.'

'Neither do I.' He tapped the file against an open hand. 'Do you want to know what my investigators found out?'

Rowan gave a little half-shrug and shook her head at the same time. No, she didn't want to see the facts of her life laid out in a file. Especially if—

'Here—have a look.'

He handed her the file, and with her heart palpitating in her chest Rowan opened it out. It was empty. Not one piece of paper. Relief mixed with something else raced through her.

He started to pace, and finally rested a hip against the
dge of his desk, arms crossed formidably over his broad
hest. He quirked a brow. 'I think I'm ready for your ex-
lanation, Rowan. Because unless you've been sitting on
 mountain top in India meditating for two years, you
aven't popped up anywhere in the world. And, believe me,
ve've searched.'

She could well imagine he had.

This was it. The moment of truth.

She carefully put down the file and went to stand by the
vindow, looking outside for a long time, praying for
ourage. When she turned around Isandro was just
vatching her, his expression guarded, not a hint of warmth,
nything. This was it. She had to tell him. He above anyone
leserved to know.

'You haven't found any trace of me because when I walked
out of the hospital that day I cut up all my cards, any trace of
paperwork. I used my middle name, Louise, and my mother's
naiden name, Miller. I moved my inheritance to a Swiss
bank account and withdrew cash as I needed it.'

Rowan knew she was talking, and looking at Isandro as she
lid so, but she felt removed, as if she were watching herself
from a long distance. She gripped the back of a chair that was
in front of her.

'That still doesn't tell me where you've been. It just tells
ne how you evaded detection.' His voice was flat. Grim.

Rowan breathed and swallowed painfully, tried to say the
words as dispassionately as possible. But she could feel her
fingers digging into the chair-back. 'I was in France—a small
own just outside Paris. I've been there since the day after I
valked out of the hospital. In a clinic.'

She saw Isandro frown, and felt a cold sweat break out on
ner brow. She prayed for the fortitude to see this through. She

closed her eyes for a second and opened them again. Took a deep breath.

'It was…is…a cancer clinic.'

CHAPTER ELEVEN

ISANDRO stood from the desk. Rowan felt shaky and light-headed, as if she was going to faint. She took deep breaths. He came close and gripped her upper arms, pulled her round to sit in the chair.

'*Explain.*'

Rowan looked up a long way and said weakly, 'Can you sit down, please? You're making me dizzy.'

He pulled up a chair and sat down opposite her, his whole body screaming tension. She focused on his eyes, which were a more intense blue than she'd ever seen before. She willed him to believe what she was about to say. She knew she wouldn't be able to bear it if he laughed or told her she was making up a story.

Shakily, she tucked some hair behind her ear. 'When I was seven months pregnant I went for a check-up. I'd been feeling more tired than usual…run down… I'd got a couple of colds…'

Isandro frowned, something flashing into his head. 'You had all those nosebleeds…'

Rowan nodded slightly, surprised that he remembered. At one point she'd been having two or three nosebleeds a week. 'That…they were a part of it too.'

Isandro looked at her. She *had* seemed more poorly in the

latter months of her pregnancy. He had put her increasing distance down to that. He nodded at her to continue, feeling curiously numbed, as if already protecting himself from something.

'Dr Campbell did a routine blood test and sent it to the lab. She called a couple of days later and asked me to come in and see her. You…you were meant to be going to New York for the week-long conference and you got delayed by a day.'

Isandro nodded again briefly. He could remember coming back from that trip and finding Rowan cool and distant. That had been the start of it. And he could also remember the pain of leaving that townhouse behind, the loneliness that would creep up on him during trips away, surprising him with its force…surprising him with its presence.

'When I went back to see Dr Campbell she had another doctor with her…' She took a deep breath. 'A visiting consultant haematologist, Professor Erol Villiers…' Rowan looked away for a moment and pressed her lips together before looking back. 'They told me that they'd found something in my blood. AML. It's an acute form of leukaemia.'

No matter how much she said it, or how quickly, the terror of that moment would always be with her.

She watched Isandro for his reaction, but he was unmoving, impassive. She recognised shock. Feeling claustrophobic, Rowan stood and walked back to the window, crossing her arms. It was easier to move, to not be so close, under such scrutiny.

'They wanted me to start an aggressive cycle of chemotherapy straight away, but I refused.' She heard Isandro stand behind her and turned around.

He was shaking his head. 'Why did you refuse?'

It was almost a relief to have him react. 'Because it could have harmed the baby. There was a risk of premature labour…malformity. There was no way I was going to put him at risk. I wouldn't do it then and I wouldn't do it now, if I had to choose again.'

'But…' Isandro turned away and paced back and forth. He couldn't even begin to articulate a coherent response. His brain, normally able to function at a level that left most people in the dust, now refused to operate.

'Just let me finish. I know…I know it's a lot.'

He stood facing her again, a raw intensity in his eyes.

'Because I refused to have the chemotherapy I knew I was severely reducing my chances of survival. But…' She shrugged. 'The most important thing was delivering Zac safely. That was all I cared about.'

'To the detriment of your own health?' He was incredulous.

Rowan nodded. 'And in case you're worried there was never any risk to Zac from my diagnosis. Not then, not now…'

Isandro looked grim, but Rowan continued. 'They wanted to start me on chemo straight after Zac was delivered, and I knew what was likely to be involved—how invasive it was going to be, how debilitating, with no guarantee of any success. Even so, Professor Villiers asked me to go to his specialist clinic in France. He was interested in my case as this type of cancer in pregnancy is rare.'

Rowan rubbed her hands up and down her arms. 'My own mother died of breast cancer when I was five. I remembered her treatment, the pain, the degradation… I didn't want to put Zac through bonding with me even for a short time, only to have me…taken away from him. I knew he'd be safe with you. You were so happy at the thought of a son…'

She reached out and held onto the back of the chair again like a lifeline.

'I meant it when I told you that I hadn't ever expected to

see you or Zac again. I truly didn't have any hope for the future. The doctors warned me that it would most likely have spread too far, too fast. Going to France was somewhere for me to go…to be…'

To die.

The unspoken words hung in the air.

'So what happened?' Isandro asked flatly.

Rowan knew that the last thing he'd have expected was to be faced with having to feel any kind of sympathy for her. So she made her words as clipped and impersonal as possible, hiding the acute pain of what she'd endured.

'They started me on the chemotherapy anyway, but as they had expected it didn't precipitate a remission. It was too late.' Self-consciously she touched her hair. 'This…my hair fell out. And the scar you noticed…it was from an intravenous line for fluids.'

Isandro was still unmoving. It made something contract protectively inside Rowan. But she went on. She had to.

'The only other possible option we hadn't explored was a bone marrow transplant. That's because it can't happen without a donor match. As all my close family were dead it was more or less ruled out, and time was running out…'

She crossed her arms tight across her chest, locked in the memories. 'But a few weeks after I arrived a perfect match became available within the clinic itself. It was from one of the registered voluntary bone marrow donors who happened to be related to a patient…however, it was going to be an extremely risky operation.'

'Why didn't you contact me then, if there was a chance?' Isandro's voice was unbearably harsh, and Rowan flinched slightly as it brought her back into the room. She looked at him unswervingly.

'Because even at this point there was only a fifty-fifty

chance. Less. You with all your money and influence could not have improved on that. And after a bone marrow transplant you're kept in isolation for up to a month, possibly longer, very prone to infections. Visitors are kept to a minimum.'

She paled. 'I contracted at least three infections. Even if the transplant is successful, and you survive the infections, there's every chance the new marrow could be rejected by the body months down the line. Don't you see?' she beseeched him. 'What would have been the point?' Her voice cracked ominously but she forged ahead, 'I hadn't expected to survive that far, and I couldn't have borne not being able to see Zac, being separated by two doors in a quarantine area…'

Isandro stuck his hands deep in his jean pockets and then took them out again. His fists were clenched. Rowan looked so vulnerable and defenceless standing behind the chair. A surge of emotion broke through the awful numbness and instinctively he moved towards her. But then abruptly he stopped again. He felt…he felt as if he was being torn in two. Like nothing else he'd ever experienced. He wanted to go over to her and crush her to him, hold her in his arms and never let her go. And yet…much to his utter shame…he couldn't. Not yet. Couldn't even hold her, because he was afraid of what might erupt out of him if he did. Unbeknownst to him, his face suddenly looked drawn and lined.

'And the note?'

Rowan flushed. 'That was to ensure you didn't come after me. I was hoping to dent your ego, your pride…'

She saw a flare of something in his eyes, but it died away, because he had to acknowledge that she'd been right. And that irked him beyond belief.

She looked down at her hands. 'I'd written other letters to you and to Zac. Letters to be sent…explaining everything.

Saying sorry. I wouldn't have wanted Zac to grow up thinking the worst of me.'

'Yet you've let me do that for nearly two months now?'

Her conscience struck her. She looked up again. Not telling him had been the only thing holding her fragile control together. 'I did try to tell you a couple of times…it wasn't the easiest subject to bring up. That day I bumped into you in London *was* literally my first day back from France. I truly had no idea that hotel was yours.' Her mouth twisted. 'It really was fate…circumstance.'

Isandro remembered his towering rage that day, remembered that she had indeed said something about wanting to explain. He remembered the other night, his cruel words, her reaction…but how could he have known *this*? He could feel himself retreating somewhere inside. That numbness was spreading through him again, and he welcomed it because it was removing him from *feeling*.

'I wanted to write you a letter through my solicitor and explain everything before we met, so that you might understand. That's why I was meeting Mr Fairclough.'

Isandro paced away and then back again. His brain finally seemed to click into gear. Every line in his body was rigid with tension. '*Why* didn't you tell me when you found out? For God's sake, I know it was just a marriage of convenience, but you were carrying my child. I would have supported you no matter what. You shouldn't have had to go through that on your own.'

Rowan turned away from the anger in his voice, the censure. She still had to protect herself. 'I didn't tell you because I was afraid you'd side with the doctors and force me to have the chemo. I can't explain how I felt…all I know is that Zac's health and safety were paramount to me. I didn't want you to feel…*obliged* to care for me. To feel you had to do the right thing—which could have possibly harmed Zac but given me a better chance.'

She turned back and her eyes were defiant. 'I made a decision to deal with it on my own. To put Zac first and then deal with it myself.' Her voice didn't hold even a thread of self-pity. 'I've always been on my own, Isandro. It's what I'm used to. And I never…never expected to be here, explaining all of this to you.' Her voice shook with quiet intensity. 'I would *never* have walked away from Zac that day if I had believed there might be a chance…you *have* to believe me.'

He did. He did believe her. The pain was etched on her face even now. In her eyes. It was the pain he'd glimpsed before. That urge to take her in his arms almost overwhelmed him with its force, but was crushed down by the weight of guilt, heavy and pervasive.

When his investigators had turned up precisely nothing on Rowan's whereabouts he knew something had happened. This had been compounded by her behaviour since they'd met again in London. Her obvious devotion to Zac, her love for him. He hadn't mistaken the emotion she'd shown around him those first few days, weeks. When he'd thought it had been an act.

He realised now how overwhelming it must have been for her, her intention to live nearby…he couldn't ignore the facts any longer. She just wasn't the person who had left that callous and flippant note.

But what did this mean?

His head reeled. More than reeled. It was spinning off into space with all these facts. He was beginning to feel so many things that he had to keep a lid on his emotions. He took refuge in attack, hating himself because he knew well it was directed at the wrong person, but he was unable to stop. He asked ascerbically, 'Did you not think I'd support you?'

She was white as snow, her eyes two huge pools of violet

in her face. The gash on her lip was stark, and made something clench in his chest, his heart.

'Of course I knew you'd support me, Isandro. But our marriage wasn't ever about that. I…couldn't face the thought of…dutiful support. You hadn't signed up for that.'

A maelstrom seemed to erupt inside Isandro. He hadn't signed up for the passionate chemistry that had exploded between them either. Hadn't signed up for the way she'd turned his life upside down in so many ways. *Was* turning it upside down. His voice was icy. '*That's* how you could justify leaving?' He knew he sounded harsh, remote, but he couldn't help it. Something was weighing him down inside.

A bleakness filled Rowan's heart and soul. He didn't understand. He'd never understand. How could he? And in the face of this cold front she knew she was still a coward. She had left that day for myriad reasons, not least of which had been Zac and his welfare. But also because she had loved Isandro too much. To see him shackled to her for the days, weeks, possibly months on end…to witness his pity…to have him witness her downward slide…his responsibility for her had been too much to bear. A painful ache lodged in her throat.

She looked away and then back. Her voice was so quiet he almost didn't hear her.

'I overheard your conversation with Ana. So you don't have to explain anything to me. I knew exactly where I stood.'

Isandro's head was beginning to hurt. 'My conversation with Ana…?'

Rowan crossed her arms. 'It was the day I'd found out about my prognosis…' She balked for a second. At the time she had intended telling him everything—until she'd overheard… She gulped and forced her mind away from it. 'Ana was angry.'

And then he *did* remember. Vividly. The way his sister had tried to back him into a corner, make him reveal himself when he hadn't even known how he felt. All he had known was that he'd wanted to protect Rowan from Ana's vitriol, which stemmed from his father's betrayal of them all.

'I hadn't meant to listen. I came home from meeting Dr Campbell and heard you…' She lifted a hand ineffectually and let it drop. 'You didn't say anything I wasn't already aware of.' She prayed he wouldn't see how badly she was lying.

The words came back to haunt him now. Clearly Rowan had heard the worst of it. Like shards of crystal, moments, snippets started to come to Isandro. The timing of when she'd withdrawn into herself, cut herself off from him emotionally and physically… But he couldn't grasp the implications of it all fully—not yet.

Her voice didn't ring with the conviction it had when she'd told him of her illness. In fact she seemed all too brittle now. He felt that brittleness spread through him too. The world was reduced to that room and he couldn't *feel* anything. It was all too huge to take in, too abstract. To have believed one thing for so long…and now this.

Rowan stood still, looking at a spot in the carpet for so long that she was beginning to feel dizzy. Then Isandro finally spoke, and Rowan looked at him reluctantly, afraid to see what might be in his eyes. But she couldn't read their expression, they were veiled.

'So…what now?'

What now indeed?

She almost welcomed the banality of words. Even though they were really far from banal. 'I have to go back to the clinic for a couple of days. I've been in remission now for some months, but Professor Villiers wants to see me for a routine check-up just to confirm that everything is okay.'

'When?'

'Tomorrow.'

'That's not much notice.'

Rowan's heart ached at Isandro's astringent tone. 'They believe me to be in London, I was going to take the train. And in truth I'd forgotten about it…with everything.' She flushed.

'You can take the plane.'

Rowan looked at him, slightly aghast at his easy offer. 'Well, I…thank you. I'd appreciate that.'

And just like that it was out. Her big terrible dark secret. And nothing had changed. They were right where they'd always been. In some kind of no man's land.

Isandro's phone rang on his desk, making Rowan flinch. He looked at her for a long moment, and then with an impatient gesture went to answer it. Rowan slipped quietly out of the room.

CHAPTER TWELVE

Two Days Later

'I CAN'T stress enough how ill your wife was, Mr Salazar. The fact that she survived at all is a testament to her strength, and the sheer luck of finding that donor when we did. She showed great courage in the face of daily pain on a level that you or I can only imagine.'

The stark words struck deep. He looked at Rowan's doctor. Isandro had arrived early that morning. When Rowan had left early the previous day he hadn't even accompanied her to the plane, unable to break out of the stasis that had gripped him since she'd told him everything. Since then his mind, his heart, had been a seething mass of pain, anger, confusion. And something else.

'Professor Villiers, I know I wasn't here…when my wife was going through her treatment—'

The doctor waved a hand. 'It's none of my business, but I knew she'd decided to go it alone for her own reasons, which is why we could never tell you. As you know, doctor-patient confidentiality is sacrosanct. As the symptoms of her illness were largely *a*sympomatic, her pregnancy disguised them. She got away with not telling you.'

He took off his spectacles and looked slightly fierce. 'I won't lie to you, though. There were times when I wished she wasn't so stubborn. She wouldn't even let us induce the baby early. She wanted to give him the best possible chance—and that, of course, reduced her own chances even more...'

Isandro reeled anew. And took a deep breath. Enough. 'I need to know. I have to know what she went through... *please*.'

The doctor looked at Isandro for a long moment and then, as if he'd seen something he could trust, he nodded briefly.

'Very well.'

Relief surged through Isandro. Professor Villiers stood up.

'Of course I can't reveal any of Rowan's specific details without her permission, but I can tell you what someone in her position might have gone through.'

'Thank you.' Isandro stood when the doctor gestured to the door.

'Come, we will walk and talk. Have you seen your wife yet?'

Isandro shook his head.

'Then I will take you to her when we're done.'

Isandro stood leaning against the open doors that led outside to a pretty garden area. It was a sunny day and patients and visitors strolled the paths.

But he didn't see that.

He saw images: the room where Rowan had had to be on her own for almost three months as she battled infections after the transplant. The equipment she'd been hooked up to.

His hands were deep in his pockets, clenched tight against the pain inside him. The pain of how close he'd come to—

And then there she was. She looked so healthy now, so vibrant, it made it hard to believe... He stepped out and walked towards her. She was sitting cross-legged with a group of children around her. She was reading a story and looked about sixteen herself, in a flowery summer dress. Bare legs, bare feet.

He sat on a bench and just watched. Drinking her in, trying to come to terms with so much. And he thought that perhaps now he understood a little.

Rowan finished the story and looked up with a smile—only to look straight into Isandro's piercing blue eyes. It was as if they'd been drawn there like a magnet. He was sitting on a bench just feet away, watching her. The breath stalled in her throat, and she could feel the colour drain from her face. Perhaps she was dreaming, because in this very spot so many times she'd fantasised… Absently, she hugged and kissed the children.

She stood awkwardly and slipped her sandals back on. Isandro stood up as she approached. He was real, not a figment of her imagination. She tried to ignore the fluttering in her chest, the aching in her heart, and called up the very real need to protect herself.

'Isandro…what are you doing here?' She sounded breathless and cursed herself.

He looked down at her and she could see his eyes flash, something swirling in their depths. 'I think I owe you this at least. I should have come with you yesterday, not let you go on your own.'

'Oh…it's fine, really. I hadn't expected it.'

A pain lanced him. He took her hand in his and looked at it almost absently. 'No, I don't suppose you did.' He looked up and gestured to where she'd been sitting with the children. 'Who are they?'

Rowan wanted to pull her hand away. She was feeling hot and bothered. And confused. 'They're…they're patients.' She had to concentrate. 'When it was finally confirmed that I was in remission three months ago I was still weak. I had to build up my strength, so I helped out with the kids…' She shrugged then, and looked down. 'I always feel so guilty for getting well again, when they should have their whole lives ahead of them.'

'It's nothing to feel guilty about.' Isandro said with a quiet fierceness that surprised her.

'Yes.' She said simply, still shocked to see him here. And then she said the words she'd thought she'd never say. 'The results are good; I'm still in remission and I'm getting stronger.' She took a deep breath. 'My prognosis is...very good.'

She searched his face but couldn't fathom what was going on in his head. It must be pity. She hardened her heart. And then he took the wind out of her sails again by asking, 'Show me the new wing they're building?'

Her mouth opened and closed. 'Dr Villiers told you?'

He nodded.

Rowan led the way, and when Isandro reached for her hand she let him take it. What was the harm? Soon enough they'd be discussing the divorce, custody... If he was doing this out of pity then she'd be a coward and take it.

They approached a building site around the back of the clinic where a makeshift wooden plaque hung on the fence. It read: *The Catherine and Alistair Carmichael Wing for the research and treatment of children's leukaemia.*

Isandro's voice sounded tight. 'Why did you use your parents' names?'

He felt Rowan shrug, and she touched the plaque briefly with a finger. 'So they can live on together...through this.'

Isandro's head reeled with her selflessness. 'All your inheritance?'

Rowan looked up at him then, and shook her head. 'Not all. I kept some back for legal fees in case...in case...' She avoided his eye and couldn't finish, but it was hard, his gaze was so penetrating, 'I knew you'd most likely pursue a divorce...I expected that.'

His eyes were too intense. She had to look away. The pain was debilitating. She pulled her hand from his and started to walk. Her emotions were threatening to erupt again. To be here, sharing this with him, was too much.

Rowan packed up her few things and said goodbye to the staff and Dr Villiers, who gave her a huge bear hug. Isandro was waiting for her.

In the car Rowan sat as far apart from him as possible. She felt as if he'd looked inside her brain, her heart.

Just when she saw that they were passing the sign for the airport, she heard him say, 'I've booked us into a hotel in Paris for the night.'

She looked over, aghast. 'Why?'

He was looking at her with an expression she couldn't decipher and she didn't like the determination in his eyes.

'Isandro, you don't have to do this. Please. I'm not a child who's just had a nasty trip to the dentist. I'd much prefer to go home.' *Not that his home was her home.*

His jaw clenched ominously. 'I'd like to take you out for the evening. We have to talk, Rowan. It might as well be here as Seville.'

Was he afraid that she mightn't be able to take the news well? Did he see her as somehow delicate now that he knew? Didn't he know how prepared she was? *Who was she kidding...?* She looked out of the window and could see that already they were on the motorway, headed for the centre of Paris. She shrugged. He was right. It might as well be here as in Spain.

They pulled up outside the Four Seasons Georges V Hotel, one of the most exclusive in Paris. Rowan felt severely under-dressed in her flowery dress. Isandro came around the car and took her by the hand, further unsettling her, and led her inside.

He was greeted obsequiously by the staff. Rowan was amused to see that for someone like Isandro checking in wasn't expected. A senior member of staff greeted him immediately and ushered them into a lift, taking them straight up to their room. Her head was spinning as they were led in and she looked around. Opulent didn't even come into it.

She wandered around while Isandro dealt with the manager. Ornate doors led out onto a private patio, with a stunning private view onto the Eiffel Tower. It was early evening by now, and the distinctive shape of the tower was set against a beautiful clear sky streaked with mauve.

Rowan went and leaned on the railing, barely noticing the table set for two. She assumed that it came with the room as standard—after all, she thought cynically, wasn't Paris the most romantic city in the world? And this one of its finest hotels? That brought her up short. What did Isandro expect? Why was he doing this? Were duty and pity fuelling these actions?

She turned quickly to find him standing in the doorway, watching her. She couldn't read the expression on his face. But it was *intent*. And it made her heart flip-flop. She had to stop this now, get a hold of herself. She was way too vulnerable after the trip to the clinic.

'Isandro…this is lovely…but crazy. Surely you haven't brought us here for some kind of…?'

His mouth twisted into a grim line. 'Romantic evening?'

She coloured. Her throat felt tight. He strolled towards her and she had nowhere to go. She had to stop him.

'Exactly. It's nice to be here, but you could have booked somewhere more…modest—two rooms…'

The bed loomed large in the background. Her heart thudded so loud that she felt sure he must hear it.

'What if I do want this, Rowan? What if I want all of this?'

She frowned. 'I don't know what you mean.'

He was so close now that all she would have to do was reach out and pull him to her. She looked up. And wished she didn't have to look into his eyes.

'Take a look around. Don't you know where we are yet?'

She shook her head, feeling seriously confused. He took her hand and led her back into the room. Suddenly it *was* clear. The room was so sensually decorative…so romantic. A bottle of champagne peeped out from an ice bucket on a nearby table, two crystal flutes beside it sparkled. She gasped, and her hand tightened reflexively around his.

'It's the honeymoon suite.' She felt sick. What kind of joke was this?

He turned her around to face him, his hands on her shoulders.

Anger surged. 'Sandro, I don't know what this is all for, but you can ring down right now and tell them we're not staying here. I don't know what you think—'

She broke free. He couldn't know, could he? Had she been so transparent? Frantically she tried to deny her feelings, deny that he might have read them.

'We do have to talk, Isandro—but does it have to be here? I mean, isn't this some sort of mockery?'

'You think that wanting to make a new start is mockery?' His voice was frigid.

Rowan looked at him in bewilderment. 'What new start? We're getting divorced. I'm moving out.'

'I've stopped divorce proceedings.'

Her jaw dropped and her heart stopped. 'You've *what*? Why?' she asked a little wildly.

'I think it's obvious now that we should stay married. There's Zac. And your safety to consider.'

Rowan felt cornered, trapped. 'So in effect nothing will have changed? It'll still be a marriage of convenience, only now you know what happened, so you can forgive me for my past sins, I'll be allowed to be a mother to Zac, and you can keep us safe if we're all together.'

'Is that so bad a prospect?' he asked quietly, a different quality in his voice.

'No...*yes*!' Rowan threw her hands up in the air. He didn't know what he was asking. It was heaven and hell. Her heart was pumping so hard that it threatened to burst from her chest. She looked at him and begged him silently to understand, not to do this.

'Isandro, I can't. I won't. It's not fair on me or you or Zac. He deserves to have two parents who love one another, and I won't stand by and watch you sacrifice your happiness just out of a sense of pity and duty. We can live a perfectly happy life divorced. I can live nearby, see Zac...'

'*No.* I won't have that.'

Rowan blanched at the vehemence in his voice.

He came and pulled her over to a silk-covered sofa, sitting her down. She could feel the tension in his body transmitting into her own. She ached for him even now, body and soul.

She opened her mouth to speak, but he got in first. 'Rowan, just...let me speak, okay?'

She nodded warily. His hands were on hers, heavy.

'Professor Villiers showed me around today, and without going into the details of your case told me what you would have gone through. I saw the quarantine room...he told me about the treatments... That was why you had the bad dreams, wasn't it?'

Rowan closed her eyes weakly. It was all coming back. 'Don't...'

'I won't. But...'

She opened her eyes again, and the pain in them nearly stopped Isandro—but he had to keep going. 'It nearly destroyed me to see what you had to endure, Rowan. No one should have to feel they have no option but to endure that alone. And I'm sorry—I'm so sorry that you felt that was your only option.'

Rowan shook her head. 'You really don't have to do all this just because—'

'I'm not. You made your own choices. I wish you'd included me, but I think I can see now why you didn't. I couldn't take it in when you told me first. I had no real concept of what you faced until today...'

That made her sit up. She looked into his eyes. He was sincere.

'When we got married I was away a lot. Too much I can see now. I saw it at the time too...but you were never meant to get in the way of my business. I didn't know why I was suddenly feeling...wanting...' He stopped ineffectually. 'We had no time to get to know one another properly. You got pregnant so quickly.'

'Which never should have happened.'

He shook his head emphatically. 'It would have happened sooner or later, Rowan. The truth is I desired you from the moment I saw you. I just hid it under very elaborate plans to marry you to further my career in Europe. I had an agenda and nothing was getting in my way. You see, I'd never planned on marrying for love or desire, after seeing what it did to my parents. When my sister and I were in our teens my father was driving home one night. He and my mother were having one of their passionate arguments and he crashed the car, leaving her paralysed from the waist down.'

An image of the tiny woman dressed in black in a wheelchair at their wedding came into Rowan's mind. The bitterness etched into her face. Isandro's voice dragged her attention back.

'My father was so racked with guilt for ruining his wife's

life that he took an English mistress and broke my mother's heart. And my sister's. That's the root of her own unhappiness at our union. But in truth I think she would have been unhappy with anyone I chose to marry. When my father failed her so badly, she put me on a pedestal instead.'

Rowan was feeling unsteady. This conversation was going into unknown territory that she wasn't prepared for. He had desired her all along? She tried to focus.

'When I saw you across that room and then found out you were Carmichael's daughter. I told myself the desire I felt was for power, pure and simple.' He shook his head, his eyes burning into hers. 'But that night, our wedding night, when we slept together that first time…'

Rowan blushed and looked away. She'd practically thrown herself at him. He guessed what she was thinking and put a hand to her chin, bringing her round to face him, 'No. It was mutual. I don't take women to bed out of pity, Rowan. And I don't keep taking them to bed unless I desire them.'

Her heart stopped.

'I…I always thought… And then when I was so…' She was blushing so hard now that her cheeks were literally burning.

Isandro rubbed the back of a hand across one hot surface. 'It was like that for me too. But then when you retreated into your shell…which I know now was after you'd been to the doctor…'

Rowan fought to stay sane despite the heated intensity in his eyes. He was guessing, *knowing* too much, nearly everything. She had to remind him before she duped herself into believing she was reading something in his eyes.

'But there was that conversation.'

His eyes didn't change; they blazed harder. 'Which was a mistake that you shouldn't have had to overhear. My sister was demanding to know how I felt about you. She's poisonous in her anger and her hatred of our father. If I had told her that I had feelings for you, she'd have gone out there and annihilated you. And, apart from that noble desire, I was an abject and miserable coward.'

Rowan frowned slightly.

'I was so confused about how I *was* feeling that I wasn't in any shape to articulate that to Ana.'

Feelings? He just meant friendship...warmth...respect.

Rowan felt as if she had to say something to avoid the awful moment when he would confirm that. 'Look, Sandro...I like you too. I liked you from the start. I had no choice but to marry you...my father...the bank. My inheritance.' *She had to convince him.*

He shook his head and sent up a silent plea. 'I don't believe you.' He held her hands even tighter.

Rowan's skin prickled and her belly fell. He wasn't going to do this to her, was he?

'Sandro, please...' she begged, trying to pull her hands away from his. 'I don't know what you want to hear.'

'You're a strong woman, Rowan. I think you've more than proved that you don't do anything you don't feel passionately about. And your inheritance? I don't think that's ever really mattered a damn. All I want to hear is the truth...'

The truth.

She shook her head helplessly, and to her chagrin her eyes filled with hopeless tears. 'You know. You *know*. That's why you're doing this...to make me agree...but I can't, Sandro. I can't.'

The blue of his eyes was hypnotic. 'Tell me,' he demanded hoarsely, not giving her an inch to back away.

And then the fight was too much. She was too tired. Did she really have the strength to walk away from a lifetime with Isandro even if he didn't love her? She knew the answer...

Her hands lay limp in his, and she looked to a spot over his shoulder. Anything to avoid the laser-like gaze. 'If I hadn't got sick I never would have left. I would have hoped and dreamt that some day you'd come to feel about me the way I felt for you.' She looked at him then, her eyes clear and true. 'I think I've loved you since our wedding night. I told myself I didn't love you any more when I saw you in London, but I knew I did. I was just trying to protect myself.'

She steeled herself. 'And I do now.' She shrugged one shoulder then, in an endearingly vulnerable gesture. 'You and Zac. My deepest most secret dream through all those months was of us as a family together...healthy and happy.'

Isandro took up her hands, and Rowan was surprised to feel his own hands shaking violently. He bent and pressed a kiss to her palms. '*Gracias, mi querida...*' He pressed another kiss to her hands, the other side. '*Mi vida...*'

Rowan still felt slightly shell shocked at what she'd just said. The urge to self-protect was still strong. Her back was still tense. 'Sandro...'

He lifted his head and he was smiling, grinning inanely. She'd never seen him look so happy. 'Rowan...*querida*...I fell in love with you too along the way. Somewhere you crept into my heart. When you gave birth to Zac—in that moment...I knew it then.'

A shadow crossed his face. He sobered. Rowan was holding her breath. Surely he wouldn't go *this* far just to get her to comply?

'When I came back and found you gone...found that note...'

He looked so bleak for a moment that Rowan had to believe. Tentative wings of joy started to take off in her heart.

'You were right. I was so angry, so incensed, that I damned you to hell and told myself I'd been the biggest fool. But the hurt didn't go. It festered. I told myself I'd been stupid to trust you when all along you'd turned out to be the same as every other money-hungry social climbing…' He stopped. 'That day when you walked away you didn't just walk out on Zac…you walked out on me, and I didn't think I could ever forgive you for it.'

Rowan's whole body and head were going into meltdown. 'I had no idea I meant anything to you at all. It was that that gave me the courage to go. I didn't want to burden you with a terminally ill wife you felt nothing for. I wanted you to be free to remarry…someone you loved and desired. And I couldn't bear for Zac to know the pain of separation…'

His hand came and cupped her jaw, his thumb catching a tear that she hadn't even been aware of. 'You're the only one, Rowan. I love and desire you, no one else. The other night…I know you read me wrong in the morning. I never meant that I didn't *want* to make love to you. I felt like a crass schoolboy when I should have been offering you nothing but comfort…yet I couldn't help myself. I haven't even been with another woman since you left. I couldn't. I told myself it was anger hampering me. I couldn't even go looking for you…the hurt was too intense.'

'Oh, my love…' Rowan's heart overflowed. If she was dreaming then she never wanted to wake up. She pressed a kiss to his palm and, unable to hold back any more, Isandro pulled her forward and crushed her against his chest.

'I love you, Rowan. You're my life.' He smiled ruefully for a second. 'I called you my mistress…that thought lasted about two minutes. I just couldn't see you like that, no matter how much I tried to distance myself.' He was serious again. 'When you and Zac were taken…when I saw you in that awful room…'

A shudder ran through his big frame, and Rowan welcomed him when his head bent and his mouth met hers in a searing kiss.

When they broke apart Rowan was crying in earnest. 'I'm so sorry I didn't tell you straight away…I just…couldn't…'

'Shh.' He kissed her again, pulling her close. 'It doesn't matter now. You're here, you're well, you're going to be well. Zac is well. We're together, and that's all that matters.'

Rowan nodded tearily.

Isandro gestured with a shoulder and sent a quick glance around the room. 'I brought you here because I want this to be a new start. We never had a honeymoon.'

Rowan shook her head in acknowledgment.

Isandro kissed her hand again. 'Well, now we will. Starting tonight. With dinner overlooking the Eiffel Tower.' He smiled a little ruefully, almost shyly, and it made Rowan's heart soar even higher. 'I know it's a bit of a cliché, the table overlooking the Eiffel Tower…the room…the champagne… I have so much catching up to do with you, Rowan. This is just the start of it…I promise.'

She shook her head vaguely, too entranced by his eyes and his words to be able to begin to tell him that it was all okay. Fine. Perfect. His words were washing over her like a healing balm.

And then he reached into a pocket and took something out. She looked down. In his palm he held her wedding and engagement rings. She watched wordlessly as he took her hand and slipped them onto her ring finger one by one. He'd had them resized and now they fitted perfectly.

Rowan reached up to touch his mouth with a finger, her eyes dropping in an innocently provocative gesture before looking back up. Her hand shook with the emotions running through her. 'You were so sure?'

He shook his head then, that vulnerable light still in his eyes, and caught her finger and kissed it. 'No, I wasn't sure at all…but I prayed to every god I know that you felt something for me…that you would at least agree to stay married.'

They shared a long intense look.

'Do you know what day tomorrow is?'

'Of course I do. It's Zac's birthday,' Rowan said huskily.

He smiled. 'So tomorrow, early, we go home, we wake up our son, and we give him a very special birthday—the first of many, *together*.'

Rowan smiled a wobbly smile. She was sure she must look a sight, but with Isandro gazing at her as if she were the Venus de Milo she didn't care. She let him take her hand, pull her up and lead her out to the terrace.

In the warm spring air of a beautiful night in Paris, they started again…

Four years later.

Rowan looked down in wonder at the small head full of dark auburn hair nestled against her breast. Watched the tiny puckered frown, the rosebud mouth suckling fiercely as if her life depended on it. A small hand curled around her little finger with a strength that was truly unbelievable. Her daughter. Alégria. *Joy*. Because that was what her pregnancy had been. One of hope and joy. There had been every chance that after the chemotherapy her fertility might have been irreparably damaged, but Alégria was proof otherwise.

The door opened with a burst, and a flash of blond barrelled in, followed by Isandro, tall and so handsome that Rowan smiled and her heart clenched as it always did. They shared a look, and then she turned her smiling attention to Zac as he clambered up onto the bed.

'Mamá, mamá—look what I drew for Légria!'

'It's Alégria sweetie…'

Zac clearly wasn't interested and chattered on, showing Rowan a drawing of Papá, Mamá, Zac and the new baby. Tears filled Rowan's eyes and Isandro saw them. He came and pressed a lingering kiss to her mouth. She just looked at him mutely, with everything written on her face, in her eyes. The moment was huge. Love blazed between them, strong and true.

Isandro just smiled at her. 'I know, *querida*…I know…'

MILLS & BOON
MODERN
Power and Passion

Prepare to be swept off your feet by sophisticated, sexy and seductive heroes, in some of the world's most glamourous and romantic locations, where power and passion collide.